FEY USED DIVE!

FEY USED DIVE!

FANTASIA

BOOK TWO

UNICE5656

Podium

Published in 2025 by Podium Publishing
www.podiumentertainment.com

FEY USED DIVE!

CHAPTER 1
WELL MET

Last coach, yay, yay, yay!" There was little to distinguish Fey's voice from that of a five-year-old anticipating the end of an overly long car ride as she and Blade drew closer to the salt air and glimmering expanse of ocean on the road to the coastal town of Seaport. (After creative gems like "Moonwood" and "Skyhaven," the author clearly put the same extreme effort into thinking up the ingenious name of "Seaport.")

The destination was relatively unpopular, and the party had the coach to themselves. They took advantage of this to continue their unconventional training.

By this point, Amethyst's Double Membrane had levelled up enough that Fey had moved to poking the slime with her newbie dagger, the sharp metal leaving temporary indents but no breaks in the slime's translucent skin. Fey herself was pale and mildly nauseated as she suffered the effects of poison mushroom poison in order to continue training Immunity.

Boris and Blade continued their battle of wills as the boar repeatedly used Glare and the warrior countered with Fighting Spirit, both abilities having reached level 6 in an arms race of psychological dominance.

Fey had (thankfully) stopped telling Magic to cast Spore indiscriminately out the window and had instead put the mushroom in charge of training the glooms. She had no idea what the training was actually accomplishing, but they seemed to be enjoying running all over the sides and the underside of the roof in a way that made it clear that gravity was just a convenient option, so she let them be.

Amidst the controlled chaos, it occurred to Fey that some of her pets were rather unsuited to underwater adventuring. How unsuited largely depending on what equipment they would need to facilitate breathing underwater, and whether they could be adapted to fit her diminutive pets.

She contacted Sirena to ask.

<Fey: Hey, what kind of breathing apparatus am I going to be using underwater? Scuba equipment?>

<Sirena: Oh, I thought I'd buy some of the magical air bubbles we use for the dolphin taxis down here. They last at least a day.>

Fey mentally inventoried her pets. Amethyst would be fine underwater with an air bubble. Boris would be fine, assuming he could swim at a reasonable pace. She did not think the glooms needed to breathe, and given their ability to shift shapes, they would probably swim quite well.

Magic . . . The mushroom was not dense enough to sink underwater, and had no limbs with which to swim.

<Fey: Bring at least ten. I don't think all my pets need to breathe but better safe than sorry.>

<Sirena: No problem, they're pretty cheap down here.>

It was time to do some experimenting. Fey grabbed the nearest gloom as it hopped by overhead (it was Inkblot, not that she could distinguish between them) and dropped it into the flask of water she had been keeping to practice enchanting water.

Inkblot sat obediently in the flask, at the surface of the superdense liquid, looking extremely cute as its head peeked out over the lip of the container.

Fey sighed and used her hand to push the gloom down until it was immersed. "Start wiggling or something if this starts to get uncomfortable," she told the shadow-rabbit.

Inkblot curled up inside the flask, looking extremely comfortable despite being the victim of an experimental drowning scenario.

"How long do I have to keep him here before I can conclude that glooms don't need to breathe?" she asked Blade.

He shrugged, most of his attention on resisting the demonic Glare coming from Boris. "Twenty minutes?"

Fey sighed. With her free hand, she picked up her dagger and resumed poking Amethyst.

Never one to miss out on new kinds of fun, Amethyst hopped off Fey's lap and joined Inkblot in the roomy flask. Paying no attention to the fact that the water inside was now enchanted, she activated Osmosis and absorbed a slime-sized volume of it.

<Amethyst has learned Potion Slime!>

"Ohmygod."

Blade looked up from his staring contest with Boris. "What?"

Fey held up a finger while she read the ability description.

<Potion Slime: Can secrete potions that it has learned the composition of. Mana consumption depends on potion type and amount of potion secreted. The slime requires a source of pure water to secrete large amounts of potion.>

<Current recipe(s): Enchanted water (24MP/mL)>

"Ehehehe—" Fey remembered that she was not alone and abruptly stopped her evil laughter, though it continued to ring out in her mind. *Ehehehehehe . . .*

While it appeared that Potion Slime would consume a very large amount of mana when it came to rare potions, it still replaced the difficulty of locating and processing rare ingredients with a naturally regenerating power, representing an endless source of profit.

Having totally forgotten that Blade was still waiting for an explanation, Fey rummaged in her pouch for other potions. She came up with her newbie minor health and mana potions, the lesser healing potion Kallara had gifted her, and the strength tonic they had brewed with the King Slime bubble.

"Here, Amethyst, osmose." She dumped all the potions in succession over the slime (much to Blade's ongoing bewilderment).

The command was technically inaccurate, as the process of osmosis referred to the movement of water across a semipermeable membrane and would exclude any active potion ingredients from being absorbed, but Amethyst was not much for pedantry and internalized each potion without comment.

<Current recipe(s): Enchanted water (24MP/mL)>

<Minor healing potion (5MP/mL)>

<Minor mana potion (10MP/mL)>

<Lesser healing potion (18MP/mL)>

<Strength tonic (100MP/mL)>

Producing enchanted water consumed a relatively high amount of mana because of the intrinsic mana cost of producing it the normal way, whereas strength tonic was expensive due to the rare ingredients and high apothecary skill needed to brew it correctly.

Unlike players' base attribute points that could be custom allocated in any proportion, pets' attributes increased in a fixed pattern with every level increase. Amethyst gained 3 intelligence points with every level and her maximum mana was at 750, almost triple that of her owner. It would still take quite a while to produce a full dose of strength tonic at 50 millilitres of potion, but Fey saw no reason to delay milking the ability for all it was worth. Using the empty bottles from the potions she had just fed the slime, she got Amethyst working on synthesizing replacement doses. She made a mental note to stock up on more bottles.

I was thinking about something else before, wasn't I? (#EndRandomTangent)

Her eyes fell upon Inkblot, who was again floating on the surface of the enchanted water after she stopped holding the gloom underwater. Her mental processes reset by the distraction, she simply asked, "Do you need to breathe?"

Inkblot shook its head.

"Oh, okay. Off you go." (Why wasn't this plan A?)

The gloom wiggled its ears (cutely) and hopped out of the flask to rejoin its brethren in their anti-gravity stunts.

"Are you going to . . . tell me what's going on?" Blade ventured, not really sure he wanted to know after the evil laughter he had heard earlier.

"Oh, uh, Amethyst can secrete potions now," Fey answered vaguely, trying to remember what else she had been thinking about before she got distracted.

Since she did not specify that the slime had gained the ability to recreate literally any potion it had the chance to absorb even once, and Blade still naively believed in the concept of "game balance," he was not particularly impressed. "Huh. Cool."

Oh yeah. Fey remembered that she was assessing her pets' suitability for adventuring underwater and grabbed Magic off the side of the carriage as he was hopping by.

No matter how she thought about it, she could not think of a way for the mushroom to function effectively underwater. *I'm going to need a pet-sitter.*

(Stop pushing! The author is *so rude*. Okay, okay, leaving, no need to pull out the "author wand of obliteration." Sheesh. As the keen reader may have surmised, the next scene is written from Leandriel's point of view.)

Leandriel sliced the head off a misshapen monster, an asymmetric five-legged wolf-creature with patches of slimy skin mixed with matted fur. Blood the wrong shade of red spurted out, and the head continued snapping at him, animated by demonic and undead forces. He stabbed it in the forehead with blessed mithril, and it finally stilled.

He was currently in the Rift, a very dangerous area in the remote reaches of the Dark Side. According to lore, a black magician had split the earth of the barren wasteland to create a deep, inescapable prison to trap his failed experiments. Over time, only the most deadly had survived.

He checked off "corrupted demon-wolf" from his encounter list. In addition to training to level 110 and his next warrior skill, he was evaluating the monsters in the area. He made a note to mention that something felt off about the creature's pack behaviour.

Just because he was done testing did not mean the monsters were done with him. More disturbingly mutated monsters attacked, driven to rage by his strong holy aura. Now that he had less need for close-up observation, he used more of his advanced skills to blast and cleave his way through the pack, fighting toward the next monster's territory.

<Fey: Hey, Leandriel?>

Though Leandriel was experienced in fighting and messaging at the same time and frequently had detailed discussions with Kevin and other programmers while defending himself against hordes of monsters, objective evidence from the last few days of exchanging greetings with Fey showed that he found their conversations much more distracting and he tended to get injured if he attempted to continue fighting. Instead, he blew through his mana reserves to cast his most powerful area-of-effect spells, turning the area into the epicentre of a holy explosion that no monster could survive.

Every monster in the area was seared from existence; the purifying energy was so strong, even the corpses and blood disappeared. Compared to the rest of the Rift, which was covered in a level of gore reminiscent of the late stages of a horror movie, the pristine area looked like a circle of paradise.

Leandriel smiled and replied, ignoring the dizzying effect from the sudden mana depletion.

<Leandriel: Yes? What is it?>

<Fey: Could you do me a huuuge favour and take care of Magic for a while? I'm about to travel underwater and I don't think he'd do well there.>

Leandriel jumped fifteen metres into the air and began winging his way out of the dark confines of the Rift. He was a six-hour flight from the nearest town with a teleportation gate, five if he pushed himself.

<Leandriel: I will take him. You are planning on bringing your other pets with you?>

<Fey: Yeah, I think the rest of them will be fine. Well, I'm not so sure about Boris, either.>

<Leandriel: I could take him as well.>

<Fey: Haha, when pigs fly. Sorry, bad puns.>

Leandriel chuckled.

<Leandriel: No need to apologize. I find you amusing.>

<Fey: Haha, I think I'm amusing, too. And modest, don't forget modest.>

<Leandriel: Indeed.>

Leandriel enjoyed the bantering style of conversation, which was similar to the silly, creative environment he was surrounded by at work, but he found he was not particularly adept at adding on to the joke to keep the banter going. He felt his lack quite keenly, much more so than his conversational partners noticed. In the absence of a witty comeback, he returned to more practical matters.

<Leandriel: When will you arrive at Seaport?>

<Fey: Mm, in about four and a half hours?>

Four and a half hours. There was no need to make Fey wait around for his arrival. He could make it.

<Leandriel: I will see you then.>

<Fey: Thank you so much! See you then!>

<Leandriel: You are very welcome.>

Closing the chat channel, Leandriel began to make adjustments for high-speed, long-distance flying. Shedding his heavy plate armour, he Ex-quipped into light, close-fitting cloth garments that minimized wind resistance.

Rapidly gaining height, Leandriel reached the thinner, cooler air at the altitudes flowing by migratory birds, finding a favourable air current to speed his travel. Downing a stamina potion, he shot through the air at a pace just short of a flying sprint.

—◦◦◇◦◦—

(Oh, so now the author *wants* snarky comments. Hmph. Okay, okay, comments are on, no need to pull out the "author wand of obliteration". So violent.)

Fey was predictably happy about the prospect of seeing Leandriel again. Over the days of travelling, she had had brief conversations with the angel through private messaging, learning to hide the silly smiles that inevitably resulted by leaning her head "contemplatively" on an arm, covering her mouth in the process.

I guess the secret is up now. While Blade could be counted on to miss the crinkling at the corners of her eyes from a silly smile, he was not so unobservant as to miss an angel with a wingspan the length of a small school bus, the feathers so white that they could cause a dazzle effect on his enemies if he fought in direct sunlight. (On a tangentially related note, in the right state of distraction, our heroine could foreseeably fail to notice something like that.)

She brought up the subject in an indirect manner. "Hey, Blade, what are you going to do with Firefly while we're underwater?" If anything, the fire-element pet was even less suited for underwater adventures than Magic was.

"Keep her at the bank, I guess."

"You can do that?"

"Yeah. They're held in magical stasis."

To a critical thinker, the availability of a simple, practical solution might have raised the question as to why Leandriel was going out of his way to help her in a far less convenient manner. Fey was not much for re-appraising previously made decisions. "Huh. Well, I asked one of my friends to take care of Magic for me."

"Who?"

Fey could tell from Blade's expression that he was thinking something along the lines of *You have more than one friend?* She narrowed her eyes dangerously, temporarily outstripping Boris's Glare in terms of threat level.

(Russian roulette of reactions . . . Roll childish.)

"Hmph!" Fey flopped back against her seat without further explanation. She resumed poking Amethyst with her dagger, but it was clear she would have preferred to be stabbing somebody else.

Blade still wanted to know who Fey's other friend was, but with the sense that he had just stepped on a land mine but miraculously survived unscathed, he did not pursue the line of questioning. Boris then Glared at him, causing a shiver of reaction as his attention was pulled back to training.

Four and a half hours later, Fey jumped off the travel coach with her usual alacrity. She stretched her arms, pretending the eagerness was due to escaping the confines of the carriage rather than the prospect of seeing a certain winged being again. She sent off a message.

<Fey: I've arrived at Seaport!>

<Leandriel: I am almost there. You should see the teleportation gate begin to activate in a few minutes.>

<Fey: Great! I'll wait for you there.>

As Fey strode toward the landmark in question, she realized she had not mentioned Blade to Leandriel at all. On the one hand, it seemed vain to think the angel would care about Blade's presence; on the other, it felt inconsiderate not to give him a heads-up, especially when she herself hated meeting new people without warning. (With warning too, but slightly less.)

Feeling rather awkward, she sent the message.

<Fey: Just so you know, I'm going to have a party member with me, a human warrior named Blade.>

<Leandriel: Okay.>

Was it just her imagination, or was the response a fraction of a second slower than usual?

She needed to stop overanalyzing everything.

He's not real, he's not real, he's not real, she reminded herself. He was able to interact with her, but in the end, he was just another handsome video game character.

Nerves settled, she found a spot by the teleportation gate and waited for it to activate.

Blade trailed Fey across town, managing to keep up with her quick strides. (It had taken two days, but he had finally learned how to walk quickly.) She seemed rather distracted and, at one point, started squeezing her pet slime like a stress ball without seeming to notice.

They stopped at a teleportation gate, presumably where Fey's friend was going to appear. Fey stopped squeezing her slime and put it back on her shoulder, again without seeming to notice what she was doing.

In a flash of blinding light, a figure materialized, a huge set of wings making him physically imposing in a way that could not be ignored.

Looking at the angel, Blade was forced to reconsider his preconceived notions on the race. He had always thought of celestials and angels as somewhat girly, but this player had a strength and grace that demanded respect.

Scrutinizing the angel's armour, Blade guessed there was a lot of blessed mithril to empower holy element attacks, perhaps even the addition of electrum lining to facilitate magic conductance.

It did not seem likely that such a high-level warrior was the friend Fey had asked to take care of her little mushroom. (Okay, well, when you put it like *that*, it does sound a bit ridiculous.)

He was forced to reconsider the thought when the angel scanned the crowd, spotted Fey, and made his way directly toward her.

Fey held to her calm while Leandriel approached, pretending that this was just another adventure in an anime she was watching. (This would make her the incredibly dense main character. Sounds about right.)

"Hello," he said, smiling.

"Hi." To say that Fey's nerves were totally settled would be a lie, but her smile was natural and unforced.

Beside her, Blade wore an expression of disbelief.

Fey incorrectly attributed the disbelief to the angel's general existence rather than the fact that she had called said existence over for such a minor errand and considered it entirely natural. She made the introduction. "Leandriel, this is Blade. Blade, Leandriel."[1]

"Hello."

"Hey."

(If you are unable to tell who said what without dialogue tags, please reread the entire story.)

Fey watched with a social science perspective as the two went through the timeless ritual of "sizing each other up". Carefully neutral expressions told her that they were prepared to dislike each other.

<Sirena: Hey, you here yet?>

<Fey: Yes, but I think I'm in "a situation.">

<Sirena: What kind of situation?>

<Fey: Leandriel and Blade appear to be engaging in a staring contest.>

<Sirena: Who's Blade?>

<Fey: Oh. Forgot to mention him. Party member.>

<Sirena: Since when?>

<Fey: Uh, second night of playing?>

<Sirena: If you were anyone else, I'd accuse you of deliberately failing to mention him.>

<Fey: Not on purpose, I swear.>

<Sirena: You know it's rude to consider people's existences beneath your notice, right?>

<Fey: I mean, only if I say it out loud, right?>

<Sirena: Never mind. Let me see.>

Fey turned on video chat with the background setting on so that Sirena could see Leandriel and Blade beside her. Naturally, audio connectivity accompanied video, a fact that Fey lamented when Sirena proceeded to squeal at a loud volume and very high pitched.

"*SQUEE!!*"

Fey winced.

Noticing her grimace, Leandriel broke the stare-off and asked, "What is it? Are you okay?"

Gingerly, Fey asked, "Can you damage your eardrums if someone screams at you through private messaging?"

"I do not believe so. Who is screaming?"

"I'm good, then. Say hello, Sirena." Fey made her video screen visible to others, and Sirena the mermaid swam into view.

Leah's avatar retained her cute facial features and short, compact body type, but looked quite different with light blue skin and an iridescent scaled tail below the waist. Despite the appearance change, Fey was sure it was her friend because of the gleeful expression the mermaid wore.

"Hello, hello!" Sirena greeted them, completely nonchalant about having just blown out her best friend's metaphysical eardrums. "I need to know: Have either of you used appearance modules?"

Both young men looked rather bemused by the question, which Fey found rather adorable.

"No," Leandriel answered. Blade echoed the response.

Sirena put a hand to her cheek. "So *cute*. I can't even."

Fey caught the moment when the mermaid's expression shifted to pure mischief but was too slow to stop her.

"Hey, Leandriel, is your wingspan proportional to your . . ." Sirena paused delicately for everyone to brace for the dirty joke. ". . . weight?" she finished in a tone of mock innocence.

Fey covered her eyes with one hand. "Say goodbye, Sirena." She turned off the video screen before the mermaid could say anything else.

Having had a somewhat sheltered upbringing, Leandriel initially reacted to answer the question literally. It was only Fey's reaction that caused him to think back and realize the innuendo. ". . . Oh," he said belatedly.

Fey covered her face with both hands. "I'm sorry, everyone."

Whereas the angel had simply talked to Sirena and would presumably have little to do with her in the future, Blade realized that he had volunteered to go on an extended set of adventures with the mermaid. For the first time, he seriously contemplated his choice of company in the game. "She . . ." He trailed off as he had no idea what he was trying to say.

Removing her hands from her face but keeping her eyes averted, Fey said, "Do you guys want to get something to eat?"

"Yes, of course."

"Uh, sure."

The three made their way toward an NPC-run seaside restaurant.

Well, that's one way to break up a staring contest.

CHAPTER 2

LAUGHTER IS THE BEST POISON

Seaport was a town made to facilitate trade between the merfolk colonies just off the coast and the human lands in the eastern part of the continent. With very few players having reached level 30—the point at which merfolk could transform and function on land—the town currently hosted far fewer players than it was designed to accommodate.

The upside of the rather deserted-feeling atmosphere was that service in the shops and restaurants was extremely fast. Fey, Blade, and Leandriel were the only customers in the seaside restaurant dubbed the Lucky Mackerel. To avoid blocking up the restaurant with Leandriel's bulky wings, they had taken seats on the second-floor balcony, which offered a great view of the tropical waters.

The staff considerately offered them a table typically meant for ten people and cleared the other furniture from the deck so the angel would have room to stretch out. Fey dropped her pets in the extra place settings while Firefly perched on the deck rail. Feypets being Feypets, they immediately hopped all over the table and grouped themselves as they pleased.

There was a noisy bustle of activity as everyone got themselves situated appropriately, but as soon as that ended, the silence became distinctly awkward.

Amethyst squeaked. ("This is weird.")

All the Feypets nodded in agreement.

Magic hopped over to Leandriel, climbing the angel's arm onto his shoulder. He squeaked. ("Fey-Fey and Lee-Lee usually talk a lot.")

Glad to have something to pay attention to, Fey watched the squeakers as if she could follow their conversation.

"Do you know what they say?" Leandriel asked, intrigued. There were some abilities that allowed players to understand pets and other creatures, but they were generally unlocked with high-level psychic or nature-based powers.

Fey huffed in amusement. "Not really, but I make it up as I go. I assume they were commenting on the awkward silence."

Prompted by the observation, Blade made an effort to be friendly. Given his generally laid-back disposition, he was not sure why his initial reaction to Leandriel had been so antagonistic in the first place. (This is probably due to an instinctive sense that the author-goddess had been *extremely* unfair in distributing positive attributes when she created the characters.)

"So, how did the two of you meet?" he asked conversationally.

Fey and Leandriel exchanged a glance that was suspiciously laden with meaning. Fey was ready to gloss over the incident, but Leandriel answered without trying to present himself in a positive light. "In one of my first, clumsy attempts at flying, I crashed into the lady, injuring her seriously."

Fey's inner fangirl was giggling madly at being called a lady, but she mustered up enough brainpower to protest, "It wasn't that serious."

"You broke several bones. I would consider that serious," Leandriel countered, his expression darkening with guilt as he remembered the crash.

Blade was starting to pick up serious lovey-dovey vibes from the argument-that-was-not-an-argument. "Are you two dating or something?" he asked.

Fey and Leandriel exchanged another glance before looking away from each other, a slight blush rising in their faces.

". . . No . . ." Leandriel finally answered. (He sounded like he would prefer the answer to be "or something.") He glanced again at Fey, who had covered her eyes with one hand.

When Fey entered into situations that were actively embarrassing, she felt a physical urge to jump to her feet and run away. She had largely mastered the impulse, but this particular situation was embarrassing enough that her quadriceps muscles tensed in preparation for jumping and running.

Certain that she would explode in a smoking pile of mortification if Blade continued on the same line of questioning, she sent him a PM.

<Fey: Stop it! He's an NPC, you idiot!>

Startled, Blade looked directly at Fey, making it obvious that they were communicating on a private channel. Leandriel politely refrained from commenting on the exchange.

<Blade: What? No way. Why is he here, then?>

<Fey: I asked him to come get Magic.>

<Blade: Not that. Shouldn't he have some kind of NPC job, then?>

Blade was making a very valid argument against Leandriel's existence as an NPC, but a single fact had Fey firmly convinced.

<Fey: He's obviously an NPC. There's no possible way a player could have reached level 100 in the time since *Fantasia* has been out. He probably has some NPC job that won't become relevant until players get to level 100 or something.>

<Blade: Oh. Good point.>

<Fey: Just stop asking awkward questions!!>

Objectively speaking, Blade had been making fairly normal conversation and he did not deserve to be yelled at, but Fey was in no mental state to behave calmly.

<Blade: Okay, okay! Dropping the subject.>

Fey had never been as grateful in her life to see the arrival of food to interrupt the conversation. Under the cover of clinking dishes, she lifted Amethyst close to her mouth and muttered, "If Blade says anything stupid, smack him."

(For amusement's sake, the reader may take a ten-second pause to consider the results of this command.)

Amethyst nodded with an excessive amount of enthusiasm and hopped over to the optimal position to smack the human warrior, right next to Blade's elbow. Blade glanced down, rather confused as to why the slime with which he had a casual enmity had chosen to sit so close to him, but when Amethyst failed to do anything else after settling down, he allowed his attention to move to his food.

"Thank you," he said to the waitress as his plate was placed in front of him.

As soon as it was safe to do so without disturbing the food, Amethyst smacked him with her bubble. (It's quite unfair that she's denigrating his display of basic manners, but she is, after all, a tamed monster.)

"Hey!" Blade yelled indignantly, glaring at the diminutive pet. "What was that for?"

Ah. Oops. Fey started to realize the probable outcome of her command and was seized with silent giggles. Her internal struggles were such that she forgot to speak, and Blade was faced with having Amethyst's incomprehensible squeaks as his only explanation.

Leandriel looked back and forth between Blade's argument with the slime and Fey's mirthful expression, not sure if he should be concerned or amused. Magic, who was sticking to the side of the angel's arm and had completely understood the squeaked explanation, chimed in with his own squeak. ("I think that counts as a stupid question.")

Amethyst squeaked ("Good point.") and smacked Blade again.

At Blade's second indignant "Hey!" Fey's silent laughter burst into audible giggles, her inner five-year-old now firmly in control of her body.

Blade glared balefully at her. "You put it up to this!" he accused.

Amethyst squeaked ("Duh") and smacked him again, which only caused Fey to laugh harder.

Owowowowow. Fey was now thoroughly out of breath and her sides were starting to seriously cramp, but the situation was so funny she could not stop laughing.

"What did you tell her to do?" Leandriel asked.

She answered breathlessly between giggles. "I . . . told her . . . to smack him . . . if he said . . . anything . . . stupid!" A renewed burst of laughter escaped after the explanation.

Leandriel (being a better person than our MC) felt rather bad for laughing at an acquaintance, but (having been infected by her evilness) had to chuckle at the explanation. "That is a bit . . . unfair," he said, the otherwise stern words ruined by his obvious amusement.

"I didn't say anything stupid!" Blade protested. This resulted in another smack. Blade yelped. "Stop that! That hurts!"

Amethyst squeaked. ("It's supposed to hurt, duh.") and smacked him again.

Fey was now experiencing shooting pains in her abdomen and sides with every inhale and exhale and tried to calm herself with deep breathing. "Amethyst . . . you gotta stop . . . I'm dying here."

Amethyst squeaked concernedly. ("Is Fey-Fey dying?")

Boris grunted. ("Her breathing is really weird.")

Amethyst left off tormenting Blade and hopped over to her incapacitated owner. Fey gained enough control to laugh silently, though the ongoing shaking of her shoulders indicated that she was a long way away from relieving her muscle cramps.

Calming down was a long, slow process. Whenever Fey thought about why she was laughing, she was struck by a renewed fit of mirth. It did not help that Leandriel started to find Fey's laughter amusing in and of itself, and his occasional chuckles created a positive feedback loop of laughter inciting amusement inciting laughter.

As their owner gradually recovered, Magic and Boris had a thoughtful conversation. A translated transcript is as follows:

Magic: Do you think Fey-Fey really would have died if she kept laughing?

Boris: Probably not. She would have fainted first.

Magic: Hmm. Do you think this "laughing" thing would make a good status effect?

Boris: Definitely. It doesn't kill, but it looks like it hurts. And it lasts a long time, too.

Magic: I'll try to make a Spore!

Inspired, the mushroom closed his eyes and focused on his internal biochemical processes.

Fey eventually sat with her head bowed and gaze fixed firmly on her plate, avoiding eye contact with anyone lest it trigger more laughter. The pose gave her an appearance of modesty and penitence that was belied by the occasional irregularity in her breathing.

Blade was unamused, grumpily digging into his food and pointedly ignoring Fey. Leandriel likewise kept his eyes away from her, but with an upward curve to his lips that suggested he was only doing so to preserve the tenuous calm.

Alas, finishing the meal in peace was not meant to be. Magic opened his eyes and squeaked. ("I think I got it.")

Boris grunted. ("Try it.")

Amethyst squeaked. ("Don't hit Fey-Fey. She's still recovering.")

Magic nodded and sent his newly formulated cloud of laughter Spore to envelop Blade and Leandriel. (#FriendlyFire)

Caught off guard by the experimental attack, Leandriel inhaled the Spore. It was indeed formulated correctly, and he was caught by the uncharacteristic urge to laugh freely. However, due to the huge level difference between him and the mushroom as well as many passive self-recovery abilities related to his race and class, he shrugged off the effect in mere seconds, the only consequence of having been hit that he established that he had an incredibly rich and attractive laugh. (The author-goddess continues to shower her chosen one with excessive gifts.)

Blade had no such resistances; he began to laugh and did not stop.

Seeing the Spore particles in the air and Blade's inexplicable mirth, Fey asked Magic, "What did you *do*?" Ignoring his explanatory squeaks, she checked Blade's status through the party menu:

<Laughter: Hinders breathing, vision, movement, and concentration. Magic are unable to cast spells that have a verbal component.>

<Duration: 1 hour.>

"One *hour?*" Fey was torn between admiration for Magic's addition to his already overpowered repertoire, dismay that her party member would be debilitated for such a long period of time, and disbelief that some game developer had actually coded such a ridiculous status effect. (#TooMuchFreeTime)

"Is there an antidote for laughter?" she asked, not expecting an answer.

Exceeding expectations (as usual), Leandriel said, "No, but it is possible to snap him out of it with a different stimulus." The angel had never encountered the status effect before and made a mental note to find out who had designed it and then stay far away from that person. (It seemed so harmless in theory . . .)

"Great idea. Blade, snap out of it or I'm going to have to do something really unpleasant." There was no malice in Fey's tone, as even her somewhat underactive conscience felt bad that her pet had done this to him, but Blade had no doubt that he was indeed in for something very unpleasant if he could not overcome the status effect by himself.

He made a valiant effort, but the small spike of fear from Fey's threat was not enough to overcome the laughing status. "Don't . . . do . . . anything . . . rash," he gasped out between bouts of laughter.

"Of course not," Fey agreed. After all, she was putting careful consideration into how to make him suffer without too much actual damage.

"Just . . . let it . . . wear off," Blade tried to argue before a renewed fit of mirth overtook him.

Fey considered it. "Nah, an hour is too long. Better to get it over with." Eyes falling on Amethyst, she realized she knew the perfect stimulus.

"Amethyst, furyweed."

Having spent the previous days almost constantly poisoned, Fey had built up Immunity to the point that she could handle the painful toxin with impunity. Having refused to undergo the same training, Blade could not.

Fey dangled the slime threateningly over Blade's arm where a previous smack had damaged his skin barrier. "Last chance," she warned with a voice of doom. She had resolved not to inflict furyweed on anyone after experiencing its symptoms herself, but the circumstances called for an exception.

Blade shrank back but was unable to mount a coherent defence in the middle of his laughing fit. "Wait," he gasped.

"One. Two. Three!" She touched him with the slime.

"Son of a [censored word]!" Blade swore, jumping out of his chair and knocking it over. The burning pain was bad enough that he did not immediately notice that he had stopped laughing.

"Um, you might want to drink an antidote," Fey suggested. "The damage is high enough to kill you."

Blade fumbled in his belt pouch and downed a vial of green antidote. Sighing in relief as the side effects disappeared, he righted his fallen chair and sank into it exhaustedly. "You really need to stop poisoning me," he complained.

(Too late; it is now a running joke.)

"Ehe. Sorry." Fey was actually meek and penitent for once, but the unusualness of her contrition made it feel insincere, even to her. She plucked Magic off Leandriel's arm and scolded, "You can't just go around casting random status effects on friends."

Magic squeaked. ("Is meat-shield-man a friend? Fey-Fey doesn't like him very much.")

Fey continued to show amazing translational accuracy despite her lack of insight into the Squeak language (or the existence of a Squeak language). "Yes, even Blade."

Amethyst squeaked ("He's on her friend list, so that counts.") while Blade complained, "Hey, what's that supposed to mean?"

"Well," Fey said, "There are friends, 'friends,' and *friends*."

". . . I don't know what that means."

"That's okay."

Blade scowled. "Do you know what she's talking about?" he asked Leandriel in a commiserating tone.

"I believe so, yes," the angel answered.

"You're kidding," Blade said disbelievingly.

"I believe she was pointing out the differences between friendly acquaintances, allies of convenience, and true friends."

Fey just had to grin at how accurately Leandriel had translated her vague nonsense as well as his well-worded, formal way of speaking. "Yup," she confirmed, her eyes curving into happy crescents.

"So what kind am I?" Blade challenged.

Fey just looked at him. "What do you think?"

". . . You know what, I don't think I want to know."

The waitress came over and discreetly cast a spell to reheat their food. Fey thanked her guiltily and actually started eating. (Somewhat unfairly, the thanks did not trigger a punishment for stupidity.)

Once they finished the meal, Fey and Leandriel stared at each other for several seconds and had a silent, polite argument about who was going to pay. Neither of them won, so each of the players ended up paying for themselves. (Fey left a large tip to apologize for creating a disturbance.)

Unable to think of an excuse to continue spending time together, they made their way back to the teleportation gate, their steps at a normal pace by average standards but quite slow given their usual walking pace.

While they were waiting for the teleportation gate to fully activate, it occurred to Fey to ask, "Magic will gain more experience if I transfer his ownership to you, right?"

". . . Yes." Leandriel hesitated, not because he was unsure of the game mechanics, but because the question implied a high degree of trust. There was no game mechanism that could force him to return the pet if she traded it away.

The concern never crossed Fey's mind. (Whether this is actually due to a high degree of trust or simply extremely poor foresight on our main character's part shall be left up to the opinion of the reader.) "Okay," she said, opening a trade dome.

Leandriel smiled and pulled out a coin. "Do you accept this coin in exchange for your pet blue mushroom?" he asked. A keen observer (which Fey decidedly was not) might have detected a trace of mischief in his expression.

"Yes."

<Trade complete.>

<Pet ownership transferred.>

<Fey gains 1,000,000 gold.>

Fey gaped at the coin Leandriel dropped into her hand. It was the same size and shape as a normal one-gold coin, but a blue sheen in its metallic hue gave away its composition as mithril, and the design minted into its surface clearly stated its value at one million. (Ah, the classic "give someone a crap ton of money they weren't expecting" trick.)

"You, you . . ." Fey floundered for words, wanting to call the angel a bad name but unable to come up with an appropriate insult for the occasion.

Leandriel chuckled. "No trading back."

Fey felt a strong impulse to hit the angel. Were they alone, she probably would have. (Haha, no public displays of affection, please.) Mastering the impulse, she settled for sulking. "I'm not spending it," she declared. (This ranked number one on the list of lamest comebacks she had ever uttered.)

"Okay," said Leandriel far too agreeably. "I should go." The teleportation gate was now fully active and waiting to return him to the Dark Side.

Fey switched mental gears to bid him a proper goodbye. "Bye! Be good, Magic!"

The Feypets chimed in with their own farewells and last-second advice. (Boris pragmatically said, "Don't die," while Amethyst repeated the Feypet motto of "Don't forget the loot!") Magic cheerfully accepted the well-wishes.

"Goodbye." Leandriel did not forget to cast Helping Hand on Fey and Blade before he disappeared through the open portal with a flash of light.

CHAPTER 3
DIVING IN

Fey did not like carrying large amounts of money on her person. It gave her the feeling that potential thieves could see the riches and target her for robbery.

Mithril coin gripped tightly in one hand, she quickly made her way to the bank. Her bank balance, previously in the thousands of gold, suddenly increased by three orders of magnitude. She decided to pretend not to see the extra digits.

While there, she and Blade took the opportunity to shed extra items, including most of their equipment, which was not designed for prolonged contact with seawater. Blade also put Firefly into magical storage.

Thus unburdened, the party made their way to the shore. The game developers had taken some (extreme) liberties with the local flora and fauna, but to the untrained eye, the sandy beach and ocean looked like a typical tropical coral reef environment.

Fey messaged Sirena.

<Fey: Are you near the surface?>

<Sirena: Nope. I'll be there in ten minutes.>

<Fey: K. We're just going to buy some swim gear and we'll meet you in the shallows.>

<Sirena: See ya.>

On the beach was a small building called the Dive Shack. Fey and Blade visited the shop and purchased diving gear: wet suits, goggles, and flippers. The gear was magically augmented to alleviate the dangers associated with diving, such as nitrogen narcosis and decompression sickness.[2] There was even a belt that adjusted to ensure that the swimmer was neutrally buoyant.

Perhaps the most important item being sold was the supply of gaseous oxygen any creature without gills would need to breathe underwater. Fey was appalled to find that each magical bubble of air cost a thousand gold, more than the rest of the swimming gear combined. She thought that Sirena, though fairly irresponsible with money, would not describe them as "fairly cheap" if they were priced similarly in the underwater towns.

<Fey: How much did you say the bubble spells cost?>

<Sirena: 50g, why?>

<Fey: They cost a THOUSAND gold up here. Buy as many as you can, we have some major merchanting to do.>

<Sirena: Wow. You have to admire that level of price gouging.>

<Fey: That's one option. I believe that the average person would react with moral outrage.>

<Sirena: Since when are you an expert on average people?>

<Fey: Hey, I've studied them extensively throughout my life.>

As the friends bantered back and forth, Fey and Blade struggled into their wet suits. With neither one of them having ever put one on before, it took considerably more time than it normally took either of them to change clothing, long enough for Sirena to reach the shallows.

<Fey: Almost.>

Fey and Blade waddled along the beach, their steps made awkward by the flippers on their feet. As they splashed into the water, movement farther in the water caught their attention.

Blade shaded his eyes to cut the glare. "What's that?"

Fey followed the line of his gaze and caught a shape jumping out of the water. At first, she thought it was a dolphin, but the colour and shape were wrong.

<Fey: Uh, are you randomly leaping out of the water like a drunk dolphin?>

<Sirena: I'm *sooo* bored.>

Fey sighed. "That's Sirena." Her friend was really not helping to convince Blade of her sanity.

Blade froze momentarily before continuing to wade forward. ". . . Oh."

"We just need to go save her from boredom and she'll start functioning like a normal person. Ish."

Just then, Sirena attempted a backflip. Having neither the strength nor coordination to accomplish it, she failed to slice through the water at a favourable angle and landed with a loud splash, the back-first version of a belly flop.

Fey winced.

<Fey: That looked like it hurt.>

<Sirena: Yup, it kind of did.>

Sirena did not continue leaping out of the water. (Thus the dangerous state of boredom claimed yet another victim.)

Now deep enough into the water that swimming was faster than wading, Fey and Blade kicked their way over to the mermaid, staying near the surface.

Hee hee. Gotta love flippers. Having small hands and feet, Fey was not used to being able to push much water and swim quickly, so the speed boost from wearing flippers was particularly refreshing.

When they reached Sirena, the mermaid was more or less waiting around like a normal person. She passed them small spheres that appeared to be air contained by a thin membrane and spoke telepathically. *Just pop them and the breathing spell will activate.*

Normal speech did not work underwater, so the game developers had given merfolk an innate ability to speak telepathically that broadcasted at about the same range as a human voice, with the same ability to modulate the equivalent of volume, tone, and inflections.

Neither Fey nor Blade had the psychic ability to respond in kind, so Fey added Sirena to the party and spoke through party chat. With some extra concentration, it was possible to send audio chat without speaking out loud.

"Sirena, Blade. Blade, this is my best friend Sirena."

Hello! Sirena said cheerfully, offering a blue hand to shake. There was thin webbing connecting all her fingers except for the thumb.

"Nice to meet you," Blade said somewhat warily. He accepted the handshake as if he expected a minor explosion to result.

"He already knows you're crazy," Fey noted.

Sirena pouted. *Oh, pooh, it's no fun that way.* She smiled at Blade. *I'm usually more normal than Fey is.*

"She is," Fey confirmed.

Blade looked like he was trying to figure out if that meant Sirena was less crazy than he thought or Fey was more crazy. "Right . . ."

Sirena let out a telepathic laugh and privately messaged Fey.

<Sirena: Why is he hanging out with you if weird people aren't his thing?>

<Fey: I have not a single clue. That being said, he's a really solid party member, so I don't question it. He can definitely be the meatshie— I mean, "tank." Yeah, he's the tank.>

<Sirena: Outsourcing your responsibilities, I see.>

<Fey: I prefer the term "delegate." It sounds more dignified.>

Fey's attention was caught by one of the glooms. With their usual rabbit forms fairly inefficient at swimming, they had been experimenting with new shapes. Ebony had hit upon copying Sirena's mermaid form and was now gliding through the water with ease. For whatever reason, however, the gloom had elected to retain its bunny ears, giving it a cute, costume-y look.

Oh, how cute! Sirena exclaimed, grabbing the gloom and hugging it to her chest.

"I'm not sure if this counts as narcissism," Fey commented dryly.

Learning quickly from each other, the other glooms adopted a similar tail to Ebony's form but found it simpler to form round blobs in the front rather than the complexity of a humanoid head and torso. The resulting shape moved quickly but unsteadily through the water.

"You need fins to stabilize your trajectory," Fey observed.

The glooms continued their clumsy swimming without any response.

Fey's eyes widened in horror. "They can't hear me!!!" she yelled through party chat.

Sirena winced (#Revenge). *Relax, I'll tell them. Glooms, Fey says you need fins.*

The five non-mermaid glooms extended three fins each, equidistant around their circumference, now resembling living torpedoes and slicing through the water with impressive precision.

"This is *so* not cool," Fey grumbled, having no way to directly communicate with her pets.

While human speech was fairly unintelligible underwater, the Squeak language sounded somewhat distorted but comprehensible. Amethyst squeaked concernedly. ("Fey-Fey can't talk to us?")

Ebony squeaked from her position trapped in Sirena's grasp. ("She can't mind-talk like crazy mermaid lady.")

Boris grunted. ("She'll figure it out.")

"Grr, let's get you levelled up so we can get out of the water," Fey said, grabbing Sirena and starting to swim toward the nearest underwater town. With a scoff and a stroke of her powerful tail, Sirena overtook her elven friend and reversed their tow-er/tow-ee relationship.

Blade swam hard but quickly fell behind. "Uh, ladies?" he called ahead.

Oops, sorry! Sirena released Fey's hand and swam back to tow Blade along. Meanwhile, Fey was already pulling out her handy-dandy rope. None of them had any advanced knot-tying skills, but they rigged up an arrangement with the middle of the rope looped around Sirena's waist while Fey and Blade each held on to one end, their swimming speed a weighted average of what each could achieve on their own. (Get it? Weighted?)

Uh, Fey, are you staring at my butt? Sirena asked, glancing back at her friend after a few minutes of swimming.

"You don't have a butt right now," Fey pointed out logically.

Okay, are you staring at my upper tail section?

"Kind of. I'm trying to figure out what kind of tail you have."

Both Sirena and Blade looked at her quizzically. As it was covered in scales, it seemed fairly obvious that it was a fish tail.

"Fish tails move left to right and marine animal tails move up and down," Fey explained. "Your tail has scales, but it moves up and down."

Huh, Sirena said contemplatively. It was one of those things she knew through observation but never consciously thought of until someone pointed it out. *So it's a fish-mammal hybrid tail?*

"I guess," said Fey. "It probably wouldn't work well to try to integrate lateral tail movement with a human spine."

With the curiosity Fey had pointed out, Blade had also glanced at Sirena's "upper tail section" and subsequently looked away, now stuck in one of those situations where trying not to think about something just made it more prominent in the mind. He resolutely kept his eyes on the seafloor.

Before long, Sirena's endurance became a limiting factor, further exacerbated by her lack of strength as a mage. *You guys are heavy*, she complained good-naturedly, slowing her pace to avoid exhaustion.

"Meh," said Fey, acknowledging and ignoring the complaint as good friends often did.

"Sorry," said Blade. He kicked harder with his flippers to reduce the drag on the mermaid, happy to have a straightforward task to focus on.

After a brief moment of surprise, Sirena smiled at the warrior. She proceeded to gossip with Fey through private messaging.

<Sirena: What a gentleman. I can't believe you "forgot" to mention him this whole time.>

<Fey: Everything is relative. You did see angel dude, right?>

<Sirena: You do enjoy your fictional characters. This is as good as it gets when it comes to real people.>

(#DramaticIrony)

Fey did not consider Blade particularly good-looking or gentlemanly, but she was aware that her perceptions were extremely skewed by fantasy fiction and did not argue.

<Fey: Noted.>

<Sirena: You're so abnormal.>

<Fey: Luv ya too.>

About half an hour later, Pearlview,[3] the merfolk starter town, came into view. The buildings were made of live coral in beautiful shades of pink, green, blue, white, and gold. Curves and spirals dominated the architecture; a keen eye (which Fey had not) would notice the golden ratio[4] everywhere. Aquatic plants were cultivated in gardens and swayed gently in the water currents. Colourful fish and merfolk swam by, scales flashing in the clear, tropical waters.

Pearlview's crowning glory and namesake was a giant pearl that rivalled Fey's height in diameter. The impossibly large sphere was mounted on the tallest tower in town, almost glowing with iridescence in the sunlight filtered from above. (Well, impossible by regular standards. Oysters get bigger in this game.)

"Pwetty," said Fey as she looked around. (*W*-spelling intended.)

Blade nodded in agreement, though his attention was not on the scenery.

In the world of *Fantasia*, male gamers outnumbered female gamers at a ratio of about 2:1. For the less classically pretty races, the ratio was even more unbalanced; for instance, dwarven players had 35 males per female.

With the merfolk colonies, the gender imbalance was completely reversed, and mermaids dominated the population 50:1 compared to mermen.

Additionally, travelling efficiently underwater necessitated tight-fitting clothing with minimal bulk and, while not limited to (extremely uncomfortable-looking) shell brassieres, fashion tended toward "skimpy."

In such an environment, any insecurities a player had about their physical appearance were heightened and exposed. As a result, the merfolk colonies had the highest rate of purchase of appearance-enhancing modules of any player population in the game.

In short, Blade was currently in an anime-style harem fantasy. Natural or not, beautiful mermaids swam in every direction. He was self-possessed enough to pretend not to notice, but he could not change the fact that he enjoyed the view.

Finally, we're here. It was with relief that a tired Sirena untied the rope from her waist and let Fey put it away. *So, what do you want to do first?*

"Weapons shop," Fey said without hesitation. (Priority 1: Be able to kill things.) Almost all of their armour and weapons were extremely unsuitable to be used in a saltwater environment and had been left in their safe-deposit boxes.

Oh, right. This way.

Sea architecture differed quite significantly from that on land. Fluctuations in temperature and weather were basically non-existent, so buildings served more to delineate boundaries than to provide shelter from the elements. In addition, a constant flow of fresh water was necessary to prevent oxygen depletion inside. As such, public buildings were completely open on top and there was no distinction between windows and doors, large openings in walls built of coral that had an organic look to them that made Fey suspect they had been conjured with the merfolk equivalent of the elves' tree-singing.

They swam into the weapons shop from the open top, rows of lethal-looking implements displayed along the walls and interior shelves the equivalent of three storeys high rather than on tables along the bottom.

Hello, said the shopkeeper, a merman NPC who seemed designed to be popular with the predominantly female player population. His telepathic voice seemed to have all the distinctive qualities of a physical voice, very clearly distinguishable from Sirena's more feminine voice.

Hi! Sirena said cheerfully. Unlike Fey, she had absolutely no problem chatting with anyone, stranger or not. *My friends here need weapons suitable for level twenty-something warriors.*

Certainly, said the sales(mer)man. Expertly maneuvering in the restricted space of the store, he took down a selection of weapons and took them up to a counter in the open upper area of the store for them to look at.

In addition to the consideration of materials that could survive in an underwater environment, weapon design had to take into consideration the increased viscosity of water compared to air. Drag would significantly hamper attempts to slash or swing in large arcs, whereas stabs and thrusts were less impaired. As such, the dominant weapons were variations on the spear, made of crystal and metals that would not rust.

Fey was drawn to a double-headed spear made from glossy obsidian and enchanted to be less brittle than the base material. One end was equipped with a standard leaf-shaped spearhead, while the other had a harpoon-like backward curve that would ensure the weapon would either stay embedded in its target or do even more damage on the way out.

Blade chose a weighted net, woven from fibres tough enough to resist cutting and tearing, as well as a titanium-coated trident, somewhat coincidentally matching the weapons used by a class of Roman gladiators, the fisherman-inspired retiarius.[5]

After paying for the purchases, they left the shop. Given the short amount of time they planned to stay underwater and the effects of drag on swimming mobility, they decided not to spend extra money on armour. (Thrifty choice or dangerous decision, we'll just have to see.)

"Where to now?" Blade asked.

"Let's go experiment on some weaker monsters," Fey suggested. Her perfectly logical suggestion somehow brought to mind fictional evil scientists with questionable morals.

How about giant lobsters? They're level 15, Sirena proposed.

"Sounds edible. Let's kill some."

CHAPTER 4
ELECTRIFYING COMBAT

The giant lobster territory was a significant distance from town and in order to avoid again being lassoed as a draft[6] mermaid, Sirena enlisted the services of a pair of taxi dolphins to tow her slow-swimming party members.

We'd like to go to the giant lobster territory, she said to two individuals waiting at a designated pickup point.

Dolphins in *Fantasia* were not a playable race due to the impracticality of not having opposable thumbs, but they possessed human-level intelligence and the same telepathic abilities as merfolk.

That's not very far, commented one of the dolphins. Her telepathic voice was clear but somewhat inhuman.

Humans don't swim very quickly, Sirena explained, pointing at her tail-less companions.

The dolphins circled Fey and Blade curiously, having never seen two-legged humanoids before.

So this is a human, the same dolphin commented.

"I'm an elf," Fey declared. She said this through the group chat and Sirena failed to relay the message, so the dolphins continued their inspection uninterrupted.

What are those tiny things? the female asked about the Feypets. She curiously poked Boris with her rostrum. (The author wanted to use the word "beak" but was caught between sounding normal and technical accuracy. Please don't judge her for being pretentious.)

Those are my friend's pets, other creatures from land, said Sirena. *That one's a miniature boar, the purple squishy thing is a slime, and these shadowy things are glooms. The glooms can change shape.*

After observing the dolphins' ease of movement in water, Shadow and Onyx chose to shift their forms from tailed torpedoes to miniature shadow-dolphins.

The dolphins chittered in laughter at the imitation. *Just for that, we'll take you for free,* said the female, who appeared to be the older one of the pair.

Fey was amused, the dolphins making her consider their appearance from a novel point of view. In terms of surviving in an underwater environment, her pets were bizarre indeed. (That makes it seem like they're not bizarre, period.)

She waved hello as she grabbed on to the kelp rope harness the female dolphin was wearing, while Blade did the same with the male dolphin.

Hello, I'm—a series of dolphin whistles and clicks. *And that's*—a series of different dolphin whistles and clicks.

Fey waved again.

You two should really go purchase telepathy stones, commented Blade's dolphin (hereafter referred to as "Click"). *Having mute riders is boring.*

Telepathy stones were designed to allow non-aquatic races to communicate effectively underwater. "Ooh, I want one!" Fey said over party chat, wanting to be able to communicate with her pets again.

Okay, let's go to the accessory shop— Before Sirena could complete her sentence, the dolphins had zoomed away, towing their somewhat startled passengers.

Even towing a person each, the dolphins made Sirena work hard to keep up. They made quick stops at the accessory shop, the bank, and then the accessory shop again. The telepathy stone, made of blue kyanite,[7] cost 5000g. Fey considered the convenience well worth the price, but Blade, who did not have any pressing need to communicate outside the party, elected to save his money.

The stone was mounted on a simple choker-style necklace. *There we go*, Fey said in satisfaction as she put it on. Her telepathic voice was recognizably Fey-like despite not having an auditory component.

The Feypets squeaked loudly ("Fey-Fey!") and converged on their owner as if reuniting after years of separation. Even Ebony wriggled from Sirena's grasp to join in on the group hug.

Why are the land-pets attacking their owner? asked Click.

This is called "hugging," answered Fey's dolphin (hereafter referred to as Whistle) in a lecturing tone, passing on her knowledge of the strange behaviour of land-dwellers. *Land creatures grab on to each other in order to express affection.*

Oh. Octopi do that to their food down here, I guess. Everybody likes food.

Fey laughed at the dolphins' conversation, amused by the idea that a mundane hug could be seen as bizarre behaviour. *Okay, let's go kill some lobsters.*

Click and Whistle led the way to the giant lobster territory, followed very closely by their passengers, and less closely by Sirena. The dolphin-shaped Shadow and Onyx raced the torpedo-shaped Inkblot, Obsidian, and Midnight, with no clear winner in speed. Ebony, straggling along behind due to her extraneous bunny ears on a mermaid build, was recaptured and towed along by Sirena.

"Hey, what spells do you have?" Blade asked Sirena as they travelled. (Being a perfectly practical question that any reasonable person might ask, it was even odds whether it would have occurred to Fey.)

My level 10 spell is an electric-type elemental bolt, Charge Jolt. My level 20 spell is a non-elemental area-of-effect attack, Magic Bomb. I also bought a spellbook and learned Ice Slice, which deals physical damage.

Merfolk had naturally high water affinity, and mermaid mages could cast water-element spells with 30 percent more effectiveness. However, all aquatic monsters also had high water affinity and took less damage from water spells. Sirena had chosen an electric-type beginner spell to exploit the weakness of most of the local monsters. Ice and water element affinities had 50 percent overlap, so she had chosen an ice spell to deal physical damage.

"Cool," said Blade. (Fey snorted at the unintentional pun.) "So what's the strategy?" he continued.

Um.

Hit enemies until they die,[8] said Fey.

"Got it."

As plans went, the best that could be said of this one was that it was "flexible." (The worst that could be said was that it's "not a plan.")

When they arrived at the giant lobster territory, Fey made an impressed sound. *They weren't kidding about the "giant" part.*

Due to certain biological mechanisms, real-world lobsters did not reach "old age" and in fact continued to grow throughout their lives.[9] Though they were known to reach over a metre in length and exceed twenty kilograms in weight after a century of growth, their size was limited by the energy requirements of molting, and they had an increased chance of dying during the process of shedding and forming a new exoskeleton as they grew larger.

Apparently, Fantasian lobsters had no such restriction. Each of the bluish-brown crustaceans was longer than Fey was tall, vaguely reminiscent of crocodiles with their long, low silhouettes. Instead of large, snapping jaws, they were armed with huge claws that looked like they could easily crush a person's head or sever a limb.

Thanks for the ride, Fey said to Whistle, letting go of the dolphin's harness to swim under her own power. Blade likewise separated from Click, and the two dolphins swam off.

Instead of returning to town, the dolphins chose to loiter in the area, curious as to how the humans would fight.

Sirena shared her previous experience fighting the lobsters. *They can't really get far off the seafloor, so don't worry about protecting me; I'll just stay up here and shoot spells. Watch out for the claws; they can seriously maim you.*

Okay. Try not to hit us. Fey swam down to engage a lobster, with Blade following close behind.

Sirena began a spell. "Charge Jolt," she intoned.

Spell-casting had a unique mechanic in *Fantasia*. Rather than individual spells having a cool-down time, they instead required a buildup of magical energy before they manifested. This minimum value was listed as the "mana intensity threshold" in each spell's information.

Accompanying this measure of mana intensity was the mage-only attribute of concentration. Unlike the base attributes of vitality, strength, dexterity, agility, intelligence, and willpower, it did not increase automatically to each level and had to be increased by assigning free stat points or spontaneous increases gained through focus exercises and meditation. Concentration affected spell-casting in two ways: one, its value was the mana intensity a mage could produce per second; and two, the higher it was, the lower the chance a mage's spell-casting could be interrupted by attacks and other distractions.

While a warrior allocated their attribute points toward vitality, strength, dexterity, and agility, a mage spent theirs on intelligence for mana reserves and magic attack, willpower for mana regeneration and decreased spell costs, and concentration for spell-casting speed.

Charge Jolt had a mana intensity threshold of 100 while Sirena's concentration was 36, so it took a minimum of 2.8 seconds to cast the spell. However, there was an option to continue building mana intensity beyond the threshold for extra attack power, and Sirena released the attack after a full 8.4 seconds, tripling the intensity of the attack. Electricity flashed between her fingertips and the nearest lobster, then arced to chain-attack two more lobsters. Instantly cooked, all three turned a bright orange-red.

<Sirena has defeated the giant lobster!>

<Sirena has gained 45 experience.>

<Sirena has defeated the giant lobster!>

<Sirena has gained 45 experience.>

<Sirena has defeated the giant lobster!>

<Sirena has gained 45 experience.>

Sirena blinked at the game notifications, which indicated that none of the kill experience had been shared with her party members. *Uh, guys?* she called out. *Why are you using individual experience allocation?*

Fey was rather preoccupied with her own target, swimming up from a posterior approach to hopefully be less noticeable. Taking a two-handed grip on her spear, she stabbed down with the end that was not barbed, aiming for the spot in the back of its head that she had seen recommended on cooking shows. Despite its sharpness, the spear barely even left a visible mark on the lobster's thick exoskeleton. Startled, the lobster fled, propelling itself backward by curling its tail in. Chasing after her quarry, Fey distractedly answered her friend. *You can change it if you want.*

Blade was the official party leader with the power to change party settings such as experience allocation. He had gotten his trident wedged under a piece of carapace, and he was being jerked along as his lobster zoomed through the water. Managing to get his feet braced on its back as it slowed, he heaved up with all his strength, freeing his weapon as well as a fairly large piece of exoskeleton. He immediately stabbed down into the unprotected flesh, killing his target.

<Blade has defeated the giant lobster!>

<Blade has gained 45 experience.>

<Blade has learned Disarmour!>

"What?" he said, his mind catching up to the conversation. "Oh." He changed the experience setting from "individual" to "weighted." "Hey, I learned a new skill!" he exclaimed.

Fey chased after her lobster, which had surprised her with its burst of speed. Finally catching up, she attacked again, this time remembering to activate Mana Edge to bypass some of its defence. With the magic, her spear sank into the lobster's brain for an instant kill.

<Fey has defeated the giant lobster!>

<Fey has gained 15 experience. Amethyst has gained 7 experience. Boris has gained 7 experience. Onyx has gained 7 experience. Inkblot has gained 7 experience. Ebony has gained 7 experience. Midnight has gained 7 experience. Shadow has gained 7 experience. Obsidian has gained 7 experience.>

<Blade has gained 15 experience.>

<Sirena has gained 15 experience.>

(This is funny because both Sirena and Blade got the full experience from their kills but Fey had to share.)

What? she said, also catching up to the conversation. Looking back on the party system notices, she saw *Disarmour. How'd you learn that?*

"I ripped off a piece of its shell," Blade answered.

Hmm . . . Fey murmured in consideration. Reversing her grip on the spear so its barbed end was forward, she swam to another lobster and stabbed down with all her might (which was still not very much).

While the attack left a slightly more prominent line than her first attack, it still failed to penetrate the exoskeleton. This lobster also zoomed backward with a flip of its tail, sending her tumbling.

In building his avatar, Blade had completely ignored dexterity and agility, considering the passive increases with level enough to get by. He had invested almost all of his free stat points into strength, with a few into vitality.

Fey's strength was over 40 points lower than Blade's. She was confident that if they ever fought, she would win (by poisoning him and running away), but in terms of brute strength, she could not compete.

Trying to use her smarts over strength, she found another lobster and carefully poked the barbed spearhead through its exoskeleton with Mana Edge before deactivating the ability. It worked quite well to lodge the weapon in its shell.

In a classic bout of premature smugness, Fey yanked up on the spear and found that ripping away a chunk of exoskeleton took even more strength than penetrating it. She was dragged along for the ride as the lobster's flight response was activated.

Help, she called out in a helpless-but-calm tone.

Maybe let go of the spear? Sirena suggested.

But what if it gets away and I lose it? I just bought this thing, Fey complained.

Let go . . . now, Sirena said, releasing a Charge Jolt on the last word.

Fey barely let go in time to avoid being electrocuted, but since she had not actually been electrocuted, she supposed she could not complain about the method of rescue. *Thanks*, she said, trying not to sound sarcastic.

Any time, Sirena answered cheerfully, trying not to sound like she enjoyed putting her best friend in mortal danger.

Blade was moderately smug at having picked up a skill that he had formed without help, and one that Fey could not learn. He cheerfully repeated Disarmour on every lobster he attacked.

Fey abandoned trying to learn the new skill and returned to using Mana Edge for precision strikes to the head, killing most of her targets in a single blow. She comforted herself with the fact that her method was faster and more efficient.

Slightly behind her ear, Amethyst squeaked questioningly.

You can help, but no poison, said Fey. *They need to be edible afterward.*

With a squeak of acknowledgement, Amethyst released her hold on Fey and caught a ride with a torpedo-shaped Inkblot. The whole gang of Feypets (the author considered many different nouns to refer to the collective of Feypets and somehow "gang" felt the most appropriate) zoomed off to do their own fighting.

A safe distance away, Click and Whistle entertained themselves with a running commentary on the action.

That's an interesting technique, noted Click, referring to Blade. *Those feet things are useful for pushing against things.*

It looks impressive, but it's slow, said Whistle. *The she-human is killing three for every two of his.*

(Clearly, the dolphins were never going to learn to distinguish between humans and elves.)

Well, if it's speed you're after, the mermaid is killing six at a time, said Whistle, watching Sirena maximize her chain lightning attack.

Well, the humans have to spend most of their time chasing after the lobsters. They're such slow swimmers, Whistle lamented.

Hey, what's that? Click asked as he saw a giant lobster suddenly jerked off the seafloor. Its tail had not curled inward to propel it, and it flailed its legs until it landed back in the sand.

An annoyed squeak followed. ("More to the right!")

This time, only the right side of the lobster jerked upward. Unbalanced, it was flipped onto its back, its legs waving helplessly in the water. In the place it had been previously standing was a gloom-riding slime.

Other glooms zipped around, confusing the lobster and hindering its efforts to right itself. Amethyst pounded away at the softer underside of the crustacean with Whip, though each of the powerful attacks sent her and Inkblot tumbling in the opposite direction, forcing the gloom to do a great deal of swimming just to remain in the same place.

Click and Whistle were impressed. The glooms were quite small, the slime even smaller, and yet they had managed to kill a giant lobster all by themselves.

In all the commotion, Boris was feeling left out. Fey had put him down in order to wield her spear with both hands, and his swim speed was not nearly enough to keep up with the other Feypets, even slower than Fey and Blade with their scuba flippers. He was rather too heavy to be effectively towed by one of the glooms, which left him stranded on the seafloor, unable to participate.

He grunted. ("This sucks.") He could walk slowly on the seafloor, but if he tried going faster, he started floating upward, losing traction until he sank down again.

Wandering slowly along, he came upon a smooth, water-worn stone that was about a third of his size and perfectly shaped to fit on his back.

Inspired, he called to the other Feypets, who zipped over to where he stood.

After listening to his explanation, Shadow and Obsidian hoisted the rock onto his back while Onyx transformed into a harness that kept it securely fastened.

Boris trotted experimentally along the seafloor for a few steps, pleased to find that he could dig his feet into the sand without starting to push himself away from the seafloor. Activating Charge, he built up speed and collided with a giant lobster, the weight he was carrying helping to increase the destructive energy delivered to the crustacean.

The lobster collapsed to one side, two legs and part of its main exoskeleton crushed.

The rest of the Feypets swarmed the crippled monster and quickly finished it off.

With a snort of satisfaction, Boris shook himself off and began another Charge.

Land creatures are kind of scary, said Click.

Whistle wholeheartedly agreed.

If such tiny ones are so strong . . . He trailed off.

Let's just be glad we swim faster than they do.

CHAPTER 5
GO FOR GOLD

(Parentheses have been allowed in Leandriel scene
for limited translation purposes.)

Leandriel flew through the air with powerful wingbeats. After some experimentation, he had found that the easiest way to carry Magic was to have the mushroom ride on his head, minimizing the additional drag generated. Fortunately, Magic showed no inclination toward falling from his nearly vertical perch, peering with interest at the lethal distance separating them from the ground.

The seemingly endless depths of the Rift came into view. Leandriel backwinged and began a careful descent into the darkness of the crevasse, summoning tiny fairy lights to illuminate his way without ruining his dark vision.

The deeper he went, the more an ominous atmosphere encroached on his holy aura. Strange shadows seemed to flit across the walls and through the air, the feeling of being watched became oppressive, and cackling maniacal laughter rang out intermittently, only to abruptly morph into screaming. The developers had, of course, turned these "imagined" dangers into very real and bloodthirsty monsters.

Magic was somehow immune to the ambience, his own aura of cute obliviousness making any feelings of trepidation seem ridiculous. When Leandriel's feet finally touched ground after many minutes of descent, the mushroom hopped down to Leandriel's shoulder, squeaking excitedly. ("Are the monsters strong here? Do they drop good loot?")

Leandriel chuckled and patted Magic briefly before hurriedly drawing his sword. He did not understand the squeaked questions, but Magic was soon answered: every monster within sensing distance, insanely enraged by the presence of holy element, attacked.

Expecting this reaction, Leandriel calmly waded through the horde, his flashing sword leaving grotesque corpses in his wake. The monsters at the entrance of the Rift were between levels 80 and 90 and well within his fighting capabilities, even in huge mobs.

<Leandriel has defeated the undead horror!>

<Leandriel has gained 276 experience. Magic has gained 138 experience.>

<Leandriel has defeated the dark abomination!>

<Leandriel has gained 310 experience. Magic has gained 155 experience.>

<Magic has reached level 21!>

Within minutes, Magic had gained a level. Each slice of Leandriel's blessed sword corresponded to a huge increase in the mushroom's experience gauge. While there were safeguards against power-levelling other players, there were none against doing so with a newly acquired pet.

Magic hopped out of the way of Leandriel's arm movements, returning to his spot on Leandriel's head to watch the fighting and commenting with happy squeaks. ("So many monsters! So much loot!")

Leandriel found himself smiling as he fought his way forward, the mood so drastically different compared to before he had agreed to pet-sit that he rather wished he had his own companion, though a pet raised in his influence would certainly have a more subdued personality than Fey's vivacious creatures.

Magic's squeaks shifted in tenor to confused ("Aren't we getting too far from the loot?") to sad ("Oh. We're not picking up the loot.") as Leandriel fought his way deeper into the Rift, toward the stronger monsters he had not yet tested.

"What's wrong, Magic?" Leandriel asked, continuing to fight and progress forward. He barely noticed the coins, minor equipment, and crafting materials he was leaving behind; they were under the purview of other testers and nothing but potential tripping hazards to him.

Magic gave a short, sad squeak ("Never mind."). He was aware that his new owner had different priorities from Fey, and resigned himself to seeing the loot vanish.

Leandriel was not one to ignore a sad mushroom (*sentence that would make absolutely no sense in any other story*). He stopped his forward advance and fought only enough to defend himself.

"Magic, I cannot guess what you are upset about. You will have to show me."

Magic dispiritedly hopped to the ground and a nearby monster corpse. He found a 500g coin and nudged it back toward Leandriel, ignoring the three monsters that tried to eat him on the way. Leandriel lunged forward and killed the monsters with clean strikes of his mithril sword.

"A coin? What about it?" Leandriel wondered. Magic hopped away again and Leandriel continued to protect the little mushroom as he added two more coins to the pile.

Understanding dawned. "You want to collect the gold?"

Magic nodded but squeaked again sadly. ("I know you're busy.")

Leandriel found himself unwilling to leave his new friend so dispirited. "Just a second. Hop on."

As Magic returned to his safe perch, Leandriel sent a message through a special PM channel linked to the outside world. The words showed up as an instant message on a certain programmer's computer screen.

<Leandriel: Hey, Kevin, could you add Gold Magnet to my spell repertoire?>

The ability to attract gold and/or other loot was a high-level racial trait of dwarves, a rogue-only class skill, and a general-use spell for anyone lucky enough to obtain the rare single-use spellbooks that etched it into memory. Asking a programmer to add it to his repertoire was cheating, but Leandriel thought it would be fine as long as he did not use the extra income.

<KevinO: Why do you need more gold? You have a couple million stashed.>

<Leandriel: I don't, but I have a new pet who apparently is a fan of gold.>

<KevinO: When did you get a new pet?>

There was a microsecond pause as Kevin looked through Leandriel's activity logs. Before Leandriel could formulate a reply, Kevin had already found the information.

<KevinO: Where did you find a level 20 blue mushroom?>

Another pause as Kevin scanned the log further into the past.

<KevinO: You fell on an elf and broke her ribs?>

Leandriel grimaced. Kevin used programs to analyze Leandriel's game activities and rarely looked directly at the logs. Since the programs focused on battle abilities and experience gain, Kevin had thus far missed the small periods of time Leandriel had spent with a certain elf.

<Leandriel: Yes.>

He answered though Kevin did not need the confirmation. He was certainly not going to try to shirk responsibility for carelessly injuring Fey the way he had.

Another few seconds passed as Kevin's skilled fingers pulled up more related information.

<KevinO: Man, you really like this girl.>

Leandriel did not know what information Kevin was using to draw such a conclusion, but he felt acutely uncomfortable, as if someone were reading his personal journal. He did not keep a journal, precisely to avoid this vulnerability.

<Leandriel: Whatever you are looking at, please stop.>
<KevinO: Okay, okay. If it makes you feel better, she likes you too.>
<Leandriel: What? How do you know?>
<Leandriel: Wait, do not tell me.>

Leandriel dearly wanted to know why Kevin had drawn the conclusion about Fey's feelings, but respecting her privacy was more important. Legally, the terms of service for *Fantasia* included a clause that released game information to developers and testers, so Kevin was free to look at whatever he wanted, but Leandriel did not feel this exempted him from basic ethical considerations given that he certainly did not need the information to do his job.

<KevinO: If you say so. This other guy, though . . . >

Apparently, the computer whiz was now looking at tangentially related data. Leandriel guessed Kevin referred to Blade, though it was certainly possible it was an entirely different player.

<Leandriel: What about him?>

<KevinO: He's pretty crazy.>

<Leandriel: In a good way or a bad way?>

<KevinO: In a somewhat masochistic kind of way. Actually, your girl is pretty crazy, too.>

The mental image that Leandriel had formed of Fey was that of someone who enjoyed a bit of harmless silliness, so he assumed that Kevin was using the word "crazy" in the slang sense. He had no idea what the developer meant in terms of masochistic craziness and mentally shrugged off the curiosity.

<Leandriel: Never mind that. Spell, please.>

<KevinO: Oh yeah. No problem.>

<Leandriel has learned Gold Magnet!>

<Leandriel: Thank you.>

Magic squeaked curiously, wondering what his new owner was doing as Leandriel spent several minutes absent-mindedly defending himself from monsters while staring at a virtual screen. As they had stayed in the same spot for a while, the attacks had largely died down. (Get it? Died down. *smacked by the author-goddess for exceeding limited translation purposes*)

"Watch this," Leandriel told the mushroom. "Gold Magnet."

<Gold Magnet: Gold within 50m will be attracted to the target>
<Duration: 1 hour>

Pieces of gold began to float off the ground and drift toward them. Leandriel had targeted the spell to the inside of his belt pouch rather than his body, so the coins streamed smoothly into the receptacle's magically augmented depths.

Starting to move again, Leandriel flowed across the battlefield, leaving defeated monsters in his wake. Large-denomination coins drifted in, quickly totalling to more than Fey's pre-mithril-coin-augmented bank account balance.

Magic had never seen such riches in his short mushroom life. Such was the depth of his wonderment that for the first time, he uttered a sound other than a squeak. "Ooooo . . ." The high-pitched sound of admiration went on and on.

Leandriel laughed. He felt like he had just performed a sleight-of-hand trick for a delighted child.

"Let's finish some work now, shall we?"

Magic squeaked in the enthusiastic affirmative.

Sirena and Blade looked at each other as Fey (and pets) disappeared through the teleportation gate on the way to deliver freshly killed giant lobsters to Tallen's tavern. (What, you thought she wanted to eat them? That would be too straightforward.) Because the gates required time to activate, Fey would not return for at least ten minutes. This was an awkwardly long time to do nothing, but too short a time for the two to go anywhere and return.

Sirena handled the situation with far more grace and ease than her friend would. No novice to the art of small talk, she deftly avoided asking about personal details that would allow her to find Blade's real identity (remember, children, practice safe Internet). Instead, her opening gambit was *So, what do you like doing in your free time?*

Blade shrugged. Sirena had settled down and refrained from doing anything outrageous after the "drunk dolphin incident," and he had largely stopped treating her like an unfamiliar explosive device. "Just normal stuff, hanging out with friends, watching TV. Sometimes I go hiking."

Sirena seized upon the most potentially interesting activity. *Hiking? The scenery must be beautiful. Where's your favourite place to hike?*

And the conversation took off (*bang of starting pistol*). With a few well-placed questions and a disarming smile, Sirena struck up a lively conversation (*author skipping dialogue because she cannot properly depict social competency*). She learned that Blade had gone hiking on the Inca trail in Peru, was not prone to altitude sickness, had an immediate family that consisted of still-married parents and an older sister, and enjoyed spicy food.

Blade was describing the differences between llamas and alpacas (llamas are bigger[10]) when Fey (and pets) reappeared.

Fey listened for a moment, then chimed in. *So you've been to Peru?*

"Yeah," said Blade.

When did you learn about llamas and alpacas? asked Sirena.

Fey grinned. *Never underestimate the randomness of the things I know. He wasn't even talking about the weirder animals in Peru, like the Andean cock-of-the-rock.*

"The *what?*" Blade asked.

Fey raised a hand as if pledging an oath. *It's a real species of bird. I didn't name it.*

(*Author trying to justify the amount of time she wastes learning trivia by inserting it into a story*)

You must have the weirdest Internet search history ever, sighed Sirena. Rather than an exasperated tone, she telepathed with admiration.

I try, said Fey in a tone of false modesty.

"You should go on *Jeopardy!*," Blade suggested.

Nah, I never know any of the answers. I hate memorizing names and dates. Fey's knowledge of trivia was dominated by the basic sciences, particularly biology.

History was always your worst subject, Sirena commented.

Only if you don't count gym class. It seemed that every single year, Arwyn had managed to get hit in the head with a basketball at least once (*–1 IQ point*). While she had fairly good endurance, flexibility, and balance from tae kwon do, she lacked the strength and hand-eye coordination required to excel at any of the activities covered in gym class.

In some (okay, most) ways, Blade's high school experience was the opposite of Fey's. He was a fairly skilled athlete and did well at team sports.

As people did when trying to fit into a group, Blade refrained from discussing the differences. "So you guys went to school together?" he asked instead.

Four years of high school, Sirena confirmed.

And then we were cruelly separated at university, Fey lamented. They had been accepted to venerable institutions several hundred kilometres apart (because Canada is huge).

And then we moved back to the same city to work, Sirena added.

Sirena deftly turned the conversation away from personal matters and asked, *So how did your lobster delivery go?*

Fey smiled happily. *Tallen gave me 500g per lobster.*

Tallen had given Fey a reasonable price for the giant lobsters, which each contained enough meat to feed a whole table. Of course, after he cooked them, he would mark up the price and turn over a hefty profit for himself. There was nowhere else within five hundred kilometres with a supply of lobster, so the tavern-keeper could overcharge as much as he wanted.

Sirena held out a hand. *Share,* she demanded casually, dispensing with manners with her best friend.

Fey grumbled but pulled out the coins. *Neither of you even produced a single sellable lobster. You, with the precooking, and you, ripping up the shell so it looked gross. Amethyst and I did all the work.*

Mm-hmm, said Sirena in an "I'm ignoring your whining" tone. She received three thousand gold in large coinage.

Since Blade had been equally useless as but not more useless than Sirena, Fey had to share with him as well. *Here,* she said as she held out a handful of coins. Not expecting the bounty, Blade was half a second late in accepting them. "Thanks."

Fey had (barely) managed to fit twenty giant lobsters into her backpacks for a profit of 10,000g. She had shared 3000g with each of her party mates and kept 4000g for herself rather than bothering with using smaller-denomination coins to distribute the gold more evenly. She thought this was more than fair, since she had killed all the sold lobsters and done the transportation herself.

Should we go get more lobsters? Sirena asked. Ten thousand gold was a hefty sum for players of their level.

Meh, said Fey. *We can gold-farm when we need gold. Let's go fight something stronger.*

"Do you know what monsters around here are level 20 or 21?" Blade asked Sirena.

Sirena had not yet fought monsters of that strength and was unaware of which ones they were. *No idea. Let's go check out the notice board,* she suggested. She swam off with an easy flick of her tail, paced by the glooms, with the taxi-less Fey and Blade lagging behind.

Pearlview's notice board was covered in posters made of pale green kelp paper. Instead of using ink, words were etched in dark brown through the application of heat. The quests offered on the board were all simple mass hunting or collection quests; to find more interesting ones, one had to explore the game world and interact with the NPCs.

Fey had a minor talent in scanning text for desired information; after a second's perusal of the haphazardly arranged posters, she reported, *Electric eels at level 20, and "nomfish" at level 21.* She pointed at the locations of the two posters she read from. They both showed the same format: a request for a hunt of five hundred monsters, basic information of the monsters, and an uncoloured illustration.

The electric eels were fairly straightforward, their physical appearance taken directly from their real-world counterparts. (Behaviour and electricity-generating abilities, not so much. Gotta make them more able to kill people.)

Nomfish were an entirely artificial construct, made by one of the developers *not* known for drawing skill. The rather simplistic fish was coded into the game by some other programmers as a joke upon finding the developer's doodle on a napkin. (You say we give the developers too much free time. They say it adds a "whimsical touch" to the games they produce. The popularity and profitability of VirtualRealities.com means we're going to go with the developers on this one. Though we're not going to give them *more* free time, as they've been requesting.)

I'm guessing my Charge Jolt wouldn't work so well on electric eels, Sirena commented. *Plus, I don't want to get shocked.*

"Our suits are pretty rubbery, so we'll probably be fine," Blade pointed out, referring to himself and Fey.

What about me? Sirena asked plaintively. Her (skimpy) aquatic mage robes boosted magic stats but offered very little physical or elemental defence.

"Well, you're the mage, so you're not supposed to be taking damage at all," said Blade.

Sirena looked at Blade, trying to determine whether his remark was an indirect promise of protection or a sign that he was indifferent to whether she was injured or not.

Fey took the remark as Blade had meant it: a factual statement of the role mages are supposed to play in combat. She replied accordingly. *That's true. However, given Sirena's magic type and how cute the nomfish are, I vote we go after them.*

The illustration of the nomfish showed a cartoonishly cute monster. Light green in colour, it had a round body wider than its height, black button eyes, and a wide mouth that looked like it was smiling. Fey preferred to go after monsters that did not look like real animals (except if they were edible), preferring the fighting to be as gamelike as possible.

Nomfish, Sirena voted.

"Sure." Blade shrugged. Either choice was acceptable to him. The only class of monster he was against was the poisonous class (*wrong choice of party member*).

As the stronger monsters were farther away from town, the party found a group of three dolphin taxis to take them to the nomfish territory.

(For the record, it's not always a good idea to go after the cute monsters. Sometimes, they have teeth.)

CHAPTER 6
YOU JELLY?[II]

*E**ugh.**

Fey's party limped back to Pearlview looking much worse for wear than when it had left. Taxi dolphins usually lingered where they dropped off their passengers in order to collect a return fare, but the trio of dolphins the group had hired to take them to the nomfish territory had immediately returned to Pearlview after dropping them off.

This should have been an obvious warning, but Fey, Blade, and Sirena had persisted on their quest to hunt five hundred nomfish.

It turned out that the reason nomfish had such wide mouths was to accommodate the excessive number of sharklike teeth they had. ("Nom" is short for "omnomnom.") When provoked, the entire school of carnivorous fish had attacked like hungry piranhas. As with many species (and people), nomfish were a lot cuter when they kept their mouths shut.

Sirena poked mournfully at a tear in her mage robes. Two warriors (well, one warrior and a Fey) had been insufficient to keep all of the nomfish away from her. Her clothing and flesh had suffered as a result; it said something about her priorities that she mourned the clothing more.

I need to up my Concentration, she sighed. While taking 8 seconds to cast a spell had seemed fast against the giant lobsters, Charge Jolt's minimum cast time of 2.8 seconds had seemed far too long in the face of the fast-moving nomfish.

"You already did, didn't you?" asked Blade. Applying some of the attribute points from levelling up toward Concentration, Sirena could now cast Charge Jolt in 2.4 seconds. (This had also seemed far too long in the face of the fast-moving nomfish.)

We should have bought armour, Fey lamented (see Chapter 3 to review the unwise decision), joining in on Sirena's self-pity fest. Her wet suit had not been enough to keep nomfish teeth away from her skin.

"Aww, cheer up," said Blade. "We finished the quest and levelled up, didn't we? Sirena even gained two levels."

Blade, Fey, and Sirena were now level 25, 24, and 23, respectively. If anything, the human warrior was even more tattered than his party mates, having taken up his meatshield (*cough* we mean "tank") duties with seriousness, despite not having been told it was his role.

We should have gone after the electric eels, Fey continued gloomily. She was not a person who let some optimistic encouragement get in the way of a good pity-fest. (Whining childishly was one of her favourite hobbies.)

"Come on," Blade coaxed. "Your glooms even learned a new skill."

Despite herself, Fey smiled. *They did, didn't they?* She glanced fondly at her adorably vicious shadow-pets, which now consisted of one rabbit-eared mermaid, two swimming torpedoes, two shadow-dolphins, and an inky nomfish. The glooms had figured out that the safest way to kill the nomfish while staying away from their teeth was to seal the nomfishes' gills shut, depriving them of oxygen. Thus, Suffocate had been born.

Obsidian swam over, temporarily grew arms to give Fey a hug, then darted off again (as a torpedo).

Love you too, Fey called after her pet. Compared to her earlier expression, she was now smilingly cheerful. Her somewhat sudden shift in demeanour was not a sign of emotional instability; rather, she had not been particularly upset in the first place. (She was also not one to let "not being particularly upset" get in the way of whining).

Seeing that she had lost her comrade-in-self-pity, Sirena also adopted a more cheerful mien after one last sigh over her damaged clothes. She gave the captured Ebony an extra hugging squeeze. Ebony wiggled slightly in a feeble attempt to escape but had mostly resigned herself to her fate as a living stuffed animal. (Psst. Shadow-bunny. If you shift to the cave-spider shape, the mermaid will probably let you go.)

As the sun set in the game world, visibility underwater became very poor.

How does anyone play underwater at night? Fey asked. Even with elven night vision, she could tell that she would have trouble seeing when the sun set completely.

A lot of monsters are bioluminescent, Sirena answered. *Still, it's a good idea to stay near town after dark.*

"Why?" asked Blade.

Sirena met a question with a question. *Ever heard of anglerfish?*

"Uh, maybe?" The term sounded vaguely familiar to Blade.

Scary deep-sea fish that use a lanternlike appendage to lure prey to them, Fey summarized. *Fun fact: several species of anglerfish practice sexual parasitism, where the male fuses with the female and is basically reduced to a sperm source.*

". . . Cool." Blade did not really think that Fey's fact was particularly fun (more like "super creepy").

Yeah, a fun fact would be something along the lines of "there was an anglerfish in Finding Nemo," Sirena commented dryly.

To-may-to, to-mah-to, said Fey, dismissing the gentle correction with a wave of her hand.

Anyway, Sirena continued. *Anglerfish aren't restricted to low depths in this ocean. They're also a lot bigger and have lures that look exactly like low-level jellyfish.*

Ooh, jellyfish. Are they cute? asked Fey.

I wouldn't exactly call them cute. They're gelatinous masses with tentacles full of neurotoxic stingers, Sirena replied.

I wanna see! Fey exclaimed (childishly). Apparently, Sirena's description of the jellyfish was appealing to her.

Sirena shrugged (after so many years, she was no longer surprised at her friend's antics). *Sure, they're on the way back to town.*

"But . . ." Blade protested, trailing off as he was met with two grinning faces.

Were you perhaps about to point out that we're going to visit jellyfish at night after being warned about giant anglerfish with jellyfish-like lures? Fey asked mischievously.

"I . . ." Blade had indeed been about to point out the danger, but seeing the girls' "laugh in the face of a possible gruesome death" attitude, the words would not come out.

In real life, of course, Arwyn and Leah took much more care with their lives and health. They avoided dark alleyways, secondhand smoke, even jaywalking (unless they were *really* late). In the game, Fey and Sirena were much more blasé about risking life and limb in the pursuit of amusement, never confusing the 99 percent realism of *Fantasia* with real life. (Considering everything that's happened, though, somebody should really ask the game developers how exactly they had come up with their 99 percent value.)

It'll be fine, Sirena reassured Blade. *If the anglerfish really does come, we can just feed it a newbie and escape.*

"You're kidding, right?" he asked.

Sirena splayed her fingers and rotated her wrist back and forth in a "so-so" gesture, the action prominently displaying the translucent webbing between her fingers. *Ehhh, kind of. I wouldn't throw a newbie at it unless there was no other way to get away.*

Swimming along as they conversed, they began to see a faint pink glow in the distance. It soon resolved into a swarm of pink jellyfish. Of the sea nettle variety, each jellyfish had a round bell with long, neurotoxin-filled tentacles trailing delicately from its edges. From its centre extended thicker, whitish oral arms. The jellyfish varied in size, but most had tentacles much longer than Fey was tall.

Aww. Fey swam over for a closer look while Sirena and Blade hung a safe distance back. The jellyfish were set at level 3 because of their extremely slow movement speed, but being sufficiently stung by the tentacles could cause death even for high-level players.

Fey carefully poked a jellyfish on its neurotoxin-free cap. Ninety percent water, the jellyfish offered very little resistance to her finger and caved in easily. *Hee hee.* (Our heroine is easily amused.)

Having fun over there? Sirena called out.

Yup! Fey called back cheerfully. Her inner nine-year-old was once again in charge of her body.

A tiny jellyfish drifted by, its tentacles the length of one of Fey's fingers. *Aww,* Fey cooed, cupping her hand around the tiny cnidarian[12] and manipulating the water currents so it would not drift away. *I shall call him Squishy and he shall be mine*, she said, quoting Dory's line from *Finding Nemo*.

<Fey has tamed the sea nettle!>

<Fey receives a pet!>

<Monster Tamer has reached level 6!>

<Please select a name for your pet:__>

Somehow, Fey was not surprised that *Fantasia*'s game developers liked *Finding Nemo*. *Squishy,* she decided, since she had already called the jellyfish by that name.

<Name confirmed.>

<Squishy, immature sea nettle>

<Time until maturity: 15 days>

Guys, I caught a baby jellyfish! Fey called excitedly. She began to fan the water, pushing the sea nettle toward her party mates.

"Seriously, how many pets do you need?" asked Blade.

Don't be jelly, laughed Fey. She normally would not use the diminution of the word "jealous," but puns often took precedence over the proper use of English.

Technically, Fey was still at nine owned pets, having transferred Magic over to Leandriel's care.

How are you going to transport it? Sirena asked pragmatically. *Jellyfish are slow.*

Dunno, Fey said with a considering twist of her mouth. She fanned the water faster, pushing Squishy along. *Oww!*

Fey had accidentally brushed the jellyfish's tentacles with her right hand. Red welts began to rise on her skin.

<Fey's hand has been partially paralyzed!>

<−10 agility to hand until healed.>

Uh-oh, said Fey. The welts stung fiercely, but more importantly, she was unable to close her hand in a proper fist. Priority one (being able to kill things) was now compromised.

Anybody know how to fix this? she asked.

Sirena swam over to inspect Fey's fingers. *I don't think you can heal this with a regular healing potion*, she said after assessing the damage.

"Why don't you just use some of that healing balm that you have?" asked Blade.

Oh yeah! Fey had completely forgotten about the salve that she and Kallara had made from slime remains and the Blessing of Health spell. (#Nostalgia) Smiling at Blade for his helpful suggestion, Fey rummaged in her carry-pouch and pulled out the correct container, which still contained about half the original amount of healing salve.

Fey was stymied for a second, unable to open the jar with only one working hand.

"Here," said Blade. He took the jar, opened it, and handed it back to Fey.

Thanks. Fey smiled and eagerly scooped out a small globule of balm, spreading it over her injured hand and sighing in relief as it took away the pain and paralysis. She closed the jar without help and put it away (making a mental note to dump out the salt water when she got back to land).

<Sirena: I didn't know you liked Blade.>

Fey glanced up in startlement at Sirena's private message. The mermaid looked slightly unhappy with the events that had just transpired.

<Fey: I don't.>

<Sirena: Then why did he open the jar for you?>

<Fey: Because my hand was paralyzed?>

<Sirena: Guys don't just go around opening jars for people.>

<Fey: Actually, I think they do. It makes them feel strong and useful and stuff.>

<Sirena: Yeah, it makes them feel strong and useful and stuff, which is why they only open jars for people they like.>

<Fey: Are we still talking about opening jars?>

After several repetitions, "opening jars" was starting to sound like a euphemism for something else.

<Sirena: Of course we're not talking about opening jars!>

<Fey: Okay then. You don't need to be jelly either. I can open my own jars, I don't like Blade, and I highly doubt that he likes me.>

(Our heroine is actually pretty good at opening her own jars. All it takes is the sudden and violent application of force.)

Blade caught his party mates exchanging meaningful looks, with the occasional glance thrown his way. "Hey, are you two talking about me?"

Sirena telepathed, *No, of course not!* at the same time Fey said, *Yup.*

Fey clarified, *Well, we were talking about me in relation to you, and whether there's any deeper meaning to the act of opening ja-ars . . .* Fey's mental voice stuttered in startlement when Sirena clamped webbed hands over her mouth. Mouth obscured, she expressed her emotions through an eloquently raised eyebrow. *You know that covering my mouth isn't going to stop me from using telepathy, right?*

It's symbolic, said Sirena in a "shut up right now or I'll pull out the blackmail material I have on you from high school" tone.

Sirena's dramatic actions successfully distracted Blade from Fey's "jar" comment. "Symbolic of what?" he asked.

Of me shutting up, said Fey in a "fine, I'll be quiet, but you don't have anything worse on me than a few pictures of me wearing braces, and we both know it" tone. Privately, she messaged Sirena.

<Fey: Wow, you're really crushing on this guy already. It's turned your brains all mushy and making you act crazy.>

<Sirena: Shut up. I hope you're worse and act like a total idiot when you fall for someone.>

<Fey: Meh, I like to stick to fictional characters.>

Coming over to defend its new owner, Squishy puffed its bell, displacing water until it reached Sirena and stung her hands where they rested over Fey's mouth.

Ouch! Sirena quickly released Fey and shook her hands out, trying to relieve the pain. Compared to Fey's accidental sting, this one was much more severe.

<Sirena's hands have been paralyzed!>

Good job, Fey told the tiny jellyfish (he's the only one who's supposed to be jelly), seeing an opportunity to allay her friend's jealousy. She again pulled out her jar of healing balm and handed it to Blade.

Here, you can open the jar for her, too, and we'll be even. (Are we still talking about opening jars? This not-euphemism is getting out of hand.)

Confused, Blade nonetheless did as bid and opened the jar. Since both of Sirena's hands were paralyzed, the human warrior even went as far as to apply salve to the ugly red welts on the mermaid's hands.

Fey winced as Blade used far more balm than was strictly necessary to cancel the status effect.

<Fey: I hope you're enjoying yourself.>

She messaged Sirena. Sirena did not reply with a private message, but her facial expression was full of enjoyment. To Fey, that was more than worth the usage (and wastage) of her expensive, powerful healing balm.

Fey looked away from her party mates, giving them "a moment." Suddenly, she noticed that Amethyst was not hanging around on her neck. Not wanting to interrupt Sirena's "moment" with a telepathic call, she looked around in all directions.

Fey finally located Amethyst by the slime's purple bioluminescence, which stood out in the sea of pink jellyfish. Riding along on Inkblot, Amethyst appeared to be eyeing a particularly large jellyfish, which had a cap fully over a metre in diameter. *She's not really going to try to eat that, is she?* Fey wondered.

Amethyst gave a commanding squeak ("Go! Go!") and Inkblot dived in. The slime's mouth opened impossibly wide and engulfed the jellyfish's main body. She then began to slurp up the enormously long tentacles like noodles until they, too, disappeared.

Jellyfish neurotoxin was not like the other poisons Amethyst had ingested, and the slime was not fully compatible with it. She winced as the jellyfish was slowly digested.

Fey was alarmed to see Amethyst's health drop below half and rushed over to force-feed her pet a potion. *This is what you get for trying to eat such random crap,* she scolded. *You're going to get yourself killed one day.*

Amethyst nodded dutifully, but Fey had no faith that the slime would change her seemingly suicidal eating behaviours. Amethyst was further justified when the system notice appeared:

<Amethyst has improved Poison Slime!>

<Sea nettle toxin: causes localized paralysis to area of contact; severe contact can cause general paralysis and damage.[13]>

Sighing, Fey grabbed both Amethyst and Inkblot and swam back to Sirena and Blade, who appeared to be done with their "moment" and were looking slightly embarrassed.

Back to Pearlview? Fey asked, completely ignoring the awkwardness to make it go away.

Mm, yup! Sirena purposely used her superior swimming speed to gain a small lead over her party mates, giving herself some time alone to calm down from her emotional agitation.

Blade returned the healing salve to Fey, and the two land-dwellers made their slow way back to town.

<Blade: Is Sirena single?>

Blade asked through private messaging rather than party chat so Sirena would not be aware of the question.

Fey grinned. Things appeared to be working out nicely.

<Fey: Yup.>

Blade nodded, trying to look casual. He glanced several times at Fey, who continued smiling and said nothing.

<Blade: Aren't you going to threaten me with bodily harm
or something if I hurt her feelings?>

<Fey: Nope. Sirena doesn't need my help to get revenge.
She's a lot more creative than I am.>

More seriously, Fey added:

<Fey: You seem like a nice guy. For some unfathomable
reason, you put up with me. I give you my "best friend
stamp of approval.">

Blade was a little surprised that Fey held him at a level of esteem that was above "contempt."

For Fey, few people could tolerate her fully uninhibited personality. Just the fact that Blade had continued to adventure with her through poison, violence, (poison,) childishness, sarcasm, (poison,) antisocial moments, nerdy and creepy fun facts, (poison,) and a truly outrageous best friend meant that she now felt comfortable around him. In her mind, he was 90 percent of the way into the "friend" category. His sanity was somewhat in question, but then again, so was hers.

<Blade: Thanks.>

Fey smiled and swam on.

CHAPTER 7

DEAD IN THE WATER

Fey ended up carrying Squishy in her pouch, putting the tiny jellyfish in an empty potion bottle. She made a mental note to acquire a larger container before Squishy outgrew the current one.

The party swam back to Pearlview, the trip so long that Fey and Blade each gained a stamina point. Since they were moving (pathetically) slowly by mermaid standards, Sirena failed to increase her stamina.

By night, Pearlview glowed beautifully with bioluminescent corals. Fey looked around with admiration. *Pwetty*, she said again.

Amethyst, who was glowing (cutely) purple in the dark, squeaked questioningly from her position dangling off Fey's neck.

Yes, yes, you're pretty, too, said Fey, giving the slime a pat. Amethyst smiled (cutely), easily pleased.

Before they had entered far into town, Sirena paused and cocked her head in a listening pose. *Do you hear that?* she asked.

Fey and Blade also paused. Faint telepathic singing could be heard, the voice male and the song a pop love ballad that was currently on the top music charts in the real world.

Nice. A bard? said Fey. Controlling telepathy was as challenging as controlling sound through vocal cords, and the voice was smooth and well-trained, perfectly on pitch.

"Probably," Blade agreed.

Let's go see! Without waiting for agreement, Sirena swam off in the direction of the telepathic sound.

As the party drew near to the source of the singing, it became more clear and distinct. Fey rather liked the music. The song was one that sounded good even without instrumental accompaniment, and the singer's performance was as good as the original artist's.

They came across a large gathering of mermaids. Unlike on land, where onlookers were restricted to a two-dimensional ring around a street performer, the mermaids formed more of a globe shape as they all tried to get a good view.

"That must be it," said Blade. With the crowd of mermaids, it was impossible to see the singer, but his voice came through easily.

I'm going to try to get a better look, said Sirena. She swam around to the other side of the crowd, looking for a gap.

You go ahead, said Fey. She hung back with Blade. Fey had an aversion to finding out the appearances of singers she liked. In her imagination, their faces and bodies were as attractive as their voices, but this was almost never the case, leading to strong feelings of disappointment whenever she was faced with the reality of their looks.

Blade had a much simpler reason for staying behind. He much preferred looking at all the attractive mermaids (and their "upper tail sections") over some random male bard.

The song ended after several minutes.

<Fey has listened to a bard's love ballad.>

<Effect: +2 attractiveness, +5 intelligence>

<Duration: 1 hour>

The performance was met with loud applause and high-pitched cheering. Fey could not decide whether fangirl squealing was more irritating as sound or as telepathic screeching direct to her mind. Nonetheless, she and Blade applauded along with the crowd, more impressed with the stat boost than the singing itself.

The crowd began to shift. Some players dispersed, presumably off to finish some training while the bard's stat boost was in effect. Some jostled for position to try to speak with the performer. Some drifted, chatting excitedly in smaller groups.

Fey and Blade were still unable to see the singer from their position, but the movement allowed Sirena to peek through. "Meh," she reported through party chat. "Not that bad-looking, but bland."

"Good to know," Fey replied. She also used party chat so she would not have to yell at Sirena over the distance that separated them. "Ready to go?"

"Hold on a sec. I want to put some coins in the collection bowl as thanks for the intelligence buff."

"Okay." Fey pulled Amethyst off her neck and prepared to train Immunity while she waited. *Amethyst, poison mushroom poison.*

Amethyst obediently secreted the requested toxin. Apparently, it was water-soluble, as a faintly purple-tinged sphere spread out around the slime.

<Amethyst has learned Poison Sphere!>

<Poison Sphere: When underwater, spreads poison effects throughout an area. Poison types available are those learned for Poison Slime.>

<Level 1: 1m radius, 10 second duration>

<Fey has been poisoned!>

<Poison mushroom poison: −4 health/20 seconds>

<Duration: 10 minutes>

<Level 7 Immunity effect: −3 damage per poison infliction>

<Net effect: −1 health/20 seconds>

<Duration: 10 minutes>

<Blade has been poisoned!>

<Poison mushroom poison: −4 health/20 seconds>

<Duration: 10 minutes>

<Level 2 Immunity effect: −1 damage per poison infliction,
−1 minute duration>

<Net effect: −3 health/20 seconds>

<Duration: 9 minutes>

"[Censored word]!" Blade yelled. He flinched and put several metres between himself and Fey (or, more accurately, Amethyst). "Stop [censored word]ing doing that!"

Sorry, Fey apologized meekly. *I honestly didn't know that was going to happen.*

Blade scowled and crossed his arms in a disgruntled fashion. The poison mushroom poison caused blurry vision but no pain, and the damage was something his health reserves could handle, so he decided to save his dwindling stock of antidotes in case Fey "accidentally" poisoned him with something worse.

"What happened?" asked Sirena. Still somewhere amongst the crowd, she had heard Blade's expletive-filled exclamations through party chat.

"Fey poisoned me again!"

"Again? How many times has she poisoned you?"

"I've lost count," Blade grumbled.

Fey hazarded a guess. "Four or five?"

(This was in fact the seventh instance in which Blade had been poisoned in Fey's presence.)

"It feels like a lot more," Blade grumbled.

"Wow. You ought to stop doing that, Fey," said Sirena.

"I'm mostly not doing it on purpose."

The conversation was cut short when Fey's still-blurry vision detected mermaid-shaped blobs approaching. "Are those people swimming toward us?"

"Looks like it," said Blade. His vision was similarly compromised.

Hey, look, humans! came an unfamiliar telepathic voice. Multiple blobs approached.

"I'm an elf," Fey muttered. She hastily pulled off the choker holding her telepathy stone and pressed it into Blade's hand.

"What?" he asked confusedly.

"Take it. You deal with them," said Fey. Once again, she was using Blade to allow herself to be antisocial.

"Okay . . ." Blade fastened the choker onto his neck. Thankfully, it automatically adjusted to its user and did not actually choke him with a Fey's-neck-sized circumference.

Several mermaids were now within conversational distance. Blade did his best to imitate making normal eye contact despite his poison-induced myopia. All he could really make out was the outline of each player and their skin colours, which varied between blue-green and turquoise.

Hello! I'm Shelly.

Several other mermaids introduced themselves in quick succession (with the author being too lazy to make up their names).

Hi, I'm Blade, and this is Fey.

Fey gave a little wave and her best bland smile.

The mermaids all said "hello" again.

When did you get to Pearlview?

What level are you?

Are you looking for a party?

The rapid-fire questions were all directed at Blade, who answered as best he could.

Fey kept a pleasant expression on her face but mentally tuned out of the conversation. *Your desperation is showing*, she mentally told the mermaids. She did not know if their efforts to entice Blade to join their party was normal behaviour (for them), or if the scarcity of male players in Pearlview had driven them to extremes.

So as not to distract Blade from his conversation, Fey talked to Sirena via private message.

<Fey: You done yet? If we don't leave soon, there is a distinct possibility that someone will entice our tank away from us.>

<Sirena: Yup, coming. Oh, look, the bard guy is coming your way. I'm right behind him.>

<Fey: Everything is blurry right now. Side effect of the poison.>

<Sirena: Right. Why are you poisoning yourself, again?>

<Fey: I'm training my Immunity.>

<Sirena: And Blade's, against his will.>

Coincidentally, it was at this point that Blade's poisoned status ran its course.

<Blade's Immunity has reached level 3!>

The system notification caused Blade to temporarily stutter in his speech, but he carried on without the mermaids noticing anything out of the ordinary.

In Fey's still-blurry vision, another blob approached. Its presence caused the blobs currently speaking to Blade to move aside in deference. Another blob, which Fey could tell was Sirena based on the mage robes, circled around to come to a stop beside Fey.

I just had to say hello to a fellow out here, came an unfamiliar male voice. Despite the cheerful delivery, Fey sensed that the merman was less than pleased to have competition of the male kind in Pearlview.

Perhaps not sensing the concealed hostility, Blade answered in a friendly way. *Hey. I'm Blade.* He offered a hand, which the merman slapped in a casual greeting style.

I'm Requiem, said the bard. Fey gave him points for having a name that combined music and death into one word.

It was at this point that Fey's poison wore off.

<Fey's Immunity has reached level 8!>

With her newly restored vision, Fey was able to examine Requiem's appearance for the first time. She agreed with Sirena's assessment of "bland." He reminded her of a fashion model; there was no feature of his face or body that had any real flaw, but she felt no "character" in his appearance. She gave a mental sigh. As usual, she preferred the singer's voice over his looks.

Belatedly, Fey realized that Requiem was looking at her rather than focusing on Blade.

And who might this be? Requiem asked.

This is Fey. She doesn't have a telepathy stone right now, Blade answered. Only Fey heard the slight but distinct emphasis on the last two words of his sentence.

"Wait, when did you give Blade your telepathy stone?" asked Sirena through party chat.

Fey smiled blandly at Requiem while answering, "When the people came over, duh. Just go with it."

No telepathy stone? And I thought she was just being shy. Requiem smiled at Fey as if expecting her to giggle.

Instead, Fey's smile became more fixed and less natural. Requiem did not appear to notice Fey's unenthusiastic response to his attempt at joking.

Sirena supplied all of the missing giggling. It always amused her whenever someone tried to flirt with her best friend, whose thought patterns were so aberrant that normal social approaches completely failed. Fey generally treated the conversation of flirting as "stupid questions and unwelcome observations," and often would not even realize someone was trying to flirt until after she had already ended the conversation with hostilely sarcastic remarks.

Oh, Fey definitely isn't shy, Blade said wryly. He could think of a lot of words to describe his party mate, but "shy" was not one of them.

Well, we'll just have to get her a telepathy stone, won't we? Come on, said Requiem. He grasped Fey's wrist, intending to lead her to the accessory shop, only to be surprised as she quickly and easily twisted her hand free. (Remember, children, pull against the thumb, which is always the weak point in a grip.)

An awkward pause at the rather hostile reaction, and then Sirena explained, *That's just a reflex she has.*

Fey's smile was now apologetic, but something in her expression warned Requiem not to try to grab her again.

The merman visibly rallied his efforts to appear charming and confident. *To the accessory shop!* he announced, then swam off alone as if that had been his plan all along.

"So . . . Is he trying to get me to buy my own telepathy stone, or offering to buy one?" asked Fey.

Sirena giggled. "Who knows? Either way, this is hilarious. We should follow him." Grabbing Fey's hand, Sirena failed to activate

Fey's so-called escape reflex and started toward the accessory shop.

When Blade started to follow his party mates, he was stopped by Shelly and company.

Don't you want to join our party instead? he was asked.

Blade glanced over at his unusual party. Fey and Sirena had heard the question and paused to listen to his response. The girls looked like they expected him to accept the mermaid party's invitation.

Rather perversely, this caused Blade to want to stay. He gently disengaged his arm from Shelly's grasp. *Sorry, I already have a party.*

Fey and Sirena both gave him quintessentially female enigmatic smiles before turning to follow Requiem. He had no idea what they meant, but he got the impression that they were happy he had not abandoned them. (Sirena was thinking, *I might just really like you*, while Fey was thinking, *Good, I won't have to find another meatshield.*)

Fey's party descended into the roofless accessory store in time to hear Requiem ask, *Don't you have any colours other than blue? It should complement her eyes.*

Fey rolled her apparently uncomplemented eyes. Light blue kyanite matched her dark purple colouring just fine.

There are other crystals that can be enchanted with telepathy, but they are more expensive, answered the shop-keeper.

That's fine, answered Requiem. *Do you have pink?*

Fey grimaced. She hated pink, which she saw as a weak, pathetic version of a proper red.

Sirena was now giggling to the point of holding her sides in pain. *This is the funniest thing that's happened since that guy tried to help you skate a few years ago*, she gasped, quiet enough that Requiem did not catch the words. She referred to an incident where a misguided acquaintance had grabbed Arwyn's arm at the skating rink and upset her balance, nearly causing her to fall onto the ice. (In Canada, the "ice" in "ice skating" is implied.)

What's so funny? asked the bard.

Sirena waved a webbed hand in a dismissive gesture. *Oh, nothing, nothing. Carry on.* Her denial was made less convincing by the fact that her giggling had not stopped.

Blade was torn between amusement at Requiem's attempts to treat Fey like a normal girl and the feeling that he was being a bad person by not clarifying things for the merman. It was mostly the fact that he was not quite sure of how he would explain Fey to Requiem that caused him to stay silent.

The shop-keeper opened a small jewellery box, revealing a pink crystal set in a silver chain. *This one is 15,000g,* he said.

Fey gasped. The pink telepathy stone was three times the price of the regular blue one. *There's no way he'd buy it, right?*

Requiem appeared unpleasantly surprised by the price of the stone, but with the pressure of eyes watching his actions, he went ahead with his intentions of buying it for Fey. *I'll take it. Just let me get to the bank and—* The bard stopped speaking abruptly as Fey swam behind Blade and began unfastening the choker around his neck.

Fey could not let this random stranger waste 15,000g on a stone she neither wanted nor needed. Requiem seemed like a good enough person, if rather misguided (and with horrible taste in colours). Unaware of how intimate the gesture looked, she removed her telepathy stone from Blade's throat and replaced it on her own neck.

This one's mine, she explained apologetically. Not wanting to deal with the awkward fallout, she said a quick goodbye and logged out even though it was early.

Still laughing her head off, Sirena said, *See you tomorrow, Blade!* and followed suit.

Requiem's expression shifted from shock to unhappiness at being made a fool of, then into an anger directed squarely at Blade. The merman's expression turned ugly as he glared at the human. *You think you're better than me? Just you wait, I'll steal that Fey girl from you.* He swam off with a violent swish of his tail that knocked over some of the small items being displayed in the accessory shop.

Blade tried to reply but then remembered that Fey had reclaimed her telepathy stone. He sighed, shaking his head at the merman's misapprehension.

The shop-keeper went about straightening his shop with a resigned look at Requiem's rude disturbance. Feeling guilty even though he was probably the least to blame for the whole incident, Blade helped the NPC straighten up before logging out himself. It did not occur to him that before meeting Fey, he never would have felt guilty for inconveniencing an NPC.

Arwyn opened her eyes groggily and glanced at the clock. It was slightly before 6:00 a.m. *Way too early.* Feeling the stuffiness in her head that told her she had not had enough sleep, she zombie-shambled her way to her bedroom and snuggled amongst her (five) pillows to go through another REM cycle.[14]

Slightly after 8:00 a.m., Arwyn yawned and sat up, still hugging a pillow. It was Saturday, so she contemplated whether she should leave her comfortable bed. With her game-playing, she was sleeping more than usual and did not feel sleepy at all.

Eventually, hunger drove her to get moving. She put down the pillow and made her way lazily to the kitchen.

Her fridge was woefully out of stock. Arwyn was forced to look in the freezer for breakfast, finding some frozen waffles she put in the toaster. *Time to go grocery shopping.*

After eating, Arwyn dressed in clothing suitable for running errands, grabbed her purse and keys, and headed for her local supermarket. She was a person who did not enjoy cooking but enjoyed eating home-cooked food. She also enjoyed sweet and salty junk foods and was paranoid about food going spoiled. This resulted in a distinctive pattern of purchases, where she bought small amounts of fresh produce, a lot of canned and frozen foods, and what seemed like far too many boxes of cookies and bags of chips for one person.

Still, as Arwyn walked up and down the aisles pushing a grocery cart, she looked fairly normal. Her actions and appearance gave no real hints as to the alien shape of the inner recesses of her mind. The only thing that an objective observer might guess about her would be that she was about to throw a party. (Nope, she really is going to eat all of those chips by herself. No, she has no idea why she's still skinny.)

After returning home, Arwyn cooked herself lunch, a process that took an unreasonable amount of time because she was extremely slow at chopping vegetables. She ate and put the leftovers away, wondering what to do with her afternoon.

No activity could hold her interest. She drifted from the computer to the television, then wandered randomly around the house, in a strangely restless mood.

Arwyn realized that she had not read a book in almost two weeks. Reading was something that she did for fun and relaxation, and she started exhibiting strange withdrawal symptoms if she went too long without consuming a book. Even fun activities like *Fantasia* could only partially replace reading to keep her mentally balanced. (Wait, she's mentally balanced?) She headed out the door, walking to her local public library.

CHAPTER 8
PATHETIC FALLACY

Out of all the sections of the library, from nonfiction to children's books, music, and DVDs, Arwyn frequented only two. The first was the magazine section, where she sometimes sat to read the latest issue of *Psychology Today*. The second was the fantasy fiction section, where she headed now.

Though the library's collection was regularly rotated with other branches and updated with new books, at any one time, a good third of the titles on the shelves were ones Arwyn had already read. She browsed the titles on the books' spines, picking up anything that caught her eye. After closer inspection, she either replaced the book on the shelf or added it to her checkout pile. She had an e-ink tablet and an extensive file collection of books, but when it came to browsing for new authors she had never tried before, nothing beat physical books and the ability to flip through the pages.

In approximately ten minutes, Arwyn had a nice pile of five books and headed to the checkout machine. She entered her fourteen-digit library card number from memory, scanned the barcodes on the backs of the volumes, and exited the library without setting off any alarms (electronic or otherwise).

Back at home, Arwyn settled into her reading chair, a fat, cushioned seat that had little aesthetic appeal but was immensely comfortable. She picked up one of her newly borrowed books. The most common subjects in the fantasy section were vampires and werewolves, followed by people with magic, elves, descendants of gods, the occasional dragon, or some combination thereof.

This time, though, Arwyn had picked up a book with an angel on the cover. She began to read.

Six hours later, Arwyn finished the last page of her novel. Closing the book, she stood and stretched muscles that had been motionless for much longer than was recommended by health professionals.[15]

After being immersed in a fantasy world, her mind felt both relaxed and engaged. Imagination still caught on angel wings, Arwyn was in such a good mood that she managed to force herself through household chores after dinner, giving everything a rare, thorough cleaning.

Day pleasantly and productively spent, she logged into *Fantasia* at 10:27 p.m.

⸻◦◇◦⸻

As soon as Fey appeared in Pearlview's accessory shop, she received two private messages simultaneously.

<Leandriel: Hello.>|<Sirena: What took you so long? I've been on for over an hour.>

No novice to simultaneous chat messaging, Fey fired off two quick replies.

<Fey: Hi! How are you and Magic getting along?>|<Fey: You mean a game hour, so only 20 minutes.>

(This isn't confusing at all.)

<Leandriel: Very well. He is a great pet.>|<Sirena: Yeah, yeah. The point is, I'm bored.>

<Fey: I hope he's helpful, too.>|<Fey: Is Blade on yet?>

<Leandriel: Oh, yes. Once he levelled up some, his Spore became very helpful.>|<Sirena: Of course not. Otherwise, I wouldn't be so bored.>

<Fey: What level is he now?>|<Fey: Where are you?>

<Leandriel: 50.>|<Sirena: I'm tormenting the water slimes right outside town.>

Fey's mind temporarily went blank. Losing the rhythm of simultaneous messaging, she sent a message to Sirena.

<Fey: Holy [censored word]! Magic is level 50!!!>

Belatedly, she remembered to message Leandriel as well.

<Fey: Wow. I am so jealous right now.>

<Sirena: Damnnn. I'd sure like to be angel-dude's pet. If you know what I mean.>|<Leandriel: Haha, you'll get there eventually.>

<Fey: You had better mean that you want to mooch half his experience points.>|<Fey: Yup. All I have to do is train, and train, and train . . . And train.>

(Now the order of Fey's replies is reversed. Still not confusing at all.)

<Sirena: Haha. Of course that's what I meant. You know what I mean ☺☻✿⌨Leandriel: You could try questing if you get bored of fighting monsters.>

<Fey: I shake my head at you.>|<Fey: Yeah, maybe I'll look for an interesting one today.>

<Sirena: Yeah, yeah, just get over here before I get really outrageous.>|<Leandriel: Have fun.>

<Fey: Coming.>|<Fey: Thanks, you too! Talk to you later.>

<Leandriel: Bye.>

(The conversations conveniently ended at the same time.)

Fey swam off toward the water slime territory, expecting a normal day of random adventures. The trajectory of her game day was dramatically altered when events of the previous night caught up to her.

Hey, Fey was it? came a slightly familiar male telepathic voice.

Fey glanced beside her to find Requiem the bard swimming along beside her. *Yes,* she answered in a neutral tone. In her mind, she thought, *Damn. I guess I could only delay the awkwardness, not avoid it.*

You logged off in a hurry last night, Requiem commented. It was clearly an opening conversational gambit designed to lead into casual small talk.

Fey hated small talk. Rather than a conversation-conducive reply, she simply answered *Yes* again. (#AwkwardSilence)

Apparently, it took more than two terse replies to deter Requiem (#AnnoyinglyPersistent). He tried again. *Where are you headed?*

Damn, he asked a non-yes-or-no question. Fey was forced to use three words to reply. *Water slime territory.*

The three words gave the merman enough fodder to continue the conversational thread. *Aren't those a bit low-level for you?* he asked teasingly.

Technically, Fey could have just answered *Yes* to this question, but she saw that that would only result in a follow-up question about why she was visiting the water slimes, so she answered, *Just meeting a friend.* Her completely neutral tone was consistent with the fact she was utterly ignoring any flirtatious vibes Requiem was emitting.

That Blade guy? Requiem asked. His tone sounded slightly darker when he mentioned the human warrior.

Nope.

Requiem appeared both happy and slightly thrown off by the reply in the negative. He took a moment to think back to the previous night. *That other girl who was with you? The one that kept laughing?*

Yup. Fey's face briefly took on a smile as she thought of her best friend. *At least she's getting some amusement out of this*, she thought.

At this point, elf and merman reached the water slime territory. Water slimes were physically identical to land slimes, except that they had small finlike appendages instead of bubbles at the ends of their arms. They used these fins to swim around in an endearingly clumsy fashion (far too slowly to get away from the newbies who wanted to kill them).

Fey scanned the area for Sirena's mage robes amongst the newbie outfits. The search was rendered (blindingly) easy when a lightning spell ripped through the hapless water slimes, the intense heat causing them to explode.

Chain attacks were the specialty of lightning magic, and Sirena's spell arced between fourteen slimes before dissipating.

Oh! So close! Sirena complained.

Fey swam toward her friend, trailed by Requiem. *Close to what?*

My next Connect Four[16] *mage feat. I need a sixteen-hit chain,* Sirena answered absently. Taking her eyes off the remains of the slimes, she saw Requiem and burst into laughter.

What's so funny? asked the merman, trying to keep grumpiness out of his tone of voice. He was starting to dislike Sirena because she was constantly laughing at him.

It's just . . . you . . . and Fey . . . More laughter followed. Requiem thought that Sirena's mirth prevented her from finishing her explanation, but that was in truth the entirety of the information Sirena had intended to convey. To anybody who had a grasp of Fey's personality, the hilarity was fairly obvious.

I'm glad you're enjoying this, Fey commented wryly.

It's like . . . a polar bear trying to make friends with a penguin.

Why am I a penguin in this situation?

Because you're smaller? Or maybe because you're awkward. Well, you're definitely too skinny to be the polar bear.

(Fey's also too skinny to be the penguin, but why quibble? Because quibbling is fun, of course.)

Despite understanding all of the individual words in their speech, Requiem felt like he was listening to a conversation in a foreign language. *What are you guys talking about?*

You'll figure it out if you hang around Fey for long enough, said Sirena (laughingly).

When Requiem looked askance at Fey, she just shrugged. *Don't look at me, I'm just an awkward penguin.*

Amethyst squeaked. ("What's a penguin?")

Requiem flinched in surprise, not realizing until now that Amethyst was more than an unusual accessory (#LazySlime).

Ignoring the merman, Fey answered the slime. *A penguin is a semiaquatic, flightless bird that lives around the South Pole.*

Amethyst squeaked again. ("Fey-Fey's not a penguin, she's an elf.")

Fey patted the slime fondly. *Thank you for noticing; I'm getting tired of being called human. The penguin thing is just a metaphor.*

More squeaks. ("What's a metaphor?")

While Fey explained metaphors to a rapt audience of pets (the rest of which Requiem still hadn't noticed), Requiem looked incredulously at Sirena. *Is she seriously talking—*

A blast of lightning sizzled past his ear, far too close for comfort. It travelled on to explode through a group of water slimes.

Damn. Fifteen. So close, Sirena muttered. Looking at Requiem, she asked, *Did you say something?*

Requiem felt like he had fallen into a parallel dimension where everything looked the same, but everyone was insane (except him, which made him the insane one). *Ah, uh, nothing.*

Requiem was seriously rethinking his plans. He was on the brink of cutting his losses and leaving when Blade appeared. Expression tightening in dislike, Requiem('s testosterone-poisoned mind) decided to stick it out.

Blade swam up to his party mates, having logged on and located them through the party map. His legs temporarily paused in their kicking upon seeing Requiem, and he continued with less enthusiasm. "Hey guys—" he began, only to dive aside as Sirena loosed another volley of lightning.

Yes! Sixteen! Sirena pumped a victorious fist in the water. *Oh, hi, Blade!*

Fey had graduated from explaining metaphors to explaining similes, then analogies, then allegory, and was just now finishing up on pathetic fallacy. *And that's why it rains a lot in romantic movies. Hi, Blade.*

Blade did not even bother asking for an explanation. "Hi," he said, repeating his aborted greeting. He nodded at Requiem, who nodded back. It appeared that while girls were present, the merman would maintain a well-behaved demeanour.

"So, what are we doing today?" Blade asked.

Well, if you guys are bored of grinding, Leandriel suggested we find some interesting quests, Fey replied.

In addition to being left out of Blade's party chat comments, Fey was now referring to a person that Requiem was unfamiliar with. *Who's Leandriel?*

Mage feat completed, Sirena was once again paying attention to the conversation. She began to laugh again. Apparently, the constant fits of merriment were taking their physical toll, because she leaned on Fey for support. *He just . . . He just doesn't even know!*

Fey tried to calm her overexcited friend down. *Deep breaths*, she advised (or whatever mermaids do). She patted Sirena soothingly on the back.

While Sirena wrestled with self-control, Blade just had to jump into the conversation. Pressing his thumb against Fey's telepathy stone, he said, *Leandriel's your competition.* This caused Requiem to look a confused kind of angry. (He's even more lost than Blade because he came into the Feyworld with a greater number of preconceptions.)

Fey rolled her eyes (still patting Sirena on the back). *Leandriel isn't anybody's competition. That'd be like putting an Olympic athlete in with a bunch of nine-year-olds.*

Blade gave Fey a funny look. "We're not talking about level here."

Fey smiled. She was not *that* dense. *I know.*

Sirena slowly straightened, assiduously avoiding looking in Requiem's direction. *So, quest?* she asked.

Quest, Fey voted.

"Sure." Blade shrugged.

The three party members swam off toward town, followed half a beat later by Requiem.

Fey watched the merman pacing them with uncertainty. Normally, either one of her party mates would be more inclined than she was to interact with strangers, but Sirena was busy trying not to laugh, and Blade seemed to be avoiding Requiem.

Requiem felt equally awkward. He was used to parties of mermaids begging him to join them, so this kind of lukewarm reception ("frigid" really, but he's got a bit of an ego) was a new experience for him, one he did not enjoy.

"So . . . Are we inviting bard-dude to join our party?" Fey finally asked through party chat.

"Up to you," answered Sirena. "After all, he's chasing after you. Pfft." Sirena placed a hand over her aching abdominal muscles and started chanting, "I'm not laughing, I'm not laughing, I'm not laughing . . ."

"I don't think it's a good idea . . ." said Blade. He was reluctant to bring up what Requiem had said after the girls had logged off the previous night because it was the kind of thing that could hurt a person's feelings.

"Why not?" Fey's tone was full of honest curiosity, and she showed no displeasure at Blade's opinion.

"Well . . ." Blade decided to just tell the story. "I think he's only after you out of competitiveness. Last night, he told me he was going to 'steal' you from me."

Rather than an expression of hurt or disbelief, Fey looked enlightened. "That explains *a lot*."

"Let's kill him," Sirena hissed, all laughter gone. Her best friend's feelings were not to be toyed with (or attempted to be toyed with).

Just when Blade thought he had gotten used to the weirdness, the girls revealed new facets of themselves. In most matters concerning the opposite sex, Fey used the computer-like part of her brain rather than the emotional side. The bubbly and sometimes outrageous Sirena turned vicious when her friends were threatened.

As Blade was struck speechless, the conversation continued on without him.

"Now, now, let's not be hasty," Fey cautioned. "If you kill him, you'll get infamy and probably have a bunch of crazy fangirls out for revenge. Plus, we could still use him in our party. Do we need a bard?"

Sirena reluctantly switched mental gears from "bloodthirsty" to "pragmatic." "Well, if the only thing he can contribute is party buffs, it's not worth it. We'd need a much larger group to make supporting a bard worthwhile."

"Well, he has to be able to do other stuff, right?" Fey reasoned.

Blade shook his head and joined in on the analysis. "We need to know if his level is close to ours."

"Good point." *Hey, Requiem, what are your level and combat skills?* Sirena asked breezily, as if she had not just been agitating for his death.

I'm a level 23 spearman. Secondary skills are group song buffs and group debuffs. There was a hint of relief in Requiem's voice. If they were asking about his skills, they had to be considering whether to invite him to join them.

Fey's party was somewhat surprised to hear that the "squishy" bard was actually a warrior, able to hold his own on the front lines. In *Fantasia*, "bard" did not fall under any of the four main combat classes and was relegated to the non-combat skill section along with many other art, trade, and craft skills. Those who wanted to be bards usually chose a ranged combat class, but ranged weapons were fairly useless underwater, so Requiem had instead become a warrior.

"Do we really need another warrior?" Blade asked.

Cool, Sirena said to Requiem. Wryly, she continued, "Well, Fey doesn't really count as a warrior, so we could use another one."

Fey did not know whether to take offence or agree with her friend. "I do melee damage, so I'm a warrior," she finally said, ". . . but we could always use another one."

"Actually, I'm starting to like this plan," said Sirena with sudden enthusiasm. "Long-term revenge is best."

"Uh, what are you planning on doing to the guy?" Blade asked with a fair amount of trepidation.

"I don't know yet," Sirena answered cheerfully. "I'll figure it out as I go. It's all about using the resources at hand."

Fey winked at Blade. "I told you she's more creative than I am," she said, referring to their conversation the night before. She issued the telepathic invitation to Requiem. *So Requiem, would you like to join our party? Blade's a level 25 warrior, I'm a level 24 warrior, and Sirena is a level 23 mage.*

With a glance at Blade that could be interpreted as "victorious," Requiem said, *I'd love to, thank you, Fey.*

Blade still had some severe doubts about this particular course of action, but despite being the official party leader, stronger wills than his prevailed in group decisions (#Bullied). He issued the official game system invitation.

<Blade has invited Requiem to the party.>

Blade felt less guilty about Requiem's probable fate when Requiem gave him a smug look before accepting.

<Requiem has accepted Blade's party invitation.>

<Blade's party: Blade (leader), level 25 human; Fey, level 24 elf; Sirena, level 23 merfolk; Requiem, level 23 merfolk.>

Sirena immediately sent Fey a private message.

<Sirena: I just realized that we can't talk about him behind his back on party chat anymore. Now what?>

Fantasia private messaging was not meant for group chat and was unable to ferry messages between three or more people. The developers had thought party chat sufficient for group conversation, and had not imagined a case where a party would want to invite someone to join them but exclude him from the conversation.

<Fey: Dunno. Just stop talking behind his back?>

<Sirena: *sigh* Really? That's your solution? Sometimes, I feel like you're not even trying.>

<Fey: Oh, please. Subterfuge takes up too much brainpower that I could be using to have fun. Why can't you just insult him to his face?>

<Sirena: Of course I can insult him to his face. What I can't do is successfully plot to make his life subtly miserable to his face.>

<Fey: Well, it's not like you need other people to plot. Just do you and give me and Blade a heads-up if you're about to do something.>

<Sirena: Good point.>

The newly enlarged party arrived in the coral streets of Pearlview.

So . . . said Fey, *Anyone know how to go about finding an interesting quest?*

It was Requiem who answered. *Just talk with the NPCs. It helps if you have high fame and charisma, too.*

How high? asked Fey while checking her fame stat. She was surprised to see it at 56; the last time she remembered, it had been in the twenties. Unbeknownst to her, a very talkative Todd back in the Moonwood tavern was spreading tales of her Wood Collector title and many pets as well as her status as the first and only permanent VIP of the tavern.

You can find quests even if you don't have any, but the higher, the better, Requiem replied in a knowledgeable tone. He was something of a local celebrity in the area because of his public music performances.

Neither Sirena nor Blade had any fame to speak of; their stats were in the single digits. *If we have to rely on Fey making small talk to find quests, we might as well give up now,* Sirena lamented.

I'm sure I can find one, said Requiem confidently. *My fame is 317.*

Sirena patted the merman on the shoulder. *Being useful already. I'm so glad we didn't kill you*, she said in a joking tone.

Fey cleared her telepathic throat to distract from that somewhat threatening pseudo-joke. *So, split up and search? Call through party chat if you find something.*

Why don't we go in pairs? asked Requiem, his intentions so obvious that even Blade rolled his eyes.

Why not? Sirena agreed, using a subtle tone of sarcasm that Requiem failed to catch. She grabbed Blade's hand and dragged him off in one direction, saying, *We'll go this way.*

<Fey: I just realized, if bard-dude's goal is to one-up Blade by making someone fall for him, he should be after you.>

Sirena was still close enough at this point that her laughter was loud and clear. It became Blade's turn to propel them through the water as the mermaid went limp with merriment. *He just, he just doesn't even know!* she repeated.

Fey's lips twitched before she looked innocently ("innocently") over at Requiem. *So, should we head this way?* she asked, indicating the direction opposite to where Sirena and Blade had gone.

. . . Yeah. Much of Requiem's usual bravado had been stripped away by the abrasive sandstorm of Fey and Sirena's combined personalities (#Metaphor). *Let's go.*

CHAPTER 9
SIREN CALL

Fey looked down at the town below her. Because citizens entered buildings from above, Pearlview lacked real streets, with shops and homes tending to cluster in natural-looking arrangements, spaced out by gardens and works of art.

Instead of the wide-open roofs designed to display wares and invite potential customers in, Fey now saw screens designed for privacy and small entrances that would only allow one person to enter at a time. She guessed that they had left the commercial district and entered a residential area.

Fey glanced back at Requiem, who was following her lead without paying much attention. She was not familiar enough with the merman to determine whether his withdrawn state was due to preoccupation and thought, or he was simply sulking.

Either way, Requiem was being useless, and uselessness was not something Fey was prepared to put up with.

Any ideas? she asked.

Hmm? Requiem blinked, then focused on Fey.

On getting a quest. Fey's telepathic tone was a quarter of the way toward the exaggerated slowness she reserved for idiots, and her left eyebrow was very slightly raised. Neither of the cues was large enough for Requiem to consciously notice, but he flushed slightly and straightened his posture.

Ah, well, I've only ever gotten non-hunt quests when NPCs heard me singing, he confessed.

That's fine, said Fey. Now that Requiem was being useful again, her speech (and eyebrow) had returned to normal. *Why don't you try that now?*

Singing?

Yup.

. . . Okay. It took Requiem a moment to shift into performance mode. As a trained singer, he automatically straightened his posture to optimize lung capacity, though telepathic singing did not require it. *Any requests?* he asked.

Something that will buff attack, said Fey pragmatically.

It took Requiem several seconds to find a song that fit Fey's vague request, but soon enough, the music began with a martial drumbeat. It appeared that one of the bard's skills was to produce instrumental accompaniment without needing instruments.

Requiem launched into a rendition of "I'll Make a Man out of You" from the Disney movie, *Mulan.* Unlike the sweet tone he used for his earlier love ballad, his telepathic voice now held the power and vibrancy of a warrior.

Fey tried not to be impressed. Her face remained calm and impassive, but her inner fangirl danced and twirled in silly circles in her mind. Requiem had unwittingly picked one of her favourite songs and, if anything, was performing it better than the original soundtrack.

It occurred to her that if Requiem stopped the flirting nonsense and simply sang all of her favourite songs as well as he was singing this one, she probably would develop a crush on him. She kept the thought to herself. (Meh, she's safe. Bard-dude is too dense to figure it out.)

The music ended with an emphatic drumbeat, and Fey applauded. She was not alone; a small crowd had gathered throughout the performance.

<Fey has listened to Requiem's battle song.>

<Effect (in-party bonus): +20 attack, +5 agility, +10 stamina>

<Duration: 1 hour>

<Requiem's fame has increased to 328 (+11)!>

Requiem bowed with a flourish and began speaking to the audience members who went up to him.

It appeared that this was an NPC neighbourhood, as the audience had a balance of ages and genders rather than the almost exclusively young, female player population.

A few of the merfolk pressed a coin into Requiem's hand in thanks before going about their business. Some requested that he sing one of their favourite songs; he was not always familiar with the song but performed it when he did, gaining himself and Fey small amounts of quest experience.

Finally, only one NPC remained, an older female with grey streaks in her (blue) hair; the word "maid" fit her no longer (so we're just going to make one up and call her a "merdame").

You sing quite well, boy were her first words as Requiem turned his attention to her.

Thank you. I practice a lot.

The modest words were lost to the NPC; her eyes had gained the dreamy, faraway expression of a person dwelling in memory.

You sing well, the merdame continued, *but nothing like what I heard one day, twenty years ago. Now that was true siren's song. It was so beautiful that I was mesmerized for hours until it stopped . . .*

Are sirens real, then? Fey asked. As far as she knew, mermaids were the closest match to the siren myth in *Fantasia*.

I don't know. The NPC sighed. *I searched and searched, but I never heard the music again. According to legend, merfolk used to have singers that could stop entire cities with their songs, but our records say the last one died centuries ago. I've never heard of anyone with that kind of ability in any of the colonies. Plenty of singers that sound nice, like you—*she patted Requiem's arm—*but nothing I couldn't swim away from if I wanted to.*

Are you saying that siren's song is a lost merfolk ability? Requiem was beginning to sound very excited. A merfolk-only singing ability would give him a huge advantage over bards of other races.

That's what the legends say. I don't know if it's true, but if you ever find it, I'd love to hear it again. The NPC looked wistful, as if she did not expect to ever again come across the music that haunted her memories.

A quest was being offered, and Requiem did not stop to think before accepting it. *We'll find it for you,* he promised.

I hope you do, boy. My name's Wellia; I'll be around here if you're looking for me. Patting Requiem on the arm a final time, the merdame swam off about her business.

Requiem turned to Fey excitedly, only to sober abruptly as he realized that he had made a major decision without consulting her. *Hey . . . Sorry about that. I guess I got too excited about the possibility of a new singing ability . . .* He trailed off awkwardly.

Fey decided that since Requiem expected her to be annoyed, she would be gracious and understanding instead (#Contrary). *Oh, it's quite understandable,* she said in her most musical tone, channelling rainbows and sunshine into her telepathic speech (in a way that was quite creepy if you knew her normal demeanour). *I'd be quite excited as well, if I were you.*

When Requiem proved to be at a loss for words in the face of her unexpected response, Fey smiled mischievously (evilly) and continued, *Why don't I tell Blade and Sirena and we can start looking for clues?*

. . . Yeah, good idea.

Fey opened the party chat at a text-only level.

<Fey: Hey guys, we found a quest to find a hidden merfolk ability, "siren's song.">

<Sirena: Ooh, how apropos, considering my name.>

<Blade: Is it bard-only?>

<Fey: No idea.>

<Sirena: I'll just have to sign up as a bard, just in case.>

<Blade: If you're going to pick a non-combat class, shouldn't it be one we don't already have?>

<Sirena: Oh, please. We're already unbalanced with a mage and three warriors.>

<Sirena: Well, two warriors and a Fey. Whatever.>

<Fey: . . .>

<Sirena: My point being that we might as well learn whatever skills and classes we want, then figure out how to work together.>

Having followed the party conversation without participating, Requiem glanced at Fey, wondering why Sirena had implied she was not a warrior.

Fey simply smiled wryly (he'd find out soon enough) and continued the conversation.

<Fey: Meet at the performing arts guild? Sirena can sign up and we can plan our next move.>

<Blade: Maybe the people there will know something about siren's song.>

<Fey: Blade, you're quite insightful, sometimes.>

<Blade: . . . Thanks?>

Fey sent a smiley face over and closed the chat. She and Requiem swam toward the commercial district of town.

The performing arts guild was modelled after a giant conch shell stuck vertically into the seafloor. Divided into three floors, the lowest level was devoted to dance, the middle to drama, and the top to music. Fey and Requiem swam directly into the third floor, where Sirena was running through scales and arpeggios while a female NPC listened critically.

In real life, both Leah and Arwyn had been through the standard piano lessons expected of them from ages four to eighteen. They were highly educated in music theory and had fairly good ears for pitch, but only passable, untrained singing voices.

Sirena, however, sounded a lot better than "passable" as she breezed through the telepathic singing exercises. Although singing using the vocal cords required specific control of the muscles related to sound production and breathing, singing telepathically only required that a person be able to vividly imagine the correct pitch and quality of "sound." Therefore, most trained musicians could sing incredibly well using telepathy, even if voice was not their instrument.

As these thoughts occurred to Fey, she toyed with the idea of becoming a bard as well. She enjoyed singing but preferred to do it where she would not bother others with the occasional off-pitch note. Being able to sing well enough that others would want to listen would be a novel experience.

She decided against committing to the non-combat class. Since telepathy was not an innate racial ability for elves, if she ever took off the stone she wore on her throat, she would be forced to rely on her vocal cords to sing, which she assumed would result in a huge penalty to any bard skills.

Sirena finished the last of the singing exercises, and everyone turned to Songsmistress Gwenna for her judgement.

Gwenna looked satisfied. *You have some talent. I would be happy for you to join our ranks.*

Thank you, mistress, said Sirena, shaking (webbed) hands with the NPC.

Work hard, Gwenna advised, *and perhaps one day, your name will be known across the land and sea.*

Requiem took the opportunity to enter the conversation. *I was told that there were once legendary singers who truly had siren's song.*

The songsmistress scoffed. *That old batfish Wellia's been telling tales again, has she? There's no special ability; if you honed your skills enough, you could bring a water dragon down with just your voice.* To demonstrate, the NPC telepathically voiced a wordless melody, each note ringing out with crystal purity.

Fey, Requiem, Sirena, and Blade were instantly mesmerized by Gwenna's song, unable to move or look away from the captivating performance. Even after the NPC let the haunting melody fade away, it took the players about a minute to shake off its effects.

Having some resistance to mesmerization due to his own bard skills, Requiem was the first to recover. *That must be it! Siren's song!* he exclaimed, enthusiastic at the demonstration of the power he might one day attain.

Gwenna sniffed. *Apparently not, according to that old batfish. Every year, she comes to the guild's summer performance, and every year, she moans about how none of us are good enough compared to that random hallucination she had.* The songsmistress was clearly offended at the insult to her skills.

Have you ever gone looking for sirens? Sirena asked.

Me and every other musician to pass through this town. We've all gone to that chasm in the southeast where old Wellia said she heard the music, but there's nothing there. Looking at the players, she sighed. *I can tell that you are going to go looking, no matter what I say, but you're wasting your time.*

It's not that we don't believe you, said Requiem apologetically, *it's just that . . .*

. . . it's every bard's wildest dream come true, if it's real, Gwenna finished for him. *Yes, I understand. Go on, then; the sooner you see for yourself that there's nothing to find, the sooner you can move on.*

The newly reunited party swam out of the performing arts guild, strongly concerned about the chance of successfully completing the quest.

Do you think she's right? Sirena asked.

Well, it's a real quest, so there has to be some way of completing it, Fey answered logically. *If there's no special ability, then the songsmistress has to be right in that if you level up your normal bard skills, you'll eventually be able to convince Wellia you have siren's song. It'll take you months or years before you pass the level Gwenna's at now, though.*

We should at least go look at the place she said she heard it, said Requiem. It was clear that he still hoped there would be a hidden ability to unlock.

It was a logical next step in the quest, so the other three agreed and the party headed toward the dolphin taxi stand to arrange for transport to the distant chasm.

Fey recognized the dolphins who had transported her and Blade to the lobster territory (in Chapter 4) based on the pattern of weaving in the harnesses they wore. The dolphins recognized her and Blade based on the fact that the players had legs.

Hey, it's the humans! Click exclaimed, swimming around the party in excited circles.

I'm an elf, Fey muttered, again ignored as more dolphins came to inspect the exotic land-dwellers.

Hello again, said Whistle as she swam up in a more dignified fashion than her younger companion. *Are you looking for another lift?*

Yup, Sirena answered cheerfully. *For all of us this time. We're going far out, to the chasm in the southeast.*

Are you bards? asked Click. *Bards always want to go out there.*

I'm a bard, said Requiem, causing Click to circle the merman more closely.

I've never seen you before, Click commented. *Are you friends with the humans?*

When Requiem said *Yes* instead of clarifying that Fey was an elf, he lost an opportunity to earn brownie points. Fey sighed, not really expecting anything else from the clueless merman. Her attention was diverted to more important matters when Amethyst squeaked inquisitively ("Req-Req isn't on Fey-Fey's friend list and Fey-Fey doesn't seem to like him, so how is he a friend?").

He's not, Fey answered in a low voice, mostly unheard by the rest of the party as they conversed with the dolphins. *He's just being delusional.*

Since Sirena had taken over the task of negotiating the party's travel fare, Blade's attention was free enough that he caught the tail end of Fey's muttered explanation. "Delusional?" he asked over party chat.

Sirena glanced over at Blade, saw who he was talking to, flicked her gaze over to Requiem, smiled amusedly, and returned to her negotiation, all within a second.

Aware that Requiem could hear party chat and was in fact paying attention to her and Blade, Fey answered by private message.

<Fey: I was just explaining to Amethyst that Requiem doesn't fall into any of the three categories of "friends" and therefore isn't one.>

Blade was still unclear on Fey's terminology for different kinds of friends (because she used the same word for all three) and focused on the part he did understand. "So you understand what it's saying now?" he asked, referring to Amethyst.

Fey grinned playfully. *Nope, still guessing. I seem to be getting it right, because Amethyst nods and stops squeaking when I answer.*

Sirena concluded her bargaining with the dolphins. *Okay, so five mackerel per person each way, and energy- and speed-boosting songs along the travel route.*

Done, said Whistle. She went to confer with her fellow taxi dolphins to decide who would go on the trip.

You pay them in fish? asked Fey.

Sirena grinned and asked, *What else would you pay them with?*

What if they're not hungry?

They go off shift. Sirena was enjoying being able to treat Fey like a slow-learning student; it was rare to find a subject that she was not already familiar with.

Fey just shook her head, accepting the playful barbs because it was the way she treated other people (mostly Blade). *I don't have any fish.*

Requiem saw and seized the opportunity to come to the rescue. *Don't worry, Fey, I'll take care of it*, he said in his most suave and self-assured tone.

Unfortunately for the merman, Fey's attention was distracted by her pets. After an excited squeak from Amethyst ("We have fish!"), Inkblot and Onyx dived into the satchel attached at Fey's hip and emerged with a dead nomfish apiece.

Fey raised an eyebrow. Her diving satchel was not enchanted for extra space. *Did I know those were in there?* she asked Amethyst.

The slime shook her head.

Are there any more in there?

Amethyst shook her head and squeaked apologetically ("No more room.").

I'm impressed you even managed to fit two in there, said Fey, patting the slime in praise. She did the same for Inkblot and Onyx as they delivered the fish to her hand.

Are those nomfish? Whistle asked as she approached with Click and two other dolphins. There was an undercurrent of delight in her tone that Fey missed.

Yeah. I don't know if you guys eat these things, but I guess I could use these to pay and borrow another three fish from someone else. Fey held the two (green) fish toward Whistle, who approached eagerly.

One of the unfamiliar dolphins shoved Whistle aside. *Oh, no way is Whistle getting all of the nomfish*, he said in a commanding voice. *We'll divide them equally.*

Nomfish! Click chittered excitedly. *I haven't had one in ages!*

So, you guys really like nomfish? Fey asked.

Dolphins in *Fantasia* were created so that the higher the combat level of the fish they ate, the more delicious it tasted. Compared to non-monster fish like mackerel, the level 21 nomfish were exotic treats.

Any fish that's hard to kill is delicious was Whistle's explanation. *They're vicious, though, so we generally avoid going near their territories.*

The nomfish were equally divided between the four dolphins, who reduced the fare to only three mackerel each because of the treat. Since neither Fey nor Blade carried fish with them, Sirena and Requiem provided the fare.

When Requiem pulled out the fish to pay for Fey, Sirena casually took the mackerel and fed them to Click as Blade gripped the dolphin's harness. She then pulled fish out of her own pouch to feed Whistle as Fey grabbed the female dolphin's harness. (#SubtleTorment)

Feigning confusion at Requiem's displeased expression, Sirena fed her own taxi dolphin and zoomed off toward the southeast. Requiem's ride, a female dolphin, gave him an impatient look at being left behind. He hurriedly fed her and they chased after the rest of the party.

CHAPTER 10
DO NOT PULL

Fey's party sped through the ocean in a southeasterly direction, individually towed by a quartet of dolphins.

Requiem and Sirena were in charge of using their bardic skills to enhance the dolphins' speed and did so by performing a medley of high-energy pop songs. Unlike Requiem's earlier performances, which granted a boost that lasted for an hour after the end of the song, the merfolk players now used their Continuous Song ability, which produced a larger buff that ended as soon as the singing stopped.

Fey thoroughly enjoyed the music during the trip. More often than not, she joined in on the singing, not to train a skill but just to be part of the music. Her telepathic voice was the idealized version of what she wished she sounded like in real life, the notes rich and pure, with a much larger range than her vocal cords could manage.

Requiem was surprised and impressed by Fey's singing. When he had a break from singing the dolphins' speed buff, he took the opportunity to compliment her. *You sing great.*

Fey shot Requiem a disgusted look at his use of an adjective where an adverb belonged (#GrammarSnob). Pointedly looking away from the (confused) merman, she joined in on Sirena's music without replying.

Not missing a note, Sirena continued singing while casting a maliciously amused glance at Requiem and his utter failure to gain a single speck of Fey's favour. (It's almost like he was designed that way . . .)

In a good mood from the music and group dynamics, Sirena boldly experimented with her bardic skills. At the beginning of the next section of music, she left the melody to Fey and launched into a harmonic line. Such an attempt would have resulted in a mess of discordant notes in real life, their voice training inadequate to stay in tune with each other, but the girls managed to meld their telepathic voices to create a hauntingly beautiful sound.

<Sirena has learned Harmony!>

<Harmony: +30% effect to all bardic skills with each additional harmonic line>

The female party members broke off singing in light of the new development, causing the dolphins' movements to visibly slow.

New skill! High five! Sirena exclaimed.

Her taxi dolphin (hereafter known as Splash) humoured her by swimming close enough to Fey and Whistle for the girls to slap each other's palms, then gently reminded her, *If you could resume singing, please.*

Oops, sorry. Sirena launched into another high-energy song, allowing the dolphins to regain their earlier speed.

Requiem naturally wanted to learn Harmony as well but was stymied by the fact that he lacked the ability to improvise harmonic lines. In fact, he had no experience singing harmony at all.

Fey caught the merman's expression and said, *Can't sing harmony? Me neither.* She grimaced in empathy. Not even two years of singing lessons had taught her to sing anything but the melody line in a group.

Yeah. Requiem was surprised at Fey's perceptive observation and uncritical attitude, especially after her earlier reaction to his compliment. (Our scatterbrained heroine had in fact forgotten about the grammar incident after being lulled into a good mood by the excellent music.)

When Sirena finished her song, Fey suggested, *Why don't you let Requiem sing melody and you sing Harmony?*

We have another harmonically challenged one here, do we? Sirena missed no opportunity to subtly belittle the merman who would treat her friend's emotions so callously. *Time to vote him off the island.*

She's joking, Fey reassured Requiem (untruthfully). *Sing something*, she urged.

After a moment's hesitation, Requiem decided that he simply did not understand Sirena's sense of humour and launched into a song. When Sirena joined in with Harmony, the two bards' skills were elevated to a new level and the dolphins surged forward with extra speed.

Fey glanced over at Blade. The human warrior appeared to be passively enjoying the music, listening appreciatively but not joining in. She judged that he was doing well without her interference and turned her attention back to the music, joining in on the melody an octave higher than Requiem. (Blade is generally in a healthier state of being when Fey's not interfering.)

Of the party members, Blade was the only one without musical training. He knew what he liked, and listened to music without singing along.

He definitely liked Sirena's beautiful telepathic voice. It was beyond his abilities to consciously articulate, but Fey's idealized voice sounded so crystalline and pure that it was a little bit inhuman, while Sirena's had a warm undertone that he could connect to.

No skill at all. One person should easily be able to sing three lines. The muttered comment came from Click, Blade's chatty taxi dolphin.

Blade frowned in confusion. He did not have enough knowledge of how music was written to understand the implications of Click's words.

He did not have the telepathy to ask for clarification, and did not consider the matter important enough to interrupt his party mates' singing, so he shrugged off the comment and returned his attention to the music.

We're here, announced Whistle. A deep chasm came into view on the ocean floor. To either side were rock and sand; occasional scraggly plants were the only sign of life. No signs of movement could be seen, nor could mysterious music be heard.

The four players gathered at the edge of the chasm. Peering into the crevasse, they could only see a few lengths down before the darkness became impenetrable.

We don't have to go down there, do we? Fey asked doubtfully. Going into a chasm of indeterminate depth and populated by unknown monsters did not seem compatible with staying alive.

It seems likely, said Sirena with a touch of regret, the same casual tone normal people would use to say *We're going to have to walk in the rain without an umbrella.*

Blade found a fist-sized rock and dropped it into the chasm. It quickly disappeared into the darkness. The players waited a full minute to hear it strike the bottom, but no sound came. (This did not necessarily indicate that the chasm was particularly deep, as one would not expect a rock sinking into wet sand to make much noise. #Indeterminate)

Well, that's reassuring, Fey said in a cheerfully ironic tone. She looked around in a last-ditch effort to find something safer to explore. The landscape did not oblige her by spontaneously creating a point of interest. She sighed and resigned herself to probable virtual death. *What's the penalty for dying again?* she asked.

"You lose a level and some items," said Blade. He looked into the chasm. "It can't be *that* dangerous down there."

Clearly, you have an underdeveloped imagination, said Fey, her voice dark with foreseen doom.

Requiem was impatient. *Let's just go already.*

Why don't you take the lead? Fey invited politely.

Requiem nodded and began descending (completely missing the fact that he had essentially been invited to be the first to die).

Sirena and Blade followed, and Fey (cowardly) brought up the rear. (Congratulations to Blade, who has apparently been promoted from "meatshield.")

Down and down they went. Light from the surface quickly attenuated, and Amethyst's bioluminescence quickly became the only source of light. It occurred to Fey to pull out the bottle containing Squishy-the-jellyfish as a second pet lamp. In terms of brightness, Squishy's pink glow outshone Amethyst's faint purple light.

As they swam, the players remained watchful of their surroundings, on alert for quest clues (or bloodthirsty monsters, depending on their individual levels of paranoia).

Ten minutes later, the party (anticlimactically) reached the bottom of the chasm without incident. They had seen nothing but bare rock walls, and the bottom was no different.

This can't be right, Requiem muttered. Of the four party members, he desired the siren's song ability the most. Casting about for clues, he picked a direction at random and began swimming along the length of the chasm.

The other party members followed, but Fey and Blade lagged behind when swimming under their own power. Requiem found his pace limited by how far he could see beyond the glow of Fey's pets.

Before long, Requiem lost patience. Swimming back to the group, he grabbed Fey's wrist and towed her along with powerful strokes of his tail. As a low-strength mage, Sirena could not hope to pull Blade and keep up; before long, the two halves of the party had a considerable gap between them.

Fey allowed the manhandling for several minutes while she considered her options. This was the second time Requiem had grabbed her without permission and he clearly needed some positive punishment[17] to discourage further offences.

All avenues of possibility were open as Fey plotted. Requiem paid her no attention while searching for quest clues along the chasm, and likely would not react fast enough to any kind of attack that Fey unleashed.

I could just stab him with my spear, she reflected idly. *Nah, that's not creative enough. I could let Squishy out of the jar and sting him. Meh, not painful enough. I could scream at him and scare the bejeezus out of him, but that might attract some scary monsters. Hmm . . .* Fey twisted her lips in consideration.

Amethyst watched alertly as she trailed along like a strange scarf, ready to participate in whatever mayhem Fey desired.

The slime's eagerness settled the matter. With a discreet hand signal, Fey shooed her other pets out of range, then said quietly, *Amethyst, be a dear and cast all your poisons into Poison Sphere.*

The slime squeaked cheerfully and complied.

<Requiem has been poisoned!>

<Slug poison: −1 health/30 seconds>

<Duration: 5 minutes>

<Blue mushroom poison: −2 health/10 seconds>

<Duration: 5 minutes>

<Thornweed poison: -2 health/5 seconds>

<Duration: 5 minutes>

<Furyweed poison: −3 health/second>

<Duration: 5 minutes>

<Poison mushroom poison: −4 health/20 seconds>

<Duration: 10 minutes>

<Gloom blight: −10% speed, −1 stamina/minute>

<Duration: 15 minutes>

<Poison Sphere has reached level 2!>

<Poison Sphere has reached level 3!>

(Excessively dedicated and detail-oriented readers may have noticed that sea nettle poison did not appear; because of the way jellyfish neurotoxin works, it is strictly a contact poison.)

Most of Amethyst's poison collection consisted of weak toxins that could easily be shrugged off without an antidote, but the combined effect hit Requiem in a wave of agony.

Blade and Sirena caught up a minute later to find Requiem contorting in obvious pain while Fey looked on with a detached-but-slightly-worried expression.

What did you do? Sirena asked in an impressed voice.

Blade did not need to ask; he knew the signs of poison (intimately). "Which poison did you use?" he asked.

All of them, Fey answered, biting her lip. Her eyes were focused on the stat window she had called up; Requiem's health bar was dropping at an alarming speed. *He's going to die in less than two minutes,* she reported. Her furyweed alone was enough to kill the average level 30 warrior; the other poisons simply compounded the pain Requiem felt and hastened his death.

Sirena slung a companionable arm around Fey's shoulders. *Good job,* she congratulated her. *I couldn't have done it better myself.*

Fey still looked worried. Her callous and self-interested nature revealed itself when she asked, *If he dies, will I get a player killer penalty?*

Sirena sobered. *Good point. Grabbing you probably doesn't count as first aggression on his side.* She sighed regretfully. *I guess we better heal him up.*

Blade was watching Requiem's death throes with a "that could easily have been me" kind of fascinated horror. It took him a few seconds to notice the girls staring at him expectantly. "What?" he asked.

Lend a fellow an antidote? Fey asked hopefully. She had never stocked up on any, given how she always toughed out the full duration of a poison effect to train Immunity.

Blade drew back defensively. "No way. I only have two left." Blade's stock of poison neutralizers had become dangerously depleted in the course of adventuring with Fey, and he was not about to risk himself in order to help a rude, obnoxious person like Requiem.

Pleeeease? We don't want Fey to get infamy, Sirena begged. Her expression was all "enormous puppy eyes," making it hard for Blade to refuse her. (#EmotionalManipulation)

I'll get you more antidotes as soon as we're back in town, Fey promised, making it hard for Blade to refuse on pragmatic grounds. (#Bribery)

"Fine," he acquiesced. With some reluctance, he dug out his second-to-last antidote.

Yaaay! Sirena cheered. She swam over and gave Blade an exuberant hug and kiss on the cheek, then plucked the antidote out of his surprised fingers and proceeded to be rougher than necessary in forcing the potion down Requiem's throat.

Thanks, Blade, Fey added gratefully. Blade had saved her the trouble associated with being a player-killer; infamy resulted in poor relations with NPCs, making it difficult, if not impossible, to obtain quests or purchase items. She did not hug him or kiss him on the cheek; her brand of affection consisted of making a mental note to buy him a lot of extra antidotes (which he wouldn't need if she just stopped poisoning him).

Poisons neutralized, Requiem was now in a state of critically low health and its attendant physical weakness. *What happened?* he asked groggily; that many concurrent poisons had somewhat stunned him and the pain had driven memory away.

Sirena saw an opportunity to further toy with the beleaguered merman. Putting on a concerned face, she said, *You must have been attacked by a really poisonous monster.*

Amethyst squeaked proudly at the compliment ("Am I really, really poisonous?"). Fey smiled fondly and patted the slime. *Yes you are,* she cooed.

Requiem missed the interplay between owner and pet. *What was it?* he asked, looking around uneasily.

I didn't see it, Fey answered. (This was truthful if one did not consider tamed pets to be monsters.)

Did you get poisoned, too? Requiem demanded.

Yes, but I have a fairly high level of Immunity. At level 8, the ability made her immune to all but the poison mushroom poison and gloom blight, and she was tolerating the blurry vision and speed penalty so well that the other party members would only notice if they looked in the party menu.

Colour slowly returned to Requiem's skin as his vitality restored his health out of the danger zone. Though his physical state was returning to pre-poison levels, his mental state was considerably more paranoid as he constantly scanned the environment for the poisonous monster Sirena had planted in his mind. (Ooh, she's so evil.)

Before Requiem could ask any more questions, Fey distracted him by saying, *Let's proceed cautiously from now on.*

Sirena nodded seriously (well, "seriously"). After being nudged by the mermaid's elbow, Blade nodded as well, though with a distinctly unconvincing look on his face.

Fey now took the lead in exploring the chasm. Requiem stuck close enough to the party that he started invading Blade's personal space, causing the human warrior to shoot him an exasperated look. "Dude, back off. The poison monster is gone."

Fey shot Blade an amused look and Amethyst waved her bubble at him. Teasing (tormenting) done, Fey now focused on the quest as she moved forward. *Tell me if you see anything interesting*, she whispered to her pets. She was amused enough by the fact that the party was relying on a person with poisoned vision to lead that she did not give up her position at the front in favour of pragmatism.

The glooms (and a gloom-riding boar) zipped off to explore. It was a gloom that found the site of interest, many minutes after Fey's poison status had worn off. Squeaks brought her attention to a rusted lever on the chasm floor.

Come look at this, she called to her party mates. They gathered around the strange object, trying to figure out why it was there and what it did.

Fey held her jellyfish lamp closer to the metal. Under the rust, she could faintly make out lettering. *Do not pull*, she read aloud.

The party members exchanged glances. They all had differing levels of desire to pull the lever.

Fey was fully against it. In her mind, pulling the lever equated with bad and probably lethal outcomes.

Sirena was of mixed feelings. She felt that pulling the lever would be dangerous, but also that it was a necessary part of the quest.

Blade was cautiously for it. He did not have a fertile imagination for unknown dangers, and felt that the party could handle whatever happened.

Requiem would normally be very eager to do whatever was necessary to finish the siren's song quest. However, in the wake of his traumatization-by-poison, his normally brash nature was temporarily subdued, and he looked at the lever with indecision.

Fey looked around the circle, saw that the other party members had some desire to court death-by-mysterious-lever, and took a calming breath, reminding herself that in-game death was (probably) not too unpleasant. *Okay, fine, let's do it.* Before she could think too hard about the stupidity of her course of action, she grabbed the lever and yanked.

The other party members tensed, then relaxed as Fey's strength proved insufficient to budge the rusted contraption. (Second anticlimax reached.)

Trying to cover her embarrassment, Fey gestured at Blade to try his strength. The human warrior planted his feet and heaved; with a creaky groan, the lever slowly changed position.

For a second, nothing happened. (Error. Anticlimax limit for the chapter has been reached. Proceed with plot.) Then a loud rumbling began from the chasm walls as they slowly moved toward each other.

Fey acted quickly, expecting something of the sort. She grabbed Requiem's arm and yelled, *Swim up! UP!*

The party raced madly out of the chasm, with Blade and Fey acting as severe handicaps on the merfolk's speed. The chasm walls inched ever closer together.

Eyeing the distance still to swim and the distance left between the walls, Fey judged the party was not going to make it. Thankful that telepathy allowed her to talk even when she had laboured breathing from sprint swimming, she called the glooms over and had them take Amethyst and Squishy with them as they escaped.

Fortunately, Fey's calculations were off. The movement of the chasm walls displaced a huge amount of water, which helped to propel the party out safely before the ocean floor closed with a deep boom.

Tumbled about by the turbulent flow of water, the party finally settled, panting from overexertion, some distance away from the chasm.

Well, that was fun, Fey finally remarked. Even she was unable to determine the ratio of sarcasm to honesty in her voice.

Sirena looked around. There was a crack in the ground where the chasm used to be, but the gap was gone. It appeared that nothing else had changed, and they were no closer in their quest to find siren's song.

Requiem was the first to remark, *Do you hear that?*

Hear what? Fey asked.

Low, low *voices.* The telepathic sound was near infrasound; though the players were not relying on their ears to hear, they were still restricted by the range of signals their brains could process.

The pitch of the voices rose into the clearly audible range, travelling up and down. *It's . . . singing!* Sirena exclaimed.

(Several hours after the close of the chasm, a small tsunami hit the town of Seaport. There was extensive property damage, especially to the buildings closest to shore, but the NPCs managed to keep any players from dying.)

CHAPTER 11
BOOM

Massive silhouettes swam into view. The shapes appeared to be moving slowly, but with just a few strokes of their tails, they arrived at the remains of the chasm.

Fey's party was awed into silence. The new arrivals were a mother blue whale and her calf, the adult about 150 (metric) tonnes[18] and her offspring a third of the size. Ignoring the (tiny) players, the mother whale circled the newly sealed chasm, inspecting the change to the seafloor while her calf tagged along.

After taking several minutes to get used to the sheer enormity of the largest animal in the world, Fey and Sirena glanced at each other.

Is this even quest-related? Fey asked quietly, so as not to disturb the gigantic creatures. Wellia had mentioned nothing about whales when giving out the quest.

Sirena shrugged. *Can't hurt to ask.* She swam forward, her pace matched by a quest-eager Requiem.

Unless we get killed, you mean, Fey muttered with her typical "take things literally" mindset. Blue whales were filter feeders that targeted tiny krill for food, but their sheer size made them apex predators. She swam forward anyway, not truly believing that the whales would kill them. (Blade also followed. #Afterthought)

Hello! Sirena called out cheerfully from approximately one whale-length (30 metres) away.

The whales did not appear to notice.

After a few seconds, Requiem tried. *Hello?*

Still no reaction.

Maybe louder, Fey suggested.

HELLO! Sirena yelled, to no effect.

Impatient, Requiem swam daringly close to the whales. He was first noticed by the whale calf.

It's a merman, he noted. His voice sounded childish despite being immensely loud and deep.

The mother whale spoke, her voice even deeper and louder than her offspring's. **What do you want, merman?**

Do you know anything about siren's song? Requiem asked.

Did you say something? Speak up, merman.

DO YOU KNOW ANYTHING ABOUT SIREN'S SONG? Requiem yelled as loudly as he could.

Both whales swam away from him with annoyed flicks of their tails. **What are you screeching for?** the mother whale asked irritably.

From Fey's perspective, she found it obvious that whales would find the normal pitch of human voices to be shrill and annoying. Reassured by the fact that Requiem had not been mauled after annoying the sea-giants, she decided to give communication a try. Swimming closer to one of the mother whale's eyes, she imagined her voice as a resonant bass, amplified as if by loudspeakers.

Hello!

The whale glanced over. **Greetings, human.**

Fey ignored the mistake about her species in order to build good relations with the possible source of their next quest clue. *Greetings, great one. My name is Fey. The merman you spoke to is Requiem. Allow me to introduce my other party members, Sirena and Blade.*

I am Laaguuna. This is my fourth offspring, Iaabaanaar. The whales' names had deep, elongated vowels.

Hi! Iaabaanaar chimed in.

The conversation appeared to be flowing smoothly. Fey continued, *If you could spare us a moment of your time, we would like to consult your wise knowledge about a mystery we are exploring.*

Laaguuna gave no indication whether the flattery had any effect, but nonetheless granted the request. **Ask.**

Do you know anything about siren's song?

The party's expressions became more alert, each member paying sharp attention to Laaguuna's answer.

The whale gave a deep-pitched snort. **The merfolk spent too much time amongst the land-dwellers**, she said, answering the question indirectly. **They confused** singing **with the noise-making that the humans do, and lost much of their ability.**

Fey felt that the whale was providing crucial information to unlock siren's song but did not quite understand what she meant. *Could you give an example of how merfolk have lost their ability?* she asked.

Another snort. **The way your Requiem screeched when attempting to speak with me. Even you, a human, are closer to grasping the true capabilities of sea-speech.**

Fey paused to reflect on the information. If "sea-speech" was telepathy, then Laaguuna had stated that Fey's telepathy was closer to siren's song than Requiem's . . .

Laaguuna did not wait for Fey to finish thinking. **If that is all, we shall be leaving.**

Hey, wait—

Fey interrupted Requiem's exclamation with a well-placed elbow and a bow (only realizing halfway through the motion how stupid it looked underwater). *Thank you very much for your aid.*

Bye! said Iaabaanar cheerfully.

Mother and calf swam off majestically in the direction they had appeared from.

What the hell, Fey? Requiem complained. *She didn't tell us anything!*

Fey was busy trying to recapture the line of thinking that had been interrupted by the whales' departure and made no reply other than an annoyed shushing gesture in Requiem's direction.

Requiem was wholly unused to being ignored by a member of the opposite sex (sorry dude, wrong species), and tried again. *Are you listening to me?*

Shut up unless you have something useful to say, Sirena snapped. She recognized the look on Fey's face as the one present when puzzling through problems.

Requiem had had just about enough of Sirena's rudeness. *Sirena, you really need to—*

SHUT UP! Sirena borrowed Fey's earlier technique and altered her telepathic voice to boom like speakers set to maximum volume. She did not bother altering it to sound deeper than her speaking voice.

<Requiem has been stunned for 5 seconds!>

<Sirena has learned Boom Stun!>

<Sirena has unlocked the Volume Overlimit requirement for Siren's Song!>

<+30% range to all telepathy-based bardic abilities>

Sirena was quite pleased with the turn of events. *Oh look, I made some quest progress. What were you thinking about, Fey?*

Well, if I was trying to catch a train of thought, your shouting certainly derailed it, Fey answered dryly. *Besides, it looks like you figured it out by yourself.*

Figured what out? Sirena asked guilelessly.

. . . What the whale meant when she said that telepathy differs from singing with vocal cords?

Comprehension failed to appear on Sirena's face. *How does it differ?*

With anyone else, Fey would suspect the person was feigning incomprehension as a joke. She knew her best friend well enough to just sigh and explain. *Volume? You couldn't be that loud in real life without a hell of a lot of training.*

Oh well, yeah. Sirena flapped her hand at the obviousness of the explanation.

HA! Requiem suddenly yelled upon recovering from the stun. The other party members jumped in unpleasant surprise. The looks they shot the merman ranged from "displeased" to "irritated."

Fey instinctively clapped her hands over her ears, only to grimace and lower her arms after remembering how useless the gesture would be against telepathy. *What the hell did you do that for?* she asked irritably.

Requiem looked confused. *Why didn't I unlock anything?*

Sirena rolled her eyes. *You're doing it wrong.*

HAA!! This time, Requiem yelled for twice as long, with a similar lack of success.

Fey grimaced. *I wish I could plug my ears,* she remarked wistfully.

Yelling for longer doesn't do anything, Sirena snapped. *Stop being an idiot and actually do it properly.* To Sirena, flexibility in telepathy came intuitively, and she had accomplished the necessary mental shift to adjust her volume without "yelling" so easily that it did not occur to her that others might require a better explanation than "do it properly."

I'm doing the best I can, Requiem snapped back defensively. As a trained singer, it was quite difficult for him to separate what his vocal cords could do from his understanding of sound and music. *You could try actually being* helpful.

And why would I want to help an incompetent playboy idiot like you?

Sirena's body language was becoming increasingly aggressive, and Requiem's rose to match it.

Blade watched the escalating situation with discomfort. He glanced over at Fey for support in defusing the argument.

Fey was observing the merfolk players with a calm "well, I guess this is happening sooner rather than later" expression on her face. She looked not the least bit stressed by the emotional environment, nor did she show any sign of wanting to stop the fighting.

Incompetent!? Requiem repeated incredulously. *You just became a bard a couple hours ago!*

(Haha, notice how he didn't refute the "idiot" or "playboy" parts.)

Yeah, and I'm already better than you! Quest answers are handed to you on a silver platter, and you can't even make them work! Sirena's pent-up aggravation had clearly burst the dams. She was not as devastatingly critical as Fey in the insult department but held nothing back in pointing out all the parts of Requiem that annoyed her.

Blade decided he should intervene, with or without (well, without) Fey's support. "Um guys, maybe we should all calm down."

Sirena disdainfully disengaged from the argument. *Hmph.* She swam away. Fey fell in behind the mermaid (and grabbed her hand, forcing Sirena to tow her friend's weight), and Blade quickly followed.

Requiem was left hanging in incoherent anger. (Poor dude, it was his turn to talk in the argument.) His pride strongly discouraged him from following after Sirena, but no matter what he wanted, he needed to return to town with the party. He gritted his teeth and caught up.

The party found the dolphin taxis still lingering in the area and hitched a ride back to Pearlview. Sirena seized the singing role the entire way in order to deny Requiem the chance to gain experience.

Instead of the cheerful pop songs of the first trip, the song selection veered toward "dark and aggressive." As often as not, this resulted in attack rather than speed buffs, but the dolphins did not quite dare to complain.

After the third inappropriate song choice, Fey rolled her eyes and intervened. *If you're going to pick angry songs, at least pick fast, angry songs. We agreed to provide speed buffs.* She made a few suggestions of songs that would fit the criteria.

Sirena patted Splash apologetically. *Sorry, guys,* she said to all the dolphins. She chose one of Fey's suggestions, causing the dolphins' speed to surge.

What has her tail in a twist? asked Whistle in an undertone.

Oh, she and Requiem got into a fight, Fey answered in an unconcerned fashion. *Group tensions and all that.*

Did the quest not go well? Whistle asked sympathetically.

Oh no, it went very well. We got enough information to almost solve the quest. It's just that Sirena figured out how to use it to improve her bard skills, while Requiem hasn't quite gotten the hang of it yet.

I see. Well, not everyone has the flexibility of mind to master the finer aspects of sea-song, Whistle replied in a knowledgeable tone.

Fey began to suspect that the dolphin knew something that would help them solve the quest. *So do you sing?* she asked casually (or, more accurately, "attempted casually"; our heroine's ability to dissemble is quite sadly lacking).

Me? Nothing anyone would want to listen to. I have a cousin who's quite good, though.

Did she take lessons? Fey asked.

Nothing so formal. We listen and join in with our families and during larger gatherings, and you either pick up the tricks or you don't.

And what tricks did your cousin pick up?

Whistle's telepathic voice was amused. *Nice try, little human. Your quest won't be as easy as asking me.*

What if I bribed you with delicious fish? Fey asked (after grumbling *I'm an elf* to herself).

This information is worth more than a few nomfish. I wouldn't give you a hint for less than a netful of water swifts.

Hmm. Fey was unfamiliar with the name of the creature Whistle referred to, but she assumed that they would be stronger than the level 21 nomfish. *I'll let you know if I'm ever in possession of these water swifts, then.*

For everyone who was more sensitive to emotional currents than Fey (i.e., everyone except her pets), the trip back to Pearlview was awkward with unresolved anger. The dolphins dropped off their passengers, accepted their payment in fish, and left as quickly as possible.

Blade rather desperately thought of something to say in order to sweep tensions under the (figurative) rug and said the first thing that popped into his mind. At the same time, Fey started talking about the water swifts.

"Oh yeah, Fey, Sirena, and I—"

So my dolphin said—

Both players paused. "You first," said Blade.

Okay. So my dolphin said that she'd give us a hint about siren's song if we got her a netful of "water swifts." I don't know what level they are, but I figure it might be a good next step in the quest.

Sirena glanced up at the water's surface. It was not dark yet, but it soon would be. *We probably don't have time to go out again before dark. Stay in town, get information, practice skills, and go out tomorrow?* she proposed.

Fey and Blade nodded, while Requiem glared in sullen silence.

What were you going to say? Fey asked Blade.

"Oh well, Sirena and I got a quest from a mermaid who wanted to see a land flower. We figured you could teleport out and get one while the rest of us worked on something else."

Yeah, sure, Fey agreed. *I'll go grab one while you guys find out about the water swifts.*

Get a nice one, said Sirena. *I'm pretty sure the reward depends on the type of flower you get.*

. . . I'm not really qualified to determine what a "nice" flower is, but I'll try, said Fey. She swam off toward the teleportation gate with a wave of goodbye.

Blade realized that his hasty speech had resulted in him being left alone with two hostile factions. (Oops.)

Sirena did not bother looking at Requiem when she announced, *We're splitting up.* (#Passive-Aggressive) Imperiously indicating that Blade should follow her, she swam off into town.

Requiem immediately swam away in a different direction.

Blade looked at the angry merman's retreating back, sighed, and followed Sirena.

Fey appeared in a flash of light in River's Bend, a town in the middle of human lands she had passed through on the way to Seaport. She judged that she would be more likely to find flowers on open plains than her native forest.

She had no idea what kind of flower would be the best for the quest, so she decided to just collect as many different kinds as she could find and present them all for inspection.

Following a trail out of town, Fey came upon a meadow full of lush grasses and vibrant flowers. In the warm afternoon sunlight, the scene looked absolutely idyllic.

"You don't fool me," she muttered. Marshalling her pets, she laid out the plan. "Got it?"

The pets squeaked in agreement.

"Okay? Go!" They burst into action.

Fey dashed from flower to flower, severing stems and collecting blossoms. When the plant and its same-species friends rose up in retaliation, the Feypets moved in. They had been told that Fey only needed one of each species; therefore the rest were simply potential experience points to be harvested (through violence).

The glooms reverted to their shadow-rabbit shapes and hopped through the meadow, biting through stems and leaves. The plants, affected by their dark-element blight, shrivelled and browned, crumbling away into dust after dying.

Amethyst handled the larger and more aggressive plants. All of their attacks bounced off of her upgraded Triple Membrane without a scratch, and she retaliated with devastating blows of her level 18 Whip. She also secreted gloom poison, leaving circular patches of dead land wherever she hopped.

Boris was in charge of uprooting the stubborn plants that retreated underground or used the soil's nutrients to replenish their health. Using his snout, he exposed plant roots and mercilessly ripped them out of the ground; the glooms took care of the rest.

<Boris has learned Dig!>

<Amethyst has achieved level 21!>

<Boris has achieved level 21!>

<Onyx has achieved level 20!>

<Inkblot has achieved level 20!>

<Ebony has achieved level 20!>

<Midnight has achieved level 20!>

<Shadow has achieved level 20!>

<Obsidian has achieved level 20!>

The level 20 mark resulted in another intelligence boost for the pets.

Amethyst squeaked nostalgically while beating a sunflower-like opponent into a pulp. ("I miss Magic.")

Boris grunted, ripping a family of wild carrots out of the ground. ("Yeah. This would be a lot easier with him around.") When Onyx hopped over to infect them with his blight, Boris stomped an impatient foot. ("Those are edible. Leave them as loot.") Onyx instead pounced predatorily (in a rather un-rabbit-like fashion) upon a creature that looked like an animated troll doll with grass for hair. It shrieked and punched at the gloom before crumbling away into clods of earth.

In the end, Fey collected fifteen different varieties of flowers, as well as miscellaneous roots and seeds that she decided to let Kallara sort through later. She praised her pets for their hard work, treated the various bruises and cuts everyone but Amethyst had acquired through combat, and packed up to return to River's Bend, then Pearlview.

She left behind a barren, devastated meadow. Some of the hardier plants respawned, but the carnage was sufficient to permanently alter the monster population of the area. Thorny, poisonous plants grew, and dark-element creatures appeared, thriving in the blighted lands.

The next players to follow the trail to the formerly pleasant meadow barely escaped with their lives.

Before teleporting back to Pearlview, Fey stopped at the local healer's and purchased a batch of basic antidotes from a Kallara look-alike named Kinsey. She had Amethyst absorb one of them through Osmosis in order to add the potion to her Potion Slime repertoire.

"There," she said with satisfaction. "Now you can fix Blade if we poison him again."

Amethyst squeaked. ("But then Blade won't learn Immunity.")

Fey sighed. "Yeah, but we shouldn't force him to train it if the side effects really bother him that much."

Amethyst squeaked judgementally. ("He's kind of wimpy.")

"When it comes to poison, yeah," Fey agreed. "But we're all wimpy when it comes to something."

Amethyst blinked several times, processing her owner's words.

<Amethyst's intelligence has increased to 64(+1)!>

. . . *Philosophizing appears to be good for my pets' intelligence. Just when I think I've gotten used to Fantasia, something weirder comes along.*

CHAPTER 12
FLIPPED

Requiem hid himself in an isolated niche in Pearlview and attempted to unlock the Volume Overlimit requirement for Siren's Song. He tried various kinds of telepathy: short shouts, yelling words, singing at high volume, anything he could think of. He was sure he was louder than Sirena had been when she succeeded, but the system message failed to appear for him.

Dammit! he swore, punching the nearest coral wall. He swore again when the rough surface lacerated his knuckles.

His frustration and embarrassment only increased when the elf, Fey, swam into view.

Requiem did not understand the girl at all. His first impression of her was of her hovering quietly behind that human warrior, Blade, the picture of a shy, passive girl.

Every subsequent interaction with her confused him more. Her reactions to his words and actions seemed so bizarre; when he tried to be nice, she reacted negatively, but at other times, she would be surprisingly empathetic and helpful.

What's up? Fey asked in greeting as she came within conversational distance.

Requiem had nothing new to report, so he made a vague sound of acknowledgement (also known as a "grunt").

He immediately regretted not talking more, as Fey took the opportunity to notice the isolated surroundings and the small cloud of blood around his scraped knuckles. When she spoke, he braced himself for a comment about his lack of progress with Siren's Song.

You're actually a singer in real life, aren't you? Fey asked instead.

Requiem's brow knitted in confusion. *Yeah?* he answered warily.

Fey ignored the question he implied. *Think of it as turning up the volume on your microphone while singing quietly.* After a pause, she said, *Okay, I'm off to find Sirena and Blade; later!* and swam away.

Requiem considered her words. After a moment, he began to sing a low, quiet song. Concentrating on maintaining the velvety tone of his singing, he gradually increased the volume of telepathy until he could be performing for a crowd of hundreds.

<Requiem has unlocked the Volume Overlimit requirement for Siren's Song!>

<+30% range to all telepathy-based bardic abilities>

Oh, they're so beautiful. The NPC mermaid cooed over the flower arrangement Fey had brought in a jar.

<Quest complete!>

<Blade gains 2500 experience. Sirena gains 2500 experience. Fey gains 10,000 experience. Requiem gains 100 experience.>

<Fey has achieved level 25!>

May I keep the flowers? the NPC asked. *I'll trade you my necklace for it.* She held out a simple chain holding an exquisitely carved piece of gem coral in the shape of a complex polyhedron.

In Fey's eyes, the pendant was clearly more valuable than her jar of common flowers. *Sure, I guess,* she agreed, not quite happy with an unequal trade that cheated the other party. *The flowers are going to die in a few days, though,* she warned.

That's fine, said the NPC, pressing the coral carving into Fey's hand. She swam off happily with the jar of flowers.

Sirena slid the chain out of Fey's grasp as smoothly as a moderately talented pickpocket. *This is clearly for me,* she said with satisfaction.

Hey, what? Fey complained. *I did all the work here.*

Sirena made a cutesy face that was completely wasted on her friend. *It enhances magic,* she explained cheerfully. *Magic inscriptions in* Fantasia *are based on geometric shapes.*

Fey opened the item description.

<White coral mage focus: This piece of white gem coral was masterfully carved into a twenty-pointed star to channel and amplify mana flows. (+10 intelligence, +20 magic attack)>

Fey sighed in defeat. There was no arguing that the item belonged with the group's only mage. Sirena grinned and slipped the chain over her head.

What's next? Fey asked.

Blade answered. (Yes, he's been there the whole time.) "Well, we asked around, and it turns out that water swifts are level 40, so . . ."

Oof, said Fey as if she had been punched in the abdomen. *I don't really want to stay down here for longer than it takes to get your land legs,* she said to Sirena.

What's wrong with "down here"? asked Sirena, hands on scaled hips.

It's wet, answered Fey. *My fingers are getting all prune-y.*

Blade looked curiously down at his hands. In the salt water of the ocean, his fingertips did not wrinkle.[19] Shaking his head free of the random thought (#Fey'sInfluence), he rejoined the conversation. "I think this is too important a quest to give up just to get back to land earlier."

Psh, who said anything about giving up? Fey made a dismissive gesture. *We should just figure out the rest of it on our own.*

Blade very nearly expressed a sentiment along the lines of "You can't just 'figure out' a quest," but realized that Fey would probably reply with something like (a raised eyebrow and) "Why not?"

He remained silent as Sirena asked, *Did you figure something out?*

The parts of Fey's brain that were supposed to be devoted to basic tasks like paying attention to her surroundings and walking without tripping over her own feet were instead used to muse over various random topics. Very occasionally, these musings resulted in ideas of material use. *So I was thinking about what the whale said. She basically implied that our minds naturally limit telepathic singing in the ways that real singing is limited.*

Neither Sirena nor Blade particularly remembered Laaguuna implying any such thing. Sirena hid the confusion better (#JustGoWithIt) and nodded encouragement for Fey to continue.

So, if we figure out what all the limits are and learn how to sing past the limits, then we'll unlock siren's song, Fey concluded.

The task sounded simple enough, except for the "figure out what all the limits are" part. Fortunately, this was one of the rare occasions that Fey's musings had amounted to ideas of material use. *Obviously, we already figured out that volume is one. The next one is probably pitch, since I already lowered my voice when I talked to the whales.*

Hmm, let's see. Sirena began to hum a descending scale from middle C. After about two octaves, she had to pause and really concentrate, but eventually she managed to produce notes belonging to the bass vocal range as she descended another two octaves.

Try high notes, too, Fey suggested.

Sirena started singing an ascending scale. Her natural voice was already soprano, so she had to travel into almost "dog-whistle" territory to really exceed her upper register.

<Sirena has unlocked the Pitch Overlimit requirement for Siren's Song!>

<Special bardic abilities can now be learned.>

Nice, said Sirena, *what's next?*

Ummm . . . Fey pondered for a moment. *Breathing?* she ventured. *I guess you can hold a note for as long as you want.*

Sirena made a face. *That seems too obvious.* Nonetheless, she began to sing a song with continuous phrases, not pausing the flow of sound where she would normally need to draw a breath. At its conclusion, several minutes later:

<Sirena has unlocked the Duration Overlimit requirement for Siren's Song!>

<+10% duration of bardic buffs>

Sirena was really excited. *Wow, we're going to finish the quest tonight! What's next?*

. . . I've got nothing, Fey admitted. She had no idea how many unlocks were required to complete the quest, and the idea of trying to think of a possibly large number of subtle limits to break was daunting.

Sirena sighed (*deflated*). *Oh well, three out of five isn't bad.*
Five? Where'd you get five from?

It just seemed like a good number for a quest.

It's probably twelve or something, said Fey pessimistically.

A long moment passed as Fey, Sirena, and Blade each tried to think of another limit of singing that telepathy could overcome.

Fey was the first to give up; she generally left this kind of thinking to her subconscious. *I'm hungry. What do people eat down here?*

Seafood, Sirena answered promptly.

"I could eat," said Blade.

Seafood was not Fey's favourite, but they had not eaten all day, so it was no time to be picky. *Let's go.*

As the party travelled to the nearest restaurant, Fey asked, *How do people cook down here?*

Very carefully.

Cooking was indeed a dangerous activity underwater. It was accomplished by using fire magic to heat the water around the food to boiling. Unless the process was very precisely controlled, a would-be chef could end up cooking their own flesh along with the fish.

To reassure restaurant patrons that they would not meet that rather unpleasant fate, they were separated from the cooking area by a wall of clear glass. Rather than conventional tables and chairs, the restaurant boasted tiered seating on a magically grown coral reef. Diners sat in loops of coral shaped like inner tubes, preventing them from drifting away on water currents.

Fey, Sirena, and Blade were about halfway through their (fishy) meal when Requiem appeared. Sirena was the first to spot the merman hovering near the restaurant entrance.

I wonder what he wants.

Fey turned to see who Sirena was talking about, then answered, *To finish the quest, I'm assuming.*

The trio was seated in such a way that Requiem had to swim up to find them; he did so, his body language somewhat different than before.

And how's Siren's Song going for you? Sirena asked with venomous sweetness.

I learned it, Requiem snapped. Visibly reining in his anger, he asked, *Fey, may I speak with you alone?*

Whoa, I thought people only did that in movies, Fey thought. Her expression clearly showed her surprise, but after a pause, she said, *Sure,* and extricated herself from her seat. Merman and elf swam to the other side of the coral reef for privacy.

Sirena leaned over and twisted at an extreme angle in order to spy on the pair. *What do you think he's saying?* she asked Blade.

Blade shrugged, taking another bite out of his fish. "I don't think it's any of our business."

Sirena gave an airy (watery?) wave. *Don't be silly; Fey totally assumes I'm spying right now.*

"What about Requiem?"

Never mind Requiem. Fey's my best friend and I reserve the right to spy on her while she's talking to idiot playboys.

Blade did not quite know how to respond to that, so the conversation fell silent until:

Ooh, look at that body language. He's totally into her.

"What? No way," said Blade, curious despite himself.

See for yourself, Sirena urged, waving him forward without looking away from her spying.

Blade found himself leaning out of his seat; his vantage point was such that he did not need to undergo the contortions Sirena was performing (which was good, because he definitely wasn't flexible enough). Indeed, Requiem's body language was quite intent on Fey, whereas Fey's was aloof (what a fun word) as she politely listened to him speak. "Huh. I wonder what's going on."

Ohmygod. Sirena managed to latch onto Blade's arm in excitement even as her gaze stayed glued to the private ("private") conversation. *He's totally fallen for her!*

Blade tried not to wince at Sirena's long nails digging into his arm. "Why would he suddenly fall for her?"

She totally flipped the trigger when she was nice to him after I stressed him out.

Sirena's words confused Blade in multiple ways. "Huh?"

Sirena released her grasp in order to poke Blade. *Someone being nice to you when you're stressed is a classic way of triggering a crush.*

Blade considered the explanation and decided it made sense. "Okay, but when was she nice to him?"

When she taught him how to do the Volume Overlimit thing, duh. There's no way that idiot could have figured it out by himself. Plus, she's really good at explaining things so even idiots can understand.

Blade thought back to all the instances that Fey had confused him with a distinct lack of explanation. "Fey is definitely really bad at explaining things."

Aww, poor baby. Sirena actually looked up from spying in order to pet Blade on the shoulder with amusement and sympathy. *Fey's really good at explaining things, but she rarely does. You have to be quick-witted around her.* She abruptly straightened as Fey and Requiem turned toward their table, wincing as her abdominal muscles protested their abuse.

Fey and Requiem arrived at the table to find Sirena and Blade paying more attention to their food than strictly necessary. Fey slid back into her seat, asking Requiem, *Are you joining us?*

Nah, I have to go practice. See you tomorrow, Fey! Requiem swam off.

The moment he was out of telepathic earshot, Sirena demanded, *So? What'd he say?*

Fey answered without stopping her eating. (Ah, the benefits of telepathy.) *He thanked me for explaining the Volume Overlimit, and then I explained the other two unlocks we figured out, and then he thanked me again.*

Oh, he totally likes you, Sirena said with relish. (No ketchup? Sad.)

"Uh, how does that prove anything?" Blade asked.

Fey sighed resignedly. *I'm afraid I'm going to have to agree with Sirena's evaluation. He touched my elbow twice while we were talking.* (Apparently, this kind of aggravation makes our heroine pull out the essay-type vocabulary.)

"What's so special about an elbow?"

To prove her point, Fey asked, *And how many times have you touched my elbow in the week we've been adventuring together?* A pause to allow Blade to recall never performing such an action. *Exactly. It's not where, it's the fact he did it at all.*

Sirena laughed at Fey's put-upon expression. *Hey, cheer up; it could be worse.*

Blade stared at Fey. He knew she was an unusual girl, but . . . "Aren't you supposed to be happier?"

Fey raised her eyebrow at him. *I'm given to understand that that's the normal reaction to being found desirable, but it seems to me that unless you like the other person, having him like you is just troublesome.*

Sirena patted Fey's hand comfortingly. *At least he's pretty normal this time.*

That's true. How did that happen?

You were nice to him after I stressed him out.

Fey narrowed her eyes at her friend. *That's right; this is all your fault. You're totally paying for dinner.*

"'Normal'? 'This time'?" Blade asked.

Sirena laughed. *Oh boy. Let's just say that Fey could write a stand-up comedy routine just by telling the unembellished tales of her interactions with the opposite sex.*

Fey sighed again. *I attract weirdos,* she explained bluntly. *Not that often, but too often for my comfort.*

Blade tried to say something encouraging. "I'm sure you . . . They can't all be . . ."

Sirena just kept laughing. *Now with Requiem, she can finally say they're not all weirdos. Though really, this probably means we're going to discover something really weird about him.*

I refuse, Fey said firmly. *We are going to finish this quest quickly, not discover that he is anything but normal, and then never see him again.*

Oh, please, he's in loooove. Sirena clasped her hands dramatically. *He shall follow you unto the ends of the earth and pledge his undying loyalty to your cause.*

I don't even . . . Wow, even other people's crushes make you stupid.

Just you wait, said Sirena. *You've reformed his playboy heart.*

Fey sighed yet again.

Amethyst squeaked. ("Fey-Fey is breathing funny.")

Fey petted the slime. *You folks have it right, with the mitosis or binary fission, or whatever you do,* she said to her pet. *Hormones are stupid.*

After the meal (which Fey did make Sirena pay for), the party left the restaurant and made plans for the next game day. Fey and Sirena would look through their music books and try to analyze the limits of singing. They decided that the next night, they would either train or find another quest to do, since the Siren's Song quest was at a dead end until they either figured it out or were able to kill level 40 water swifts.

Oh, before I forget. (*cough* before the author forgets *cough*) Fey dug around in her belt pouch and handed Blade a batch of antidotes. *It's not that many, but I'll make more if you need it.*

"If you would stop poisoning me, I wouldn't need it," Blade sighed, stowing the potions in his own bag.

Bidding each other good night, they logged off.

CHAPTER 13
EVOLUTION

Sunday morning found Arwyn in tae kwon do class as per her weekly routine. After warm-up and stretching, the class was split up by belt rank; each group was assigned an assistant instructor who led them through the appropriate pattern practice.

Tae kwon do patterns, or forms, were sets of linked kicks, punches, and blocks in a pre-set order. The movements were balanced and symmetrical; if performed perfectly, one would end in the exact same spot in which the pattern was begun.

Arwyn loved performing patterns. There was a unique grace and dignity to the ancient movements, passed down through the martial art for centuries. She herself was not a graceful person, but when she flowed through the twenty-plus movements of a pattern, it felt like she was.

The head instructor wandered between groups of students and observed. Generally, he nodded in approval and moved on without comment, but he would occasionally intervene to change a stance, shift the angle of an arm, or give brief instructions to the assistant instructor.

He paused to observe the red belts moving through tae geuk yook jun,[20] the sixth pattern learned by students under the

World Taekwondo Federation. (WTF.[21] The author didn't even make this up.)

Arwyn always felt nervous when being observed by the head instructor. He was a compact, mild-mannered man who did not really "look like he did tae kwon do" unless you noticed the intense focus in his eyes. She was not sure whether he had five or six stripes on his black belt (because after four, they became hard to count and she was too intimidated to stare for more than a second). There was no real reason for her to be nervous, as all the instructors were supportive and patient teachers; it was mostly her imagination that told her they could see a dozen things she was doing wrong that they were too polite to mention.

Legitimate cause or not, Arwyn's nerves meant that when she was being observed by the head instructor, her kicks, punches, and blocks gained an extra measure of snap. Her mind went into overdrive, looking for and eliminating any minor errors in technique. Having already memorized the pattern she was practicing, she moved through its thirty-one movements without error or pause.

"Very good," the head instructor said in approval. "How long have you been a red belt?"

"Uh . . ." Arwyn hesitated as if trying to figure the time in her head, but really she was stalling because she did not like the direction the conversation was taking. Her last belt exam had been before she started university, five years ago. Moving away from her hometown, she had kept up her fitness by joining her school's tae kwon do club, but as it catered to beginners trying the martial art for the first time, she had forgotten most of the knowledge she was supposed to know as a red belt. Only after graduating and moving back had she started relearning everything.

The head instructor searched his own memories of recent belt exams and did not find Arwyn. "It's been a long time, hasn't it?"

"Yes, sir." Arwyn could foresee her doom.

The head instructor nodded decisively. "You'll go for your black stripe in December," he announced.

Doom. Arwyn had three months until she would be called up and examined on everything she was supposed to know. She was not feeling enthusiastic, but respect for her teachers was deeply engrained. There was only one possible response: "Yes, sir."

The head instructor patted Arwyn's shoulder reassuringly. "You'll do well." With a few words to the assistant instructor, he moved on to other groups.

Arwyn knew she was being melodramatic with the pronouncements of doom. In reality, no one ever failed the belt exams; if the instructors did not think you were ready, they simply did not let you take the exam. It was only the combination of her love of the sport, her nerves when being observed by a panel of masters, and her habit of getting good grades that made her want to score one hundred percent on tae kwon do exams.

Even with the goal of getting a perfect score, three months was plenty of time to learn everything. Arwyn's ability to learn and memorize was several standard deviations above average. Going to classes regularly and spending a few hours at home studying would be sufficient if she applied herself properly.

Better start now. She concentrated with ferocious attention as the assistant instructor began to demonstrate a different pattern she needed to know.

◊◊◊

"Ready, buddy?"

Magic squeaked an enthusiastic affirmative. He and Leandriel were about to walk into the lair of the main boss of the Rift. At level

120, Leandriel would have left it alone for another few months of training if not for his new companion. With Magic's help, he thought he could defeat it now, but it was a risky endeavour. With the current difference in level, any stray hit was likely to earn him a quick trip to the rebirth point.

Walking forward, Leandriel felt rumbling in the ground. "No turning back now," he told his pet. "It has caught our scent." Bending his knees, he leapt into the air just in time to avoid a lashing tentacle.

If the other monsters in the Rift were failed experiments, the boss was an amalgamation of leftover parts. Blobs of flesh connected innumerable limbs of all kinds. Eyes and mouths were everywhere, with or without heads. Internal organs decorated its outsides: loops of bowel, bone, and sickly, beating hearts. The entire mass was easily bigger than a dozen dragons, glistening with bodily fluids, and torturously held to life by heavy-duty demonic and undead magic.

It wanted to add Leandriel to its parts. He narrowly avoided shots of acid, grasping limbs, and once, an eye laser. Hissing at the close call as the laser singed a dark line across one wing, he muttered, "Nobody told me it could do *that*."

Having successfully survived the first burst of attacks, Leandriel began his counter.

"Purifying Light." Brilliant white light pierced the monster with holy energy. The spell was far too weak to do any real damage, but it helped blind the multitude of eyes aiming deadly attacks his way while at the same time strengthening him due to his high holy affinity.

"Drain Spore, please," he requested of his companion. "Do not bother aiming; just lay as thick a layer as you can."

Magic complied, trailing a dense cloud of spores as Leandriel ducked and dodged through the air. Leandriel was far too busy avoiding death to look down and see the effect of the spores on the monster, having to trust that they were doing some damage.

Many of Magic's Drain Spores failed to attach to the boss, swept aside by the violent movements of its limbs or dissolved in acid as they landed. Some, however, were able to land safely; the monster was so large that a considerable number found safe areas to touch down.

Upon beginning to use Drain, another chunk of the spore population died, undead and demonic energy being rather toxic to other creatures. Still, a hardy few persevered, collectively draining a few health points per second and using the life force to fuel their own growth. Meanwhile, Magic continued to release new Drain Spores every second, adding to the population sucking away the monster's health.

The monster paid no attention to the diminutive fungi, focusing its energy on Leandriel and his stinging holy attacks. The spores took this time to mature into small mushrooms, which allowed their Drain ability to begin levelling up. One HP per second became two, then three, then four . . . times a hundred mushrooms, two hundred, three hundred and counting. With so much surface area, the monster was uniquely vulnerable to the carpeting of Drain Spores.

When its health started to become noticeably depleted, the monster finally tried to deal with its mushroom infestation. It used its limbs in clumsy attempts to scrape them off, but they were firmly anchored and refused to budge. Even if the monster hit them directly, anything but an instant kill was ineffective, as Drain quickly restored their health to full.

Leandriel took the monster's distraction as an opportunity to swoop in and destroy several of its external hearts. Hundreds of discordant voices shrieked and howled in pain.

Right next to the monster, the wall of sound hit Leandriel like a physical blow. Stunned and disoriented, he faltered in flight, stalling in the air. By the time he recovered, he was in the grasp of a crablike claw that pinned his arms to his sides and was trying to pinch him in half. His armour groaned in protest and began to buckle.

Magic came to the rescue without prompting, disappearing into Leandriel's magically expanded belt pouch and emerging with a flask of holy water. The mushroom quickly dropped the flask before it expanded to its normal size and it shattered on the monster's claw with a sizzle.

The monster flinched back from the burning liquid, allowing Leandriel to wrench himself free and escape into the air. "Good job, buddy."

Magic squeaked happily and went back to casting Drain Spore.

By this time, the monster was losing over a thousand health per second to the Drain Spore mushrooms. Its movements were noticeably weaker as it tried to rid itself of parasites. Displaced mushrooms determinedly hopped back into place and re-anchored themselves, and the monster caused itself more damage than it saved using its deadly limbs on its own body.

Leandriel flew in evasive circles around the boss. When it focused its attention on the mushrooms, he sent lances of holy light spearing through the monster, leaving smoking holes behind. When his attacks drew its attention, he focused on defending himself, letting the mushrooms sap away its health.

Before too long, the boss began to look distinctly dried out and feeble. Leandriel judged that its health was as low as it could fall with minor attacks. For a boss of the Epic calibre, such as this one, only a finishing blow that would destroy at least 5 percent of its health would have any effect beyond this point.

Leandriel flew higher and higher until even the huge bulk of the monster looked like a tiny speck below.

"Into the pouch, buddy," he bade Magic. The mushroom squeaked encouragement to his owner and disappeared into the magical storage pouch.

Leandriel cast his ability as he began his dive.

"Holy Impact."

A spark of bright white appeared at the tip of his sword, brightening to sunlike brilliance as Leandriel steadily gained speed.

Hurtling through the air at a devastating pace, he sent a quick PM to his programmer:

<Leandriel: I really hope the physics of this works out as you claimed it would.>

There was no time to wait for a reply; his sword pierced into the boss as he continued diving with no attempt to slow down or change direction.

Without intervention of magic, such a maneuver would certainly be fatal, his momentum carrying him headfirst through the monster and into the ground. Even relying on the explosion of his attack to blow him backward would likely result in whiplash that would snap his neck. Thankfully, the attack worked as programmed: the holy energy of the explosion recognized Leandriel as one of its own and gently cancelled his momentum before buoying him back from the boss's death throes.

As Leandriel ascertained his survival and lack of crippling injury, he received a reply.

<KevinO: Worked perfectly, just like I said.>

<Leandriel: You are the man.>

From the air, Leandriel observed the damage he had inflicted. Approximately one-fifth of the boss's flesh had disappeared in a craterlike hole. Another three-fifths of flesh surrounding the impact site was charred and blackened. Still, the lack of system messages told him that the boss still clung to life.

Leandriel did not feel up to a repeat of the death-defying version of Holy Impact; it consumed a lot of stamina and mana and also required a lot of mental energy to convince his body to continue forward when all of his instincts shrieked for him to slow down. He decided to finish the job the old-fashioned way. Landing, he cast a blessing on his sword and began to hack his way through the monster.

Leandriel had to chop the boss in half before it finally succumbed.

<Leandriel has defeated Drykkan's Parts Monster!>

<Leandriel has gained 1,422,490 experience.>

<Leandriel has achieved level 105!>

<Leandriel has earned the title Cleanser!>

<Leandriel's holy affinity has risen to 125% (+50%)!>

<Leandriel's fame has increased to 27,300 (+15,000)!>

<Magic has gained 1,422,490 experience.>

<Magic has achieved level 66!>

<Magic's Spore has reached level 13!>

<Magic's Spore has reached level 14!>

<Magic's Drain has reached level 9!>

<Magic's Drain has reached level 10!>

<Magic's Drain has reached level 11!>

<Magic's Drain has reached level 12!>

Sensing that the battle was over, Magic hopped out of Leandriel's belt pouch and squeaked victoriously. Suddenly, the mushroom began to glow.

Frowning in confusion, Leandriel picked up his pet for examination. Under his hands, Magic began to change shape. With a chiming sound, his stem thinned and elongated, while his cap spread out like an opening umbrella. (#Pokémon)

With Magic's transformation completed, his glow dimmed and disappeared, revealing his new appearance. His overall size remained roughly the same, but his aesthetic was drastically different. Rather than a fat, squat, cartoonish mushroom, he was now tall and elegant. His cap had faded from a vivid blue to milky white to match his stem, though one could see the faintest tinge of blue if one looked for it. The gills on the underside of his cap looked delicate and feathery.

<Magic has evolved!>

<Magic, level 66 death angel mushroom[22]>

"Mm?" Magic made a questioning noise quite different from his former squeak; it was much lower in pitch and sounded like a human voice without vowel or consonant sounds.

Leandriel had a sinking feeling in his stomach. He did not think Fey would be pleased with Magic's change in appearance. Intentional or not, all of her pets had a common "cute and cuddly" appearance that Magic no longer shared.

He messaged Kevin.

<Leandriel: What happened to my mushroom?>

<KevinO: Like it? We all thought that this guy suits you better. Plus the whole "death angel" thing.>

If Magic were his pet to keep, Leandriel would not be displeased at the transformation, but . . .

<Leandriel: Could you change him back? I don't think his owner would like it.>

<KevinO: . . . You can't give it back to the elf girl, it out-levelled her a long time ago. I mean, you could, but you'd have to reset its stats as if it died.>

The sinking feeling grew more pronounced. Leandriel had not even considered the fact that players could not gain a pet of higher level than them. This was a prudent safeguard against power-levelling. He had essentially stolen Fey's pet when he agreed to take care of it.

<KevinO: Sorry man, I thought you knew the rule or I would have warned you.>

<Leandriel: I did, but I somehow did not think of it in this instance. Not your fault.>

"Mmm?" Magic's questioning sound now held a note of worry that Leandriel was not pleased with his transformation.

Leandriel sighed and patted the mushroom. "It will be fine, little buddy. I am sure Fey will not be mad at me forever." His words aimed to convince himself more than the mushroom.

"Mmmmm." Magic smiled and made a reassuring sound, trying to convey that his old owner would not be angry with Leandriel. Unfortunately for Leandriel's nerves, he lacked Fey's uncanny ability to understand her pets and thought Magic was merely trying to comfort him.

Putting his worries aside—he would deal with things when Fey logged on—Leandriel began the walk out of the boss's lair. He was accompanied by a stream of Drain Spore mushrooms hopping past him, presumably looking for new food. Demonic and undead forces had dramatically altered their development: while their general shapes were similar to blue mushrooms, some were the sickly grey of dead flesh and others vivid shades of red and yellow.

Leandriel wondered what species they were.

<Leandriel: Do I need to do anything about these mushrooms?>

<KevinO: Nah, they'll fit themselves into the ecosystem.>

<Leandriel: If you say so.>

Magic paid no attention to his strange offspring, already wanting to know what the next adventure would be.

CHAPTER 14
OVER THE TOP

Darkness. "Scanning. Player detected. Welcome back to *Fantasia*, Fey E'lan." Blinding light.

◊◊◊

Fey logged into *Fantasia* slightly earlier than usual. A quick survey of her friend list showed that neither Sirena nor Blade were online yet. As usual, Leandriel's name was written in the green that indicated he was online. Fey had never seen the angel offline, as would be expected of an NPC (or an employee who played ten to twelve hours a day and lived in the same time zone.)

Within a few seconds, Fey received a PM.

<Leandriel: Hello.>

It was the angel's habit to greet her whenever she logged on. Fey smiled and replied.

<Fey: Hi! What's up?>

<Leandriel: I need to tell you something.>

Fey's eyebrows rose in surprise.

<Fey: Is something wrong?>

<Leandriel: Not exactly.>

Leandriel sent a request to initiate a video chat. When Fey accepted, he appeared on a virtual screen. At the sight of his angelic glory, Fey blinked three times in succession as her primary personality and inner fangirl wrestled for control of her body. (Fey won the battle for voice, facial expression, and most of her motor control but was forced to cede control of her hands to the fangirl, who made her fingers twist in agitated excitement.)

Amethyst was the first one to notice the difference. From her position on Fey's shoulder, she squeaked in surprise. ("Magic's all tall and fluffy!") The other pets all scrambled to see for themselves, swimming around Fey's head and making their own excited comments.

Whether Fey understood her pets or noticed the transformation on her own was up for debate. Either way, she looked at the mushroom perched on Leandriel's shoulder and asked in an amused voice, "Is that a death angel?"

Leandriel was surprised she recognized the species, and it showed in his voice when he answered, "Yes, it is."

Fey answered his unspoken question by explaining, "Alpha-amanitin is a toxin used in biochemical experiments involving RNA polymerase." (This really raised more questions than it answered.) She continued, "Does this mean Magic's poison has changed?"

Taken aback by the unexpected course of the conversation, Leandriel replied, "Ah, let me check. Yes." He read off, "'Death angel poison: starting at 1 damage per minute, damage increases by 1 per minute every minute. Poison does not wear off and can only be cured by a greater antidote. Requires level 30 Immunity to negate its effects.'"

"Wow, talk about a slow and painful death. Remind me to collect a sample next time." Speaking directly to Magic, she said, "Congratulations on evolving, Magic!"

The mushroom murmured a cheerful reply. His happy expression was at odds with his owner's uncomfortable look.

"There is something else," Leandriel confessed. He sounded guilty and repentant.

Fey could not really imagine an in-game scenario that warranted the angel's tone of voice. "What is it?" she asked, starting to worry.

After a pause, Leandriel's words came out in a rush. "Since Magic has outstripped you in level, I cannot return his ownership to you without reverting him to his starting state."

"Oh." Fey took a moment to process the information. "That's okay."

"You are . . . okay with it?" Leandriel asked cautiously. The word "okay" sounded strange, not matching the angel's formal speech patterns.

"Yeah. Magic can stay with you. That is, if you don't mind keeping him."

"Of course not. But . . . You are okay with it?"

Fey smiled. Leandriel was normally quick-thinking and articulate, but he was clearly finding it difficult to understand her reaction. "Yeah. He's happy with you." Fey did not think of her pets as equipment to be used in battle, but companions whose preferences mattered. Recalling how well Magic and Leandriel had gotten along the few times she had adventured with the angel, she did not even feel surprised to learn that her pet would not be returning to her. It felt like her subconscious (or a certain author) had long ago decided that the two belonged together.

Leandriel stared at her for so long that even Fey, with her unique brand of oblivious self-confidence, could not help but feel discomfited. "Is there something wrong?" she finally asked, looking away from his bright blue eyes.

Leandriel blinked. "Ah, no, my apologies. You . . . your reaction is not what I expected."

Fey smiled. Randomness was her specialty. "That's me," she said cheerfully.

Before the conversation could continue, Fey looked up at the sound of her name. Looking off into the distance, she could see Requiem swimming toward her. (*sigh* That guy really does ruin everything.)

"Looks like my party is starting to log on," Fey said to Leandriel. "Talk to you later?"

"Of course. Goodbye." With a smile that tripled the power of Fey's inner fangirl (giving her control up to the elbows), Leandriel ended the video chat.

Fey turned rather impatiently toward the incoming merman. Talking to Requiem felt like a poor, poor substitute for her previous conversation. (On the bright side, Fey regained full control of her body as the fangirl took one look at Requiem and fell into a stupor.)

The merman appeared energetic in his demeanour. *What are you so excited about?* Fey asked.

I mastered the two overlimits you told me about last night.

Fey was not even slightly impressed, as extending range and duration of notes were the two easiest things she could possibly imagine using telepathy. *Congratulations.*

Fey's utterly neutral tone took much of the wind from Requiem's (figurative) sails. Rallying his spirits, he offered, *And I think I came up with one of the other requirements.*

That garnered a slight bit of interest. *What is it?*

A (melo)dramatic pause, and he answered, *Harmony!*

. . . Oh, you mean singing multiple notes at the same time. Sounds about right. Once Requiem pointed it out, it seemed like the most glaringly obvious limitation to singing, and indeed most instruments. One of the reasons Fey enjoyed playing piano was

because it allowed her to create multiple lines of melody and harmony without the help of other players.

Exactly, Requiem said with satisfaction.

I don't think singing multiple notes can be done without a lot of talent and practice, Fey pointed out. She could not imagine simultaneously focusing on two notes well enough to sing them both.

It can't be that hard, Requiem disagreed.

Fey raised an eyebrow. *Go for it, then.* Her challenge was issued in the same tone as she would to a five-year-old who insisted he could open a heavy door by himself. *I'll be over here.* Fey swam several metres away so that she could train Immunity without affecting Requiem with Amethyst's Poison Sphere.

Requiem watched Fey swim away, feeling yet again that things were not going correctly between him and the elf. He could not figure out what he was doing wrong that she always reacted with cool neutrality.

Requiem was surprised when Fey settled into a nondescript patch of water and pulled out her slime. She muttered something to it that caused her other pets to swim away. Strangely enough, they all began to circle their owner at a set distance; there were enough of them that they marked the boundaries of a sphere several times his height.

Curiously, he swam up. He could see no difference in the water at the boundary line. Stretching out a hand—

I wouldn't do that if I were you, Fey warned.

Why not?

I'm training my poison Immunity. Cross the line, and you'll be joining me. A sweet smile made the hairs at the back of his neck stand up. Something about Fey's eyes did not match the expression. (This was because under the myopic influence of poison mushroom poison, Fey could not see properly.)

Requiem swam backward away from the invisible sphere. *I'll, uh, be practicing over here.* He ended up much farther away than the original distance Fey had put between them. He tried to convince himself that his retreat was because he needed to work on the Siren's Song quest.

Clearing his mind, he hummed a note, then a major third above it. With a frown of concentration, he attempted to hum both pitches at the same time.

The attempt did not work very well, resulting in him switching abruptly between the notes rather than singing them at the same time. He tried again and again. The task occupied his attention enough that he did not immediately notice the arrival of the rest of the party.

Sirena and Blade logged on within a minute and a metre of each other. Sirena glanced over at Requiem, then Fey. Clearly dismissing the merman in her mind, she hooked elbows with Blade and propelled them both toward her best friend.

Stay out of the Poison Sphere, Fey warned. Sirena and Blade stopped at the edge of the pet-marked border.

Hi, greeted Blade, following social etiquette for entering people's presences.

So I asked a bunch of people what they thought the quest overlimits might be, and I got two answers we didn't already figure out, Sirena announced, ignoring the aforementioned etiquette.

Mm-hmm? Fey made a questioning noise. *Hi, Blade,* she tacked on as an afterthought.

One was the ability to sing multiple notes at the same time, and the other to change the quality of your voice.

Bard dude over there already figured out the first one, Fey indicated with a tilt of her head, *but what do you mean by the second?*

Allow me to demonstrate. Sirena did the telepathic equivalent of clearing her throat, then mimicked, *What do you mean by the second?* in a voice indistinguishable from Fey's.

<Sirena has learned Imitate!>

<Sirena has unlocked the Tone Overlimit requirement for
Siren's Song!>

Blade jerked back at the sound of Fey's voice coming from
someone else. "That is *so* creepy," he complained.

Fey and Sirena grinned at each other, completely in accord
without the need for telepathy. *What's creepy?* they asked in perfect
unison, Sirena still projecting Fey's voice.

Blade shuddered. "Stop that." Fey in stereo was more than he
could handle.

Fey could not resist. *Okay!* she answered in Sirena's brighter,
higher-pitched voice.

<Fey has learned Imitate!>

<Ability only available through telepathy.>

Blade was starting to feel seriously disoriented. "I do not like
this ability," he muttered.

Taking pity on the hapless warrior, Sirena patted him on the
shoulder and said, *I'll go torment lover-boy over there instead*, in her
own voice. She swam off toward Requiem.

<Amethyst's Poison Sphere has reached level 5!>

Amethyst squeaked. ("Another 1.5 metres out!") The other
pets adjusted their swimming accordingly, now marking a sphere
5 metres in radius.

Blade was disadvantaged by the fact he did not speak Squeak,
and was caught in the newly expanded *Poison Sphere* that Amethyst
cast. (What, did you really think he was going to get out of this
scene without being poisoned?)

<Blade has been poisoned!>

<Poison mushroom poison: −4 health/20 seconds>

<Duration: 10 minutes>

<Level 3 Immunity effect: −1 damage per poison infliction,
−1 minute duration, +5 seconds between poison inflictions>

<Net effect: −3 health/25 seconds>

<Duration: 9 minutes>

"[Censored word]!" Blade backed out of the poisonous waters. "Stop doing that!"

Ehe. Sorry. Fey held Amethyst in front of her face and said in her best stern voice, *Try not to poison Blade anymore.*

Amethyst paused, then squeaked dubiously. ("I'll try.")

Blade sighed and settled down to wait out the poison effect.

<Immunity has reached level 4!>

Blade glared at Fey. "You'd better not say 'you're welcome.'"

Fey wore an innocent look. *I wasn't gonna.* It was not in Fey's nature to force people to do things "for their own good." (She believed it was everyone's right to screw up their own lives.)

Sirena swam toward Requiem while humming a song titled "Playa."[23] She doubted the merman would recognize the tune but figured that his ignorance would be just as irritating to him.

The merman was busy humming something himself and did not notice Sirena's approach until she was within arm's reach. Irritation flashed across his features as he saw her.

How's it going? Sirena asked in a singsong voice.

Better before you got here was the aggravated reply.

Sirena affected an expression of disappointment. *I heard you figured out the fourth overlimit. Guess you don't want to know about the fifth.* She turned to return to Fey and Blade.

Requiem growled, *Wait.*

Sirena turned back around. *Yes?* she asked as if she did not know what the merman wanted.

Tell me.

Sirena put her hands over her hips (or where her hips would be if she had legs). *How rude. Is that any way to ask for a favour?*

Requiem looked like he might explode. Sirena did it for him, bursting into laughter in a way that defused his temper and left him confused. *You're too easy.* Deciding she had met the "aggravate Requiem" quota for the day (or at least an hour), she mimicked his tenor voice. *It's changing the tonal quality of your voice.*

Sirena laughed again at the merman's surprise. *You can do it!* she encouraged in Fey's voice, causing Requiem to startle even more.

At this point, Sirena saw that she had seized such a huge lead in their verbal sparring that Requiem had no chance of catching up. Deciding it would be boring to continue, she broke off hostilities. *Well, that's all I wanted to say*, she said in her own voice. *Bye!* She swam off again, intending to return to Fey and Blade.

Looking beside her, she paused. *Why are you following me?*

Requiem rolled his eyes. *We're in the same party.*

Don't you have to practice singing or something?

Don't you? he countered.

Good point.

Sirena paused in the water and Requiem followed suit, confused. She sang the three notes that made up a major triad in succession, then all at once.

<Sirena has unlocked the Self-Harmony Overlimit requirement for Siren's Song!>

<It is now possible to invoke Harmony bonus effects in a solo performance.>

<Sirena has unlocked all the overlimit requirements for Siren's Song!>

<Siren's Song will be learned when all overlimits are exercised in the same performance.>

How the [censored word] *did you do that!?* Requiem demanded.

Sirena looked at him confusedly. *I just did it.* Sirena was naturally gifted at music, and a quirk in the way she processed it made it easy for her to perform all of the overlimits without practice. She was unable to explain how she did what she did, as she had never experienced music through the mind of another person and did not understand the difficulties Requiem faced.

Resuming her forward motion, Sirena reached Fey and Blade. *. . . Did that sphere get bigger?*

"Yeah." Blade sounded rather aggravated as he answered.

Not-so-subtly changing the subject, Fey asked, *How's the singing going?* from within her poisonous domain.

Looks like I've unlocked all the overlimits. It says that Siren's Song will work when I use all of them in a single performance.

What? No way. How did you sing multiple notes? Fey asked.

Um, like this. Sirena sang a major triad again.

Fey wore an expression of intense concentration. When she heard chords, they did not sound like the sum of individual notes but rather a new sound that blended the notes. This made concentrating on and projecting multiple notes all but impossible. *Unless . . .*

Sing it again, will you?

Sirena complied. When she sang the triad, Fey did not attempt to pick out the individual notes, instead focusing on memorizing the way the blended chord sounded to her.

Taking a deep breath, she projected the chord out through telepathy. It worked, though not being a bard, Fey did not gain any abilities.

You did it! Sirena exclaimed. *High five!* She held up a webbed hand.

Fey bade Amethyst to stop casting Poison Sphere and swam over to slap her palm against her friend's.

Sirena glanced sideways and said, *Whoa, what's with that face?* Requiem looked sour enough to clean pennies.[24] He was not pleased that both girls had succeeded where he had failed, even with almost half an hour of practice.

Are you bullying Requiem? Fey asked. It seemed that her friend had moved from subtle digs to full-out verbal attacks. She did not entirely approve; the obvious approach lost style points and generally resulted in inconvenient group dynamics that lowered productivity.

Only a little bit, Sirena said with her most endearing look. Fey was unmoved (#100%CutesinessResistance).

Sirena was suddenly inspired by the forces of diabolical mischievousness. Turning to Requiem as if chastised, she sincerely apologized. *Sorry, Requiem. We seem to have gotten off to a bad start.*

Somewhat mollified, Requiem graciously replied, *No worries.*

It's no problem if you can't learn this stuff by yourself. Fey's a really good teacher. In fact, why don't Blade and I go find something else to do while you guys have a private tutoring session? The diabolical trap had been sprung.

Fey's expression flitted from distaste to resignation. *Nine out of ten*, she rated Sirena's level of diabolicalness, causing both Blade and Requiem to look confused.

Laughing, Sirena hooked elbows with Blade. *Shall we?*

". . . Sure." Noticing Fey's distinct lack of enthusiasm for the plan, he asked, "You okay with this?" (Aww, he's so nice. Fey should really stop being mean to him.)

Yup, Fey answered with studied neutrality. *After all, it's the logical thing to do.* She was fairly sure she could explain the remaining two overlimits to Requiem in a way he would understand.

Requiem seemed happy with the suggestion, both because he would be free of Sirena's presence and because he would be alone with Fey. *Cool. Thanks, Fey.*

Swimming away with Blade in tow, Sirena could not resist sending Fey a PM.

<Sirena: It's a win-win situation; I get to have Blade all to myself.>

<Fey: How is me being alone with Requiem a "win"?>

<Sirena: Well, he wants to be alone with you. It's more of a win-lose-win-win situation, so it's rounded up to win-win.>

Fey beckoned to Ebony (the bunny-eared mermaid-shaped gloom) and murmured a low-voiced request before sending her after Sirena.

Aww, so cute. Thanks, Fey! she called back to her friend.

Ebony morphed into a monstrous cave-spider and landed on Sirena's head.

Fey winced at the incredibly loud shriek that rang through the ocean, but the pain did not stop her smile. *Shall we?* she said cheerfully to Requiem.

CHAPTER 15

PET TRAINING

S o where are we going?" Blade asked.

Good question, Sirena answered cheerfully. *We should go train or something.*

"Okay," Blade agreed. As the pair swam to the edge of town, he asked, "How long do you think they're going to be?" referring to Fey and Requiem.

Sirena smiled wickedly. *As long as it takes that idiot to learn, so probably a couple of hours.* She petted Ebony, whom she had convinced to morph out of arachnid shape.

"Is it okay to leave them alone for that long?"

Yup. There's a ninety-nine percent chance that nothing interesting will happen. Sirena sounded rather disappointed in her friend's lack of scandalous behaviour.

"What about the one percent?"

That's to account for the possibility that Requiem will do something extraordinary, or extraordinarily stupid. I'm leaning toward stupid. Changing the subject, she continued, *So do you want to look for a hunting party or just train by ourselves?*

"Whichever one's easier, I guess."

Blade had no problems with working with strangers, and neither did Sirena. They quickly found a party that welcomed the addition of a warrior and a mage, setting off toward the territory of level 23 bladefins.

Right before Sirena left Fey's party to join the new one, she sent a message to the group.

"Blade and I are joining a hunting party. Have fun, you two!" As farewells went, it was perfectly innocent and appropriate (except for the insidiously suggestive tone of the "have fun"; to be fair, only Fey detected it).

Bladefins were fish whose name was perfectly suggestive: their dorsal, pectoral, and pelvic fins were hard, sharp, and metallic silver in colour. Small and agile, they travelled in schools of around fifty and were not safe to hunt unless one belonged to a large hunting party.

Aquatic battle formations were different from their land-based counterparts; due to the three-dimensional nature of the milieu, a well-balanced party required more front-line fighters to defend players with high attack but lower defence. However, the principle was the same: tanks (meatshields) protected the more fragile players, who focused on destructive output.

Blade and Sirena settled easily into their respective roles. Their party, which, other than Blade, consisted entirely of female merfolk, was reasonably skilled. It was not long before the fighting became predictable and Sirena started to get bored.

Thankfully for everyone involved, Fey sent Sirena a PM before she found a way to alleviate her boredom. Barely an hour into hunting:

<Fey: Where are you guys? We'll join you.>

Sirena devoted half her concentration to the conversation. (The other half focused on mercilessly electrocuting bladefins into lifeless husks.)

<Sirena: Done already? Bard dude must have more talent than I thought.>

<Fey: Not really. I taught him like five two-note intervals because he couldn't sing a triad. He can do a bunch of different voices, but only male ones. I got the overlimits unlocked, but I really don't see him being able to use them all at once.>

Sirena snorted as she released chain lightning upon a new school of fish. It sizzled past the head of one of her party members with less than a hand's breadth to spare.

<Sirena: So he's just as talented as I thought. It'll be a challenge for him to learn Siren's Song, then.>

<Fey: Not my problem. I only need one of you to learn it so I can finish the quest and get back on dry land.>

<Sirena: Oh, your cold, cruel heart. If only lover boy knew, his spirit would be crushed.>

<Fey: You planning on telling him?>

Sirena knew her friend well enough to apply the correct hopeful tone to the words. She released another spate of lightning before replying.

<Sirena: He wouldn't believe me. To him, you are the angel of benevolence who rescued him in his moment of need.>

<Fey: Training is getting boring, huh?>

<Sirena: Like you wouldn't believe. We already figured out the best attack sequence. I just cast lightning every six to eight seconds until forever.>

<Fey: Any room in that perfect attack sequence for two more?>

<Sirena: Sure, they'd love to have you. Or at least Requiem. They seem really starved for male company.>

<Fey: Haha, are they getting all touchy with Blade?>

<Sirena: It's aggravating. "Blade, will you show me how to hold my spear?" "Blade, do you want a snack?" "Blade, do you think our positions are okay?" It makes me want to apologize on behalf of all females.>

<Fey: Ehe, to be fair, males also do very stupid things under the influence of hormones. Exhibit A is currently to my immediate right.>

Sirena forgot to cast magic, too absorbed by the hint that her predicted 1-percent-chance-of-Requiem-doing-something-extraordinarily-stupid event had occurred.

Sirena! one of the mermaids called out sharply.

Oops. Sorry! Sirena called back meekly. She was actually quite irritated at her gossip being interrupted, and her next chain of lightning was proportionately more lethal.

<Sirena: What did bard dude do?>

<Fey: Well, I'd tell you, but you left me alone with him for an hour, and that kind of behaviour shouldn't be rewarded.>

<Sirena: Whaaat? Pleeease? It was just a harmless joke.>

<Fey: You not knowing won't do you any harm, either.>

Sirena viciously let her Charge Jolt build for an extra-long period. When she released it, it annihilated an entire school of bladefin without any of her party members' participation.

<Sirena: Heartless monster.>

<Fey: That's me ^_^>

(Hey wait, are we really skipping over what happened with Fey and Requiem? That doesn't seem like a good narrative choice. #OverruledByAuthor-Goddess)

Fey and Requiem arrived at the hunting grounds (waters?) by taxi dolphin and were welcomed into the fighting formation. Both were classified as warriors and took positions on the outer perimeter; there was subtle maneuvering as Fey attempted to put distance between herself and the merman, while Requiem attempted the opposite. Fey by herself might have lost the battle, but she was aided by the fact that several mermaids wanted to fight next to the handsome bard. She ended up as far away from both Blade and Requiem as the geometry of a sphere would allow. (She wasn't trying to avoid Blade but definitely wasn't willing to fight hormone-crazed girls to be near him.)

At the first break in fighting, Fey sent her pets away to train separately. With their small bodies and lack of magic, they were unsuited to joining the hunting party's battle formation.

Go find a good place to train, she told them. *Take care of each other and don't let anybody die.*

With various (adorable) gestures of affection, the Feypets bade their owner a temporary goodbye and set off to find a suitable training ground.

Having surpassed the level 20 mark, Fey's pets had gained a boost in intelligence and also developed more distinct personalities, drawing traits and patterns of behaviour from their owner.

Generally speaking, pets below level 40 would be quite unable to act effectively on such vague orders as Fey had given. The Feypets, being patterned after their eccentric owner, were unique in several ways.

First, their intelligence was distributed extremely unevenly. They were incredibly logical and pragmatic for their level; in converse, they had simplistic and reductionist views of the world. They had also failed to gain the basic language skills most pets developed at this stage, relying on the fact that Fey seemed to understand their squeaking.

Second, the Feypets were naturally independent. Their owner rarely issued them commands and they had had to rely on their own initiative to even keep up with her from day one. Even if their personalities were not taken from Fey herself, the experience they had gained under her loving-but-absent-minded care would have forced their development in this direction.

Third, they had very good memories for things they considered important. (They tended to forget trivial things, such as "Try not to poison Blade.") All of Fey's actions and battle strategies had been carefully observed and analyzed, pondered and distilled into their purest form. The Feypets had found several common themes, such as "be unexpected" and "hit them where it hurts," but all had independently arrived at the conclusion that Fey's battle strategy could be summed up into one sentence: Pick a monster weaker than you, then spam your most effective attack until it dies.

With this master plan in mind, the pets set out to find the perfect (victim) monster to train on.

The glooms squeaked suggestions. ("It swims slower than us.")

Boris chimed in. ("Preferably land-bound.")

Amethyst squeaked. ("Poisonous!")

All the pets turned to look at the slime (except Inkblot, who was carrying her. The gloom extended the length of its neck so it could stare.)

Boris snorted. ("Why? Your poison won't work well on them, and we can't get near them.")

Amethyst squeaked earnestly while the other pets listened on. ("I've been thinking. You guys should all learn Immunity. Fey-Fey won't make you because it's uncomfortable, but it would make everything convenient.")

Obsidian was the first to squeak agreement. ("You're right. Fey-Fey's doing it, so we should, too. We're not wimpy like Blade-Blade.")

Boris and the other glooms nodded, united by the notion that they were made of sterner stuff than Blade.

Amethyst squeaked a warning ("I'm doing it, then.") and released her weakest slug poison through Poison Sphere. No system notices appeared due to the lack of players in the vicinity, but the pets were each aware of their own statuses.

Boris absorbed the minor discomfort of the poison and put it out of his mind.

A beat later, Onyx squeaked confusedly. ("Did you cast it yet?")

Amethyst squeaked, likewise confused. ("Yeah. Didn't it work?")

Boris grunted. ("I'm poisoned.")

Each of the glooms reported their lack of status ailments.

Amethyst put forth a hypothesis. ("Are you guys immune to poison?")

Inkblot squeaked. ("Looks like it.")

Amethyst squeaked cheerfully. ("Well, that's convenient.")

(Probably too convenient, but hey, they don't need oxygen and don't have blood or nerves, so it's plausible.)

Amethyst was full of plans. ("We can kill a lot of monsters quickly if we swim around poisoning stuff.")

Onyx squeaked. ("Boris still has to learn Immunity.")

Much squeaking followed as the Feypets attempted to create a viable plan.

In the end, the pets decided that planning was too much trouble. They swam through the ocean looking for monsters with the intention to deal with issues as they came up.

Shadow was the first to spot a group of black starfish on rocks below. Unknown to the pets was the fact that the monsters were level 30 ninja starfish. Inkblot carried Amethyst over to the sea stars while the other pets hung back cautiously. Amethyst reached out with a furyweed-infused Poison Sphere.

Enraged starfish immediately leapt upright onto two points and launched themselves through the water at much higher speeds than the glooms could swim. Inkblot dodged sideways, avoiding one spinning starfish, but squealed in pain as a second flew past, leaving a deep gash in her shadow-flesh.

The Feypets scattered, frantically dodging spinning death. Onyx, burdened with carrying Boris, was particularly slow; both the gloom and its passenger suffered extra damage.

Amethyst and Inkblot formed the rearguard of the retreat. Amethyst was able to use Whip to deflect many of the attacks, though she inflicted little physical damage.

The starfish were easily able to keep up with the group's travel speed and were relentless in their attack. Enraged by furyweed, they continued attacking past the edge of their territory. Amethyst was beginning to worry about disobeying Fey's "no dying" rule when the black sea stars began to visibly weaken. The (ridiculously OP) poison had done its work, eating away at the monsters' health. As they died, they stiffened and hardened, becoming perfectly balanced throwing weapons.

Amethyst squeaked. ("Not good for training.")

The other pets nodded vigorously. They collected the loot and moved on.

Several mishaps and close calls later, the Feypets were ready to give up. Because they had started off in bladefin territory, the monsters in the area were between level 25 and 30, slightly too strong for the pets. They decided to make a wide loop into unexplored waters and then return to Fey if they found no promising targets.

Luck (or statistical probability) was with them as they came upon a group of strange-looking fish. Rather than having the sleek lines of more agile fish, these looked rather round and slow.

The pets were cautious, knowing that appearances were usually deceiving when it came to monsters. Rather than provoking a whole group of them with Poison Sphere, Midnight bravely volunteered to perform a high-speed flyby (swim-by?) attack of an individual fish. He clipped the fish with jarring momentum and continued by in fast retreat.

The retreat was unnecessary. Rather than pursuing aggressively, the fish reacted by inflating itself to almost spherical shape, revealing the spines that had formerly lain flat against its skin. Its appearance now clearly matched that of a pufferfish. As the Feypets had no education in biology, this meant little to them.

A moment of waiting made it clear that the pufferfish reacted only defensively. The Feypets' mood rose collectively as they saw the possibility of a good training spot. Other glooms dived at the fish, knocking it this way and that. They took no damage, but it was clear that they inflicted little as well.

They switched attacks, deciding to use Suffocate. After they plastered themselves to the fish, the pufferfish revealed another defensive mechanism, spinning rapidly around. The action would have torn flesh, except that the glooms simply spun with their victims. They felt slightly dizzy but were able to cling on.

The glooms with passengers hung back. Amethyst bade Inkblot to take them forward, as it looked safe to use Poison Sphere on multiple monsters. However, when she cast furyweed into the water, they failed to react.

Amethyst became excited. The resistance to poison meant that the fish were likely poisonous themselves.[25] With an excited squeak, the slime opened her mouth and engulfed an entire pufferfish.

What happened next was not pretty. Amethyst was fairly transparent, so the entire digestive process was visible to observation. (Fortunately, nobody was paying attention, so the gruesome details can be skipped and this story can retain its family-friendly status.)

The end result was that she learned the recipe for pufferfish poison.

It occurred to Amethyst that she need not restrict her eating solely to poison collection. The skill Engulf was born.

Boris and Onyx were the last ones yet to join the fray. Boris was pragmatic; the creatures were poisonous and his Immunity was only level 2 after training for a few hours.

He grunted. ("Put me down and go fight.")

Onyx hesitated, but logic and pragmatism won. The gloom delivered Boris down to the sandy seafloor before attacking the nearest pufferfish.

Boris wandered along, feeling slightly lonely and out of place. He was of very little help in underwater fighting, and in fact was more of a hindrance to Onyx, who had to carry him. Feeling morose, he looked up at the fighting as he passed a medium-sized rock.

He was jolted into a more immediate state of mind when a powerful suction force tumbled him off his feet. The rock was in actuality a rockfish waiting for unsuspecting prey.

With a desperate twist, Boris managed to avoid having any of his limbs caught in the fish's gaping mouth. His main body was too large to fit, and stopped up the mouth quite nicely. The rockfish released the suction for a second attempt, and Boris lashed out with his sharp tusks.

In the end, Boris was battered and bruised but victorious. He enjoyed the rush of experience points, picked up a coin, and began nosing around more carefully in the sand.

CHAPTER 16
TOXIC

Fey and the temporary hunting party quickly racked up experience points. The hunting was so good that they ended up staying in bladefin territory for the entire day, each player gaining three levels. Only when the sun had truly set did they pack up to leave.

One by one, mermaids said their goodbyes and (reluctantly) swam off. Blade and Requiem received and declined numerous party invitations, all under the gazes of (a coldly wrathful) Sirena and (a bored) Fey. Finally, the original party of four re-formed.

Fey silently relaxed, releasing the small but not insignificant amount of self-control she required to act normal and unremarkable. It had been a good day for training, but the experience points had come at the cost of her relaxation time; she preferred to just be herself in the game. Still, she was satisfied with the day's results: in addition to her three character levels, she had used her normal warrior's skills extensively, raising Arc Slash to level 5 and Mana Blade to level 6. The day's hunting had also yielded a good amount of gold and loot in the form of bladefin meat and bladefin fins, which were (improbably) made of high-grade steel.

Getting ready to return to town, Fey looked for her pets. *Looks like they haven't come back yet.* She sighed and opened her system map to locate her wayward companions. She brightened considerably when she saw eight dots moving toward her location at high speed, saving her the need to actually go collect her pets.

Before long, a small purple glow heralded the arrival of Amethyst (and company). The Feypets swam at maximum speed in their rush to reunite with their owner, slamming into her in a way that would have been quite painful if not for their diminutive sizes. As it was, Fey drifted backward several metres, plastered in pets from neck to ankles.

Hi guys. Did you miss me? she asked jokingly. She rather regretted the joke when the Feypets responded by tightening their respective holds on her; most of them were quite tolerable, but Amethyst had wrapped her bubble-arm into its customary position around Fey's neck. (#AffectionateStrangling)

Amethyst, save that for the monsters, okay? Fey's telepathic voice sounded slightly choked because of the mental state associated with obstructed breathing.

Amethyst loosened her hold and squeaked questioningly. ("Am-Am should hug monsters?")

Not hug, Fey corrected, *strangle*.

Sirena swam in and plucked Ebony off Fey's left knee. *Where's my hello?* she demanded of the bunny-eared-mermaid-shaped gloom. Ebony reacted by going floppy like a doll.

Sirena wrinkled her nose in annoyance. *She acts just like you*, she complained to Fey.

Fey looked up from the process of detaching pets from her body. *Huh?*

Sirena gave the floppy Ebony a small shake to illustrate her point. *Does this look like a proper reaction to being hugged?*

In Fey's eyes, Ebony's "play dead" approach to being captured by a predator was a legitimate one. She chose to disagree on another point. *What does that have to do with me?*

You're like the most physically unresponsive person ever.

Fey considered the accusation for a moment, decided it had merit, and silently conceded the point, returning to the process of peeling Inkblot off her left shoulder. It was true that her body language was very often neutral, reflecting her inner confidence and emotional equilibrium. (The only time she would initiate something like a hug with a friend was in the wintertime, in order to leach body heat.) She had moods when she felt more playful and expressive, but in general, she had the range of gestures and expression of a moderately realistic robot.

Sirena flounced off (with her Feypet captive) while Fey released her pets into the water with a pat of affection.

Greetings complete, they began to disgorge loot. Following Amethyst's example, the glooms had managed to make pockets out of themselves, carrying items and coins in volumes that equalled their size.

The entire party was stunned at the quantity and variety of items. Shells, fish, plant life, crafting items . . . "Are those ninja stars?" Blade asked incredulously.

It appears so, said Fey, after examining one; it appeared to be a five-pointed, sharp-edged star made of a mysterious black metal.

There was far too much loot to carry in Fey's unenchanted bag, so she made the glooms pick it back up. Looking carefully at each shadow-rabbit-turned-aquatic-creature, she saw that they did not appear to expand enough to match the volume of the items they contained. She shook her head, thinking, *Laws of physics are just mild suggestions in this game.*

Any other surprises for me? Fey asked her pets. It was meant to be rhetorical, but the pets were still at the stage in development where they took everything literally.

Amethyst took the opportunity to debut her new pufferfish poison. The Poison Sphere she cast was limited to encompass

Fey's head (proving that she had poisoned Blade all those times on purpose).

<Fey has been poisoned!>

<Pufferfish poison: −10 health/30 seconds>

<Duration: 1 hour>

<Causes increasing paralysis>

<Level 8 Immunity effect: −3 damage per poison infliction, −3 minutes duration>

<Net effect: −7 health/30 seconds>

<Duration: 57 minutes>

<Rate of paralysis will be slowed.>

Oh boy, said Fey in a "this is rather bad" voice. She could already feel her lips and fingertips going numb. The damage from the poison would not kill her, but it would leave her with less than 10 percent of her health bar. Combined with the paralysis, she was as good as dead away from the safety of town.

Amethyst saw that her owner was less than pleased and squeaked with trepidation. ("Bad poison?")

Fey petted the slime, not really able to feel the action with her numb hand. *A little bit troublesome. Maybe wait until I gain a few more levels of Immunity before we practice with it again.*

Are you dying? Sirena asked interestedly.

Kind of. If we can get back to town without being attacked, I'll probably be fine.

Blade rolled his eyes. "You could just take an antidote, you know," he said, pointing out the obvious solution.

Fey blinked. *That had not occurred to me.* Her telepathic speech was still crisp because it did not rely on the movement of her numbing lips. She took the green potion Blade held out, but paused before opening it. *On the other hand . . . If I survive this poison, I'll probably gain a lot of experience in Immunity.*

Requiem made a choking sound. *Are you serious? Take the antidote!*

It was clear to Fey that Requiem was concerned for her well-being, so she did not take offence.

Sirena took offence on Fey's behalf. *She can do whatever she wants. Come on.* Sirena took Fey's hand and began towing her toward town.

Fey did her best to minimize the burden on her friend, kicking strongly though she could no longer feel her feet. She stuck the antidote in her pouch before it dropped from her numb fingers.

Blade's falling behind, she noted. Requiem could easily keep up with Sirena's speed, but Blade was not equipped with a tail. Sirena slowed and looked back.

Requiem made an exasperated noise. *I'll take her ahead.*

Sirena did not like the merman, but she had to concede that he could swim faster than her. *Fine.*

Requiem grasped Fey's wrist and began swimming strongly toward town. He began singing to enhance his speed from the first stroke of his tail.

Fey gradually lost the ability to kick as numbness travelled up her extremities. The sensation of being paralyzed was rather claustrophobic, but she was able to ignore it fairly well. She drifted in Requiem's wake, enjoying the music he sang to speed their travel.

Third time really is the charm, she reflected. Here Requiem was, pulling her along by the wrist without her feeling the slightest bit of hostility.

He really is a good singer. As always when she heard music she liked, she felt the urge to join in. She refrained because she did not feel close enough to Requiem to do so.

Requiem glanced back at Fey, cursed internally, and swam faster, never breaking his singing. He had not thought that her moon elf skin could be paler, but as she lost health, it became chalk-white. Her normally self-possessed expression had gone slack, and she drifted along behind him with little more animation than a doll.

They reached Pearlview in forty minutes, a time that rivalled the speed of a taxi dolphin. Requiem pulled up, chest heaving with exertion (or whatever merfolk did when they were out of breath), and realized that he had somehow fooled himself into thinking that arriving in town would cure the poison. He looked around, not knowing what to do next.

Let's just find somewhere out of the way and wait it out, Fey suggested. Her telepathic voice sounded calm and self-assured as usual, jarringly at odds with her state of paralysis.

Requiem sat Fey against the wall of a random building and began the swimming equivalent of pacing back and forth.

So have you thought about what you're going to do for Siren's Song? Fey asked.

Requiem gave her an incredulous look.

Fey's expression did not change, but he could almost *hear* the raised eyebrow. *This isn't an emergency, you know. It's going to wear off in*—she consulted her status screen—*seventeen minutes.*

Still. She was only getting paler. *How can you be so calm?* he demanded.

I'm almost always calm, came the (calm) reply. *So, Siren's Song?*

Requiem shook his head. *No idea.* He had not really considered the challenge, and he was in no state for clear thinking now.

I was thinking, the easiest way to combine all five overlimits would probably be to mimic a choir performance, or an orchestra, or a piano piece.

Requiem nodded in distracted agreement. He was not really paying attention, though it did seem like a useful suggestion.

Calm down. Now Fey sounded amused. *I really will be fine.*

You look like you're dying.

The math is clear. Fourteen damage a minute times fifty-seven minutes is seven hundred ninety-eight, and I have eight hundred and sixty-five health. I'll be fine.

Fey's unswervingly analytical mindset made no sense to Requiem. He did not live in a way that could be divorced from emotion. Obviously, he knew he was in virtual reality, but everything still felt real.

Fey chuckled telepathically.

What? Requiem demanded.

It struck me as funny that I'm the one doing the comforting. In multiple ways.

Requiem did not know quite what to say to that. It was true that he should be the calm one in this situation. *Maybe if you were less calm, I wouldn't have to do all the worrying,* he retorted.

She chuckled again. *Why don't you sing something to boost vitality or something?*

He could do that. All he had to do was think of the right song.

He hummed the five-note theme from the Pokémon Centre.

<Requiem has learned Heal Song!>

<Heal Song: Use the power of music to heal your allies in battle. Consumes mana.>

Relieved he had something useful he could do, he repeated the melody until his mana bar was exhausted and Fey had regained her usual rosy complexion.

Fey PM'd Sirena.

<Fey: We may need to keep him.>

<Sirena: What, as a taxi dolphin? He did get you to town ridiculously fast.>

<Fey: He's currently healing me by humming the Pokémon Centre theme song.>

<Sirena: . . . Damn, now I have to like him.>

Thank you, Fey said when Requiem was done with his healing. *Also, the Pokémon Centre thing? I approve.*

Heh. Requiem rubbed the back of his neck, rather embarrassed that the childish tune was the only one he could think of.

Calmer now that Fey looked healthy. Requiem settled himself next to her against the wall. *Isn't it uncomfortable?* he asked curiously.

What is?

Not being able to move.

A little. I'd probably be freaking out if I were the kind of person who couldn't stand small spaces or tight collars. Oh. Just then, Fey lost control over her neck, and her head flopped to the side. *Okay, well, that's pretty uncomfortable.*

Requiem carefully propped her head against the wall so that it was upright. *I still can't believe you're putting yourself through this.*

It doesn't really hurt, and it's only for a little while. I probably wouldn't do it again unless I could get rid of the paralysis, though. It's pretty inconvenient.

And dangerous.

If Requiem had been hoping for Fey to say something like "Oh but you're here to protect me," he was disappointed. *My pets could probably take down a small whale with the proper motivation,* she said instead. Amethyst squeaked threateningly to emphasize the point.

Requiem glanced around at the small pets with clear doubt about their offensive capabilities.

I have to confess something, said Fey. *Amethyst was the one who poisoned you yesterday.*

Requiem gaped at Fey, then the slime on her shoulder.

I probably shouldn't have done it, but I really don't like it when you grab me without permission. I should have probably told you that instead of resorting to poison, Fey continued. *So, sorry. But yeah, my pets are pretty OP.*

. . . I'll try not to grab you without permission.

Um, aren't you supposed to be mad at me for poisoning you and lying about it?

Probably, Requiem agreed. *It's hard to get mad at a paralyzed person, though.* Fey still looked quite helpless, even without her previous deathly pallor. Requiem did not add that she had quite the emotional advantage over him because he had a crush on her.

A pause. *What are your plans after this quest?* Fey asked.

Requiem shrugged. *I haven't really thought about it.*

We're planning on leaving the ocean as soon as Sirena hits level 30. If you want to come . . .

Requiem smiled broadly. Somehow, he had gotten on Fey's good side. *Yes.*

Twelve minutes later, Fey regained feeling in her limbs.

<Fey's Immunity has reached level 9!>

She flexed her arms and legs, then got up. *Good as new,* she said cheerfully. *Thanks again.* Speaking to her pets, she said, *No other surprises, right? I think the next one might kill me.*

The Feypets squeaked in unison. ("No. Except . . .")

Fey sighed. *Hit me with it.*

With more squeaks, Fey was directed to open her pet menus.

She blinked to make sure her vision was working correctly, then sighed. *Wow. I'm the dead weight in this team. You guys could have conquered the world by now if I weren't holding you back.* Her pets, which had been at level 20 and 21, were now level 28. It appeared that the only reason they had not grown more was because their levels were capped at whatever hers was.

In addition, they had all made various skill level increases. Amethyst had learned a skill called Engulf, which sounded self-explanatory. Boris had gained an ability called Danger Sense. The glooms' pocketing of the loot had been turned into an ability called Shadow Space.

Requiem sensed Fey's attention slipping away. Not wanting to return to being an afterthought, he said the first thing that came to mind. *Wanna go get something to eat?*

Now that you mention it, I'm starving. Is there anything to eat other than fish?

He smiled. *I'll see what I can do.*

Looks like bard dude is joining the party permanently, Sirena commented to Blade.

"What? Why? I thought you guys didn't like him."

He went and sang himself into a healer.

"If that's the only reason, couldn't you do it, too?"

You keep making good points today. Sirena chimed the Pokémon Centre theme like a xylophone, singing chords rather than single notes.

<Sirena has learned Heal Song!>

"Really? That's the tune?"

I know. And bard dude thought of it, too. Sirena sighed. *We probably have to keep him.*

"Don't I get a vote?"

Sirena patted his hand. *Of course you do.* A pause. *Fey and I each get three votes, though.*

". . . Are you joking?"

Blade, Blade, Blade. The thing you need to learn in this party is that we're always joking. And partly serious.

CHAPTER 17

UP WHERE THEY WALK

The hauntingly beautiful notes of the first movement of Beethoven's Moonlight Sonata resonated in the minds of every sentient mind in Pearlview, halting all thought and motion.

The music was both like and unlike every rendition before it: while the notes stayed the same, it had never before been performed through telepathy.

Sirena, Requiem, Fey, and Blade were gathered on the top floor of Pearlview's performing arts guild, along with Songsmistress Gwenna and the quest-giver Wellia. The NPCs were as enraptured as the rest of the town as Sirena and Requiem wove music into magic.

It was a masterful performance. At Fey's request (she's such a softie), Sirena had arranged a piece of music to be performed as a duet with Requiem so that they could simultaneously complete the quest. Requiem's part was much simpler, barely complex enough to fulfill the overlimit requirements for Siren's Song and within his mental limits for creating harmonic lines.

Over his steady accompaniment, Sirena played with the melody. Intuitively matching the mood of the music, she smoothly transitioned in instrumentation, tone, volume, and harmony. At times, she sang with the pure sweetness of a single violin, then swelled into a full orchestra. She borrowed the crystal clarity of Fey's idealized voice, then dazzled with the brilliance of a four-part choir. Mesmerizing and powerful, the music held all who heard it under its sway until the very last note faded away into silence.

<The merfolk ability Siren's Song has been rediscovered by Requiem Deemin and Sirena Unda!>

Throughout Pearlview, players buzzed over the townwide system notice.

In the guild, Wellia was the first to speak. *That was it. You did it, boy, and your friend there, too. I—*

The older merdame was almost knocked over by Songsmistress Gwenna's enthusiasm as the master bard rushed toward Sirena and Requiem. Seizing a hand from each player, she clasped them together excitedly. *I can't believe it! This is amazing! Literally the stuff of legends! You brought back a lost art!*

<Requiem has gained the title Siren Returned!>

<Requiem's fame has increased to 10,321 (+10,000)!>

<Sirena has gained the title Siren Returned!>

<Sirena's fame has increased to 10,005 (+10,000)!>

Sirena gingerly attempted to rescue her hand. *Glad to help, songsmistress.*

Gwenna let them go and took a deep breath (or whatever mermaids did), visibly calming herself. *There's only one way to reward such a deed. I will summon each of you a companion music sprite.*

What's that? asked Sirena.

They are spirits of music that strengthen and aid their chosen. They are a mark of true mastery, as only great skill can summon them. The songsmistress petted the necklet of pearls she wore, a mesh net piece that covered her neck, shoulders, and upper chest in nacreous iridescence.

Those pearls are a music sprite? asked Requiem.

Gwenna nodded. *They take a form that harmonizes with their chosen.*

Do they get one? Sirena asked, gesturing to Fey and Blade. *We couldn't have solved the quest without them.* (Well, Fey anyway.)

The songsmistress pursed her lips in consideration. *I do not know if a sprite would agree to accompany them. I will open the door, and if the sprites find music in their souls, they will bond.*

Fey shrugged at the fancy way of saying "I'll try, but don't get your hopes up." She had not expected to gain great rewards from a merfolk racial quest. *Anything we need to do?*

Please gather together and stay quiet. Gwenna raised her arms as if welcoming something from above. A clear, continuous ringing note began, as if someone drew circles along the rim of a fine wineglass. A second and a third joined it, forming an eerie chord.

Tension built as the chord grew in volume. Finally, Gwenna joined in with a wordless melody.

The space above the master bard began to ripple and distort, opening a spherical gate to another dimension. Four sparks of light drifted out from the sphere, each travelling toward a different player. Upon contact, they flashed and transformed.

Gwenna lowered her arms and let the music fade away, allowing the dimensional rift to shrink away into nothingness. *I've never summoned four at once before,* she remarked with satisfaction. *The muses are smiling upon us today.*

The players examined their new sprite-items.

Requiem took a small gold circlet off his head. *A tiara?* he complained.

Gwenna looked offended at his griping. *The outer form matters little, sir. Do not insult your soulbound companion.*

He opened the item description.

<Music Sprite's Circlet (soulbound): The embodiment of a music sprite that has decided to become your companion, it will lend you its power and grow as you gain experience.>

<+5% strength, +5% vitality, +10% to all music-related skills.>

<Cannot be traded or sold. Loss or destruction will incur the wrath of the muses.>

Requiem shut up and placed the circlet back on his head.

Sirena examined the new, intricate arm ring spiralling around her left biceps (and triceps) with much more pleasure. Delicately wrought silver metal formed the five lines of a musical score, decorated by the notes of a short melody. *Twinkle Twinkle Little Star?* she recognized. *How silly.*

At her words, the notes rearranged themselves into the opening of "Für Elise," She laughed and patted her new accessory.

<Music Sprite's Arm Ring (soulbound): The embodiment of a music sprite that has decided to become your companion, it will lend you its power and grow as you gain experience.>

<+5% intelligence, +5% willpower, +10% to all music-related skills.>

<Cannot be traded or sold. Loss or destruction will incur the wrath of the muses.>

You rock, buddy, said Sirena to her sprite. It replied by shifting to display the melody associated with winning a battle in a popular classic RPG.

Blade turned his left arm this way and that, examining the sleeve that now encased it from palm to shoulder. It looked and felt like thin, black metal, but the sleeve had full flexibility at the joints without any visible hinges or breaks in its material.

<Music Sprite's Sleeve (soulbound): The embodiment of a music sprite that has decided to become your companion, it will lend you its power and grow as you gain experience.>

<Provides defence equal to the player's level, +10% bonus to battle cries. Will fit over or under all clothing and armour.>

<Cannot be traded or sold. Loss or destruction will incur the wrath of the muses.>

"Cool," was Blade's laconic assessment.

Where's mine? asked Fey. She had definitely seen a sprite spark touch her, but there was no new item on her person.

Sirena glanced over at her friend and smiled in amusement. *You've got a little eighth note next to your flower.* Instead of tapping the equivalent spot on her own face, she poked Fey's face where the new tattoo had appeared. ("Personal boundaries"? She knows not what you speak of.) The music note appeared to have nudged the mana blossom sideways so that the two tattoos harmoniously centred around Fey's left eye.

Fey took a screenshot of herself and examined her face with a grimace. *A flower and a music note. All I need is a little heart and I'll be all set to join a magical girl squad.* After a pause, she added, *Please let the powers that be not take that as a suggestion.* (As if. She totally doomed herself.)

<Music Sprite's Tattoo (soulbound): The embodiment of a music sprite that has decided to become your companion, it will lend you its power and grow as you gain experience.>

<+10% to one stat (will vary depending on the player's actions), +10% to all battle cries.>

<Cannot be removed.>

<Current bonus: +10% vitality>

"Cannot be removed?" Why couldn't I have gotten a nice little hair tie or something?

It's probably a commentary on your propensity to lose things that aren't physically attached, said Sirena.

I don't lose things that often.

At least one umbrella and one to two neck-warmers[26] every year I've known you, not to mention gloves and socks.

. . . Nothing important, anyway. Reminded of her tendency to lose small accessories, Fey was rather glad that her sprite had made sure she could not earn the wrath of the muses. Instead of admitting it, she said, *Oh well. At least it doesn't take up an equipment spot.*

Politely waiting for the players to finish examining their sprites, Gwenna spoke. *Thank you for your effort and diligence. If you ever need any assistance regarding the arts, you will always be welcome here.*

<Quest complete!>

<Requiem gains 250,000 experience.>

<Requiem has achieved level 27!>

<Requiem has achieved level 28!>

<Requiem has achieved level 29!>

<Requiem has achieved level 30!>

<Sirena gains 250,000 experience.>
<Sirena has achieved level 27!>
<Sirena has achieved level 28!>
<Sirena has achieved level 29!>
<Sirena has achieved level 30!>

<Fey gains 100,000 experience. Amethyst gains 50,000 experience. Boris gains 50,000 experience. Onyx gains 50,000 experience. Inkblot gains 50,000 experience. Ebony gains 50,000 experience. Midnight gains 50,000 experience. Shadow gains 50,000 experience. Obsidian gains 50,000 experience.>
<Fey has achieved level 29!>
<Amethyst has achieved level 29!>
<Boris has achieved level 29!>
<Onyx has achieved level 29!>
<Inkblot has achieved level 29!>
<Ebony has achieved level 29!>
<Midnight has achieved level 29!>
<Shadow has achieved level 29!>
<Obsidian has achieved level 29!>

<Blade gains 25,000 experience.>

<Requiem has learned Siren's Song!>

<Sirena has learned Siren's Song!>

Blade blinked in startlement at the sudden reversal of level rankings. Before starting the quest, his level had been the highest in the party, and now, at level 28, it was the lowest. Even Fey's pets had out-levelled him. His experience reward for the quest was low because of his lack of contribution to its completion. He would have to work hard to catch up to his party mates.

Yay, level 30, Fey cheered, referring to the merfolk players. *Now we can get out of here.* (#Convenient)

Bidding goodbye to the NPCs, the party swam out into Pearlview. They passed quite a few players going in the opposite direction, aiming to learn the newly unlocked racial ability. Fey was thankful that their avatar names were not displayed to the public, or she doubted they would be able to get away from people wanting to talk to Requiem and Sirena.

So how do you transform into a two-legger, anyway? asked Fey.

Go see the sea witch, duh, said Sirena.

Straight out of the fairy tale, I see. So where does the sea witch live?

Sirena made a vague motion that encompassed many directions. *Out in the middle of nowhere. Actually, I don't think you can do the quest while in a party. I'm going to go get my level 30 advancement and then do the quest. I'll definitely be ready to go by the end of today. See you later, guys!*

<Sirena has left the party.>

Sirena's words jolted Requiem into action. *I'd better get my stuff done, too. I'll message you when I'm done, Fey. Bye.*

<Requiem has left the party.>

Fey looked at her remaining party member. They had logged on just prior to turning in the quest, so there was a whole game day ahead of them. *Train?*

Blade resettled his grip on his trident. It was time to catch up in level. *I'll find us a party.*

By the time Sirena rejoined the party in the early afternoon, Fey and Blade had both reached level 30. By the time Requiem was ready to go, Sirena, Fey, and Blade had all reached level 31. Fey and Blade decided to postpone their warrior advancements until they returned to land because the available subclasses in Pearlview were geared toward merfolk aptitudes.

Sorry for the wait, said Requiem as he swam toward the party. *I had to do a few warrior feats before I could unlock my next skill.*

Sirena tsked judgementally. She had quite a few mage feat points saved up because she often chose a feat to work on while hunting. Class advancement for her meant simply visiting the mage trainers for a few minutes to learn a new spell.

As previously planned, Sirena had begun to specialize in god-sourced magic, declaring her allegiance to Thrain, god of storms. The power of spells related to wind, water, and lightning were strengthened, while all others were weakened. Her newest spell was Splash Heal, a water-element healing spell.

So what did you specialize in? asked Fey.

Pole arms. Requiem twirled his spear to emphasize the point. (Pun unintended.) *My new skill is called Heavy Sweep.*

Nice. Fey's tone was fairly interested, but she was already swimming toward the shallows, eager to get back to land. (#Priorities)

They stopped when it was shallow enough for Fey to stand and have her face above the water. *Do your thing.* She was curious to see what the developers had done for the transformation process.

Sirena and Requiem began at the same time. Out of nowhere came a wordless vocalization (a tune that would be familiar to anyone who had watched a certain Disney movie featuring a certain redheaded mermaid #CopyrightInfringement). Veils of light coalesced and wrapped themselves around the merfolk, turning them into featureless sculptures of light. At the peak of the music, their tails split into legs and the light began to dim.

Sirena's and Requiem's new forms were revealed. They retained their blue skin but otherwise looked human, the webbing between their fingers and gills on their necks having disappeared. Shimmery silver garments that brought to mind the transformative veils of light (and the dress at the end of the *Little Mermaid* movie) covered the (bare) minimum required to conform to public decency laws in North America.

The party sloshed out of the water, taking deep breaths of fresh air. Boris trotted happily along the sand, once again able to move under his own power. The glooms reverted to their normal rabbit shapes and hopped along beside him. The pets ended up making wobbly circles around the party as the players walked at a slower pace off the beach, resulting in a bizarre pattern of footprints, flipper prints, hoofprints, and pawprints sure to give any potential tracker a headache.

An hour later, everybody was properly dressed and equipped for adventuring on land. Sirena purchased a blue mage robe that boosted her affinity to water, having eschewed the white of a wind robe or the yellow of a lightning robe because the colours would clash with her skin (#Shallow). Requiem equipped himself in heavy leather and chain mail, medium armour that fell in between Fey's reinforced leather and Blade's metal plate.

Blade also took Firefly out of stasis. Fey's pets regarded the level 15 fyrfalcon with bemused pity.

Amethyst squeaked in an undertone, careful not to let Firefly hear. ("Birdy's been frozen this whole time; how boring." Yes, she knows how to use semicolons now.)

Obsidian squeaked in agreement. ("Waste of training time, too.")

Boris grunted pragmatically. ("It's not like she could go underwater.")

Midnight chimed in with a squeak. ("Birdy could've gone with Lee-Lee like Magic.")

Boris countered. ("But then she'd be gone like Magic.")

All the Feypets acknowledged the point. They saw nothing wrong with Magic's migration away from them but could see how it would be inconvenient for Blade if his only pet was gone.

Amethyst squeaked. ("Fey-Fey wouldn't go somewhere if she had to put us in storage.")

The Feypets nodded sagely, confident in their owner's superiority over Firefly's.

Blade regarded the conversing pets with suspicion. "What are they talking about?" he asked Fey.

"Oh, just about how I'm a much better pet owner than you are," she said airily.

He snorted. "What are they really talking about?"

Fey gave him a look. "It's not like I actually understand squeaking. If you don't like my translation, just make one up yourself."

Amethyst jumped onto Fey's head and squeaked earnestly at Blade. ("Fey-Fey is a *much* better owner than you.")

Blade attempted to translate. "Um . . . 'I'm sorry for poisoning you so much'?"

Fey and all of her pets snorted in unison.

Sirena walked up with Requiem, holding a huge bag of coins. *Sold all of the bubble spells*, she said cheerfully, having completed her plan to buy and resell the essential breathing magic at a huge profit. She had made Requiem aid her in selling the magical air bubbles they had brought from Pearlview due to the fact that their blue skin lent authenticity to the sales pitch.

"You have vocal cords now," Fey pointed out. "Use them."

Sirena swung the bag of coins in front of Fey's face. "I would think you'd be distracted from nitpicking by all of this *gold*." Her physical voice sounded exactly the same as her telepathic one unless she made an effort to change it.

"If I could be distracted from nitpicking, I wouldn't be me," said Fey, tilting her face out of the way of the bag. "You sold all of them already?" The party had invested almost all their savings (not including the million extra gold in Fey's account that she resolutely pretended wasn't there) into the spells, buying about a thousand.

Requiem answered. "Most people bought batches of ten to twenty." Not so modestly, he added, "Bard skills are pretty useful for attracting buyers."

Fey frowned in confusion. "Why so many?" she asked, ignoring the boasting.

"They only last a day," Sirena pointed out.

"Yeah, but you only need one to last you until you get to Pearlview, where you can buy more."

"Shhh." Sirena melodramatically looked around as if to make sure nobody else had heard Fey's sensible words. "Honestly, it's a good thing I didn't bring you. You're such a horrible salesperson."

"I'll take that as a compliment," Fey said loftily.

Amethyst squeaked. ("What's a nit?")

Due to the lateness of the question relative to the conversational flow, Fey misinterpreted the slime's question for the first time, answering instead, "What's bad about salespeople?"

"They're persistent annoyances that are hard to shake off."

Serendipitously, her explanation fit both nits and salespeople quite well.

"*Excuse* me, but I happen to be an excellent salesperson," said Sirena.

"And I haven't managed to shake you off for ten years," Fey pointed out.

"Ladies, ladies," Requiem said in a soothing tone, trying to calm a situation that was not tense to begin with.

Both girls turned their heads to look at him. "Just who are you calling a lady?" Sirena said in a highly offended tone.

"Uhh . . . Sorry?" Requiem apologized confusedly, wondering when "lady" had made it onto the list of terms that could offend people.

"You'd better be," Sirena scolded. "How would you like it if I called you a 'gentleman'?"

". . . Okay? . . ." Requiem was practically spouting question marks above his head. He looked to Blade for help.

"Don't look at me, man," Blade said, holding a hand up defensively.

Fey smiled fondly. Blade had come such a long way from constantly getting tangled in verbal snarls when she had first met him (#Nostalgia).

"Hmph." Sirena flounced off toward the bank with her gold.

"She's twenty to thirty percent joking," Fey reassured Requiem (leaving 70 to 80 percent unexplained) before catching up to Sirena and saying, "That'd better not be all going into your account."

Blade gave Requiem a sympathetic look, feeling slightly guilty at the relief he got from being the target of the girls' dizzying conversational turns. "Just stay out of it," he advised, following the girls toward the bank.

"Out of what?" Requiem pressed, wanting specifics.

". . . You'll figure it out." (Eventually. Maybe.)

CHAPTER 18
DIVERSION

Tuesday night saw Fey logging into *Fantasia* at her usual time. Of the party members, only Blade was already online. Making her way toward the human warrior, Fey received a PM.

<Leandriel: Hello.>

<Fey: Hi! What's up?>

<Leandriel: Nothing special. How are you?>

<Fey: Great; I'm back on land.>

(Yes, our heroine will actually use semicolons in chat.)

<Leandriel: Great to hear. Where are you planning on going next?>

<Fey: I actually hadn't thought about it. Any suggestions?>

<Leandriel: There are many adventure areas suited to your current level, so it really depends on your preferences.>

<Fey: Anywhere near you?>

<Fey: ~~Anywhere near you?~~>

Fey hastily erased what she had written without sending it, and replaced it with:

<Fey: Hmm, what would you recommend for two warriors, a bard, and a storm mage?>

<Leandriel: Hmm . . . Based on your mage's elemental proficiencies, I would stay out of the western deserts. She might not do as well in the elven forests, either, but you have the advantage there, and water magic is neutral against earth. You have no particular advantage or weakness in the northern areas. Your mage might do well in the southern volcanoes against the fire-element monsters, but you might need holy element to deal with the demonic monsters.>

Based on Leandriel's detailed analysis, there was no major area of the continent in which it was particularly advantageous to go next.

<Fey: Hmm. I'll have to think about it. Where are you right now?>

<Leandriel: I am in the Transcendental Mountains.>

<Fey: Where's that? I didn't see it on the world map.>

<Leandriel: It is a pocket dimension accessible from certain areas in the Oré Mountains.>

<Fey: Cool. What does it look like over there?>

<Leandriel: Very magical in a cliché sort of way. A lot of fairy-tale creatures live here, but only the cute ones.>

<Fey: Haha, sounds like a tourist trap.>

<Leandriel: Yes. Not much to do around here other than take charming pictures. I will probably leave before the end of the day.>

<Fey: Where are you going next?>

<Leandriel: Probably into the Undermountain. There is a lot of unexplored territory underground.>

<Fey: Cool. Maybe I'll see you around.>

<Leandriel: Are you free today? I happen to be near a teleportation gate. Magic seems excited to see you and the pets.>

<Fey: Yeah sure! I'm still near Seaport.>

<Leandriel: Meet in an hour or so?>

<Fey: I'll be there. See you!>

Fey was on the verge of skipping when she arrived at her destination. It appeared that Blade had found a field that was a rodent monster territory in order to train his fyrfalcon. Firefly circled and dived, more often than not coming up with a dead mouse or rat.

"Hi," Blade said in greeting.

"Hi! You look busy. How about we all take a day off to regroup before deciding on going anywhere? Besides, Sirena's going to be late today; she has a work thing. Okay? Okay, let Requiem know when he logs in. Bye."

". . . Wha . . . ?" Blade had his index finger raised in a "wait a moment" gesture, then slowly lowered it as Fey (literally) skipped out of sight.

<Fey has left the party.>

Sensing her owner's distraction, Firefly descended to perch on his arm. Blade stroked the fyrfalcon with a gentle finger. "At least I have one female who's not crazy," he said to the bird (#Naive).

He launched his pet back into the air, and she promptly struck at a field mouse.

Blade blinked. It might have just been his eyes playing tricks on him, but it looked like there had been a spark at the moment of impact.

His sight was confirmed accurate when Firefly brought back the mouse with a scorch mark and the distinct smell of burning hair.

Not too long later, Requiem manifested in the world of *Fantasia*. Not having Fey on his friend list, he could no longer find the elf after she left the party. He had no other choice than to find Blade instead.

"Where's everybody?" he asked.

Blade looked up from watching his falcon. "Apparently Sirena's going to be late today. Fey declared it a free day and ran off somewhere."

Requiem's curiosity was piqued. "Where?"

Blade shrugged. "She was going in that direction the last time I saw her." He pointed toward town.

". . . Well, I'll see you later," said Requiem. He took the path back to Seaport, leaving the human to train his pet.

Requiem wandered through the streets of Seaport, trying to imagine where Fey would go. The town was busy with new travellers as well as construction projects to repair the damage from the recent tsunami. Just walking around, he was offered two quests to collect construction materials, which he turned down.

Requiem's head swivelled in all directions as he walked through the crowds. Unfortunately for him, Fey's appearance was not particularly flashy. Countless players were equipped with the same armour, and neither her hair nor skin tone were anything to draw the eye.

A blinding flash of white caught his eye. An angel, whose folded wings easily topped three metres in height, appeared at the teleportation gate far in the distance. Requiem watched until the angel leapt into the air and disappeared from sight, then went back to looking for Fey.

Almost an hour later, he still had not found her. She was not in any of the restaurants or shops, and the town was too large for him to search each building within a reasonable period of time. He sighed.

"Hi! Are you looking for a party?"

Requiem looked down. The speaker was a pretty human girl with a longbow slung over her shoulder. Next to her stood another girl in mage robes.

"You're a warrior, right?" she continued. "We want to go hunt striped buffalo. Want to join us?"

Requiem hesitated, then said, "Yeah, sure."

Requiem proceeded to leave Blade's party to join the other.

"Hi!" Fey smiled brightly in the general direction of Leandriel's face, still somewhat blinded by the flash of the teleportation gate.

"Hello." Fey heard more than saw the smile on Leandriel's face.

Any further humanoid greetings were interrupted by a lot of excited squeaking and murmuring. Deciding that the angel had more surface area than the elf, the Feypets held their reunion on Leandriel's shoulders and wings.

Fey began to feel hemmed in by all the stares from curious strangers. She wanted to have a nice get-together without all the lightbulbs[27] everywhere.

Leandriel was likewise not a fan of the audience. "If we walk out of here, the chances of not being followed are next to zero," he murmured in an undertone.

Fey nodded. "So . . . ?"

"I propose we fly."

"'We'?"

"I am unable to bear your weight in sustained flight, but I can see two options to escaping from here. One, I pick you up and jump, then control our descent; two"—Leandriel made an apologetic face—"you go into my carry-pouch."

Fey stared at the small pouch on Leandriel's waist. "People can go in there?"

Leandriel nodded. "It should be fine. Magic goes in and out all the time."

Magic murmured a cheerful agreement, hopping into the pouch and reappearing a moment later. At another murmur ("Come look at all the loot in here!"), the rest of the Feypets followed posthaste.

Fey grinned. "You must have some amazing stuff in there, for them to be so eager."

Leandriel smiled in return. "Magic really does like it in there, but I have never been, myself."

A mysterious lure that was irresistible to Fey. "I gotta see this," she said, moving forward.

She paused. "How do I actually go about getting in there?" While the Feypets were around the same size as the pouch and could easily hop into it while shrinking, Fey was considerably taller.

Leandriel grasped her wrist. "Just put one hand near the opening and you'll begin to shrink. I will take care of the rest."

"Alice in Wonderland time," Fey said, reaching forward with her free hand.

The first thing she noticed was herself growing shorter, Leandriel's face getting higher and higher in her perspective. Then Leandriel's grip tightened, and she stopped dropping, dangling from one arm. Leandriel looked like he grew into a giant until he was gently pinching her whole arm between thumb and index finger.

"Ready?" his voice boomed.

"Ready." Fey's voice sounded tiny and squeaky. She was now a hundred times smaller, with still more to shrink to enter the pouch.

Leandriel moved his hand and the now-enormous pouch opening engulfed her.

Fey landed gently on her feet in an enormous, dark space. There was no visible source of illumination, nor visible walls or floor. All she saw were items laid out in a gridlike pattern, sometimes singly, sometimes in enormous piles, depending on how many Leandriel was carrying. The items seemed to illuminate themselves and themselves only, providing no reflected light to their surroundings.

Amazed squeaks drew her attention and Fey wound her way past piles of potions to come upon a truly impressive heap of coins, several times her height. What freaked her out even more was that all of the denominations were 50g or higher, and the number of mithril coins was not insubstantial. Ever since learning Gold Magnet, the amount of wealth Leandriel had accumulated had graduated from "staggering" to "obscene."

The Feypets gathered a step (or hop) away from the unfathomable riches, appearing too in awe to actually approach. Magic was murmuring the story of Leandriel's gold-collecting magic, causing the other Feypets to murmur their first non-squeak sounds: "Ooooooooh."

Fey felt somewhat the same way. Hesitantly, she approached the heap of gleaming coins, then reached out and poked a mithril coin. The dislodged coin fell with a handful of others, scattering with a flurry of pinging sounds.

The handful of fallen coins triggered a bucketful, then a tubful (as if that's a word) of more fallen coins, until Fey had a veritable avalanche of metal happening. The Feypets climbed the only higher ground they had (Fey) while Fey attempted to wade out of the mess. However, when the coins hampered her up to her thighs, she could no longer move.

<Fey: Um, Leandriel?>

<Leandriel: Are you enjoying yourself in there? I should land in a few minutes and I will be able to let you out.>

<Fey: You wanna hurry things up out there? I may have kind of triggered an avalanche and may suffocate in the near future.>

<Leandriel: An avalanche? Is there snow in there?>

<Fey: No, just a ridiculous mountain of coins. Is there a reason you don't keep money in the bank?>

<Leandriel: I do. This is simply what I have collected since the last time I was able to visit the bank.>

Fey blanked out for a little while, trying to imagine several times this wealth stored somewhere else. By the time she recovered, the coins were well past her waist.

<Fey: Erm yeah, so do you think you can let me out soon? The coins are up to my chin now.>

<Leandriel: I am not quite there yet, but let me try something.>

A golden light shone upon the pile of money, which reverted to its former, uncollapsed state. A single coin floated up and out of sight, falling back down a moment later.

Fey slowly backed away from the gold, carrying her pets. Most of them chose to walk (or hop) under their own power now that the danger had passed.

<Fey: Well, that worked. How did you do that?>

<Leandriel: I withdrew a coin from the pouch. I guessed that the pouch's organizational system would re-sort the items if I needed them.>

<Fey: Nice. I'm going to explore more.>

<Leandriel: Let me know if you get into any more trouble, haha.>

<Fey: Will do :P>

Fey strolled through the seemingly endless room, gazing at the rows of items, most of which she did not recognize.

She came upon a thick pile of furs, presumably collected from the bodies of ferocious monsters. She sat down, petting a luxurious black pelt with green rosettes.

It's quite comfy like this. The inside of the pouch was neither cool nor hot and made quite a decent hangout. The glooms in particular enjoyed the lightless conditions, blending in seamlessly with the dark background.

<Fey: You should put some furniture in here, and then it would make the perfect camping place.>

<Leandriel: Haha, I do not think I would be able to get out if I entered the pouch without someone to pull me out.>

<Fey: What do you mean? Doesn't Magic do it all the time?>

<Leandriel: Yes, it's quite strange. I am given to understand that it has something to do with his gravitational abilities.>

<Fey: This I need to see.>

"Hey, Magic, do me a favour and pop out of the pouch for a sec?"

Magic murmured cheerfully and hopped up. Instead of falling down, he became inverted and began falling up, eventually disappearing the same way the coin had. Moments later, he returned to what passed for ground inside the storage pouch, apparently able to choose the direction in which gravity pulled him.

<Leandriel: So? What did he do?>

<Fey: He began falling up. It was very strange. I think you could get out by flying up, but I'm definitely stuck in here.>

<Leandriel: I have landed. I will be letting you out immediately.>

Almost concurrently with receiving the message, Fey began to float up. Weightlessness turned into reverse gravity, and she sped toward a pinprick of brightness that eventually expanded into the outside world.

Fey winced and blinked as her eyes adjusted from almost complete darkness to the brightness of direct sunlight.

"Are you all right?" Leandriel asked somewhat anxiously.

"Yeah, yeah, it was just really dark in there."

"I do apologize. It had not occurred to me that conditions inside might be uncomfortable and—"

Fey blinked some more, this time in confusion. "What are you talking about?"

Leandriel frowned in puzzlement. "Were you not feeling claustrophobic?"

"Mm, nope, not at all. I don't get claustrophobic. The only thing that really gets me is bugs."

"Ah. I must have misconstrued your comment about being trapped."

"Yeah, I was only saying I couldn't get out by myself, that's all."

"Ah, yes." Leandriel looked down in a posture that Fey would call "endearingly embarrassed." She smiled at the cuteness.

"So where are we going?" Fey asked in order to change the subject.

"Hmm . . . How about the local infinity dungeon?" Leandriel replied.

"Sure," Fey agreed, following the angel to the centre of what appeared to be an unremarkable grassy plain. She was glad to get away from the crowds of Seaport, revelling in the quiet and her ability to swing her arms freely.

"What are you looking for?" she asked when Leandriel began rooting around in the grass.

"A trapdoor," he answered.

It was Boris who located a thin rope the exact colour of the surrounding grass. Leandriel gave it a heave, revealing a trapdoor hidden under a thick layer of dirt and grass. Inside, a root complex provided a way to climb down.

Fey stuck Boris in her backpack with his head sticking out and began to descend.

⸺◦◦◇◦◦⸺

Sirena logged into *Fantasia* three real hours, nine game hours later than usual. Checking her status screens, she saw that Blade was the only other person left in her party.

She found Blade training his pet in the same clearing that Fey and Requiem had. The fyrfalcon was now reliably demonstrating her fire powers, briefly manifesting flame on her talons when she struck her prey.

"Hey, Sirena," Blade greeted, looking up from collecting the latest dead rodent's loot.

"Where is everyone?" Sirena asked.

Blade ticked off the party members on his fingers. "Fey showed up first, announced that you were going to be late, then called it a free day and ran off somewhere. Then Requiem came. I think he went to look for Fey, but he left the party without telling me anything."

"Oooh." Sirena wore a look of intrigued eagerness. "You wouldn't happen to have added Requiem as a friend, would you?"

Blade grimaced a negative ("As if I would add *that* guy."). "No. Why?"

Eagerness turned into (rather impolite) glee. "Heh heh heh. Requiem's gone and got himself all separated. He'll never find us now."

Blade was quick enough to follow why Requiem would be unable to find players he was neither friends nor party mates with, but he did not quite understand Sirena's gloating. "I thought you guys liked him now?"

Sirena flapped a dismissive hand. "Only technically."

"How do you 'technically' like someone?"

"He did something really amusing and awesome, which Fey and I are bound by our moral codes to like, but that doesn't undo all the previous dislike."

"Moral code?" Blade's tone was somewhere between "You have a moral code?" and "I'm curious about what your moral code is."

"You know. It's under the same rule that says you have to go out with a guy if he buys you the perfect gift without you telling him.[28] But only if he asks you on a date after giving you the gift."

". . . Yeah." Blade was not quite sure whether Sirena was joking, but he filed the information away anyway. (Yeah, real subtle, Sirena.)

The conversation was interrupted by the sound of enormous wings. Leandriel appeared in the sky, backwinging a landing that generated enough wind that Blade and Sirena had to brace themselves to avoid falling over.

"Hey, Leandriel, looking for Fey?" Sirena asked casually. Her feigned calmness was belied by the quiet-but-definitely-present telepathic *EEEEEEEEEEEEEEEEE* going on in the background.

Leandriel smiled, politely ignoring Sirena's fangirling (mostly because he couldn't think of how to address it). "I am here to deliver her, actually." Reaching into his belt pouch, he withdrew an action-figure-sized Fey, which quickly grew into a life-sized Fey.

Sirena's eyes almost bugged out of their sockets. "Don't tell me . . . You've seen the inside of a Pokéball??"

Fey shrugged. "I mean, I have no way to tell whether the inside of a Pokéball is the same. This doesn't transform you into magical red light."

Sirena swatted Fey's arm. "This is no time for technicalities. I want to see, too."

Fey looked up at Leandriel with a "sorry my friend is crazy" expression. "Would you mind?"

Leandriel smiled. "Of course not." He held out a hand and helped Sirena into the pouch.

"Would you like to see as well?" he asked Blade.

Blade shrugged and said, "Sure, why not?" entering as well.

Almost immediately:

This is so cooooool! Unlike her physical voice, which would now be produced by vocal cords ten thousand times smaller than normal, Sirena's telepathic voice was unaffected by the pouch and could be heard in the outside world.

Ready to come out now? Fey asked dryly. Not having another necklace for equipment, she continued to wear her telepathy stone. Her physical voice would now be in Sirena's infrasound range, so she resorted to telepathy as well.

No way. Ooh, so pretty.

Whatever you do, don't touch—

<Blade: Help! Avalanche!>

—the coins, Fey finished lamely.

Leandriel chuckled and fished Blade out of the pouch.

"Thanks, man," said Blade, brushing himself off.

Look at all of these potions! And magical items! And accessories! Sirena exclaimed.

If you're done gawking, Leandriel has places to be, Fey said, her voice even drier than before.

Oh, pooh, fine. Leandriel, I'm ready to come out now.

When everyone was safely out of magical storage, Leandriel bowed. "Farewell for now."

"Bye!" said Fey, her voice much brighter than normal.

"Bye!" said Sirena, her voice bright as it usually was.

"See ya," said Blade (the only person acting like a normal, calm adult).

With a huge leap and gust of wind, the angel was gone.

Sirena nudged her friend suggestively. "So, how was your day?"

"Very well, thank you." Fey randomly decided to adopt a faintly European accent to respond.

Sirena pouted. "You know I'm going to get answers out of you one way or another."

Fey scoffed. "I am impervious to your tricks. I divulge no information I do not wish to."

"I'll tickle you," Sirena threatened.

"I'm wearing armour," Fey countered, unfazed. She was ticklish, but less than average. The key, she found, was staying calm; the ticklish sensations strengthened when she was excited.

Still, she changed the subject. "Don't we have anything better to do? I mean, look at Firefly over there, training so hard without her owner. We should go help her out."

Indeed, the fyrfalcon had amassed quite the pile of dead rodents while Blade was distracted. Reminded of his duties, Blade returned to training. Fey and her pets helped by flushing the rodents out of hiding, gaining experience by killing any monster too slow to get out of the way.

Sirena settled down to fill her new Prayer bar. There were multiple ways to do this, the most basic being simple prayer, which she tried now.

Several hours later, a gentle rain began to fall.

"I did it!" Sirena exclaimed. Another benefit of being devoted to a god was the ability to summon small miracles, the scale of which was dependent on the amount of favour one had curried with the god. A newly inducted follower like Sirena could only summon weak rain in a small area.

"Couldn't you have picked something else?" Fey complained. She hated getting rained on.

"Like a bolt of lightning?"

"I was thinking more along the lines of a gentle breeze."

"Erm, Sirena, is there any way for you to stop the rain?" Blade asked. His fire-based pet was looking distinctly bedraggled and unhappy.

"I could, but that would constitute another miracle, and I just used up my whole Prayer bar. By the time I refilled it enough, the rain would already be gone."

"This is clearly a sign that it's time to take a food break," Fey announced.

The party made their way back to Seaport to eat at a restaurant, confusing their fellow diners with their wet apparel.

CHAPTER 19
EVOLUTION

During the meal, Sirena realized that Fey had almost successfully diverted her attention from the appearance of a remarkably handsome angel in her life. Determined to get some answers, Sirena pestered Fey about it throughout their meal and afterward. Despite Fey's most skilled efforts, no amount of distraction was able to get the mermaid permanently off the topic. Finally, Fey resorted to the non-confrontation method of resistance, making only vague sounds in response to Sirena's questions.

"It was a date, wasn't it? Admit it," Sirena said as they left Seaport.

"If you say so." Fey sped up her walk to make it hard for her shorter friend to keep up.

Sirena was having none of it. She hooked her elbow around Fey's arm and latched on. "You can't escape my questions by running."

"One, I totally could, and two, I'm not running."

"Um, where are we going?" asked Blade. Feeling sorry for Fey, he had attempted to change the subject quite a few times, to even less effect than Fey's distractions (#LowManipulationLevel).

"Yeah, where are we going?" Sirena repeated teasingly.

Fey gestured ahead with her free arm. "That way."

"Are you *sure* you're not running? Methinks[29] that you're running."

"Positive." Fey did indeed have an intended destination, but to reveal it would add more fuel to Sirena's pestering fire.

Sirena began to hum the chorus from the song "U Got It Bad."

Fey rolled her eyes. Other than the title (which didn't count because it wasn't spelled correctly), none of the lyrics applied to her.

When she received no response, Sirena ended up singing through the entire song. She switched to telepathy because it sounded better.

<Song completed successfully. Monsters in the area have been attracted.>

Fey sighed in exasperation, drawing her punching blades and letting Amethyst off her shoulder. "Good job, Sirena."

Sirena snorted, raising her arms in preparation for spell-casting. "As if you aren't relieved."

Fey was indeed relieved at the distraction from conversation—right until it arrived in the form of a swarm of giant bees, each the size of her clenched fist. Their collective buzzing was deafening.

Fey screeched and swiped erratically at the air around her. Most of her strikes missed, a few batted bees aside without inflicting damage, and one managed to separate a bee's head from its body. It promptly exploded with a small boom that stung Fey's arm (but fortunately didn't leave her covered in bug guts. She failed to see the bright side).

<Fey has defeated the bomblebee!>

"That's—not—[censored word]—funny!" Fey snarled between swipes. (The programmers, who created the monster from an amusing typo, beg to differ.)

Blade, whose sword had a longer reach than Fey's punching blades, fared slightly better against the bees. "Just how many monsters have to self-destruct?" he grumbled, absorbing numerous small explosions with his arms.

Sirena fared worst of all. She had no weapon to strike out with, and a successful spell required that she maintain concentration from the moment of spell invocation until the mana intensity threshold was met. After her fifth spell was interrupted by a bee in her face, she was well on her way toward hysteria-induced rage. "Cover me!" she screamed.

Fey glanced at her pets to see which one she could assign to Sirena's protection.

Amethyst was being her usual insouciant self, merrily swatting away with her bubble-arm extended to its full 1.8-metre length while a bee that had unwisely attempted to sting her triple membrane sat digesting within her cytoplasm.

"Keep the bees away from Sirena, Amethyst!"

The slime squeaked cheerfully, changing the trajectory of her bubble to smash a bee aiming for the mermaid.

Sirena taken care of, Fey continued checking on her pets to see if they needed help.

Boris was unable to do much damage to creatures that could fly out of his way, but he kept himself out of trouble, neatly dodging any incoming stingers. Occasionally, he hit a low-flying bee with Glare, the resulting flinch bringing them low enough to trample.

The glooms were holding their own, leaping into the air and wrapping themselves around a target in order to use Suffocate. Being stung did not seem to affect them much.

Spotting the opportunity, Fey sheathed her blades, picked up a gloom-wrapped bee, and compressed it as if crumpling a piece of paper.

<Midnight has defeated the bomblebee!>

<Midnight has learned Crush!>

Immediately after, the bee exploded, causing Midnight to squeak in pain.

"Oh no! Sorry, baby." Fey petted the gloom as it uncurled, checking for damage. As this was difficult to visually assess on a shadow-creature, she ended up checking the pet menu, sighing with relief that Midnight had only lost 10 percent of his health. "Sorry, baby," she apologized again as she released her pet to the ground.

Showing off under his owner's attention, Midnight immediately leapt into the air and captured another bee, using the newly learned Crush skill and uncurling at once, which considerably lessened the damage from the resultant explosion.

The other glooms would not be overshadowed (haha, puns). Copying Midnight's actions, they each learned Crush and commenced a competition to see who could kill the most bomblebees.

Fey smiled and watched her pets' antics—

Then a bee landed on her face.

She screamed and swiped it away with extreme violence, actions sufficient to activate Terrify and Vicious Strike (respectively) without conscious intent. The bee in question died immediately (*boom*), and the entire swarm flinched back.

Sirena was reminded of her bardic skills. Switching to telepathy, she poured all of her agitation into the loudest possible Boom Stun, shouting **DIE!**

<Sirena has defeated the bomblebee!>

<Sirena has defeated the bomblebee!>

<All monsters in the area have been stunned for 5 seconds.>

<Sirena's Boom Stun has reached level 2!>

<Sirena's Boom Stun has reached level 3!>

Sirena had actually managed to kill the closest monsters with nothing but her telepathic voice. The rest of the swarm dropped to the ground, immobile.

Boris immediately began trampling the bomblebees at a rate that qualified for the word "rampage." Fey and Blade belatedly copied his actions, albeit at a slower pace. Sirena then incinerated the remaining insects with a Charge Jolt.

<Boris has achieved level 32!>

Boris was in fact only catching up to the other Feypets in level. Because of his disadvantages in underwater combat, his experience bar lagged behind. Unlike the other Feypets, he was frustrated with the limits of his body.

Boris began to glow.

Fey gasped as she watched a process she had only seen in a cartoon. With a chiming sound, the boar's outline expanded considerably before the glow faded, revealing Boris's new form.

<Boris has evolved!>

<Boris, level 32 iron boar>

Boris lifted a hoof and grunted ("Much better."), the sound much deeper and more resonant than before.

"Wow," said Sirena. Blade matched her sentiment.

Boris was now level with Fey's hip at the shoulder and several times as heavy as his owner. In addition, his tusks had elongated, even relative to his size, and he bore thick plates growing out of his chest and along his back. His tusks, hooves, and defensive plates had a metallic sheen that earned his new species the word "iron" in its name.

Fey had yet to say anything, and Boris looked as nervous as an armoured tank of a creature could look (on a scale from one to "kid around their first crush", around a three). He definitely did not qualify as "cute" anymore.

Fey knelt down and hugged him around the neck. "We're going to kick some ass, aren't we?" she murmured.

Anticipation gave way to a celebratory air as the other Feypets ran (hopped) around, and then over, their newly enlarged comrade. Boris turned his head to look and dragged Fey with him, causing her to fall onto her derrière. (The author is so snooty. A butt is a butt.)

"Oof. You're a lot stronger now, buddy," Fey said as she stood and dusted herself off. Boris nudged her gently in apology, and she patted his head. "That's okay. Growing pains." (Erm, people don't generally inflict growing pains on others.)

Blade looked from Boris to Fey, frowning as he tried to connect the two in his mind. The other pets' "cute and deadly" appearances fit how he viewed the elf, but Boris's new "strong and deadly" look clashed badly.

"Does this make sense to you?" he asked Sirena, gesturing at the massive boar and delicate elf.

Sirena raised an eyebrow. "Why not? She does have a red belt in tae kwon do."

"She *what*?"

Sirena's other eyebrow joined the first. Raising her voice to carry farther, she asked, "Hey, Fey, just how have you been killing things in front of this guy?"

Fey paused to think. "Mostly by stabbing, I guess. Some poison may have been involved. Why?"

"He seems to be physically unable to accept the fact that you do tae kwon do. Why haven't you been kicking things?"

"Well, I mean, most of the beginner monsters are really small, so it doesn't work properly. Then we went underwater. I did fight a couple monsters with kicks, but he wasn't there."

Fey glanced down at her lightly used kicking blades. "Huh. I should really find more opportunities to use these." Just because she could, she slammed an Axe Kick down into the ground, feeling the impact travel up her leg.

Boris performed his version of the same, revealing the new skill he had gained upon evolution. Rearing up, he slammed his front feet into the ground. Several metres away, Blade and Sirena stumbled at the resulting earth tremor.

"What was that?" Sirena asked.

Fey checked her pet menu. "Quake," she read aloud, "causes an earth tremor to unbalance opponents. Allies in the area will also be affected. Level 1: safe zone 2m radius, quake zone 5m radius." She looked at the ground under her feet, which had stayed still. "Handy. Good job, Boris." She patted the boar again.

Hmm . . . Fey felt like she was still missing some implication of Boris's evolution. She stared down at his broad back as she thought.

Boris waited patiently, while the other Feypets stared at their owner expectantly, perched around the iron boar's head and neck.

It was the fact that she was leaning against Boris's sturdy bulk that finally clued her in. Standing up on her toes gave Fey enough height to slide onto his wide, comfortable back.

Once she had arranged her legs to not drag on the ground, Boris took off at a walk, then a trot, careful not to dislodge his rider.

"Hey!" Sirena yelled indignantly, breaking into a run to close the gap with her party mate. Blade followed with a muffled laugh.

Fey laughed outright. This was a *very* good way to avoid Sirena's questions. "If you're going to run away, do it in style," she told her pets.

Leandriel flew through the air on his way back to the Oré Mountains region, unaware of the warm smile he wore. On his head, Magic murmured cheerfully away, the sound soothing to his ears, if completely unintelligible.

The murmuring suddenly stopped.

"What's wrong, buddy?" Leandriel asked.

"Lee-ann-dree-ell" came a cute voice. Magic pronounced the name with exaggerated slowness.

Leandriel plucked the mushroom off his head. "You learned how to talk?" After level 40 had come and gone without a single word on Magic's part, he had assumed it would never happen.

"Lee-ann-dree-ell did not un-der-stand Ma-jic," said Magic slowly. The mushroom's delivery was stilted, as if he had trouble forming the correct sounds, but otherwise correct in pronunciation and intonation.

Rather than going through the stages of speech development gradually, he had decided to learn speech, allocated some of his level 84 intelligence toward the task, and immediately jumped to high-school-level English. Why Magic had not learned speech earlier was partly because of his formative levels with Fey, and partly because his new owner was not particularly talkative. When Leandriel *did* speak, however, it was always with impeccable diction, so Magic now strove for the same.

"Sorry, Magic. Did you need to tell me something?" Leandriel was quite fond of his pet, and it bothered him to think that there had been something Magic wanted this entire time.

"Leandriel should marry Fey-Fey." Perfect diction or not, Fey would always be "Fey-Fey" to Magic.

Leandriel's flight dipped erratically before he got it back under control. "Ahm . . . That is . . ."

"Leandriel doesn't want to marry Fey-Fey?" Magic asked. His speech was gaining fluency, but still slow. The pace lent a gravity to his words that Leandriel found extremely uncomfortable.

"That is not . . . It is that— I cannot answer this and fly at the same time." Leandriel dove sharply toward the ground, landing much less smoothly than usual. The level 50 monsters in the area took one look at him and fled without him noticing.

Leandriel held his pet up and looked him in the eye. "Now, Magic," he began in a poised tone that quickly degenerated into awkwardness, "I think Fey is . . . very nice, but we are not going to suddenly get married."

Magic blinked and cocked his head sideways. "Leandriel is going to get married gradually?"

"No, you are either married or not married. But yes, relationships develop gradually."

"So . . . Leandriel is going to marry Fey-Fey later?"

"No! I mean, I don't know! Maybe!" Leandriel made a sound of agitation, looking away from his pet.

Magic looked at his owner worriedly. Even in the most dangerous of situations, the mushroom had never seen Leandriel display even close to this level of stress. "Is Leandriel mad?"

"Crazy maybe, but I am not angry." Leandriel's shoulders drooped slightly with emotional exhaustion. He took a deep breath in and out, trying to calm himself.

Magic wiggled determinedly until Leandriel let him go, then hopped up the angel's arm and leaned against his cheek in an armless hug. "Sorry."

Leandriel sighed and patted the mushroom. "You did nothing wrong. Let us be on our way, shall we?" He launched himself into the air, flying slightly faster than was comfortable, trying to leave his thoughts behind.

CHAPTER 20

ROGUISH

ey looked back and forth between the sturdy-but-not-built-for-heavy-cargo travel coach and her newly enlarged boar. "Uh, nope, not happening." Boris was now six to seven Feys[30] in weight, and the carriage was designed to carry no more than six people.

Fey stuck her head into the carriage, where Sirena and Blade were already seated. "Hey, I think I'll just take the teleport gate ahead and wait for you in the Moonwood. Might as well get my warrior advancement done while I'm at it." Blade had already completed his advancement while in human lands, choosing the heavily armoured path of the tank (with minimal prodding from Fey and Sirena).

Sirena nodded her agreement to the plan without even questioning the reasoning behind it. "Okay! We'll meet you there."

Blade nodded as well. "Sounds like a plan."

Fey glanced at Blade, huffed in amusement at Sirena's poorly hidden motivation to spend time alone with the warrior, and backed out of the coach.

"Wait!" Sirena stuck her head out after Fey. "Leave your bunny with us."

Fey glanced down at her glooms, who had taken evasive measures at the mermaid's words by lining up side by side and then melting into formless piles of shadow, essentially looking like a single puddle. "Which one?"

Sirena flapped a hand. "You know which one. The cute one."

Fey was pretty sure that if she dug through the pile of glooms, she would find Ebony at the very bottom, but she was not about to hand her poor pet over to Sirena's clutches.

An idea popped into her head. Digging into her belt-pouch, Fey pulled out Squishy in his potion bottle (whom the author totally didn't forget about for the last ten chapters). The immature jellyfish was now noticeably bigger and looking distinctly cramped within the glass. (More like Squished than Squishy. Ha ha ha . . . ? #TerriblePuns)

"Here, you can have Squishy." Fey used the game's gifting system to transfer the jellyfish's ownership to Sirena.

<Ownership transferred.>

Sirena took Squishy's bottle with a peeved look. "I want the cute one."

"Hey, Squishy is adorable. Don't be jelly. Besides, he's a water element."

Sirena looked ready to argue further, but the coach driver came over to shut the door. "We're off!" he announced. Climbing up to the driver's seat, he flicked the reins and headed out at a steady trot.

Waving a cheerful goodbye, Fey proceeded to lead her pets back to Seaport and its teleportation gate.

One of the benefits of having a massive pet, she discovered, was that crowds parted where he walked. Conversely, Fey drew more attention than she really wanted. She brazened it out, keeping her posture straight and confident, trying to project an air of "don't bother me; I'm an important person with important things to do." It (apparently) worked, as she managed to reach the teleportation gate without incident.

Fey pulled out her teleportation key. As a cash shop item, it could not be lost and appeared whenever she wanted to use it.

The key did not look like it would fit into a lock; rather, it was a flat, silver disc delicately etched with geometric patterns. Fey laid it against one of the stone pillars comprising the gate. As the pillars and the circle of ground between them began to glow, a map appeared to Fey's vision. The teleportation circle she stood on was represented by a blue dot, and the ones she could travel to by green dots.

Fey selected Moonwood village, then settled down to wait, making sure all of her pets were within the circle. A few minutes later, the light flashed for a blinding moment, and she was in the Moonwood.

From Fey's perspective, it seemed like the land outside the teleportation gate had been swapped out rather than her moving anywhere. Quickly regaining her bearings, Fey strode out of the circle, ignoring the gawkers who had gathered around. It was her experience that people were less likely to bother you if you looked like you were going somewhere, so she quickly headed down the path toward the warrior trainers. Boris (with the glooms sitting cutely on his back) followed with a heavy tread, dissuading the bolder of the gawkers from bothering her.

As she walked, Fey checked to see if she had enough warrior feats to learn her next skill. Somewhat to her surprise, she did. Perusing the completed feats, she saw:

<Follow from the Front: Belong to a party for a total of 25 hours. Must be in physical proximity to party members—10 points>

<Been There, Killed That (I): Kill 50 different monsters—10 points>

<Quantity over Quality (I): kill 1000 monsters—5 points>

<To Pieces (I): Execute 5000 slashing attacks—5 points>

Fey supposed that all of her pets' activities contributed to her achievements because she could not quite remember killing fifty types of monsters. (*cough* Is the non-parenthetical narrator supposed to start pointing out the flaws in the author's writing?)

Since she had the 30 points she needed to learn her next skill, Fey walked directly to the warrior trainers.

Both Irrilana and Irrilathan were on duty when Fey arrived.

Irrilana spoke first. "Well met, warrior. Have you come to take the next step in your journey toward combat mastery?"

Fey felt the need to match the NPC's formal wording but was unable to quickly think of a suitable reply. What came out was "Er, yes."

"The path to becoming a warrior is manifold; you must discover your own unique style and pursue it to the end. Do you have an idea of the sub-class you wish to specialize in, or would you like us to analyze your current abilities and make recommendations?"

When playing video games, Arwyn generally went with whatever class looked the coolest, usually ending up with a "glass cannon"[31] build. She knew that she had to be much more careful in virtual reality because choosing a class she was physically or mentally unsuited for would end up with her dying.

"Recommendation, please."

The warrior trainers' eyes focused on a status screen invisible to Fey as they looked over her attributes, skills, and abilities.

Fey shifted uncomfortably (in embarrassment) as the NPCs' expressions shifted from focused to confused.

"Ranger . . . ?" Irrilana said uncertainly to her partner.

"Assassin," Irrilathan disagreed. "Or maybe general."

They stared at each other for a long moment, communicating in a way that was silent to Fey.

Finally, they turned as one to regard the (strange, strange) player in front of them.

Irrilana spoke. "You have very . . . disparate skill development that points to many different class affinities, so we are unable to recommend a single sub-class or set of related classes. Due to the same disparity, our recommendations are all hybrid classes."

"What are hybrid classes?" Fey asked.

"These are sub-classes that can only be unlocked by belonging to two of the main classes. They require more extensive training, as you must complete feats from both classes for every advancement, but offer a wider variety of skills and abilities."

The trade-off sounded pretty good to Fey. "So what are the classes?"

Irrilathan answered, "Warrior-rogue is assassin. We recommend this due to your affinity to poison, as well as the spontaneously learned skills Bleed, Vicious Strike, and Isolate.

"Warrior-archer is ranger. We recommend this due to your high dexterity as well as your Monster Tamer ability.

"Warrior-mage is spellblade. We recommend this because of the spells you have learned and your spontaneous intelligence gains."

They all sound pretty cool. Coolness factor aside, Fey attempted to figure out which sub-class was the most suitable for her.

Dexterity or no, Fey did not see herself as having any talent with a bow, as it required upper-body strength and hand-eye coordination, two things she distinctly lacked.

The other two sub-classes both sounded promising, so she asked, "Could you tell me a bit more about assassin and spellblade?"

Irrilana spoke as if reading off a written description.

"The assassin knows one thing: the kill. Stalking from the shadows, she specializes in critical hits and status effect damage. She can strike from medium distances with thrown weapons. Between her stealth, critical damage, and blinding speed, she has often moved on to her next target before her current opponent realizes that death has arrived.

"The spellblade is the ultimate hybrid class, overcoming the limitations of the warrior and the mage to become proficient at both physical and magical combat. Using special casting techniques, she is able to use magic at full efficiency while wearing heavy armour. Spells that temporarily enhance her equipment give her extremely high base attack and defence in both the physical and magical domains. In combat, she seamlessly integrates skilled weapons-work with fast, simple magic attacks, giving her great adaptability to fight a large variety of opponents."

. . . *They both sound really cool.* Having two amazing choices before her made the decision both very easy and extremely difficult. On the one hand, Fey was sure that she would be happy with either sub-class, so it did not much matter which one she chose. On the other hand, neither choice was obviously better than the other, which paralyzed her with indecision.

The more Fey thought about it, the more that she thought spellblade would be the best class . . . for somebody else. Having both magic and physical attacks was a huge advantage, not to mention both magical and physical defence. However, the class seemed like it would require a lot of on-the-spot critical judgement to determine the best course of action in combat, as well as the ability to multitask. It would clearly have a steep learning curve to master, especially for Fey, who was not particularly good at tactics.

In contrast, assassin seemed to match exactly what Fey was already doing (sneaking around and using underhanded methods to gain an advantage over her opponents). The sub-class did not have as much versatility as spellblade, but she thought that it fit her so well that she could take full advantage of its special characteristics and perform better than if she chose spellblade.

"I choose assassin."

Irrilathan nodded and held out his arm, dropping a small token into Fey's hands. "Take this. When you earn a similar item from the rogue trainer, put them together and they will lead you to the assassin trainer."

Fey glanced at the token, a circular disc of grey metal that was smooth on one side and printed with a sword and shield on the other. Tucking it carefully into her belt pouch, she thanked the trainers and bade them goodbye.

"Wait," Irrilana called. "Would you like to learn Ex-quip?" As Fey turned back, the trainer added, "It's a completely optional ability that is not a prerequisite for anything, merely for convenience. It requires 30 feat points to learn."

"Ex-quip? As in, change my armour with a spell?" Fey recalled seeing Leandriel do this.

"And weapons and accessories," Irrilana agreed. "You can switch out a piece at a time or designate whole sets."

"Sounds good. I'll learn it," said Fey.

Irrilana hefted her spear. "Watch carefully." The weapon turned the luminous white-gold of the trainer's mana, then began to morph, elongating and becoming flexible until its tip hit the ground. When the light dimmed and disappeared, Irrilana was holding a lethal-looking whip.

"Clearly imagine the item that you want," she instructed, "then trigger the Ex-quip skill. You may call any item that you claim ownership to, including ones in storage."

Fey still had her beginner weapons; since every player received a dagger and every warrior a short sword, they had next to no sale value. Holding up her right punching blade, Fey clearly visualized the short sword currently sitting in her safe-deposit box, then said, "Ex-quip."

The sensation of mana flowing down her arm accompanied the (purple) glow and transformation of her weapon. 10 MP was consumed, a negligible amount at her level.

<Fey has learned Ex-quip!>

Irrilana nodded in approval at Fey's success. "If you find Ex-quip in your Abilities menu, you can designate sets of equipment to be switched at once."

Fey nodded her understanding. "Thank you," she said to both trainers, then headed off to find the rogue trainer, switching the sword back to a punching blade. The higher-levelled weapon required 20 MP to summon.

Irrilathan eyed the massive iron boar trotting after the player. When she was out of earshot, he said, "Maybe we should've recommended lancer," referring to warriors who specialized in mounted combat.

"Nah, you were right the first time," said Irrilana. "Did you *see* the level of her Immunity? She didn't even have the rogue class to make it level up faster. With those other offensive skills, she's been an assassin the whole time." Irrilana paused, then added, "But yeah . . . that skill set was *so* random."

CHAPTER 21

GEARING UP

Fey followed the system map to the place designated for rogue training. Unlike the warrior trainers' area, there was no clearing in the trees to mark the spot. If anything, the shadows here were darker than the rest of the forest, as if to encourage people to move along.

There were no visible trainers, either. Fey was expecting this, so she (almost) did not jump when a voice out of nowhere said, "What brings you here, warrior?"

Fey answered. "I wish to join the rogue class so that I might start on the path of an assassin."

"Oh?" The voice sounded mildly intrigued. It had a whispery quality that disguised gender and location, seeming to come from the rustling of the trees in all directions.

A figure coalesced out of the shadows, as mysterious as its voice. A mottled grey mask covered its face above the mouth, and a matching cloak disguised the contours of its body. An aura of shadow made its features even harder to make out.

"And what makes you think you can be an assassin?" the voice continued, still seeming to come from all directions. The figure's lips did not move.

Fey kept her body language calm and confident even as goose bumps rose on the back of her neck. "It seemed like a good fit," she answered. "The indirect battle suits me best."

"Ah, but the way of the rogue is not always so indirect," the voice countered.

A cold, metal wire slid lightly across Fey's throat. She jumped back, but of course, nothing was really there.

"What say you to that?" the voice asked tauntingly. The figure had not yet moved.

Fey summoned all of her self-discipline to stifle her creeped-out reaction and answered normally. "If it were always indirect, it would be predictable."

The figure smiled. "Quite right." It removed its mask and flipped the cloak behind its shoulders; at the same time, the shadows lightened to a more natural level.

Only when the camouflage dropped did the game system notify Fey that this was R'shelle, the rogue trainer. Fey was surprised to see that the elven NPC was slightly shorter than her; apparently, the shadow cloak had made R'shelle look taller and more menacing.

"All right," said R'shelle, "I'll let you give it a shot, but I won't take it easy on you. After all, you had the bad taste to join the warrior class first."

Though it was technically possible to join every class and learn every profession in *Fantasia*, in practice, it was nigh impossible. (Really, "nigh"? You couldn't have just used "almost"? What century are we in?) The trainers preferred to see loyalty to their own class and made joining each successive one more difficult, both in terms of being convinced to allow a player to attempt the quest and the actual quest requirements. If Fey had not answered to R'shelle's liking, the rogue trainer would never have even appeared.

"I look forward to the challenge," Fey said politely, though of course she would have preferred an easy quest (#Lazy).

"We'll see," said R'shelle with a(n evil) gleam in her eye. "The regular quest is to successfully sneak attack ten monsters and then defeat them. For you . . . Let's make it kill a hundred monsters before they notice where you are. Oh, and of course, the monsters have to be your level or higher."

I think I can, I think I can.[32] "I will do my best," said Fey, none of her (severe) misgivings apparent in her tone or posture.

"We'll see." R'shelle sounded confident in something, and that something was not Fey's success. Without a word of goodbye, the NPC disappeared back into the shadows.

Fey sighed and started walking deeper into the forest, where the higher-levelled monsters would be. She was currently at level 32; the monsters at this level were considerably faster and more intelligent than newbie monsters, and she was not looking forward to trying to sneak up on them.

The way Fey saw it, there were two ways to kill a monster to satisfy the quest requirements: one, stay hidden and inflict damaging status effects from afar; two, sneak up to it and deal fatal damage on the first strike. She had skills and abilities that might help her with both methods, but she was not confident that they dealt enough damage to be fatal before a monster noticed her presence.

Fey sighed again and reversed direction, heading back to the Moonwood. She needed some equipment upgrades.

Fey's first destination was the weapon shop(-tree). Sylvannos was busy with another customer, so she wandered over to the throwing weapon display and began to browse.

The variety was somewhat bewildering. Throwing daggers, darts, throwing stars, and chakrams were all displayed in their deadly glory. Fey even saw a boomerang propped against the corner.

Fey had no idea which kind of throwing weapon had optimal physics for dealing damage, or if one kind even had an advantage over another.

Amethyst squeaked up helpfully. ("We already have star-stars.")

"Good point, Amethyst." (Pun intended.) Fey dug around in her backpack for the throwing stars her pets had brought her during their underwater (mis)adventures.

Made of a mysterious black material, the five-pointed stars did not resemble any of the throwing stars on display, which all had an even number of points, presumably because it was easier to make them that way.

Hefting her stars experimentally, Fey decided that she liked their weight and shape and could use them as weapons. Just to be sure, she checked their description.

<Ninja starfish stars: these stars are made of a unique carbon-based polymer that is very tough but cannot be repaired if damaged.>

<Durability: 150 (not repairable)>

<Recommended minimum dexterity: 60>

<Recommended minimum strength: 20>

<Recommended maximum strength: 200>

Other than the five base attributes of vitality, strength, dexterity, agility, and intelligence—plus class attributes like mages' willpower—stats in *Fantasia* were reflective of performance rather than determinants of performance. The durability of an object was a function of its material and shape, and the stat simply reflected the amount of force or energy it would take to deform or break an object.

In a related fashion, weapons did not have minimum level or attribute requirements and conferred no set "attack power" to weapon strikes. Instead, there were recommended attribute ranges in which the weapon functioned optimally; outside that range on the low side, the weapon would do little more damage than a lower-quality item, and on the high side, the weapon was likely to exceed its durability and break.

Fey's dexterity was 67 and her strength 95, making the ninja starfish stars ideal throwing weapons for her. This was not just a coincidence (unlike every other convenient thing that's happened that the author couldn't think of an explanation for); the level 30 ninja starfish became level 30 weapons with attribute ranges corresponding to those expected of a level 30 player.

"Too bad I can't buy more of these," Fey said wistfully to Amethyst, the item description (that she only checked how many days later?) telling her where her pets had obtained them. There were only five stars, and she would have liked to have a set of eight to twelve.

Amethyst squeaked in sympathy but was actually happy there were only five stars, as they had once been really scary monsters that had nearly killed her.

"Can I help you, miss?" Sylvannos had finished with his previous customer and now turned his attention to Fey.

"How would you carry these," she said, showing him her stars, "in a way convenient for throwing?"

After carefully examining the unusual weapons, Sylvannos reached into the cupboard under the throwing weapon display and came up with an interesting pouch-box made of hardened leather. The four vertical faces were at right angles to each other, while the bottom was sharply slanted. The top was a soft flap that fastened shut with a hook. Halfway up the box on one side was a slit that spanned the width of the box, a width that exactly matched the circumference of the throwing stars.

"If I may," said Sylvannos, taking Fey's stars and dropping them into the pouch. The bottom-most star poked partway out of the side slit, ready to be drawn for throwing. Sylvannos pulled it out, and the next star slid smoothly into place. "It's designed to hold up to twelve," he explained.

Fey took the pouch and pulled out a star, watching its successor slide into place. It was quite fun, so she repeated the action. The only thing that saved her from being absorbed in the activity for the next several hours was that she ran out of stars to pull out (#InnerTwo-Year-Old).

"Very nice," she said (while the two-year-old said, "Funfunfunfunfun . . ."). "I'll take it."

Sylvannos attached the pouch-box to its accompanying harness and demonstrated how it was designed to swivel into any orientation. "In case you're lying flat or hanging upside-down or something." ("In case." Get it?)

"Wow, they thought of everything," said Fey admiringly.

Sylvannos deftly scooped up Fey's stars and slid them back into the pouch before handing it and its attached harness to Fey. "Will that be all today?"

"Actually, I'd like to see your level 30 punching blades," said Fey. She had been intending to get to level 40 before upgrading because of their high cost and the fact that she was still within her blades' recommended strength range, but she needed as much of an edge she could get with the rogue quest. ("An edge." Warning: you have reached the chapter maximum of lazy, terrible puns.)

"Of course." Sylvannos went over to the punching blade display. With a whistle, he opened a nook behind the shelves and casually reached in as if living wood parted like water all the time. The punching blades he pulled out were identical in size and shape to Fey's present weapons.

Fey hefted the new blades experimentally. If she squinted (and exercised her imagination), she could see that the metal was a slightly different shade of silver-grey, and they felt slightly heavier than her current set. She checked the description.

<Quality steel punching blades: Forged by the Moonwood's skilled blacksmith, these punching blades were crafted from Grade A steel and will perform admirably in combat.>

<Durability: 60>

<Recommended minimum strength: 60>

<Recommended maximum strength: 150>

I might as well get them. Thanks to her training not-a-date with Leandriel (#Denial), Fey was even carrying enough money to pay for them.

"The total will be 4500g."

Before Fey had even properly concluded the transaction, an enraged squeal sounded from outside. Fey unceremoniously dropped the correct coinage on the counter and rushed out to see what had happened to her pets.

("Bye . . ." said Sylvannos.)

Outside the tree-shop, Boris and the glooms faced off against an elven player that pointed a drawn longbow at them. Boris's eyes glowed red as he used Glare to prevent the player from attacking, and the glooms had shaped themselves into a mane of menacing spikes around the boar's neck. An arrow shaft was embedded in the ground next to Boris's feet.

With a single glance at the situation, Fey sprinted at the player, putting herself directly in the path of the arrow as she ran.

<Fey's agility has risen to 69 (+1)!>

The player barely avoided loosing his bow in startlement. It might have been better if he had, as Fey proceeded to yank the arrow out of his grasp, snapping it in half with the force of her grip as she threw it to the ground.

The player yelped as the bowstring recoiled with a painful snap. Before he could take offence, he was faced with an angry Fey.

"What the [censored word] do you think you're doing!?" she yelled. Due to her deeper vocal range and tae kwon do–trained breathing muscles, the sound carried quite the distance through the village, attracting attention despite the background chatter of dozens of players.

"I—"

"Pet!" Fey continued to shout, her voice still perfectly (and angrily) modulated despite the volume. "Pet! Pet! Pet! Pet! Pet! Pet! Pet!" Each repetition corresponded to an actual pet, but this was not obvious to any of the observers (or the guy being yelled at).

Fey glared at the bowman in wrathful silence for another five seconds, just to make sure the fear really set in properly, then stalked off, her steps full of violent energy that made people get out of her way. Boris gave the player one last Glare and followed. One of the glooms (Midnight) made a good approximation of a certain rude hand gesture as it was carried away. (Where did it even learn what that meant?)

The bowman's friend and party member, an elven warrior, nudged him with an elbow. "Told ya you should have left it alone. Iron boars don't just sit around town for no reason."

The bowman just nodded, in too much shock from the auditory assault to carry on a conversation. "She's scary" was all he could say.

"Yup," the warrior friend agreed, unbothered because the scariness had not been directed at him. "I wonder where she got the iron boar?"

Fey's next destination was the accessory shop. Instead of having Boris wait outside, she ushered him into the tree-shop. Its arched doorway was generously wide by human(oid) standards, but Boris had to maneuver himself carefully to avoid brushing its edges.

The appearance of a massive iron boar followed by an elf wearing a coldly furious expression made the shop-keeper blink in surprise, but she recovered quickly. (This game breeds strangeness.) "Welcome! How may I help you?"

The system notice told Fey that this was Treisillia, owner of the accessory shop. "I'd like to get something that makes it clear that he's"—she indicated Boris—"a pet and not a monster." Fey quickly shelved her anger for later and treated the NPC politely; after all, Treisillia had not done anything wrong.

"How about a saddle?" Treisillia suggested tentatively.

"Great idea!" Fey embraced the suggestion with enthusiasm, as it was greatly superior to her own vague ideas of a (useless) collar.

Treisillia pulled out her longest tape measure and approached Boris, showing remarkable composure at coming close to his intimidating bulk and sharp tusks. She even failed to startle when the glooms hopped off his back in a shadowy wave.

Fey absent-mindedly shifted her weight to compensate for the glooms who decided to climb her instead, preoccupied with ideas for the saddle. "What's it going to be made of? Can it double as armour?" she asked.

Treisillia laid her tape along Boris's spine and measured from shoulder to rump as she answered. "The standard material would be leather made from non-specific animal hide from a level 30 monster. You can, of course, bring in your own material for us to work with or order more expensive leather." Gesturing at the iron plates covering Boris's chest, back, and sides, she added, "I wouldn't think this gentleman needs any additional armour."

Boris snorted at the "gentleman" appellation. Other than the commentary, he was a model mannequin, staying patiently still while Treisillia looped her tape around various parts of his body.

Fey answered, "Not his back, but he doesn't have armour everywhere. Could we make something to protect his belly?"

Treisillia paused in the act of looping the tape around Boris's neck as she considered. "The standard design does not cover the belly, but we could certainly add additional straps for protection. We could also fasten the saddle with metal links, though that will cost more."

"Let's do that, then," Fey agreed. There was a time and place to save money, and this was not it.

"It'll still be comfortable, right?" Fey asked after she thought about the metal. "I wouldn't want him to be uncomfortable." (#MotherHen)

Treisillia draped her tape across Boris's back, then bent down to collect the ends. "Oh yes. The metal will be wrapped within leather. Our design will ensure your pet can wear it constantly without discomfort."

"Great." Fey settled back quietly (and poisoned herself) while Treisillia finished her measurements and sketched out the design of the saddle.

Fey peered at the completed drawing. The saddle seat resembled what she knew of horse saddles, albeit wider to match Boris's considerable girth. The complex harness holding the saddle seat consisted of straps that secured themselves around each leg and then crisscrossed in a woven pattern to cover his abdomen. It looked like it would be quite a hassle to put on, but once that was accomplished, it would evenly distribute the weight of the saddle and not require tight cinching to remain in place.

"I like it," Fey approved.

Before she could finalize the order, Amethyst squeaked up helpfully.

"Oh yeah. Could we add a couple of saddlebags?" (Carrying loot is far more important than carrying riders.)

"Certainly." Treisillia sketched them in.

"Also a saddle pack in the back." (#Storage)

After the extra pack was added and Fey selected Grade A steel for the straps, the total came to 7500g. Fey handed over the correct coinage (and reassured herself that this was an investment that would pay for itself. Eventually). With the promise that the saddle would be complete "in three days," the next night she logged in, Fey left the accessory shop in a much better mood than she entered it. Seeing the advanced hour, she decided to log off and tackle her rogue quest the next night.

CHAPTER 22

THROWAWAY

Arwyn dragged herself home Thursday evening, physically exhausted and sweaty. Due to her upcoming exam, she had decided to start going to tae kwon do classes twice a week. Her body was reacting the way it always did to increased exertion, lending her the energy and then charging interest like a loan shark. Arwyn did not speak Korean, but it seemed to be the language her calves were currently using to swear at her.

She was faced with her usual dilemma after an exhausting class: shower first or food first? Food almost always won because she did not wish to drown in the shower from a lack of energy.

Arwyn logged on to her laptop while she ate. She deleted some emails and browsed the news between bites.

Her messenger application flashed.

Leah-IfIHadAMillionDollars...: Look!

Leah sent a link to a video. Arwyn clicked it and proceeded to watch a transformation sequence that seemed pretty typical of every anime containing magical girl powers that Arwyn had ever seen.[33] The difference was, instead of cartoon art, the graphics were incredibly realistic. The title over the video read: *"Fantasia—ForeverHeaven's Ex-quip."*

Arwyn snorted. It was one thing to have a silly avatar name in normal games, but in virtual reality, you had to actually listen to people call you by name.

Getting back to the conversation, Arwyn wrote:

ArwynTheElf: That's not what happened when I used Ex-quip

Leah-IfIHadAMillionDollars...: You have to set it in your Abilities menu or use the transformation sequence designer on the VirtualRealities website

ArwynTheElf: I don't really see the point. I mean, that's a whole minute where someone could be shooting you

Leah-IfIHadAMillionDollars...: You're invincible during the transformation. I checked

ArwynTheElf: Meh

ArwynTheElf: Oh. You just want to design my transformation sequence

Leah-IfIHadAMillionDollars...: You're so smart ^_^. Now log in for me so I can

ArwynTheElf: Fine. I won't use it if it's too stupid

Leah-IfIHadAMillionDollars...: As if. It's gonna be AWEsome

Arwyn sighed and went to grab her game helmet. She plugged it into her laptop and used it to log in to the VirtualRealities website while Leah did something complicated with their Internet connections so that she could gain remote access to Arwyn's account.

Leah-IfIHadAMillionDollars...: Purrfect 3

ArwynTheElf: Are you going to be late onto *Fantasia* tonight?

Leah-IfIHadAMillionDollars...: Naw. Usual time. This will take at least a week to design

ArwynTheElf: You have too much free time

Leah-IfIHadAMillionDollars...: I have no time for your petty complaints. Time to choose the music!

ArwynTheElf: I'm going to go take a shower. Later

Leah-IfIHadAMillionDollars...: See ya!

Arwyn dragged herself out of her desk chair and into the shower, her muscles stiff after sitting still. After she turned the water to almost painfully hot, her body became relaxed and floppy instead.

Arwyn flopped her way out of the shower and got dressed for bed. The state of almost-numb exhaustion she often reached after tae kwon do class was actually fairly pleasant for someone whose mind was constantly in overdrive, but it was not conducive for any tasks that required concentration or willpower. Arwyn curled up with a cup of hot chocolate and the third of the five books she had checked out of the library.

Several hours later, Arwyn paused in the middle of a chapter, glancing at the clock. She found it easier to stop reading in the middle of a chapter because chapter ends were always designed to have cliff-hanger elements that prodded you to keep going. Snagging a random piece of paper from the nearest table, she bookmarked her place and went to log in to *Fantasia*.

◊◊◊

It was now Fey's habit to check her friend list upon logging in. As usual, Leandriel's name glowed green. Blade was likewise online, while Sirena had yet to appear. This was fairly typical for a game night.

Also typical, but never ordinary, was Leandriel's nightly greeting and short conversation with her. Fey walked to the accessory shop while exchanging PMs with the angel.

<Leandriel: Hello.>

<Fey: Hi! How are you?>

<Leandriel: I am well. What are you up to today?>

<Fey: I have to go sneakily kill some monsters so I can join the rogue class and become an assassin.>

<Leandriel: Assassin? A suitable choice for you.>

<Fey: Are you casting aspersions on my character?>

<Leandriel: Never. Your character is flawless.>

<Fey: You, sir, are a smooth talker.>

<Leandriel: All the credit goes to my lovely conversational partner.>

<Fey: Hahaha. Do you have anything special planned today?>

<Leandriel: Not particularly. I am training to level up.>

<Fey: Have fun.>

<Leandriel: I will, as Magic often says, not forget the loot.>

<Fey: Did he actually say that?>

<Leandriel: Yes. He recently learned to speak. It is his favourite phrase.>

<Fey: Hahaha. My pets just automatically collect everything and stick it in my bag now.>

<Leandriel: I am sure Magic would do that if he could carry items properly.>

<Fey: Aww, poor thing. I guess he'll just have to do with nagging you.>

<Leandriel: I live to serve.>

<Fey: Talk to you later?>

<Leandriel: Certainly. Goodbye for now.>

<Fey: Bye!>

Fey entered the accessory tree-shop wearing a much more agreeable expression than the first time she had visited. As promised, Treisillia was waiting with a completed saddle. The metal-and-leather contraption was much heavier than Fey would want to carry around on a constant basis, but Boris bore the weight easily.

Thanking the shop-keeper, Fey set out into the forest to complete her rogue quest.

Walking along the forest trails, Fey pondered the task ahead. It was extremely difficult to kill monsters of the same level in one blow, and even more difficult to remain undetected while attacking. Fey found it rather unfair that she had to complete a task that required rogue skills in order to join the rogue class and learn the skills. (Now that's a true "prerequisite.")

As she walked (and pondered), Fey practiced with her throwing stars. Pinching one point between her thumb and the side of her index finger, she sent them flying with an overhand flick of the wrist.

Her aim was terrible to the point that the monsters she aimed for did not always notice they were under attack. (She did occasionally hit one far to the side of the one she was aiming for.) Without the help of the glooms, she would have lost her stars to the undergrowth after the first throw.

With enough repetition, her aim progressed from "terrible" to "pretty bad" (i.e., the monsters actually noticed they were under attack). When the monsters retaliated, she defeated them with kicks and stabs.

Though her stars were still completely ineffective at inflicting a non-negligible amount of damage, Fey's practice did not go entirely unrewarded.

<Fey's dexterity has risen to 68(+1)!>

<Fey's dexterity has risen to 69(+1)!>

"Pretty bad" had now improved to "mediocre," and Fey was now reliably hitting her target with every throw. She added Bleed to increase the damage from the minor flesh wounds she generally inflicted, and the resulting fight gave her the opportunity to exercise her other skills. The monsters above level 20 started growing to a decent size so that fighting resembled actual combat rather than bullying small creatures.

<Bleed has reached level 6!>

<Kicking has reached level 4!>

Fey was training her skills effectively, but she was not any closer to completing her rogue quest. Fighting her way deeper into the forest, she was almost to the monsters at and above her level, so she needed to figure out a plan soon.

Fey stopped beside a tree. (In the forest, it's impossible not to stop beside a tree.) Placing her hand on its trunk, she looked up consideringly. Not including her slug-hunting adventures (in Chapter 6), Fey had never climbed a tree. The ancient giants populating the Elvenwood were an intimidating way to start, their lowest branches well beyond her reach.

"I don't suppose you could reel me up there?" Fey asked Amethyst jokingly.

Amethyst squeaked cheerfully and hopped from Fey's shoulder onto Inkblot's back. The gloom carried the slime up the tree to the lowest branch, gliding upward the way a shadow did with a moving light source.

Extending her bubble-arm to its fullest length, Amethyst looped it once around the branch and let the rest dangle toward the ground. She squeaked again. ("Ready.")

Fey looked up at the slime, whose bubble-arm was still too high to reach. "I don't think—"

An excited squeak interrupted her. Inkblot emerged from Fey's backpack holding her rope. (Really, that thing is super useful. People should carry rope around more often.) Carrying one end, the gloom raced back up the tree, over the branch, and returned once again to the ground.

Boris trotted over without being asked and Inkblot tied the rope to his saddle, using the butterfly knot commonly used to tie shoelaces.

"Where did you learn that?" Fey asked.

Inkblot squeaked, reminding Fey of the time the gloom had stolen a player's shoelace.

Fey laughed, shaking her head at her pets' resourcefulness (or whatever you call it). "Unfortunately, that one is going to come undone if you pull on the end of the rope." She demonstrated a more secure knot.

Inkblot proffered the free end of the rope and Fey accepted with a grateful thank-you. With Boris balancing her weight on the other side of the rope, Fey walked herself up the tree and onto the lowest branch. Amethyst wrapped her bubble-arm around Fey's ankle as a living safety rope.

"Thanks, guys," Fey called down to her pets, putting the rope away after a gloom untied the knot. "Think you could drive some monsters into throwing range?"

With a chorus of squeaks and a single grunt, the pets ventured away.

Fey crawled amongst the tree branches, looking for a good place to settle and throw stars at the ground. As if playing a strange game of Statue,[34] Amethyst stayed securely wrapped around a branch while Fey was moving, then pulled herself forward when Fey paused. Finally, Fey settled into a (relatively) comfortable position and poisoned herself while waiting for monsters to arrive.

Fey heard the monsters before she saw them. The glooms had adopted the method of "poke and run" in order to lure what appeared to be lynx made of living wood into the vicinity. In contrast, Boris had used his intimidating size to chase a herd of giant chipmunks toward her.

The two groups of monsters collided; while the giant chipmunks were larger than the wood lynx, the lynx had sharper claws and made its displeasure felt. The glooms took advantage of this distraction in order to slip out of the way and headed out to lure more monsters. Likewise, Boris veered off his Charge to do the same.

There were now plenty of targets below Fey. She threw a star down, the change in orientation making her clumsy. Of her first five throws, three hit a monster, causing it to look around before being drawn back into the fray. Fey was mostly hidden by the thick tree branch she lay on, so she was hard to spot unless she moved.

When the glooms returned with more monsters to add to the chaos, Fey had Shadow stay behind to collect her throwing stars. The gloom slid unobtrusively between the monsters, just a dark puddle in an area that had more than one streak of blood on the ground. Shadow did not just collect the throwing stars but also dropped off a hefty handful of coins with each delivery. (#Don'tForgetTheLoot)

Fey's throwing accuracy and power slowly improved, but she failed to do the kind of damage required to get credit for a kill. She added Bleed to her attacks, which added a little more damage, and then poison. She chose to use poison mushroom poison rather than a faster-acting one because its side effect was blurred vision, which seemed like a good thing if she was trying not to be noticed.

Things went smoothly until Fey hit the same wood lynx for a third time. It decided that the threat from above was too great to ignore, even if it could not see its attacker. Long claws digging easily into bark, it began to climb Fey's tree.

"[Censored word]," Fey swore, gripping her branch tightly and trying to figure out how she was going to defend herself without falling to a messy death.

Amethyst squeaked cheerfully. ("I got it!") Releasing her grip on Fey's ankle, she Whipped her bubble out with terrifying speed.

The wood lynx failed to see it coming. The bubble impacted with an audible *crack* that made Fey wince. Not just stunned but truly unconscious and possibly comatose, the lynx dropped heavily to the ground, a visible dent in its skull.

<Amethyst's Whip has increased to level 19!>

"Did I know you could do that?" Fey asked her oldest pet. Amethyst squeaked cheerfully ("Dunno") and regained her grip on Fey's ankle.

The strength of Amethyst's bubble-arm had long been unbalanced relative to her negligible body weight. She could generate force equivalent to Fey's kicks but had the mass of a large orange (or small grapefruit, if you prefer). Because of this, she had to carefully modulate and angle her Whip to avoid flying backward with each strike.

Securely anchored to a massive tree, all such considerations became moot. (Even if you dislike fancy vocabulary, you have to admit that "moot" is a fun word.) Amethyst had just demonstrated the full, deadly potential of her Whip, which helped the skill gain experience faster than a carefully controlled activation.

No longer worrying about being spotted, Fey threw her stars as fast as Shadow could retrieve them. It took over a hundred throws, but she managed to hit a giant chipmunk at exactly the right place between the base of its skull and its first vertebra, getting an instant kill.

Fey decided that she had had enough practice; much more and she would level up. Dropping to the ground, she finished off the remaining monsters, collected the loot, and headed off to find the level 32 monster territory. Another hike up a tree and she was ready for action.

The level 32 monster in the Elvenwood was a species of wolf that had grass for fur. A pack of these wolves was currently eating the carcass of an unfortunate deer that had wandered into their territory. Fey (awkwardly) climbed from tree to tree until she was within throwing range. Settling into a good spot for throwing, Fey nudged Amethyst with her free foot, and the slime squeaked.

The wolves looked up at the sound but were quickly distracted by Boris and the glooms as they charged in at the signal. (If we want to be honest here, it was Boris providing all of the distraction.) Rather than trying to kill the wolves, they aimed to distract and confuse them long enough for Fey to get the kill.

Fey was still not completely sure of her aim, so she tried to target wolves who were not immediately next to one of her pets. This tactic was less successful than she liked, as the less-distracted wolves would look up at the attack; from her current angle, she was not completely hidden from view, and she would be spotted before the wolf's attention was taken by one of the pets.

Hoping that she would not hit one of her pets, Fey aimed carefully and threw at a wolf just as it was slammed aside by Boris's shoulder. It worked, the small impact of the throwing star disguised by the much-larger impact of a six-Fey iron boar. (Apparently, a Fey is a standard unit of mass now.) After some internal debate, Fey added furyweed poison to her throwing stars because it had the highest and fastest damage of Amethyst's repertoire. The affected wolves went into berserker frenzies, but Fey's pets managed to avoid major injury.

Fey failed to land any critical hits, but by the time the wolf pack was defeated, her quest progress menu showed two kills. Fey (awkwardly) clambered between trees to find another pack, foreseeing a long and tiring day.

A couple of hours later, Fey was still in the trees when Sirena sent her a PM.

<Sirena: Hey, are you done advancing yet? Blade and I are in Meadowcircle taking a break if you want to join us.>

<Fey: Not even close to done.>

Fey explained the warrior trainers' recommendations and her current quest.

<Sirena: Spellblade sounds way cooler than assassin.>

<Fey: Yeah, but I'm sure its skill and spell repertoires have to be very limited to avoid unbalancing the game. Plus, I'm so bad at multitasking.>

<Sirena: Yeah, you'd probably be terrible at it. I bet I could be a good spellblade.>

<Fey: You may be good at multitasking, but you'd have to learn how to fight.>

<Sirena: Hmm, good point. Meh, mage robes are more stylish than armour, anyway. I'll just rely on other people to do the sweaty stuff.>

<Fey: Speaking of meatshields, how's Blade doing?>

<Sirena: Good. I made him buy me ice cream.>

<Fey: They have ice cream?>

<Sirena: As long as they have cows and sugar, I don't see why not.>

<Fey: I wasn't aware of sugar cane being a major crop in human lands.>

<Sirena: Pfft. In all likelihood, there's an adorable sugar cube monster that they farm for sugar.>

<Fey: That sounds like the kind of pseudo-logical thing the game designers would do.>

<Sirena: Too bad you can't come eat ice cream. How many more kills do you need?>

<Fey: Around 40. I'll probably be done by the end of the day, depending on whether I can keep doing this when it gets dark.>

<Sirena: I'll let you get back to it then. Later!>

<Fey: Bye.>

Very late in the *Fantasia* night, Fey returned to the rogue trainer area, tired and sore but triumphant.

The area was even creepier by moonlight.

"So you've returned."

Fey jumped and turned. R'shelle was directly beside her, inside the invisible bubble of personal space that people generally kept between each other.

"I've completed my task."

"And how did you manage that?"

Fey patted Boris and the glooms that sat on his back. "Very good distractions." If she was tired from staying in awkward positions in trees all day, they were exhausted from actually having to run around and fight for the same period of time.

R'shelle smiled. "Sound and stealth are relative. I am glad you know that. Truly, you belong to the rogue class."

<Quest complete!>

<Fey gains 500 experience. Amethyst gains 250 experience. Boris gains 250 experience. Onyx gains 250 experience. Inkblot gains 250 experience. Ebony gains 250 experience. Midnight gains 250 experience. Shadow gains 250 experience. Obsidian gains 250 experience.>

Fey considered complaining about the measly experience reward compared to the difficulty of the quest but decided it would be futile. The reward for the initial class quest remained the same whether or not the trainers decided to make it harder.

A long knife and sheath appeared in R'shelle's hands. "I grant you the honorary rogue knife"—she handed it to Fey—"though your current weapons greatly exceed it in quality.

"I will also teach you the basic ability Shadow Cloak."

Fey nodded to show she was listening and R'shelle continued.

"First, gather your energy tightly in your centre. You should be used to concentrating your mana from your warrior training. Yes, like that. Now, *invert it*."

Something about the way R'shelle said "invert" opened a locked pathway inside Fey's mind, and the colour of her mana changed from a bright glow to a dark shadow. (It was still purple, though.)

"Very good. Now release it slightly to diffuse around you and hide your presence."

<Fey has learned Shadow Cloak!>

Fey released the ability, shivering at the way the magic felt.

"This is a passive ability that requires no mana consumption and will not improve with use. The size of the Shadow Cloak you can cast depends directly on the size of your combined mana and health pools. If you concentrate it close to your body, it will muffle sound as well as light. While it is active, your mana will be inverted, and you cannot activate mana-requiring skills unless they are specialized rogue skills that also consume inverted mana. Questions?"

Fey blinked at the inundation of information. "Uh, no."

R'shelle smiled. "Welcome to the shadows. Come find me when you have enough rogue feats to advance." This time, she disappeared Cheshire Cat–style, her smile fading last.

So creeeeeepy. Fey decided that she had worked hard enough for the day and went to hang out and eat at Tallen's tavern until it was time to log out.

CHAPTER 23
CONVERSE

Leander settled his tray at a table in the dining hall and took a seat. The VirtualRealities campus offered its employees full amenities, including an all-day supply of fresh, cooked food prepared by talented chefs and designed to be both delicious and nutritionally balanced. People could cook their own food and eat in private if they chose to do so, but Leander took most of his meals in the dining hall.

Across the table, another tray settled with a clatter, and a short, vivacious woman dropped into the chair. It was Lacey, one of the company's many talented artists and also his friend Kevin's girlfriend. "Hey, Leander. I heard you got a girlfriend."

Leander blinked. "I beg your pardon?"

"Oh, don't even try to deny it. I got it from Kevin, and he's a terrible liar. 'Fey,' that was her name, right?" Lacey tucked her chin-length hair—blue today—behind an ear.

Leander took a breath and focused on his food. He could feel his face heating up, and could only hope that the blush was not obvious. "Obviously, she is not my girlfriend."

Kevin dropped into the seat beside Lacey, and Leander took the opportunity to shoot him a stern look.

Kevin raised his hands defensively. "Hey, it's not my fault. She has some freaky mind-reading powers. I barely said two words and she figured it all out."

"So? Details!" Lacey demanded.

"I think not," said Leander, tucking into his meal.

"I'll get it out of you one way or another," Lacey threatened, pointing her fork at him.

Leander did not know how to respond, so he remained silent.

A pause. "Ugh!" Lacey exclaimed disgustedly. "Honestly, you're impossible. I don't see how any girl would like you when you're so boring."

Leander's hand paused halfway to his mouth before resuming movement.

"Hey, chill, Lacey," Kevin chided. "He's cool."

Lacey waved a careless hand in Leander's direction. "I mean, yeah, he has a lot going for him in the looks department, and he's pretty talented at a lot of stuff, but you have to admit you're boring, Leander."

"Indeed," Leander agreed, striving for a light tone. He apparently succeeded, as Lacey made an exasperated sound and changed the subject.

Leander failed to follow the conversation as it continued, thinking about Lacey's comment.

He *was* a somewhat boring person. When it came to jokes and banter, he lacked the ability for quick wordplay required to participate in the fast back-and-forth most of his colleagues—all highly intelligent and creative—enjoyed. He enjoyed routine over more chaotic adventures, and most of his favourite activities were fairly quiet by the standards of his age group.

Leander was long past the age where he thought he should change his personality to fit in with others. It did not bother him if people thought he was boring, as he found his own life quite interesting, the exploration of game worlds and meticulous checking of details to ensure no bugs made it through to the release version suiting his physical talents and serious personality.

At least, it did not bother him if most people found him boring.

His mind drifted to Fey's vivacious smile and incredible mental agility.

"I don't see how any girl would like you when you're so boring."

Leander was in a rather sombre mood when he logged into *Fantasia* that evening.

Fey logged into *Fantasia* and looked over the possible rogue feats she could pursue to qualify for her next advancement skill.

The rogue feats seemed similar to warrior feats in that their titles were all puns of varying cleverness. They differed in the fact that almost half of them had little to do with combat or killing. Instead, many focused on sneaky tasks such as walking around undetected and reaching improbable-to-reach areas with acrobatic skill. (The other half, of course, involved killing large numbers of monsters in sneaky and underhanded ways.)

Fey flicked back and forth through the list, trying to decide which feats she should aim for first. She wanted to try for ones that would not take too much time, while avoiding the ones she was likely to accomplish without even trying (such as killing large numbers of monsters in sneaky and underhanded ways).

<Reach for the Top[35]: climb to the highest point in a city—
10 points>

That sounds doable. It was definitely a feat that Fey would not incidentally accomplish through regular adventuring, and she did not think climbing a tree in the Moonwood would take too much time.

Fey peered up and around the village, trying to gauge where the highest point would be. The building parts of the tree-buildings were mostly one and two storeys in height, but the trees themselves reached much higher into the sky, blending together in the canopy above.

After some consideration, Fey decided to ask an expert and wandered into Kallara's potion shop.

The elven healer looked up and smiled. "Fey! How are you today?"

"I'm good, thanks. Do you have any idea what would be considered 'the highest point' in the Moonwood?"

Rather than replying, Kallara pulled out one of her many tomes on potion ingredients and began leafing through it. "Here." She proffered the book, opened to a page on some kind of thin, golden vine.

Fey read the description.

Dawnling—This rare plant is surprisingly hardy and can survive in a large range of temperatures so long as it can find a place that meets its sunlight requirements.

The dawnling needs to absorb the first rays of light at sunrise, and can usually only be found at places of highest elevation. It has powerful holy properties and can be used to enhance the potency of a large variety of potions.

Fey looked up at Kallara and asked, "So, does this plant mark the highest spot in the Moonwood or something?"

"Oh, no, that would probably be just above the top level of Tallen's tavern, but do me a favour and climb that tree all the way to the top to collect a sample, would you?"

Fey rolled her eyes in amused exasperation and accepted the atypically offered quest. "Yes, Kallara." Returning the book, she headed over to Tallen's to begin the climb.

On the walk over, it occurred to Fey to find it strange that Leandriel had not yet messaged her this game night. It had become a predictable pattern over the past week that the angel would contact her almost exactly five minutes after she logged on, just enough time for her to get her bearings in the game and have the leisure to focus on a conversation.

She checked her friend list; as usual, Leandriel's name was listed in green to indicate his online status.

This left her in somewhat of a quandary (#Dither). Logically, Leandriel was likely to have a reason for breaking his pattern of behaviour, such as being involved in a task that would not take well to interruption. However, equality in relationships demanded that Fey not wait around and force Leandriel to take all the initiative in their interactions. If he generally used her logging on as a prompt to initiate a conversation, he was likely to forget today even after finishing whatever task he was currently occupied with.

Fey rolled her eyes at herself. She hated dithering. *Over an NPC, no less.* She decided that she would wait a couple of hours to give Leandriel a chance to finish whatever he was doing and then PM him (#Decisive). In the meantime, she had a tree to climb.

Climbing a tree that doubled as a tavern did not begin the same way as climbing a normal tree. Sending Boris and the glooms out to amuse themselves in the forest, Fey entered the tavern through its open archway and began climbing stairs.

"Hi, Miss Fey," piped the twelve-year-old Todd, falling in beside her as she climbed. "Will you be dining with us today?"

"Maybe later," Fey answered. "Do you think Tallen will mind if I climb out the window?"

"Oh, lots of rogues have already done that. Dad usually charges a 10g fee for insurance purposes, but since you're a VIP, you can probably just go for free."

Fey chuckled. "For 'insurance purposes.' Your dad has a keen business sense."

Reaching the top of the first flight of stairs revealed a second set; the tavern had expanded to a third floor. "Wow, when did this show up?" Fey murmured.

"A week ago," Todd answered proudly. "I helped." He pointed to a section of railing that was a little bit warped compared to the rest of the building.

"Good job," Fey praised sincerely, continuing up the stairs. The work might be imperfect, but since Fey had never created anything out of living wood, she was not qualified to criticize.

The third floor of the tavern was much the same as the first and second, dominated by long tables and benches. Four arched openings acted as open windows.

"Which one should I take?" Fey asked Todd.

He pointed to the window behind the stairs. "I think less people fall when they try that one."

"Oh, joy," Fey said dryly at the prospect of falling to her doom, heading toward the indicated aperture. Leaning out, she looked down to see the significant distance to the forest floor, then craned her neck in the opposite direction to see the even-more-significant distance to the top of the tavern-tree.

"Do me a favour and keep any items I drop if I die," she said to Todd.

"Oh, you won't die. Nobody else had more than a couple of broken bones," Todd said reassuringly.

"I'm climbing to the very top to collect a plant for Kallara," Fey explained, her tone that of one who had come to terms with the inevitability of death.

"Oh," said Todd. "Okay, I'll take good care of your stuff, Miss Fey."

"Thanks." Fey slid out the window and stood on its bottom ledge, looking for handholds. Fortunately, the third floor of the tavern was high enough that a tree branch was within reach. Fey wrangled herself onto that branch and began the slow, tedious-and-yet-dangerous process of climbing to the top.

With careful attention to detail, Fey made it up to the point where the branches began to sag under her weight. Looking up, there was still a ways to go before reaching the actual treetop.

The situation called for a lighter touch. "Amethyst, I choose you!" said Fey jokingly, not accompanying the words with a throwing motion.

Failing to understand the Pokémon reference, Amethyst nonetheless looped her bubble-arm around a branch and began travelling upward, swinging herself from branch to branch in a loopy path that was dizzying to watch.

Fey was notified of her pet's arrival at the tree's peak by a cheerful squeak. A section of golden vine began drifting downward, and Fey had to scramble to catch it before the lightweight plant was scattered by a random draft of air.

"Phew." Fey relaxed after catching the dawnling sample—

—only to be startled almost to the point of falling out of the tree by Amethyst's daredevil plunge straight onto her shoulder. The slime jumped as soon as she saw a clear path through the branches, landing with enough of an impact that she made a splatting sound.

"Son of a—!" Fey exclaimed, cutting off the profanity right before it escaped. After regaining her balance, she scolded her pet. "What did you do that for?"

Amethyst squeaked sheepishly. ("It looked fun.")

Fey sighed and began climbing down.

Sirena and Blade sat in a travel carriage heading northwest for the second day in a row. Sirena was exercising her Prayer bar and beseeching Thrain to change the weather. Thrain, being a storm god, obliged by sending rainclouds, making the weather rather gloomy.

Beside each player was a pet. Firefly the fyrfalcon perched miserably on a stand Blade had purchased for her, feathers fluffed and looking generally miserable in the damp atmosphere. In contrast, Squishy the jellyfish—now a full-sized adult—floated in a tank beside Sirena, looking inscrutable (due to the lack of face, facial expression, and body language). Presumably, rain did not bother it.

Despite the weather and the monotony of being stuck in a carriage, the players' mood was decidedly animated.

"Did she really?" Sirena asked. "That's diabolical." The words were accompanied by a giggle.

Blade was chronicling some of his childhood adventures, waging war against his older sister as only siblings could. He grinned. "Well, I got her back the week after by washing her new clothes and putting them all in the dryer."[36]

"You didn't!" Sirena gasped, truly aghast at the idea of an entire load of ruined clothing.

"Three pairs of jeans that wouldn't fit anymore," Blade confirmed. "Best of all, I didn't even get in trouble with our parents. 'Honest mistake,'" he added with mock innocence.

Blade and Sirena were having one of those effortless conversations that flowed naturally from topic to topic without losing interest on either side. As part of the magic of the conversation, they were completely at ease with each other as only longtime friends usually were, except that all of their anecdotes were fresh and interesting.

"I shudder to think what she did to you after that," Sirena said. She sighed. "I wish I had a sibling."

"That's only because you've never had one," Blade countered.

"Well, you've never *not* had one," Sirena returned.

Blade shrugged. "Yeah. Everything has its good and bad parts, I guess."

"So philosophical," Sirena teased. "Oh, the rain's about to let up."

Firefly immediately perked up at the words, and Blade opened the carriage window to let her fly outside, ready to hunt.

"So, what's it like, being an only child?"

The conversation flowed endlessly on.

⸺◦◦◦◦⸺

Fey returned from an expectedly disconcerting visit to R'shelle, the rogue trainer with the level 20 skill Shadow Strike. It was somewhat similar to Vicious Strike in that it added extra damage to her blows, but it was not limited to the first attack of a fight and had a chance to stun the opponent. It could only be used with the inverted mana created by Shadow Cloak.

Looking at the system clock, Fey saw that several hours had passed in the game. Leandriel still had not sent a PM.

Stop being an awkward turtle, she told herself. Resolutely, she opened the message interface and sent:

<Fey: Hey, are you busy?>

She received an immediate reply.

<Leandriel: Nothing that can't be interrupted. What can I help you with?>

<Fey: Oh, nothing. I just wanted to see how you were.>

<Leandriel: I am well. How are you today?>

<Fey: Great! Just a couple more rogue feats and I can get started on this whole assassin business.>

<Leandriel: Glad to hear it.>

Fey frowned at her conversation history. Leandriel's wording was still obviously characteristic of him, but something was off. He was not adding his own thoughts and information to the conversation, instead just replying directly to what she wrote.

If he's not busy . . . then he simply doesn't want to talk to me. The thought was surprisingly painful.

<Fey: I'll let you get back to what you're doing, then.>

A slower reply this time.

<Leandriel: Have a good day.>

<Fey: Bye!>

Fey closed the interface, feeling a tightness in her chest and throat that she took a deep breath to dispel. The attempt was only marginally successful.

Resolutely, she pulled up the list of rogue feats and headed into high-level monster territories.

"Leander, you are a first-class idiot," Leandriel denigrated himself. "You literally could not have sounded more inane."

Lacey's words echoing in his mind, Leandriel had not had the nerve to message Fey when she logged in. When, wonder of all wonders, Fey had actually been caring enough to contact him . . . "Leander, you are a Grade-A idiot."

Magic asked worriedly, "What's wrong with Leandriel? Who is Leander?"

"I am Leander, and what's wrong with me is I am a lack-witted, slow-thinking, awkward *fool*."

Magic shook his head. "Leandriel is smart."

"I fail to see any evidence of your claim, sir."

Magic blinked. "Um . . . Leandriel knows a lot of words."

Leandriel sighed and conceded the point. "Yes, yes. However, having a vocabulary is really quite useless if I am too moronic to string words together to form basic conversation."

Magic blinked again. "Um . . . This is a basic conversation?"

Despite himself, Leandriel huffed in amusement. "Yes, I suppose it is." He patted the mushroom affectionately, loving its literal but surprisingly creative thought processes.

Those behaviour patterns definitely came not from him but rather Magic's original owner.

Leandriel pinched his temples in one hand, calling himself an idiot silently so as not to worry his pet.

CHAPTER 24
FUNK

S aturday morning found Arwyn in a rather restive mood. Despite taking out her bad mood on over a thousand monsters the previous night and levelling up, restless energy made her unable to relax or sit still. She wanted to hit something. Unfortunately, tae kwon do class was not until tomorrow.

Arwyn was entirely unused to dealing with strong emotions because she rarely felt them. She dealt with problems promptly and rationally with evidence-based solutions, then just as promptly forgot about the problem and moved on to more pleasant matters.

The situation with Leandriel was neither a real problem nor easily forgotten. Her mind kept obsessively returning to dwell on it, and attempting to not think about something simply made it worse (#Perseverate). The desire to get her brain off the repetitive and useless line of thinking grew with every passing minute.

Arwyn exercised in only two ways (neither of which involved being outdoors). Tae kwon do was out of the picture for today, so she went into her games room and turned on one of her game consoles. A few minutes of loading time, and the television blared

"Welcome to *Dance Dance Revolution!*" Electronic dance music pulsed from the speakers.

When it came to physical abilities, Arwyn rated herself two standard deviations below the mean. However, with enough repetition, even she could gain a measure of proficiency at specific tasks. When she had started playing DDR as an awkward preteen, she failed even Beginner-level songs. Over a decade of practice, four game consoles, and a dozen different versions of the game later, she occasionally scored AAA on Difficult-level songs. (Her ability to complete Expert songs was limited by physical stamina. #Wimpy)

Arwyn stepped onto her metal dance pad, which was always laid out in front of the television. She selected the first song, then another, then another, letting the driving bass drum and synthesized notes wash over her, focusing on nothing but the complex pattern of arrows flashing across the screen. (The author does not recommend playing DDR if you have photosensitive epilepsy.) Her feet moved faster than conscious thought could direct them, tapping multiple panels for every beat of the music.

As her breathing deepened and her muscles warmed up, she was relieved to find that her mind escaped its obsessive pattern of thoughts. Arwyn welcomed the fatigue that calmed her racing mind. In *Fantasia*, stamina replenished itself so quickly that the deep tiredness that required hours of rest never manifested, so all of her fighting and training failed to impact her ability to worry.

Not wanting to lose the sense of flow[37] she was experiencing, Arwyn pushed herself well past the point of pleasant tiredness, playing continuously for four hours and stopping only when she began to miss steps because her legs refused to react quickly enough. Turning off the console, she prepared herself a late lunch, aware that she was going to regret overdoing it tomorrow. For now, she had finally gotten rid of the knot of tension in her gut and was content.

(Warning: Gooey feeling stuff ahead. Feel free to skip to the next set of parentheses.)

While she ate, Arwyn's subconscious delivered the results of the psychoanalysis it had been working on since the moment she had begun to feel upset: Her reactions were consistent with her being in love with Leandriel.

It was not just the uncomfortably strong attraction that accompanied infatuation—though she felt that as well. No, this was a deeper feeling, one that was dangerous in its ability to leave an emotional scar. Apparently, knowing that the angel did not exist in real life had not prevented her from falling for him, perhaps the opposite, causing her to relax and be herself around him. "Stupid programmers," she muttered, blaming them for creating such a perfect NPC. Handsome, intelligent, kind, and powerful; she was almost annoyed with herself for falling for such a cliché.

Having admitted her feelings to herself, Arwyn was aware that she had to let them go. There was no future to the relationship; there was not really a relationship at all. Her feelings were real, but the person who inspired them was not.

In her mind, Arwyn bade a silent goodbye to Leandriel. She was sure that she would still interact with him from time to time in the game, but she would no longer do so with an unguarded heart. Outwardly, her expression remained unchanged from its usual calm. Inside, she mourned for what could never be.

(Okay, gooey stuff over.)

After a lazy day where she avoided doing anything even remotely productive, Arwyn did not particularly feel like playing *Fantasia* when bedtime rolled around. However, she did not want to fall behind her friends in level. With a sigh, she got into the recliner and put on the game helmet with much less enthusiasm than normal.

◊◊◊

"Scanning. Player detected. Welcome back to *Fantasia*, Fey E'lan."

◊◊◊

Fey materialized halfway between the rogue trainer and the Moonwood, where she had logged out the night before. In her hand was the rogue token—inscribed with a mask and dagger—that could be combined with the warrior token she already had to lead her to the assassin trainer. In her Abilities menu was the newly learned Weapon Recall, which would return thrown weapons to her possession one minute after being thrown. Neither of these filled her with the proper satisfaction she should have felt after making such great progress.

Fey sighed, aware that she was going to be in a terrible mood for at least two weeks, in all likelihood over a month. She began walking toward town.

On her shoulder, Amethyst squeaked concernedly.

Fey patted the slime. "Don't mind me. I'm going to be annoyingly sigh-y for a while, but this too shall pass. It might pass like a kidney stone, but it will pass."

Amethyst squeaked questioningly. ("What's a kidney?")

Fey grinned, taking comfort in the uncomplicated affection she had for her pets. They were not real, either, but she did not want more from them than their help and company while she adventured. She launched into an explanation of the wondrous blood-filtering organ that was the kidney.

Five minutes later, Fey was describing the action of erythropoietin when the PM came in.

"So if you're going to dope,[38] you should keep your hemoglobin levels under 160—"

<Leandriel: Hello>

Inhaling sharply, Fey replied as normally as she could.

<Fey: Hi>

<Leandriel: How are you today?>

<Fey: Not bad. I'm probably going to finish my assassin advancement today.>

<Leandriel: Good luck. I believe that the first assassin skill requires some practice to use effectively.>

<Fey: What is it?>

<Leandriel: It is called Critical Sight>

<Fey: Cool.>

A long pause. Fey was aware that she would have normally found something to prolong the conversation, but she was not feeling up to it today.

The request for video chat was completely unexpected. Startled, Fey accepted the call and Leandriel appeared on a virtual screen. His handsome features were . . . uneasy, she was surprised to see. In contrast, Magic sat on his shoulder with cheerful unconcern, watching his current owner with curiosity. "Is something the matter?" she asked.

"Fey, I—" Leandriel made an agitated movement before turning back to lock gazes with Fey. "I want to apologize for my rudeness during our last conversation."

Fey gave a puzzled frown. "What are you talking about?" He may have been slightly distant during that conversation, but still impeccably polite, and not in a cold way, either.

"I . . . I was in a bit of a mood last night, and ended up being rather terse. I am sorry." Sincerity beamed from Leandriel's blue eyes.

Despite her mood, Fey could not help but smile at such a classically "Leandriel" speech. "You have nothing to apologize for," she reassured the angel.

Leandriel scrutinized her expression before asking, "Are you sure? You sounded . . . upset today."

Fey was surprised; she thought that she had been able to hold a reasonably normal conversation. "How could you tell that through PM?" she asked.

Leandriel paused to consider the question before answering. "You just sounded less cheerful. Hmm . . . You were perhaps using fewer exclamation marks than normal."

Fey huffed in amusement. "Do I really use that many exclamation marks?"

"The ideal number," Leandriel reassured her solemnly, a warm smile in his eyes.

sigh *He really is irresistible.* Fey really could not blame herself for her feelings. Moving to close the conversation, she admitted, "I'm in a bit of a mood tonight, but I'm not mad at you at all."

Leandriel's posture relaxed slightly. "Is it something I can help you with?"

Fey smiled, though her dominant emotion was sadness. "No. Something didn't work out, but there's nothing to be done about it."

"'Nothing to be done'," Leandriel echoed with a crooked smile. "That is actually what made me stop worrying and escape my own mood last night."

"What were you worrying about?" Fey asked curiously.

"Someone called me boring," Leandriel admitted wryly.

Fey could not quite believe that someone would label Leandriel as "boring," or that he would be bothered by such a blatantly false accusation. "You're perfect," she stated.

Leandriel was speechless. Fey's words were not said in the shy tone of someone confessing her feelings, in effect, a qualified

"You're perfect to me." No, her tone was as matter-of-fact as if she were saying *The sky is blue.* As if the matter of his perfection were an obvious truth, and anyone who disagreed was simply incorrect. "Ahm, thank you," he managed.

Fey grinned at his flustered reaction. "No problem."

Leandriel scrambled to find a conversational thread. "So, we're good?" He said the contraction like the foreign, borrowed phrase it was to him.

"We're *perfect*," Fey confirmed, continuing to tease.

"Excellent. I hope you find yourself in a better mood soon."

Fey's amusement faded, that sad smile resurfacing. Before he could find another comment to distract her, she said, "Me too. I'll feel better in a few days. Talk to you later."

"Goodbye," Leandriel bade, and the virtual screen winked out.

"So, would you say that went well?" he asked Magic, who was his resident expert on Fey.

The mushroom looked concerned. "Fey-Fey is sad."

"Yes. I wonder why." *Something didn't work out* was what she had said. That was vague enough to apply to almost anything. He felt frustrated that he could not help her, especially when she had used two simple words to destroy the last of the self-doubt lingering in his mind.

You're perfect.

"I should have said it in return," Leandriel muttered. Shaking his head at Magic's questioning sound, he lifted into the air, travelling to the next testing area.

━◦○◇○◦━

Fey was unclear on what exactly would happen when she combined her rogue and warrior tokens, so she decided to prepare as if she were going on a long, dangerous trip. She replenished her supply of travel food and deposited extraneous items at the bank.

While on her errands, Amethyst began squeaking excitedly and pointing toward the slime territories.

"King Slime again? Aren't you tired of eating the same thing over and over?" Fey asked.

Amethyst squeaked. ("No.")

Fey shrugged and headed in the indicated direction.

As before, the giant King Slime wreaked havoc upon the newbies training in the slime territories. Fey paused to make sense of the chaos. Idly, she wondered how many batches of healing salve one could make with a King Slime.

Or, we could find out. Fey decided that doing something utterly ridiculous, like dragging a live King Slime several kilometres through the forest to Kallara's, was exactly what she needed to feel better. Striding out into the open, Fey dodged running players and ended up in front of the boss monster. When it brought its bubble whipping down toward her, she reached up to intercept.

"Oww," she winced as the strike bruised her forearm even through her armguard. The pain did not prevent her from grabbing the King Slime's bubble-arm slightly below the bubble. "Gotcha," she said with satisfaction. Closing her other hand around the ropelike limb, she began to pull—

Fey went airborne as the King Slime swung its bubble in the other direction. It could not use its limb as if she weighed nothing, but it could definitely lift her off her feet. "A little help here," she said to her pets as she was dragged along.

A squeaked conversation and then the Feypets went into action. Amethyst retrieved Fey's rope from her backpack and passed it to Shadow, who tied it to the King Slime's bubble. Grasping the free end, the gloom jumped onto Boris and fastened it securely to the iron boar's saddle.

Fey let go as Boris backed up until the rope went taut, immobilizing the King Slime. It squeaked angrily and hopped toward the boar to give itself slack. Boris turned and began trotting back to town, chased by an angry boss. Fey laughed and followed. *I'm baaack.*

Fey's plan showed itself to be incomplete when she actually arrived in the Moonwood. "Drag it in a big circle!" she said hastily when Boris made as if to stop in front of Kallara's shop. Players scrambled out of the way of both King Slime and boar as Boris obeyed; each of them was easily of a weight that could crush bone.

Kallara came outside at the commotion, immediately spotting Fey and raising an eyebrow. "What is the meaning of this?"

"Does King Slime make better healing salve?" Fey asked impishly.

Kallara smiled; as usual, the expression looked slightly scary. "As a matter of fact, it does." Turning toward the King Slime, she cast "Deep Sleep."

The King Slime went instantly unconscious, flattening against the ground, bubble-arm flopping.

"Bring it inside." Without a glance at the gawping crowd, Kallara disappeared back into her tree-shop.

It took quite a bit of shoving to force the King Slime through the entrance archway. Fey and her pets had gotten it about halfway through when Kallara absent-mindedly sang a note and the archway abruptly widened, creating a graceless pileup of elf, pets, and King Slime.

Fey scowled and picked herself up.

Kallara was busy rummaging amongst the cupboards for her largest containers, singing other notes to open the storage areas she rarely used. "You can start filling the containers with slime," she ordered.

Fey picked up the first pot and used Bleed to create a small gash in the King Slime's membrane. Whenever she needed to switch containers, she made Obsidian seal the gash with his shadowy body.

(*cough* Please ignore the fact that the King Slime is still alive, making this scene immeasurably creepy.)

It turned out that one King Slime could make twenty extra-large batches of healing salve. Kallara promised that Fey could have a pot of it when it was done brewing. Amethyst was happy because she was able to eat the bubble membrane after Kallara collected its contents. Best of all, Fey exited the healer's abode in a much lighter mood.

Deciding it was best to take advantage of the temporary reprieve in mopey-ness, Fey travelled far enough away from town to gain some privacy, then pulled out her rogue and warrior tokens. "Ready?" she asked her pets.

Affirmative sounds, and she pressed the tokens together.

The small metal discs fused with a flash of silver light. The engravings changed, turning into a garrote on one side and a poison symbol on the other. Floating into the air, the assassin token began to rotate until it blurred. The air began to warp.

Fey examined the transdimensional gateway that appeared. Mist on the other side prevented her from seeing exactly where she would be going. "Let's do this."

Deciding it would be best if they all passed through together, Fey sat on Boris and collected all the pets together. Boris calmly walked into the unknown.

CHAPTER 25
CREATIVE KILLING

Boris's hooves clicked against mist-shrouded stone. The portal disappeared as he passed through it, leaving Fey and her pets somewhere in a low mountain range.

Fey surveyed her surroundings. The stone-cobbled path before her led up one of the small mountains, surrounded by lush vegetation that took advantage of the humid air. The mist shrouded the sun enough to cool the air, tinge the area grey, and muffle sound, creating an atmosphere of hushed serenity. The overall effect would not be out of place in a movie where the protagonist was undergoing "secret training at a mountain retreat."

Near the top of the mountain was a compound built of the same plain, grey stone as the walkway that led up to it. She could only see the outer wall, but it looked austere enough to qualify for the word "monastery."

Since there was no other visible human-made structure in sight, Fey got off Boris's back and began walking toward it. The ascent was an easy climb of half an hour, the path never rough or particularly steep.

The outer wall had a set of double doors three times Fey's height. One leaf was open wide enough for several people to walk in side by side, so Fey slipped in and found herself in a square courtyard of packed dirt.

A low, one-storey building formed three sides of the square, again built of grey stone. The mountain rose steeply up just beyond the building's walls, giving the impression that the compound was dug into the mountainside. Not a single person could be seen or heard, but the meticulous tidiness of the area told Fey that this dwelling-place was not deserted.

The door in the centre of the building slid open along its grooves. Fey caught her first glimpse of a werebeast.

Werebeasts in *Fantasia* were designed with a mix of realism and attractiveness in mind. They were not the cute, cat-eared-but-otherwise-human girls often depicted in anime, nor the grotesque, distorted creatures seen in horror movies. (The author can only assume that's what creatures in horror movies look like, as she's too wimpy to actually watch them.) Rather, the humanoid base shape was blended harmoniously with animal traits that did not detract from its visual appeal.

The NPC before Fey was some kind of werecat without spots or stripes; based on the sand-coloured fur and natural black eyeliner, she was guessing cougar.[39] His pointed, furry ears were farther up his skull than where human ears were located, though not as far forward as where people wore decorative animal-ear headbands. Other than his scalp, which had normal hair, his skin was covered in fur short enough that it looked like bare skin from a distance. Large amber eyes tilted up attractively at the outer corners, their vertically slit pupils intensifying the inhuman impression he gave off. Dressed in a dark leather outfit that did nothing to disguise a leanly muscled physique, the NPC looked dangerous and exotically handsome, everything combining to reinforce the image of a badass assassin . . . Except for the tail. Fey resolutely kept her eyes away from the long, fluffy tail that twitched semi-independently of its owner's will, knowing that she would begin to giggle helplessly the moment she paid it any attention.

As the system informed her that this was Rreowar (pronounced "rawrwar," hahaha), the assassin trainer, he spoke, revealing the pointed canines of a carnivore. "So. Warrior and rogue, why are you here?"

"To become an assassin," Fey answered.

"And what is an assassin?" he challenged.

"A killer," she stated simply.

Rreowar gave her a look of approval that vanished into a serious expression. "Indeed. If you choose this path, you will learn nothing else. You will never lead troops in battle, or gain skills to solve dungeon puzzles. Every skill will be dedicated to killing faster and more efficiently. You will walk alone in the shadows. If this is not what you want, there is still time to choose a different sub-class."

Honestly, the whole deal sounded delightful to Fey. *Teamwork is overrated.* "I am committed."

"Prove yourself, then. To be an assassin is to kill in countless ways. Show your aptitude by slaying ten monsters your level or higher with different methods. You must complete this task alone; not even your pets may help. You may return to your original location or hunt the monsters in these mountains. Shadow bless you." With that, Rreowar turned and disappeared back into the building.

(Fey managed to turn her amusement at the sight of his tail into a quiet exhale.)

"So, mountains or forest?" Fey asked her pets (#Poll).

She received a chorus of squeaks with mixed opinions, and chuckled. "'Kay, I'll just decide, then. Back to the forest." Since she had to complete her quest without her pets' help, she thought it would be safer to send them off to train independently in a familiar territory. (Is it ever really safe to send your pets off unsupervised? Oh well, plot armour and all that.)

Fey pulled out the assassin token, which had disappeared into the same un-lose-able, manifest-at-will space as her teleportation key after use. Flipping it into the air opened a portal back to the same spot in the Elvenwood that she had left the hour before.

Stepping through, Fey made her way to the deeper monster territories that matched her level of 33 and began to experiment.

The first monster was poisoned to death. Fey confirmed her guess that using Amethyst to poison her weapons did not count as outside help. Using different poisons, however, still only counted as a single method of killing. With that, Fey sent her pets off to train (/explore/create general mayhem) without her and began brainstorming creative ways of killing things.

I wonder if this is what screenwriters for horror movies feel like, Fey reflected as she strangled a hapless monster to death. (We could probably retitle this story as *101 Uses for Rope*.) It rather creeped her out that her brain could conjure up so many weird ways to kill things. As the quest progressed, the methods only became more bizarre. (In order to maintain this story's family-friendly rating, the rest of the methods will be left to the reader's imagination.)

In the end, Fey judged that this quest was actually easier than the one she had to complete to become a rogue. She killed over fifty monsters trying to find methods different enough to contribute to quest progress. Some of those methods were quite time-consuming, so by the time the quest bar read *10/10*, night had fallen and Fey was ready for a break.

Fey took the trail leading back to town and called her pets with the signal she had pre-arranged. Using her telepathy stone, she emitted a very high-frequency sound. Although easily audible to most people under the age of thirty,[40] it was the kind of droning background noise commonly produced by electronics that people had learned to ignore from a young age. The sound was more conspicuous in an untamed forest, but Fey's hope was that she could broadcast it loudly enough to summon her pets without attracting too much outside attention.

As far as she could tell, it worked. Nothing attacked her, no players came to investigate, and Boris joined her in walking back to the Moonwood. (#Success) As per their new habit, the smaller Feypets hitched a ride on his back. In the nighttime conditions, the glooms were almost invisible against the boar's dark bristles, while Amethyst stood out with a faint, purple glow.

Wait a minute . . . There were actually two glowing objects. Her eyes had been momentarily fooled because they were close together and the second glow was a pale blue that almost blended into Amethyst's purple.

Fey stopped walking and Boris halted beside her with his extra passenger. "Where did this guy come from?" she demanded. She was referring to the second slime blinking (cutely) up at her from beside Amethyst.

Amethyst squeaked. ("It just started following me around. I think it's the crown.") She tapped her trophy from the King Slime with her bubble for emphasis.

Inkblot also chimed in. ("It was fan-sliming pretty hard, so we decided to bring it along.")

Amused and exasperated, Fey bowed to the inevitable and picked up the new slime.

<Fey has tamed the slime!>

<Fey receives a pet!>

<Fey has attained level 3 Slime Mastery! (details in Bestiary)>

<Please select a name for your pet: ___>

"Aquamarine," Fey decided, keeping to her gemstone theme.

<Name confirmed>

<Aquamarine, level 1 slime>

<HP: 5/5, MP: 5/5>

<Exp: 0/10>

<No skills>

"Gah, not again," Fey grumbled. Slimes were really too fragile at level 1. She hurried back to the Moonwood before something could accidentally kill her new pet.

Back in the village, Fey headed to Tallen's tavern for a meal. She usually ate one meal a day there, relying on travel food at other times in order to save trips back and forth from the monster territories. The "VIP table" was still on the second floor, so she made her way there without waiting to be seated. Ever since the incident of Boris nearly being shot, she had taken to bringing the (massive) boar indoors with her; Tallen had considerately shortened one of the table's long benches to give Boris somewhere to sit. (This may or may not have to do with the fact that more people paid to sit at the VIP table when there was something interesting already there, such as a six-Fey iron boar.)

Shortly after Fey took a seat, Todd appeared. He held an order pad, but not with the posture of someone preparing to write on it. "Hi, Miss Fey. Are you eating?"

"Yes, please," Fey answered. She did not bother specifying her meal preferences, as she preferred to be delightfully surprised by Tallen's mind-reading ability and culinary skill.

"Just a minute." Todd disappeared downstairs and returned with a platter.

". . . Sushi?" Fey questioned, recognizing the distinct cylindrical shapes of the seaweed-wrapped rice rolls. "Where did you get fish from?"

"We didn't," Todd answered. "These are all sweet potato rolls."

Fey sighed dreamily. "Tell your dad he's literally the best." As much as she liked potato-based foods, sweet potato was another three levels up in deliciousness. She picked up the chopsticks that came with the platter and lifted a maki roll to admire before popping it into her mouth.

Todd chuckled. "You say that every time."

"Because it's true," Fey mumbled through her food, covering her mouth with her hand while she spoke.

Amethyst hopped onto the table to inspect the food. As if copying an idolized elder sister, Aquamarine did the same. Though the slimes were largely the same in size and appearance, Amethyst was noticeably stronger and more intelligent just from watching her actions.

"Did you get a new pet, Miss Fey?" asked Todd.

"Yeah, I guess." Fey's response lacked enthusiasm. She really did not need another slime, and training it up from level 1 would be a hassle. Suddenly, an idea occurred to her and she perked up. "Hey, Todd, want a pet?"

"What kind of pet?"

"This one." Fey grabbed Aquamarine and dumped it into Todd's startled hands.

Boy and slime examined each other. "It's kinda cute," Todd said doubtfully, clearly concerned with maintaining a manly image.

"Oh no, slimes are super fierce once you train them up," Fey assured him. "Just look at Amethyst here." Pulling out one of her throwing stars, she jabbed the triple-membraned slime with one of its sharpened points. Amethyst ignored the attack and ate one of Fey's pieces of sushi. "I'd show you how strong her attacks are, but Tallen would yell at me for damaging the tavern," Fey continued.

Todd looked impressed at Amethyst's durability. "Okay. How much are you selling it for?"

"Oh, it's a gift," said Fey. She was starting to feel guilty about all the free meals she was eating (despite the fact that Tallen usually managed to profit from her presence in one way or another) and thought this would be a good way to give something in return.

"Really? Thanks, Miss Fey."

<Pet ownership transferred.[41]>

"What should I name it?" Todd asked.

"Whatever you want," Fey said with a verbal shrug. "Aquamarine" was really too much of a mouthful to be a good name, though it nicely matched the slime's colour.

Todd spent a while making various contemplative expressions. "I'll go ask my dad."

Thus began a weeklong event to suggest names for the tavern's new "official mascot." To enter a suggestion cost only 5g.

CHAPTER 26
CHOICES

Fey returned to the assassin trainer to turn in her quest. Climbing a mountain at night was generally a foolhardy thing to do, but the wide, paved path allowed her to reach her destination with her ankles intact.

The compound was unlit as Fey entered the courtyard. Between the moonlight and her elven night vision, she could see, but the atmosphere was still unsettling.

"So you've returned."

Fey jumped and turned to where Rreowar stood within conversational distance on the right. *Sneaky bastard.* "Yeah."

"Completed within a day. You show promise. I will begin to teach you the assassin's arts."

Before Fey could worry too much about what would have happened if she had taken longer to complete the quest, the system notice popped up.

<Quest complete!>

<Fey gains 5000 experience. Amethyst gains 2500 experience. Boris gains 2500 experience. Onyx gains 2500

experience. Inkblot gains 2500 experience. Ebony gains 2500 experience. Midnight gains 2500 experience. Shadow gains 2500 experience. Obsidian gains 2500 experience.>

<Fey has advanced to the assassin sub-class!>

"The first ability you must learn," Rreowar continued, "is to identify the weaknesses in your targets. Assassins do not fight 'fairly.'" A verbal sneer at the concept. "Leave that nonsense to knights and their ilk. No, always strike to inflict maximum damage and gain the upper hand in combat. For this purpose, I grant you Critical Sight."

Red spots appeared in Fey's peripheral vision. Turning to look, she saw that they appeared to highlight the vulnerable areas on her pets' bodies, such as eyes and necks.

"Right now, your Sight only serves to show the most obvious of weak points," Rreowar explained. "As you grow as an assassin, it will reveal more subtle findings."

Fey looked back at Rreowar. Her Critical Sight did not show any red areas on his body.

Catching her glance, the assassin trainer smiled in amusement, revealing his long canines. "You will need much deeper Sight to find weakness in me."

Fey nodded in vigorous agreement, trying to convey her absolute lack of contemplation about how to attack the werecougar assassin. There were more painless (though not necessarily faster) ways to commit suicide.

Rreowar huffed in amusement, the sound distinctly catlike. "Welcome to the path of shadows and blood. Return here when you are ready for your next stage of training." The spot where he stood darkened, and when the lighting returned to normal, he was gone.

". . . Bye," Fey said to the empty spot. She was not much of one for extended greetings and farewells, but she thought Rreowar and R'shelle took things to the opposite extreme.

Shaking her head, Fey first figured out how to untarget her pets from Critical Sight, then headed back to the Elvenwood to test out her new ability.

◊◊◊

"Hai!" Arwyn executed a 540-degree jumping roundhouse kick and then stood panting in front of the target, posture slouched in fatigue.

Her partner for the day, a cheerful, middle-aged first-dan black belt, slapped his free hand against the target he held to create a loud booming sound. "Come on, five more!"

Arwyn did not waste breath replying, shuffling back to the starting position, two paces back from the target. Her state of exhaustion was long past pain and well into numbness. All of her concentration was focused down to drawing enough breath to stay conscious and forcing her muscles to obey her commands.

Staring at the target, she locked its location in her mind's eye and set her fighting stance. A deep breath. Her posture straightened for a fraction of a second— Launch.

"Hai!" Arwyn's foot slapped across the centre of the target with impressive speed, and then she was back to panting, hands on her knees this time, appearing far too frail and tired to have accomplished the kick.

"Four more!"

It took a full two seconds after her mental command for her muscles to begin moving back toward the starting position.

Ninety minutes later, Arwyn was flopped on her couch, trying to eat lunch despite the fact that she could barely feel her limbs. Her phone chimed. It was within arm's reach, so Arwyn checked the message.

Leah: Get online and choose between the options for your transformation sequence

It took Arwyn a few seconds to remember what her friend was referring to. Normally, curiosity would have her booting up her laptop immediately to see what Leah had come up with, but in her current condition, the five metres between her couch and her desk was an insurmountable distance.

She texted back:

Arwyn: The laptop is too far away. I'm probably going to pass out on the couch and nap for two hours.

Leah: Wimp.

Leah: I sent everything over chat

Leah: Let me know by the end of today

Arwyn: k

Arwyn finished her lunch and considered her options. She had been (mostly) joking about napping on the couch, but as her adrenaline level fell and took her ability to move with it, the idea rose in merit. Snagging the blanket folded on the back of the couch, Arwyn surrendered to gravity and lay down.

Physically exhausted but not really sleepy, Arwyn drifted, her thoughts wandering.

Wonder what Leah came up with. Hope it's not too crazy.

Figures that we have a crazy class in tae kwon do the one day a year I exercise outside of class.

Critical Sight is a really useful ability. I just hit the red spots and the monster dies. Fey had managed to level up twice in the few hours left before logging off.

Inevitably, thoughts of Leandriel drifted in.

(More sappy, mopey stuff. Skip to the next parentheses if you're not into this kind of thing.)

Never thought I'd fall for someone who apologized so much. A small, involuntary smile turned up the corners of Arwyn's mouth. In her experience, having someone apologize too frequently generally forced her into the dominant position as the expert or manager, something not conducive to forming a relationship of equals. *It works for him because he's so perfect.*

She sighed and snuggled deeper under the blanket.

Arwyn honestly had no idea how long it would take to get over the angel. There was not a single trait about him that she disliked and could focus on, and talking to him every game night made distance impossible.

Dryly, she thought, *I suppose I could just keep liking him until somebody better comes along, i.e. forever.* Other than the melancholy moods, her feelings did not impact her daily functioning. She supposed they could theoretically affect her hypothetical dating life, but she was so determinedly anti-people that worrying about that possibility seemed unnecessary.

Arwyn shrugged mentally. She would either get over her feelings or not, and did not think anything she could consciously do would change the outcome. Until then, she knew that thoughts of Leandriel would pop into her head at irregular intervals. The image of his smile accompanied her as she drifted into a dreamless sleep.

(Moping over. On to the actual story.)

Contrary to her earlier claim in her text, Arwyn's nap lasted only for one hour. However, if one included the time spent lazing on the couch before and after the nap, the total came closer to two hours.

Eventually, Arwyn booted up her laptop and looked at the files Leah had sent over. There were four songs and four backgrounds.

Arwyn put on her headphones and listened to the songs first. All four were high-energy electronic music without lyrics, but within that category, they were quite different.

The first song was an ultra-fast tune with a catchy, sugary-sweet melody that reminded Arwyn of her favourite J-pop[42] songs to play on *Dance Dance Revolution*, the ones that were too fast to process consciously (and hilarious to watch beginners try).

The second song had more of a rock influence, with the powerful sounds of electric guitars and drum sets. Arwyn did not think it exactly fit her personality, but she could see how it would help create the image of "badass assassin."

The third song had an otherworldly quality created by wordless female vocals over synthesizer notes and a bass drum. Arwyn quite liked it, and thought she would choose it—until she heard the fourth song.

Electric violin was quite possibly Arwyn's favourite sound in the world. She loved its power and sweetness, its range and resonance. The fourth song featured one such instrument over an irresistibly catchy, syncopated beat. "We have a winner," she murmured to herself. Arwyn made a mental note to look up the artist later and download all their music.

Music chosen, Arwyn turned to the background options. She did not recognize the file extensions displayed; the only reason she knew they were backgrounds was because they were named "Background 1—Void," "Background 2—Dark Flame," "Background 3—Starscape," and "Background 4—Night Clouds." Fortunately, her computer knew what to do and ran the correct program when she selected the first file.

"Whoa." Arwyn was impressed. The background was not a single still image but rather a three-dimensional space that she could rotate and move. She could see why it was called "Void." It consisted of utter darkness that seemed to stretch into infinity, with only the faintest trace of sourceless light to distinguish space. That space was slightly warped in a way that implied a centre was pulling everything toward it.

Arwyn found that she could toggle a button to insert the image of her avatar. Dragging it around the background, she saw that the spatial distortion became more pronounced close to the middle of the area, though there was no visible object causing the effect. *This is probably the closest I'll ever get to seeing myself sucked into a black hole.*

After a few more minutes of exploring, Arwyn opened the second background.

". . . Really, Leah?" was all she could say. The "Dark Flame" area consisted of an endless floor of black marble overlaid with lines of dark fire depicting intricate runes and geometric patterns. In the centre of the pattern was a ring of fire containing what looked like a sacrificial altar. Arwyn could not decide whether it looked more like a fantasy hell or the set of a fancy BDSM movie. (Why not both?)

Not wanting Leah to accuse her of not giving the option a fair chance, Arwyn made a face and inserted her avatar into the set. It appeared right next to the altar.

"Nope, nope, nope. Nope."

Chance given and failed, Arwyn opened the third background.

The "Starscape" background appeared exactly as its name suggested, an endless sky dotted with twinkling stars. Arwyn's avatar was swallowed by the vastness of outer space and yet looked oddly at home amongst the stars. *It's because I'm really an alien*, she (half-)joked to herself.

Keeping "Starscape" in mind as a strong contender, Arwyn opened the fourth background. It came with an annotation from Leah: "For when you have wings."

Arwyn could see the potential. "Night Clouds" was set above the cloud line on the night of a full moon. Above, the air was utterly clear, the stars so close they looked almost reachable. Below, the thick carpet of clouds was painted silver by moonlight. Her current avatar looked utterly out of place so far off the ground, but it would be a spectacular setting for an avariel to swoop and dive.

Arwyn sighed, thinking about how long it would take to earn her wings. The fifteen remaining levels until level 50 would take longer than the thirty-five she had already gained. *Friggin' exponential curves.*

Arwyn messaged Leah with her choices, noticing that her friend had changed her display name.

ArwynTheElf: The song with the electric violin and Starscape. Definitely Night Clouds once I can fly

Leah-SirenaTheMermaid: I thought you'd go with those.

ArwynTheElf: Could you add a moon to Starscape? Also, what the [bleep] was up with Dark Flame? Also, are you making fun of my display name?

Leah-SirenaTheMermaid: "Could I" add a moon. What a silly question. Dark Flame is totally a cool background. No, I'm following the practice of "flattery through imitation."

ArwynTheElf: There was a SACRIFICIAL ALTAR

Leah-SirenaTheMermaid: It's just an altar unless you kill something on it.

ArwynTheElf: . . . What exactly were you planning?

Leah-SirenaTheMermaid: *innocent* Nothing.

ArwynTheElf: Innocent people don't use *innocent*

Leah-SirenaTheMermaid: Never mind that. I need to go work on the choreography. I'll have to redo everything when you get wings.

ArwynTheElf: I'd apologize for the trouble except that you're the one who wanted to do this in the first place. Also, don't put anything in that I wouldn't do.

Leah-SirenaTheMermaid: Muahahahaha

ArwynTheElf: Oh boy.

Leah-SirenaTheMermaid: Kekekekeke

ArwynTheElf: Now you're just being creepy

Leah-SirenaTheMermaid: Heeheehee

Arwyn sighed and let her friend be. After all, she did not actually have to use the transformation sequence.

A(n evil) thought occurred to her that she seized with enthusiasm.

ArwynTheElf: Hey, did you consider making a transformation sequence for Blade?

Leah-SirenaTheMermaid: ZOMG THAT IS SUCH A BRILLIANT IDEA I LOVE YOU

ArwynTheElf: ♥

Leah-SirenaTheMermaid: *sigh* I don't think it would be possible for me to log on with his account, though.

ArwynTheElf: You can make it in game as well, right? Might as well put those carriage rides to use

Leah-SirenaTheMermaid: I was going to meditate and improve my Prayer bar, but this is much more important.

ArwynTheElf: Lemme know if you need help convincing him

Leah-SirenaTheMermaid: I'm sure he'll say yes if I ask really nicely

ArwynTheElf: Looking forward to it

There. Arwyn was satisfied that the majority of her friend's exuberant tendencies would now be channelled toward someone else. (Poor Blade. Mercilessly thrown under the bus.)

CHAPTER 27
RAGE

"Did you miss me?" Sirena asked as she swept dramatically forward in a swirl of mage robes and engulfed Fey in a hug. (#Glom)

Fey bore her friend's weight stoically. "Not really," she answered (cruelly). She had spent Sunday night productively training as an assassin, reaching level 38 and improving Critical Sight to level 5, the point at which she began to see blue spots indicating heavily armoured areas. As part of her developing fighting style, Isolate had reached level 6. If Sirena and Blade had not arrived in the Moonwood for another day, Fey could have easily spent another day training without getting bored.

Sirena gasped in indignation and withdrew (which was the reaction Fey was going for). "I rushed day and night without rest to hasten our reunion, and this is how you treat me?" she lamented, clearly in a theatrical mood.

"I seem to recall an ice cream break or two," Fey commented dryly.

Blade caught up to Sirena at a much slower pace. This was likely due to the fact that he was weighed down by a large water tank strapped to his back, which contained the now-adult Squishy. The jellyfish's long, trailing tentacles were somewhat cramped, even within the spacious tank. Firefly perched on one of the warrior's already overburdened shoulders, resolutely ignoring the affront to her owner's dignity.

Fey raised an eyebrow at the burdensome arrangement. "Packhorse?" she asked cryptically, aware that Blade could hear her.

Sirena understood the implied question ("You're using him as a packhorse *and* a meatshield?") and answered in an equally abbreviated fashion. "Multipurpose," she said cheerfully.

Blade briefly considered attempting to figure out what his party members were talking about, but decided he was too tired to make the effort (especially when he'd just get talked into confusing circles, anyway), and instead let the water tank slide to the ground. "I'm not carrying this around while we're hiking all over the forest," he said firmly (as if afraid he'd be overruled).

Sirena pouted (and Blade's fear of being overruled grew). "How am I supposed to train it if we leave it behind?"

"Have you been training Squishy at all?" Fey asked in a faintly disapproving tone. (Blade was uncertain as to what this did to his chances.)

"No," said Sirena sulkily. "Why'd you saddle me with such a use—"

Fey jumped forward and grabbed Sirena's arm, startling the mermaid into silence. "Don't talk like that," Fey hissed. "No wonder it hasn't evolved into anything more suited to land." She frowned disapprovingly and crossed her arms. "You're a bad owner," she accused.

"Am not!" Sirena disputed. "I got it a nice tank, didn't I?"

From Fey's shoulder, Amethyst squeaked derisively at such a low standard of pet care, earning a glare from Sirena.

"Give Squishy back," Fey demanded. "I'll take care of it myself."

Faced with an opportunity to get rid of her somewhat unwanted pet, Sirena paradoxically began defending it. "No! Hmph." She seized the tank—it was far too heavy for her mage strength to lift—and began dragging it toward the magic shop (at a pace rather too slow for a dramatic exit).

Blade stared after Sirena uncertainly. (Looks like he's not going to have to lug the tank around.) "Should we follow her?" he asked Fey. He was not quite sure what to call the interaction he had just witnessed. Not a "fight"; there was not enough anger for that. "Disagreement" was closer, but still not on the mark. The closest he could come to describing it was a mix of "parent tricking you into doing something good for you" and "best friend egging you into doing something stupid," but even that was inexact.

"No," Fey answered complacently. (She'd probably describe it as "helping her friend along the path to self-actualization" if she stopped to think about it, which she didn't.) "You hungry?" She headed off toward the tavern without waiting for an answer.

"Sure," Blade agreed (belatedly), falling into step beside the elf with a last glance at Sirena (who still hadn't made it all the way to the magic shop, hahaha).

Todd appeared beside Fey as she made her way to the usual table on the second floor. On his shoulder was his newly named pet slime, who had been dubbed Terry[43] in a mash-up of suggestions. The name did not suit the blue slime particularly well, but Terry did not seem to mind. "Good afternoon, Miss Fey," Todd greeted in his adorably formal manner. "Party of two today?"

"Yup," Fey answered casually. "Is it okay if he sits at the VIP table?"

"You and your guests are always welcome." Turning to Blade, Todd asked, "Would you like to see a menu, sir?"

"Yeah, thanks." Blade, having been out of the Moonwood for a while, had forgotten about the strangely symbiotic relationship between Fey and the tavern, so after Todd had disappeared downstairs, he asked, "Why are you a VIP again?"

"I collected a lot of wood for them." The memory triggered a moping spell about Leandriel, and Fey exhaled in a long, long sigh. (*siiiiiiiiiiiiigh*)

"Er, is everything okay?" Blade asked.

Fey sighed again, this time because there was something so obviously wrong with her that even Blade could tell. "*Emotions*," she said disgustedly, which concurrently accomplished the three tasks of expressing her present sentiments, answering Blade's question, and confusing Blade with an insufficient amount of information. Obscurely comforted when Blade became so predictably and reliably perplexed, Fey was overcome by a wave of affection (eew, more emotions) and reached over to pat him on the head. "You're a good guy," she praised him (90 percent serious, 10 percent to discomfit him).

Blade shifted uncomfortably at the sincere compliment. "Wow, you must be really off today," he joked in order to change the mood; the attempt at humour fell flat (*splat*) because his observation was so precisely on the mark.

Acting as if she had been shot (by a tranquilizer dart), Fey let her head fall onto the table with a dull *thunk*. From her shoulder, Amethyst slid smoothly onto the table. Hopping over her owner's head, the slime went to hang out with the rest of the Feypets. By now, they were all used to their owner's periodic mopey moods and showed no concern at their owner's behaviour. (Incidentally, in the Squeak language, "mopey" and "floppy" are the same word, so falling onto the table was well within expectations.)

"Er." Blade stared at the floppy Fey with the same sense of panic as if he had just broken an expensive piece of technology (after the warranty had expired). He was used to abrupt shifts in topic and tone from the elf, but the underlying calm he had always felt from her was now fractured and he did not know what to do.

A menu waving from knee level distracted Blade from the situation. He picked it up to reveal Terry the slime, who had returned sans owner (#FrenchVocabulary). "Thanks," he told it.

Terry squeaked and remained in place.

"He's waiting for your order," Fey interpreted, voice somewhat distorted by the table surface.

"Oh." Blade quickly skimmed the menu and said, "I'll have a burger and a beer."

Terry squeaked again, took the menu back, and hopped downstairs.

By this time, Fey's face was growing unhappy at being pressed against a hard surface, so she tucked her arms under her head, looking as if she might decide to take a nap.

". . . So, what do you want to do this afternoon?" Blade asked.

"Dunno. Kill things, I guess," Fey answered morosely, staring at the wood grain of the table.

". . . Right."

Blade was all out of conversational topics, so it was a relief when Todd arrived with their food.

The boy deftly avoided Fey's head and long hair as he placed their plates on the table. From his shoulder, Terry used his bubble-arm to lower Blade's beer with the precision of a helicopter drop. (Is it okay for a minor to serve alcohol?)

Fey's table manners (belatedly) made her sit up properly. "Thanks, Todd."

Todd pointed to her plate. "Dad made that to cheer you up."

Next to Fey's ideal burger—thin patty, sautéed mushrooms and onions (#MoreFrench), mayonnaise, and ketchup—was a cute custard bun decorated with a chocolate syrup smiley face and mouse ears.

Fey inhaled through her nose in a way that would qualify as a sniffle. Both Todd and Blade were alarmed to see her make an expression that indicated she might cry.

"Thanks, Todd," she said with a catch in her voice. She drew the boy into a very uncharacteristic hug before letting him escape and picking up her mouse-bun with a sentimental expression. Putting it down, she began to eat her burger with periodic glances at the bread, still wearing a very un-Fey-like, soft expression.

Blade had progressed from surprise to alarm at Fey's state of mind. Moping was one thing, but the fact that she was expressing sentimentality without even a hint of ironic humour was simply out of character.

Searching for an explanation, Blade's mind unfortunately hit upon a hypothesis guaranteed to get him into trouble. It also failed to foresee the danger in speaking it out loud.

He considered. Circumstantial evidence seemed to support the hypothesis: it had been approximately three weeks since he had met Fey, and her behaviour had been predictably unpredictable until now.

"Are you . . ." he ventured.

(Danger! Abort, abort!)

"Am I what?" Fey said, looking up from her mouse-bun.

(Last chance! Abort!)

"Like, getting PMS?"[44]

(. . .)

A deafening silence grew amidst the chatter in the busy tavern, which gave Blade's mind the time to process Fey's changing facial expressions without distraction. Blank surprise. Disbelief. Fury that went from infernally hot to blisteringly cold.

Fey opened her mouth to answer. She closed it again. Picking up her mouse-bun, she very precisely and deliberately bit it in half. Blade's sense of impending doom grew exponentially by the second.

Fey's moping mood had been seared out of existence, burned away like a wart treated with liquid nitrogen. The competing desires to verbally dismember Blade, physically dismember Blade, and cut all ties to Blade held her paralyzed on a knife edge of rage. The like/dislike graph of her time with Blade plunged so far into the negatives that it had to change to a logarithmic scale.[45] If there was one thing that she hated more than having her intelligence questioned, it would be the implication that her emotions were mere artefacts of a monthly hormone cycle rather than legitimate feelings born of a rational human mind.

As a way to snap her out of her mood, nothing could have been more effective. (As a way to continued survival, well . . .)

Eventually, cold logic prevailed. Obviously, the thing to do would be to make Blade's life unremittingly miserable for a month and show that her emotions were not prone to fluctuation. Banking the fury (i.e., making sure it wouldn't burn out for a good, long time), she finished the remains of her mouse-bun and went back to her main meal.

<Rage has reached level 3!>

<Rage has reached level 4!>

<Rage has reached level 5!>

<Rage has reached level 6!>

Fey blinked in surprise at the system notifications. She had not used Rage since the day she had formed the ability (Chapter 8 in volume 1) because of the penalty to accuracy. At level 6, it now boosted attack by 15 percent with only a 10 percent loss of accuracy. This unexpected gain almost restored her to a pleasant mood, though a glance at Blade kept the rage at a steady burn in the back of her mind.

Blade sat very still, as if in a room full of motion-activated explosives. Appetite gone, he waited for Fey to say something, growing only more apprehensive as seconds stretched into minutes without a response on her part.

Todd arrived with Blade's bill and a wooden take-out container as Fey finished the last of her food. "Would you like me to box that up for you?" he asked, gesturing to Blade's mostly uneaten burger.

Blade cleared his throat. "I can do it, thanks." He paid Todd for the meal and the boy wished them, "Have a good day!" before trotting off cheerfully. By now, Fey's expression had mostly returned to its usual neutral position, so he could not be faulted for leaving Blade alone to face his fate.

Fey silently rose and strode toward the exit without acknowledging the existence of her dining companion. Blade hastily boxed up his lunch and followed. (Run away! Honestly, Blade is actually the most abnormal person in this whole story.) He caught up as Fey began descending the stairs—

"Oof." Blade's breath rushed out of his lungs as a six-Fey iron boar deliberately shoved his way in front of the warrior. The Feypets were fully aware of Blade's current state of disgrace (though they had no idea what kind of heinous condition their owner was being accused of) and were now demonstrating exactly how difficult walking could be when they did not stay considerately out of the way. Blade nearly fell down the stairs when he stumbled over several patches of solid shadow. He seized the railing and desperately halted his forward momentum to avoid crashing into Fey, or more accurately, to avoid having Amethyst bash his skull in before he crashed into Fey. The slime gleamed with a fresh coat of the poison du jour (#BonusFrench), guaranteeing that what blunt-force trauma started, biochemistry would finish. On his shoulder, Firefly screeched in outrage at the affront to her owner, but Boris silenced her with a single Glare.

Fey smiled a goodbye to Tallen on her way out of the tavern before walking onto a forest trail, where the expression slid easily off her face.

With a lot of non-verbal negotiation with Boris, Blade managed to maneuver himself next to Fey. The fear engendered by silence was now greater than the fear of speaking, so he said, "Hey, I'm sorry."

Fey glanced sideways at him. "For what?" Her tone implied not that he had done nothing wrong, but that she wanted to know if he understood his transgression.

Blade chose his next words very carefully. "For . . . assuming . . . you were—no, I mean, your behaviour was . . . due to PMS."

Fey smiled a smile that said *Perhaps you're not too stupid to live, after all*. The sincere and self-aware apology went a long way toward lessening her wrath. She patted him on the shoulder. "I'm still going to make your life miserable for a month."

"What? 'Still'? I'm really sorry, for real!"

"It's the only way to prove that I don't have PMS," Fey said in her most reasonable tone, back to her usual mix of seriousness and joking.

"No, it's not! Plus, I believe you!"

"Belief without evidence is just superstition," Fey said scornfully, though her (evil) grin somewhat ruined the delivery. "Consider it an object lesson."

Blade groaned in defeat and accepted his fate. Now that Fey was joking and had real facial expressions again, he was fairly certain that he would survive whatever diabolical revenge she came up with.

Fey was feeling much improved and not at all mopey. In fact, if Blade had claimed to have made his PMS comment in order to provoke this specific response, she would have forgiven him and forgone her object lesson. (Unfortunately for him, that had not been his purpose and he was too honest for the thought of lying about it to cross his mind.) She walked lightly on the trail that would lead to the level 30 through 40 monster territories, well familiar with the area after several days of training. On a whim, she broke into a jog.

"Why are we running?" Blade asked, his footsteps considerably heavier than Fey's. In contrast to her stealthy, speed-dependent assassin class, he (with only a little manipulation on Sirena's part) had advanced to the tank sub-class. This was a generalized heavy-armour sub-class that could further develop into subspecialties such as mounted knight, paladin, and the truly fortresslike shield knight. His equipment weighed at least double hers, and running was not exactly a casual undertaking.

"To raise our stamina?" Fey suggested. Her feet felt as light as her restored mood, and she bounded for a couple of deerlike leaps before settling into a balanced jog, weight mainly on the balls of her feet.

Blade grunted. He was not used to running around, so his stamina was not as high as Fey's, but his strength was double hers and while he made an unconscionable amount of noise by assassin standards, he was able to keep up.

Fey's stamina was now 125 and she was easily able to talk and jog at the same time. She described the monsters she wanted to train on, the level 37 grey wolves that were in between her level 38 and Blade's level 34; he and Sirena had fallen behind after a week of mostly travelling.

The grey wolves were a monster Fey had skipped in her solo training. They hunted in large packs, and their strong pack bonds made them resistant to the effects of Isolate. However, with a tank like Blade to attract their attention, their lack of defensive abilities made them an attractive target.

Blade nodded his understanding, saving his breath for running. "Sirena?" he asked.

"She'll join us when she's ready," Fey answered, then began dropping back.

Amethyst hopped from Fey's shoulder to Boris's back, while the glooms dropped to the ground to run beside their owner. Boris began to trot more noisily and sped up in preparation to use his Charge.

"Take care of Boris!" Fey called.

(Boris grunted derisively at the idea that he needed a meatshield like Blade to take care of him.)

Blade unslung the large shield from his back and focused on not falling too far behind the boar.

Fey and the glooms encountered the grey wolves about two minutes after Blade and Boris's noisy attack. One wolf lay on the ground with a large, hoof-shaped indent in its ribs and Fey finished it off.

The rest of the wolves were now clustered around Blade and Boris, who had formed a defensive stance against a tree.

Blade's level 30 skill had been Shield Bash, and he used it now to great effect, smashing the wolves to the ground when they leapt in attack. The move was powerful and had a stunning effect but lacked the decisive damage required to make a kill.

Fey slipped into the fight, hidden in her Shadow Cloak. Blade could see her because they were in the same party, and he was taken aback at the intent, merciless expression she wore as she looked at the wolves.

Until reaching the assassin class, Fey had done her best to avoid fighting monsters that looked like real animals. She was well aware that she was in a game, but it was too realistic for her taste. After all, the monsters had not done anything to deserve being killed, and here she was, exterminating them for experience and loot.

Gaining the Critical Sight ability had increased Fey's offensive capabilities far more than it was designed to. Anyone with a basic knowledge of mammalian anatomy could identify the weak points on most of the monsters in *Fantasia*. Critical Sight was mainly intended to help with the more unusual monsters in the game.

What Critical Sight did for Fey was to simplify monsters down to coloured blobs she could easily interpret. One of the things she excelled at was absorbing and processing simplified visual schema with almost computer-like speed and precision. She could read at high speed with full recall and understanding, solve simple logic puzzles such as sudoku and nonograms faster than the mean time, and process tables and charts to find desired information without having to read them in their entirety.

Now at level 5, her Critical Sight showed her subtle variations in red: dark red for soft spots, brighter red for critical weaknesses, translucent red for critical spots protected by armour or bone, and pink for stun points. She now also saw blue in hardened areas that were poor targets to strike. With her mind now busy interpreting and acting upon the patterns she saw, killing monsters became a game not unlike the *Dance Dance Revolution* she so enjoyed.

Fey was aware of how much faster she killed monsters, but not how scary she looked while doing it. One could see from her expression that she no longer saw the coloured targets in front of her as living creatures. She kicked and stabbed her way through eyes, underbellies, and throats with brutal efficiency, eerily silent within the muffling effects of her Shadow Cloak. The wolves became aware of her after being attacked but rarely had the chance to act upon it before dropping dead from massive blood loss and paralytic injuries. Blade was distracted enough by the disturbing sight that he occasionally had some close calls, but the Feypets covered for him.

Boris and Amethyst had formed an extremely effective fighting partnership. The slime had found a convenient strap in Boris's saddle to tuck herself into, and now she used the boar to counterbalance the huge forces she generated with Whip. She now frequently broke skin with her strikes, so she added bomblebee venom for an additional 50 explosion damage to each attack. Boris barely noticed the shifts in momentum, and effectively gained a shield two metres in radius that left him free to Charge around, trample monsters, and cause Quakes without worrying about personal safety.

Unable to keep up with the sheer offensive output of Fey, Amethyst, and Boris, the glooms had abandoned the slow-working Suffocate and were diligently training Crush. The skill was currently not strong enough to do more than bruise and break the thinnest of bones, so they targeted the feet of the wolves to cripple their movement speed.

At the rate they were now destroying monsters, Fey and her pets were used to jogging between three to four spawn sites with only small breaks to collect loot. Blade pushed himself to keep up and was rewarded for his exhaustion with small stamina increases. When he occasionally had enough energy for stray thoughts, he was glad that Fey had seemed to have forgotten about making him miserable for a month. (Did she? Did she really? What a hopeless optimist.)

CHAPTER 28
SPLASHY

Fey and Blade had each gained a level by the time Sirena messaged them to say she was coming to find them. They were expecting some kind of change regarding Squishy, but nothing quite like what they were actually confronted with.

Sirena had undergone what must have been an expensive transformation, wearing an entirely new set of equipment. Her robes were a complex weave of four different shades of blue, aquamarine accessories decorated her ears and hair, and she carried a long staff carved to resemble a narwhal horn,[46] topped with a large, faceted orb of aquamarine. Whereas her former equipment was balanced between water, wind, and lightning bonuses to reflect the specialties of Thrain, the storm god, the new set focused exclusively on water and offered a staggering 250 percent bonus to spells of that element.

The new equipment was very distinctive (and blue), but nothing that would cause anyone to stare for long. No, the staring was due to the fact that there was a huge ball of water suspended in the air above Sirena's staff, one easily large enough to engulf the entire party, including Boris. Squishy floated within the magical sphere, still not quite able to extend its tentacles to their fullest length.

Sirena was casting the newly purchased Water Mace, a spell designed neither to be maintained continuously nor expanded to such an extent. Only the expensive new equipment and her innate merfolk affinity with water allowed her to maintain it without draining her mana stores faster than they regenerated.

"So? What do you think?" she asked.

Fey stared up at the preposterously sized ball of water. ". . . Well, that's one solution." One that seemed to create more problems than it solved. "Can you still cast other spells while maintaining that thing?"

"No, but I don't have to. Watch." Sirena raised the arm holding the staff, causing the sphere of water to rise in tandem.

"Waitwaitwait!" Foreseeing disaster, Fey grabbed Sirena's arm before the mermaid did any reckless swinging. "Don't damage the trees unless you want to be murdered by the forest rangers," she warned. (The statement was somewhat inaccurate, as the word "murder" implied an illegal act. "Executed" would probably be the better choice.)

The globe of water was simply too large not to cause random destruction everywhere it went. "Shrink it down," said Fey.

Sirena complied, reducing the mana powering the spell until it was approximately the size of an exercise ball. Squishy's tentacles were forced to curl several times to remain within the water, but the jellyfish otherwise suffered no ill effects. There was no way to tell how it felt about the change in its housing situation.

Fey judged that the forest would be safe from Sirena's magic and removed her restraining hand.

Sirena resumed her demonstration, shifting her grip so that she held the lower third of her staff. "Watch," she repeated. She whipped the staff sharply downward, stopping with its orb-topped end a handsbreadth above the ground.

The Water Mace spell was fairly simple in concept: A sphere of water of variable size was conjured with a fixed position relative to a magical implement, such as a wand or staff.[47] When the mage moved the implement, the kinetic energy required to move the water was supplied by magic rather than the mage's physical strength. This allowed her to manipulate the heavy mass of water at the same speed as she could move the much-lighter staff or wand.

What occurred when the water met an object depended on the speed of impact. At slower speeds, objects passed into the sphere. The spell only had power over water, so dense objects would fall out when the sphere was lifted. Jellyfish, being 95 percent water, stayed in suspension. This aspect of Water Mace could be used to drown opponents if the sphere was of sufficient size.

High-speed collisions were what the spell was primarily intended for. Much like falling into water from a great height, there was little difference between liquid-solid and solid-solid collisions when there was enough speed involved. The spell subtly increased the cohesion of the water so that the threshold for this was lower than in real life.

While Sirena's staff stopped short of hitting the ground, the Water Mace anchored to it collided with a sound between a splash and a boom, creating a deep, rounded indent. (Miraculously, this rough handling somehow left Squishy unharmed.) Sirena quickly lifted her staff so that the water would not begin to seep into the ground.

Blade squatted down to examine the impression. He whistled. At its centre, it was deeper than his fist. "Nice," he said. (#Impressed)

Fey wore an absent-minded expression, busy analyzing the mechanics and utility of the spell. While a warrior armed with a heavy weapon that could be moved as quickly as a light weapon would be a cheat-level ability, mages were limited by the fact that their stats and equipment made them unsuitable to fight in close quarters. "How far from the staff can you extend the ball?" she asked.

"Depends on how much mana I want to spend," Sirena responded. "For a short time, probably five metres or so. Keeping it up continuously, probably no more than two metres for a sphere this size."

Fey nodded distractedly, running attack simulations inside her head. She nodded again, having come up with some kind of decision. "Let's go level."

Thus began a long afternoon of training. Sirena was set to the task of learning to extend her Water Mace away from the staff at the same time as she swung downward. Results were hit-or-miss as she taxed her Concentration attribute to its fullest. The mermaid kept her attacks slow, so no one sustained any crush injuries, but the rest of the party frequently had a limb or whole body soaked from a mis-aimed swing. Boris, being the only one with a large amount of skin not completely protected by armour, sustained frequent stings from coming into contact with Squishy's tentacles. He bore the surface wounds stoically (and secretly enjoyed all the fussing Fey did over him).

<Boris's Immunity has reached level 10!>

Boris grunted in satisfaction as all of his welts disappeared. Being a reflection of the more diligent side of his owner, he had been constantly training Immunity during breaks and meal times and had now surpassed Fey's level 9 ability. In reaching level 10, Immunity evolved to provide invulnerability to the non-damage side effects of poisons, including pain, paralysis, and stat penalties.

Squishy also inflicted severe neurotoxic injuries upon the completely unarmoured monsters they were fighting.

<Squishy has achieved level 26!>

<Squishy has achieved level 27!>

While fighting, Amethyst kept an eye on the Water Mace (or as she thought of it, the "Squishy-water-ball"). It did not actually matter whether the slime was hit by the spell, as she was immune to the poison, waterproof, and almost crushproof as well. No, Amethyst was not worried about the danger from the Water Mace. It just seemed . . . not fully optimized (or as she thought of it, "stupid-weak").

The solution came to her as the magical globe of water came splashing over her and Boris yet again. She activated Poison Sphere and filled the Water Mace with furyweed poison.

Lost in the flurry of system messages associated with party combat against multiple opponents, Fey, Sirena, and Blade failed to notice the initial skill activation. Fey noticed the multiple poison notifications first, and sent Amethyst an approving look without saying anything. Sirena noticed next and accordingly adjusted her strategy from targeting one monster at a time to trying to get them all drenched at least once.

Blade paid little attention to system notifications about his party members and their pets, adjusting his settings so that anything involving him or Firefly was highlighted. It wasn't until one of Squishy's tentacles stung him at a small gap in his armour that he noticed the Water Mace's new properties.

<Blade has been poisoned!>

<Furyweed poison: −3 health/second>

<Duration: 5 minutes>

<Level 4 Immunity effect: decrease 2 damage per poison infliction>

<New effect: −1 health/second>

<Duration: 5 minutes>

"[Censored word]!" Blade swore as the burning pain of furyweed poison spread through his body. "Fey!" he yelled.

Fey winced apologetically while still delivering deathblows to the nearest monsters. "I really didn't think anything would happen to you," she said. After all, with all of his armour, the chances that he would get cut and allow the poison to enter his body were small.

Blade gritted his teeth as he deliberated over whether to use an antidote. The reduced-effect furyweed would not kill him, but it was quite painful. "Couldn't you at least pick something I'm already immune to?"

Amethyst squeaked an explanation, and Fey nodded in agreement. "All of the other ones would damage Squishy as well. The only other that needs to break skin first is bomblebee venom, and that would cause a small explosion and 50 damage every time it hit you," she translated.

Somehow, Fey had logic on her side with this poisoning incident. Sensing that the combination of Water Mace and Poison Sphere was something he would have to deal with for a long time, he decided to endure and train Immunity until he could resist furyweed poison. In pain and aggravated about it, he growled as he ploughed into the monsters arrayed against him.

<Blade has learned Growl!>

<Level 1: −10% attack, −1 initiative against all attacking opponents, +1 morale to all allies>

"Hey, cool skill!" Sirena congratulated, noticing that it was slightly easier to control her magic now.

Somehow, benefiting from being poisoned made the whole situation more aggravating. He Growled again, though the effects did not stack.

◊◊◊

Leander alternated between one- and two-handed grips of his sword as he flowed through the swings and thrusts of a battle pattern he had learned in a real-life sword academy. In preparation to test the sword-and-sorcery world of *Fantasia*, the company had paid for him to take swordfighting lessons. Fighting mostly quadruped monsters armed with teeth and claws and the addition of a seven-metre wingspan had necessitated huge adjustments in technique, but he liked to maintain his original skills, both in case he encountered humanoid opponents and because it was a fun form of exercise.

Repeating the pattern and two others at quarter speed, half speed, and full speed, he was breathing hard and sweating by the time he finished. He took a drink from his water bottle with a relaxed sigh. Exercise felt more invigorating in the real world now that his game avatar had so much stamina that it took flying to even deepen his breathing.

Leander's cell phone, a wrist model that looked like a plain black band, chimed discreetly. Tapping it, he activated the holographic display and read the campuswide notification that the morning shuttle leaving for the city would be departing in half an hour. He took a shower and was seated in one of the shuttle's comfortable seats well before the last call for passengers.

VirtualRealities was a company that took very good care of its employees, providing optimized living and working conditions for employees and their immediate families. Internationally, they had three main company campuses, each of which was a small, self-sufficient town that offered enough amenities that people did not feel the need to leave very often.

Aware that creating an isolated community that did not integrate with mainstream society would result in a loss of innovation and relevance in their games, company policy dictated that employees spend at least one day a week off campus, doing something not directly related to work. They even provided complimentary shuttles to and from the nearest urban centre, vehicles whose interiors looked more like first-class cabins than buses.

Leander was signed up to play laser tag with other company employees that evening, but he had several hours to kill until then. Stepping off the shuttle, he waved goodbye to the other passengers and wandered into the city without a particular destination in mind.

There was a peculiar kind of serenity to be found in having a pocket of silence within a bustling space. Putting in earbuds, Leander played his favourite music and lost himself in the crowd. He found himself doing this approximately once a month, just exploring, letting his feet take him toward anything that looked interesting, people-watching while his earbuds insulated him from real social interaction. He used to also finish part of his online work during the day so that he could go on walks around campus at night, enjoying the hushed quiet, but he had not done so since he had met Fey, wanting to synchronize with her play schedule.

Leander found an out-of-the-way café and purchased a morning coffee, manners dictating that he remove his earbuds while he ordered. Smiling at the friendly barista, he retired to a table next to the window and sipped at his drink, prepared in a real cup rather than a disposable one. The café was fairly quiet, so he left the earbuds out.

As he finished, the barista came over to clear the table. "Are you new?" she asked. "I haven't seen you around before."

"I'm from out of town," Leander answered truthfully.

She looked disappointed for a moment. "Oh . . . Well, how about I give you my number, and you call me when you're in town. I can show you the fun spots nearby," she said with a wink.

Leander was mildly surprised at the invitation, as he was dressed casually in a sweatshirt and jeans, nothing that hinted at wealth unless you were familiar enough with technology to see that his cell phone was a custom model. Still, he had an excuse ready. "Sorry, I have a girlfriend."

As Leander left the café and resumed his wandering, he realized something: For the first time since he had begun using that excuse to avoid awkward conversations, it had not felt like a lie.

CHAPTER 29

HOTSHOT

S canning. Player detected. Welcome back to *Fantasia*, Fey E'lan.

"There is a new notice for an event happening in one month. Would you like to read it?"

Suspended in the nothingness that was the login screen, Fey raised an eyebrow and said, "Yes."

A virtual screen popped up.

Introducing *Fantasia's* first serverwide event: a player-versus-player laser tag tournament!

Teams of four players will battle it out for fabulous prizes with every match. Limited-edition pets and equipment can be won during individual matches, while the tournament winners will receive legendary evolving weapons to match their class!

Tournament Rules

Teams of four players must register to compete at least 24 hours before the start of the tournament. Unregistered teams can participate in individual matches to win basic prizes but will not qualify to compete for the grand prize. Registered teams can continue to change composition up to 24 hours before the start of the tournament.

Teams will be placed in level brackets based on the mean level of the four players. Level brackets are every 5 levels from 10 to 60 (10–14, 15–19, 20–24 . . . , 60+). Players below level 10 or who have not joined a combat class will not be eligible to compete. Players above level 60 will be returned to level 60 stats and abilities for the duration of matches. Players will be returned to their stats and abilities at the start of the tournament for the duration of matches if they gain levels/abilities during the tournament period.

The tournament will consist of two rounds. In the qualifying round, teams will compete in ten matches against randomly selected teams from the same level bracket. The teams with the highest win count and aggregate skill score will move on to the final round, a 128-team knockout-style tournament to determine the overall winners in each level bracket. Teams that do not qualify for the final round can continue to participate in matches for basic prizes.

All match footage will be available for livestream and playback. In participating in a match, players agree to have their image recorded and released on the VirtualRealities website.

Grand prize winners may be interviewed and featured on the VirtualRealities website.

Match Rules

Players must wear transparent vests and helmets that detect magical laser fire, and will be equipped with magic guns that hold 100 shots. Other than the mandatory equipment, players are free to wear/carry their own equipment.

Regular equipment (e.g., capes) and body parts (arms, legs) cannot block magical laser fire.

Potions, pets, and live accessories are not allowed in matches.

Once-a-day skills and abilities will be disabled during matches. Other than these, all skills and abilities that do not deal direct damage are allowed. Dealing direct damage to other players will result in forfeiture of the match and a gain of 50 infamy.

Each combat class has a different set of abilities during the match:

Warrior: 10 lives, equipped with a small round shield that can block laser fire

Mage: 2 lives, each hit consumes 2 lives, can recharge guns

Archer: 5 lives, laser sight is invisible to opponents

Rogue: 1 life, no bonuses

*Players belonging to multiple classes will have the number of lives of the class with fewer lives, but otherwise the abilities of both classes. Each additional class that players belong to will result in +2 to their average (arithmetic mean) team level.

Players will be informed of the opposing team's composition 15 minutes before the start of the match and be given a private space to strategize.

Matches last until all players on one team are knocked out or 1 hour. If neither team has a mage, matches will also end when both teams are out of shots. If not ended by knockout, the winning team is determined by the number of players remaining, followed by the percentage number of lives remaining on surviving players, followed by the hit accuracy of each team.

At the start of the match, teams will be transported to starting positions at opposite ends of the arena. Players are free to move within the arena until all their lives are consumed, at which point they will be transported out of the arena with all their equipment. Upon being hit, players will be invincible to laser fire for 30 seconds and also have their guns disabled for 30 seconds.

Arenas will be selected from the following settings:

Size: 50m x 50m, 75m x 75m, 100m x 100m

Time: noon, sunset, midnight (full moon), midnight (new moon)

Land: forest, mountains, plains, desert, underground tunnels

Additional elements: None, moving elements, weather, roaming monsters (can be shot for temporary buffs)

Good luck and have fun! Practice arenas and equipment can be accessed through any teleportation gate for a small fee until the registration deadline.

Time until deadline: 30 days

Still absorbing and processing the information, Fey logged into the game.

◊◊◊

Fey flashed into the Moonwood and was immediately pounced upon by an excited Sirena.

"Whaddya think?" the mermaid asked excitedly. "This is going to be great! We'll kick ass."

"We're terrible at laser tag," Fey pointed out. In real life, they occasionally played laser tag when the occasion came up, and winning was more of a matter of identifying the skilled players and contriving to be on that team than anything else.

Sirena dismissed the pessimism (realism) with a wave of her hand. "That's real-life laser tag. This is magical laser tag. We can cheat. I bet I can use Water Mace to diffract shots."

"We'll see," said Fey. She foresaw extensive experimentation with the laser tag gear in the upcoming month to see how it interacted with their existing skills and abilities. "Where's Blade?"

By this point in their gaming lives, Fey, Sirena, and Blade had fine-tuned their logon times to be almost simultaneous. The three had in fact turned on their gaming helmets within a real-life minute of each other. The difference in time when it came to appearing in the game world was due to reading the announcement. Sirena finished first, briefly skimming the notice and coming away with only superficial details of how the tournament was going to work. Fey, on the other hand, read through the entire thing in detail and came away with near-perfect recall of all the rules.

Blade also read through the entire notice with care. Being somewhat more pedestrian in his reading skills, he took more time and came away with less comprehension than Fey. (Unaware that he was being judged, he was unbothered by this.) He flashed into being a few minutes later, excited about the upcoming event. "You guys want to enter the laser tag tournament, right?" Unlike his party mates, he was actually good at the physical pastime in real life, and was somehow under the impression that Fey and Sirena had equivalent skill.

"Yup! We're totally doing it," said Sirena.

"Well, first of all, we need a fourth team member," said Fey.

Blade's party (#Technicalities) stood several metres back from the Moonwood's notice board, which was as close as they could get with the crowd of excited players all looking to join teams or recruit members. Fortunately, the notice board had a virtual version, which allowed them to scroll through pages of posted requests.

"What kind of player are we looking for?" asked Sirena.

"Well, if we want to stay in the level 40–44 bracket, someone level 44 or less, assuming they're not a dual class like me," Fey answered, having done the calculations on the handy calculation program the game developers had installed. After a week of serious training (interspersed with breaks for silliness), the party members had each gained 6–7 levels and made various skill gains. Belonging to two combat classes could give considerable advantages during laser tag, but by adding 2 to the team's calculated level average, it came at the cost of the equivalent of 8 player levels to stay in the same level bracket.

"Okay, but what class are we looking for?" asked Blade. "If we want one of each class, it should be an archer, but I don't think having one necessarily gives us more of an advantage than doubling up on something else."

Fey and Sirena exchanged looks, silently arguing over who would be the one to give Blade the bad news.

Fey lost. "Considering me and Sirena are on the team, someone with good aim is a necessity," she finally said.

"Oh, come on. Your aim can't be . . . that bad." Blade trailed off when his party mates' expressions failed to reassure him. He cleared his throat. "Right. Archer it is."

"We wouldn't blame you if you wanted to find a different team for the tournament," Fey offered. "Well, Sirena would pout," she added, not having to turn her head to look at her best friend's petulant expression, "but we wouldn't blame you."

Blade shook his head without pausing to consider the idea. (Aww, so loyal. People should appreciate him more.) Turning on the correct filters on the request page, he announced, "Level 44 archers," and shared the virtual display. The list of names numbered in the hundreds just for the local area as players scrambled to find teams for the tournament.

Fey's eyes glazed over in boredom. She was adept at scanning data for information of interest, but only if the information she wanted was actually there. Names and sub-classes would not tell her if the player was sensible, or reliable, or any of the other necessary traits to be a good team member.

Unnoticed by the party or anyone else in the crowd, a lone player had been quietly moving around clusters of chattering players, listening and observing. She made no visual or physical contact and moved with calm purpose, blending in almost to the point of invisibility.

Catching Blade's words about recruiting an archer and Fey's subsequent joking/not joking answer, the player paused, intrigued.

When Fey said, "Okay, let's go down the list and message the first name we unanimously decide doesn't sound stupid," the loner made her decision and approached.

"Excuse me."

Blade jumped and turned as a voice spoke from his flank.

"Are you looking for a fourth team member?" The speaker was a moon elf in leather armour, holding a small crossbow in her left hand. Within the bounds of game race and gender, she was very different in appearance from Fey. While Fey was relatively tall and extremely thin, the newcomer was almost a full head shorter and of normal weight, making her body look considerably sturdier and less androgynous. Her hair was plain black, confined to a neat braid, her eyes a normal brown, her posture neat and reserved.

Fey and Sirena immediately liked what they saw. The player stood with a quiet air that suggested self-assurance without arrogance, which, in their experience, was a strong predictor of competence. (Blade is too nice and willing to give anyone a chance, so his first impressions don't count.)

"Hi!" Sirena greeted. "Yes, we were! I'm Sirena, a level 41 mage-priestess. This is Fey, a level 44 assassin—that's a warrior-rogue hybrid—and this is Blade, a level 42 tank. Are you interested in joining us?"

The player nodded. "I'm Mimi, level 43 sniper, archer-rogue hybrid."

"Perfect! Consider it done," Sirena exclaimed, though Mimi's dual class would take them into the next level bracket. (That being said, an archer-rogue hybrid is the perfect class to play magical laser tag, though Sirena hadn't actually thought it through.)

Fey elbowed Blade. "Send her a party invite."

Blade obliged, and Mimi accepted the invitation.

<Mimi Dart, level 43 moon elf sniper.>

<HP: 1634/1634, MP: 925/925.>

"Want to head over to a training arena and see how it goes?" Fey suggested.

Mimi nodded, and the newly enlarged party headed over to the teleportation gate. Walking into its centre and paying 10g per player caused the gate to send them to a newly generated practice arena.

Blade's party appeared in the centre of the arena, the default settings being 50m x 50m, noon, forest, no additional elements. Beside them was a pile of gear.

Sirena lifted a loose, off-white vest made of a light cloth and pursed her lips critically. "Not flattering."

Fey grabbed two vests and handed one to Mimi before slipping into her own. The magical cloth shimmered for a moment before shrinking to fit her thin frame perfectly and taking on the colouration of her underlying equipment. Glowing green lines flashed into being, outlining circles on her chest and back. "I mean, nobody looks good in neon green,[48] but it's not that bad," she answered. The accompanying helmet, which resembled a transparent motorcycle helmet, complete with visor, was lit with three matching green lines along its length.

Fey and Blade were also provided with small, transparent round shields that could be strapped to the forearm. They were just big enough to cover the head or chest target, never both at the same time. Fey was flexible enough to reach behind herself and cover the back target, but Blade was not.

The team geared up, a process that involved removing a lot of their existing equipment. In a game where direct combat was forbidden, heavy armour with high defence was just a hindrance to movement speed. Blade resorted to changing into his newbie outfit, his tank equipment entirely unsuited to laser tag.

Finally, they swapped their weapons for laser guns. Being magical weapons, they were actually modified wands the size of a handgun. Made of wood, they were considerably lighter than the two-handed guns the players had handled in real-life laser tag, easily carried and shot with one hand. The triggers were standard: half pressure activated a red laser sight, while full pressure triggered a shot.

Fully geared up, Fey saved the new equipment set so that she could Ex-quip into it next time. Then her mind moved on to experimentation. Lifting her gun, she shot at Blade's vest outside the target circle, with no results. Shooting inside the circle caused his vest and helmet to flash red.

"Hey!" he protested.

"You have to shoot inside the target circle," Fey reported.

Sirena lifted her weapon and shot at Fey's helmet, causing it to flash red. "Looks like anywhere on the helmet is okay," she said with an impish smile.

While Fey, Sirena, and Blade shot at each other, Mimi familiarized herself with her new weapon, getting a feel for its heft, grip, and shape. Holding it in one- and two-handed grips, she sighted along its length with and without the sighting aid, then squeezed the trigger repeatedly, finding the maximum shooting speed. By the time the other three had more or less confirmed that anywhere on the helmet was a valid target, she was ready and waiting, gun held securely in one hand.

Seeing Mimi's stance, Fey quickly called out, "One, two, three, go!" and sprinted into the artificial forest, activating Shadow Cloak as she went. In the bright lighting, the ability did little to hide her from sight, but turned her into a dark blur and smothered the light coming from her vest and helmet, making her an uncertain target. She ran in one direction until she reached one wall of the arena, then travelled along it, listening for a sign of her party mates.

The first sound came not from the environment but the party audio chat.

"Hey! Who was that?" Sirena complained.

"Me" came Mimi's voice.

A minute later, Blade swore. "Who was that?"

"Me" came Mimi's voice again. (It's becoming obvious why she's called "Mimi.")

Fey was struck with a sense of impending doom. She was next.

Keeping her shield covering her head, Fey darted from tree to tree, taking cover under the assumption that Mimi was closer to the centre of the arena than she was. One minute passed without being hit. Two. Five.

Fey heard the sound of footsteps. Peeking around a tree, she saw Sirena trudging along with a disgruntled expression. Grinning, she activated her laser sight. As usual for her, the red dot appeared outside the hit zone and she had to take a moment to correct her aim. She pulled the trigger all the way and Sirena's gear flashed red. Fey took a second to gloat—

Then she was hit. "Son of a goat!" she yelled, half a beat after Sirena's equally disgusted exclamation. (We shall leave it to the reader's imagination whether she actually said "goat.")

Fey looked around but could see no sign of Mimi's presence. "Okay, you got us all, Mimi. Regroup and discuss?" she said over audio chat. Everyone agreed and began heading back to the starting area.

Fey finally spotted Mimi as the sniper dropped out of a tree. She trotted up to walk with the other elf. "How did you get up there?" she asked curiously.

Mimi showed her fingers tipped with claw-shaped shadow. "My level 30 ability is Climbing Claws."

"Cool! Mine is Critical Sight. Speaking of . . ." Fey activated the ability, which had been set to untarget party members. In her vision, the helmet and vest targets on her party mates filled in with solid red, very easy to see in the browns and greens of the forest. "My level 40 ability is Brittle Edge, which sacrifices defence for attack power," she continued. "It's pretty useless for laser tag, though. How about yours?"

Mimi's lips curved into a small smile. "Guided Shot."

Fey's eyes widened. "As in . . . ?"

"I can shoot around corners."

Fey broke into an exuberant smile and raised her hand for a high five. Mimi obliged, still wearing a more reserved smile.

It was at this point that Blade spotted the two rogue hybrids on the way back to the starting area. They were somehow perfectly in sync despite major differences in appearance and personality.

"There are two of them now," he muttered to himself.

NOTES

1 The rules of etiquette state that the person of higher status is spoken to first during an introduction.

2 Decompression sickness occurs when a diver ascends from deep water too quickly; gases that were dissolved in the bloodstream and tissues separate and can form bubbles that can damage tissue and block blood vessels.

Nitrogen narcosis refers to a state of impairment similar to alcohol intoxication, which can occur when diving in deeper waters, where the increased pressure increases the concentration of gas dissolved in the blood.

3 This creatively uncreative name was brought to you by karami92. <You have earned the title *Fantasia* Game Developer!>

4 The golden ratio is a relationship between two numbers (e.g., *a* and *b*) where the sum of the two numbers (*a* + *b*) has the same ratio with the larger of the two numbers; this value is approximately 1.618. This ratio has been shown to be found in nature, and the most typical image of it is the golden spiral.

5 According to Wikipedia, the retiarius was considered the lowliest kind of gladiator. The author had no prior knowledge of this fact before writing this chapter.

6 The word "draft" has numerous unrelated meanings; in this case it refers to the act of pulling, as in a draft horse.

7 This crystal was chosen by searching "stone associated with telepathy" on the Internet.

8 This is a humorous pro tip from the flash adventure game *Epic Battle Fantasy 3*.

9 In organisms without circular DNA, chromosome ends are capped with areas of repetitive DNA called telomeres that do not encode genes but instead act as buffers to ensure that no genes are lost during the process of replicating DNA for cell division, during which a small piece of the end of the DNA molecule is lost. When these telomeres reach a certain threshold of

shortening, cells enter a phase called senescence, when they no longer divide, thought to be protective against the development of severe DNA changes, including cancerous cells. A protein called telomerase is responsible for lengthening telomeres; in many organisms, including humans, this is only active in germ cells to restore telomere length in the next generation, but in lobsters, it is active throughout the lobster's life, ensuring that cells never reach senescence and are able to continue growing and dividing.

10   There are quite a few differences between llamas and alpacas. Llamas, bred to be pack animals, are larger and stronger and have coarse coats not valued as fibre. Alpacas, bred for fibre, are about half the size and have dense, fuzzy coats that are highly valued for textiles. However, llamas and alpacas can interbreed, blurring the differences between the two.

The parenthetical comment here is meant to be a humourous oversimplification.

11   Chapter title credit goes to deathbypingvin.

12   Cnidarians include jellyfish, anemones, hydra, and corals, and are characterized by the cnidocytes, specialized cells that shoot neurotoxins for self-defence and/or the capture of prey.

13   In real life, sea nettle stings in humans usually cause only a mild rash unless there is severe contact, in which case muscle cramps and breathing problems could occur.

14   When sleeping, people cycle through different stages of lighter and deeper sleep. REM stands for "rapid eye movement" and is the stage of sleep in which dreaming occurs. It takes approximately 90 to 120 minutes to go through a complete sleep cycle.

15   According to modern guidelines, people should not remain sedentary for more than half an hour at a time unless sleeping.

16   This refers to a two-player game where players take turns dropping coloured discs onto a grid with the goal of connecting four discs in a vertical, horizontal, or diagonal line.

17   In the theory of operant conditioning, there are four ways to induce a desired behaviour. These are (1) positive reinforcement, where the desired behaviour is reinforced by a pleasant reward; (2) negative reinforcement, where the desired behaviour is reinforced by the removal of an unpleasant stimulus as a reward; (3) positive punishment, where the undesirable behaviour is punished by an unpleasant stimulus; and (4) negative punishment, where the undesirable behaviour is punished by the removal of a pleasant object/stimulus.

18   A "ton" is the equivalent of 2,000 pounds, while a "tonne," or "metric ton," is the equivalent of 1,000 kilograms.

19   People's fingertips will wrinkle in fresh or low-osmolarity water as the skin absorbs water and swells. In high-osmolarity water, such as the salt water of the ocean, the skin does not absorb water and will not wrinkle.

20   Look up "tae geuk 6" if you would like to see the pattern in this scene.

21   Since the writing of this chapter, the World Taekwondo headquarters has realized the unfortunate acronym created by "World Taekwondo Federation" and the organization is now just called "World Taekwondo."

22   This refers to three species of mushrooms collectively known as "death angel" or "destroying angel," *Amanita bisporigera*, *Amanita virosa*, and *Amanita verna*. They produce a toxin known as alpha-amanitin, which blocks RNA polymerase and the synthesis of new proteins in the body; ingesting this toxin leads to a slow and painful death.

23   "Playa" by Hamel and St. Croix feat. Jules Mari is a song featured in *Dance Dance Revolution X* for PS2.

24   Pure copper, as on the surface of pennies, will react with oxygen in the air; the resulting copper oxide results in old pennies' "tarnished" appearance. Soaking them in mild acids such as vinegar or lemon juice is a common way to dissolve the copper oxide, renewing the pennies' appearance. This process can be accelerated by adding salt to the acid.

25   Pufferfish contain tetrodotoxin, which blocks sodium channels in neurons and prevents impulse conduction. This toxin is not produced by the fish itself but rather by symbiotic bacteria that live within the animal.

26   Neck-warmers are Fey's (and the author's) preferred alternative to scarves. A single tube of fabric, they cover the neck and lower face without the hassle of wrapping and tying a scarf.

27   In Chinese, the equivalent of "third wheel" in dating slang is literally "lightbulb." The author thought that this would make more sense in the context of a staring crowd than "thirty-fifth wheel."

28   As far as the author knows, only she and her best friend obey this rule. The author absolutely does not recommend taking dating advice from this story. However, she does point out that most people have a deep-seated desire to receive the perfect gift as an indication that they are truly understood.

29   The Old English translation of "methinks" (actually "mē thyncth," from "thyncan," "to seem") is actually, "it seems to me" rather than "I think."

30 One Fey is approximately 50kg (110 pounds), depending on whether she has eaten recently and whether clothing and equipment count.

31 This refers to having extremely high attack power and next to no health or defence. Glass cannons generally rely either on killing opponents in the first move or having meatshields to survive.

32 The motto of *The Little Engine That Could*, a children's story about an anthropomorphic small train engine that manages to pull a train over a mountain with the power of positive thinking.

33 As far as the author is aware, Sailor Moon is the prototypical example of magical girl transformation sequences.

34 In this children's game, players must attempt to sneak up on the "it" player while their back is turned. If the "it" player turns and looks, players must freeze until the "it" player turns away again. Players caught moving by the "it" player are sent back to the starting line. This game has many names and variations of the rules throughout the world.

35 *Reach for the Top* is a general trivia quiz show for high school students in Canada. Credit goes to Dethati for this achievement, which was originally named *High Perch*. <You have earned the title *Fantasia* Game Developer!>

36 The author does not recommend ruining other people's clothing as a method of punishment or revenge. As a much-less-destructive laundry-related alternative, she suggests you consider taking the used dryer sheet and placing it in the other person's socks.

37 This is a psychological concept as a state of being fully immersed in an activity, sometimes called being "in the zone."

38 In athletics, the practice of blood doping involves using exogenous erythropoietin to increase red blood cell production in order to increase the oxygen-carrying capacity of the blood, leading to increased performance. The author does not recommend or endorse this practice.

39 *Puma concolor*, referred to as cougar, mountain lion, and puma, is a felid species native to the Americas.

40 People are born with a hearing range from approximately 20 to 20,000 Hz. With aging comes mild sensorineural hearing loss that especially affects the upper range, so that the average person can only hear up to approximately 14,000 to 15,000 Hz by the time they reach middle age.

41 This is a plot event planned a long time ago in response to a review back in 2014 from one SfaKngWeTodd:

"Amethyst is my favourite!

I want a pet slime *threatens unice5656* give me one, or I change my rating to 0 stars."

Please note that the author takes all suggestions and plot ideas into account and that threatening her with low ratings will not actually increase the likelihood that your idea will make it into the story.

42   J-pop is short for Japanese pop. K-pop is Korean pop. Other places don't get a short form because they're not cool enough.

43   Several people suggested a variation of Berry, and someone said that it should follow the pattern set by Tallen and Todd, so Terry was decided upon.

44   Premenstrual syndrome is a collection of unpleasant physical and psychological symptoms that women are supposed to get before the onset of menstrual bleeding that includes bloating, food cravings, fatigue, headache, breast tenderness, constipation/diarrhea, acne flare-ups, irritability, anxiety, depression, poor concentration, and social withdrawal. Estimates of the prevalence of this condition vary extremely widely due to the non-specific criteria. The author personally doesn't notice any of these and thinks the actual cramping and bleeding part of the whole thing is the time everybody should be irritated and depressed about.

45   Logarithmic scales are used to describe measures that have huge ranges in variation, where each unit increase corresponds to a multiplication of quantity. Examples of this include the pH scale for acidity, the Richter scale for earthquake magnitudes, and the decibel scale for sound.

46   *Monodon monoceros* is a species of small Arctic whale whose males have a long spiral tusk extending forward from the upper jaw. In earlier centuries, these tusks were passed off as unicorn horns.

47   The basic premise for this spell was inspired by a magic weapon from *The Irregular at Magic High School* (*Mahouka Koukou no Rettousei*).

48   Neon lighting is the name given to a type of gas discharge lighting that produces bright, coloured light by electrifying mixtures of gases. Neon itself has a characteristic red-orange emission spectrum, while mixtures containing xenon and argon can be used to create green, though this is more commonly done by using mercury vapor to emit ultraviolet light that is then fluoresced to green by a coating of phosphor.

ABOUT THE AUTHOR

Unice5656 is a gynoid robot designed to pass the Turing test. She writes fiction with elements of comedy, adventure, and fantasy, but which is ultimately thinly disguised romance.

Podium

DISCOVER MORE

STORIES
UNBOUND

PodiumEntertainment.com

www.ingramcontent.com/pod-product-compliance
Lightning Source LLC
Chambersburg PA
CBHW030935120726
47906CB00002B/578